The Brother

ALSO BY E.V. SEYMOUR

STANDALONES
My Daughter's Secrets
The Widow's Boyfriend
My Lying Husband
The Nanny's Secret
The Brother

KIM SLADE THRILLERS
Book 1: The Patient
Book 2: The Housekeeper's Daughter

THE
BROTHER

E. V. SEYMOUR

JOFFE BOOKS

Joffe Books, London
www.joffebooks.com

First published in Great Britain in 2025

Cover art by Cherie Chapman

ISBN: 978-1-80573-126-9

For Ian

PROLOGUE

The van was barely stationary when I threw the passenger door open and exploded out onto the wet road. Tearing through the pouring rain, I plunged down the bank, slipping and sliding, oblivious to fern, nettles and brambles clawing at my skirt. A deep, deadly scar had been cut into the landscape by the other vehicle. I couldn't tell how many young trees it had mowed down, how many times it had overturned, how badly its occupants were injured.

Oh God, oh God.

Gripped with maternal madness — this had to be karma, punishment by the universe. My guilt. My fault. One life for another.

But not Rufus, whose life has only just begun.

Not my baby.

Not my son.

Drenched through, my clothes were plastered to my skin and mud splattered the backs of my legs, weighing down my shoes, turning them to concrete. I could barely see through the driving rain. Terror of what I might find scythed through me like a sharpened blade. Close behind, the van driver was calling the emergency services, his deep voice edged with alarm, barely keeping it together as he rattled off details. *Location. RTA. Two occupants. Baby. Five months old.*

A slip down the vertiginous slope could prove fatal. Still, I hurtled, rolling an ankle on the way, the pain so eye-wateringly intense I gasped, but kept moving.

Halfway down the steep scree I spotted the wreck. It had travelled an astonishing distance and into a clearing. Surrounded by glass and debris, the mangled car was upside down, smoking in the pale wet morning light. Cold crept into my bones.

I scanned for movement.

Nothing.

I prayed for sound, however faint, however brief, yet all was quiet as if every bird had fallen silent in mourning.

Bile flooded the back of my throat. My pulse hammered and my chest felt tight. There was a weird sensation in my head, like I was going to stroke out. Closer now, on solid ground, I sped up and then my eyes flared and my legs almost gave way. At a distance, a body lay face down in the dirt, one arm flung out as if reaching, too late, for redemption. No sign of my son — he must be trapped inside the vehicle.

This was bad but not as bad as the smell from a full tank of petrol. It clung to the wet air, dark and noxious and threatening, like a death sentence waiting to be delivered.

'Christ,' the van driver let out. Right behind me he had caught its poisonous odour too.

I had to get to Rufus; had to before the whole thing went up. Cold fear coursing down my spine, I started forward. No more than a few paces, a body slammed into mine, knocking the air out of my lungs and bringing me down. I was pinned to the ground with earth in my eyes, blood and iron in my mouth.

'Let me go, you bastard.'

'It's about to light up, woman.'

I didn't care. I couldn't survive without Rufus. I couldn't live in the knowledge that I hadn't tried to reach my baby. 'LET. ME. GO.'

'There's nothing you can do,' he pleaded.

Lifting my chin, searching through a blur of tears, my anguished cry, feral and inhuman, ripped from the back of my throat. In agony, I screamed, 'RUFUS.'

CHAPTER ONE

Six weeks earlier

'It says here that big changes can occur in babies' sleep patterns at four months.'

I was holding a parenting book in one hand and Rufus, busily feeding, in the crook of my other arm. 'Do you think it means we're going to be up half the night?' So far, and in contradiction to the many horror stories I'd heard from new mums with colicky babies, or babies whose time clocks didn't synch with adults, we'd been dead lucky.

'Babies do what babies do, Sophie,' Ben replied, his standard response to any of my many questions regarding child development. Admittedly, as a first-time mother in my forties, I tended to be overly conscientious and protective.

'Bet you don't tell that to your patients.'

'Only anxious mummies.' With a wide grin, Ben chucked a fold-up changing mat, nappies, muslins, baby wipes and breast pads into my 'go-to' bag. 'Do we seriously need to take a baby monitor?' he asked.

We were due at my parents for Sunday lunch in Cheltenham and we were running late.

'Probably not but chuck it in anyway.' You could never have too much stuff.

Dressed casually in jeans, a new check shirt and walnut-brown leather trainers, Ben looked effortlessly immaculate while, despite my best efforts, I was distinctly rough around the edges. My shoulder-length blonde hair could do with a cut. I was sure the floral notes in my perfume bore the faint odour of breast milk and baby poo. Since having Rufus, I wore less make-up because life was too short to spend with mascara and lipstick, yet I felt woefully underdressed without it. Fortunately, my spring-green dress was newish and, more importantly, I could get into it. Breastfeeding, which I'd found tricky to get the hang of — throbbing boobs and sore nipples — had its advantages. With each feed, I was shifting excess weight put on through my pregnancy.

Ben sat on the end of the bed, watchful and smiling. 'Rufus is such a chilled little chap, very much like his daddy,' he said. Which was absolutely true and one of the things that struck me first about the father of my son. Younger than me by almost nine years, Ben Taylor was a far cry from what I'd expected when a mutual friend had set us up on a blind date fourteen months before. A generation apart, I didn't fancy a toy boy and said as much to Louise.

'We won't have anything to talk about,' I protested.

Louise countered with a big eye-roll. 'Who said anything about conversation?'

The thought of sex with an enthusiastic young lover had frankly made me nervous.

'Fair enough, but he won't have the slightest interest in me.'

'Who says? A strong independent woman with her own business, what's not to like?'

I could think of a few things. My childhood moniker was *Sensible, By the Book Sophie*. To my mind, this roughly translated as *dull*. 'We won't share the same interests,' I said doggedly.

'The good doctor,' as Louise mischievously referred to Ben, 'loves books, nice clothes, good food and travel. An absolute sweetie, he's kind and compassionate and a proper grown-up.'

'Sounds too good to be true.'

'You need to get out more,' Louise chided. 'You can't work twenty-four seven, Sophie.'

'But . . .'

'It's a casual supper at ours, nothing grand. You don't even have to stay beyond the pudding course.'

So I went *and* stayed way after dessert.

It wasn't so much Ben's striking prematurely grey hair that faded to mercury at the tips, his deep-blue soulful eyes, his winner of a smile, the attentive way he listened, the gorgeous scent from his aftershave (or oud), his naturally lean body (not pumped up from hours cross-training in a gym) that beguiled me. It wasn't the interesting scar, creating a slit through his left eyebrow that I found so sexy. Committed to helping the sick and dying, Ben was steady, a man of conviction and passion and whom I could trust. Still, I had not reckoned on falling so hard and so fast. And it was mutual. For a couple of weeks, apart from work, we were inseparable. I was careless and he was reckless. Within a month of our relationship, I was pregnant, something that could have gone either way: kiss of death or the start of something beautiful. Three months later, and blissfully loved up, I moved from my flat in Cheltenham to the cottage Ben was renovating in Poulton. A traditional Cotswold village, named originally in the Domesday Book, it had a village hall, church, football and cricket pitches and, at its heart, a popular pub, the Falcon. With a vibrant community, lots of activities were on offer: Pilates, yoga, art classes, a book club and film club, none of which I'd sampled due to chronic nausea, swollen ankles, indigestion and, to mitigate pregnancy sickness, an obsessional desire for ginger cookies in the morning and carrot cake, (which I'd lamely tried to kid myself was part of my five a day) in the afternoon. Luckily, I was in the cake business. Through it all, Ben loved and cared for me and was excited about having a child. Dutifully, he'd attended all my antenatal classes and did everything to allay my fears about giving birth.

'Any idea how long you're going to be?' Ben asked, staring at my boobs, not in a salacious way, I might add.

'You'd better ask him.' I gazed down at the top of Rufus's downy head.

'Could be a while. He's a greedy little devil. Do I need to drop your mum a text?' Like me, Ben was used to making adjustments. Fortunately, my mum, who'd missed her true vocation as a peacekeeper and diplomat, was as easy-going as the man I'd chosen to share my life with. It was because of her that we were eating at the family home and not at The Ivy, my dad's first choice. An antiques dealer, he'd acquired a new role as a minor TV celebrity after being invited to participate in a rip-off of *The Bidding Room*, a programme in which dealers made offers for pieces of unique interest. I loved eating at The Ivy but didn't fancy trying to discreetly breastfeed there.

'Shouldn't be too long,' I said, unlatching my son, wiping milk from his sweet little rosebud mouth with a muslin cloth. Rufus's eyes were closed, the eyelids tinged smoky blue. He had that dreamy, satiated expression on his face that spoke of a full tummy. I loved moments like this, when the world was in warm fuzzy focus, and I felt as if I were doing something important and inherently good. I gently parked Rufus, warm and snug, against my shoulder and rubbed his back until he gave a satisfied burp.

'You two,' Ben said proudly, adoration in his eyes.

'It's great, isn't it? I never thought I could be this happy.' The second the words left my mouth an insidious, obsessional voice, as dark as the interior of a Cotswold cottage in winter, whispered, *You don't deserve it.*

Banishing it from my mind, I stood up, walked Rufus up and down before then slipping him upright into his baby car seat.

'Okay,' I said to Ben. 'Let's get out of here.'

CHAPTER TWO

Awash with good memories, my family home in Cheltenham instantly had a warm and calming effect. I'd lived there from childhood to adulthood and it was only when I left to go to university I realised that, as much as it was the place where I grew up with my younger sister, Saskia (Saskia had never moved out) it was also a monument to my father's great love of beautiful things — including his daughters, he'd once sweetly told us. An end-of-terrace four-storey townhouse, it was on one of the spa town's most prestigious roads. According to family legend, my grandfather, Dad's dad, lent his only son money to buy it forty years before. Unusually not listed, the house had gone through a lot of changes over the years. In the early days of Cake That, my online cake and patisserie business, Saskia and I had worked out of the lower-ground-floor kitchen, a common architectural quirk of some of the posher properties. I couldn't walk inside the family home without memories of recipes that had gone so right, after which Saskia had cried and others that had gone so wrong, after which Saskia had also cried. Fortunately, Saskia had become less emotional and more confident since ditching hospitality and joining the business as my right-hand woman. Knowing she was temporarily at the helm had made taking six months of maternity leave a lot easier.

'Look at you,' Saskia said, bounding out to greet us. Small, dark and energetic, with a faintly exotic Cleopatra hairstyle and the build of a gymnast, she wrapped her arms around me and gave me a bone-crushing hug.

'Eugh! You smell of baby sick.'

'Mare,' I said, poking her scrawny ribs.

'Be grateful it isn't worse,' Ben chimed in behind us. I'd left him to carry Rufus. 'Where shall I dump our stuff?'

'Christ, are you three moving in?' Saskia said, in wide-eyed amusement.

'In the sitting room,' I heard Mum holler from the kitchen and then she appeared.

How my mother could look composed in an apron while cooking a roast for five people defied all laws of logic. Her hair, more white than grey, was pinned up. Wearing minimal make-up, she had an even-featured face, calm blue eyes that instantly told you she was a woman to be respected. I'd seen the photographs of her with Dad when they were young; Dad looking hilarious with his long hair and moustache and loon pants; a slimmer Mum kitted out in a long flowing dress, a silk scarf around her head from the original Biba store on Kensington High Street. Even at that tender age, she looked stately, composed, as if she knew exactly where she was heading in life.

'Darling,' Mum exclaimed, sliding past Saskia in the narrow confines of the hall, Dad fast closing in behind. She kissed me on both cheeks, as was her way.

There were more kisses and hugs, sturdy handshakes (Dad and Ben) and haphazard greetings before we all piled into the sitting room where we parked Rufus in his Moses basket, and Dad, being Dad, ceremoniously popped open a bottle of champagne to toast his and our good fortune. I wasn't drinking and Mum thoughtfully handed me homemade lemonade while Ben accepted a small glass of the hard stuff. He didn't drink much, not because he disapproved, but because he didn't much care for it. Consequently, he was a popular designated driver with our friends.

'To little Rufus,' Mum said, raising her glass.

Dad beamed and glanced over at his grandson with a pride that melted my heart.

'To the lovely lot of us,' Saskia said, laughter lighting up her face.

We sipped and they chatted and I watched. Motherhood had had a strange effect on me. I was always more of a leader and go-getter, a talker than a listener. Now, I liked to observe, appreciate and reflect. Having Rufus made me see the world in warm, positive and vibrant colours. Viewing my family now, their happy smiling faces, I felt overwhelmed with joy, not in an 'all my numbers have come up on the Lottery' kind of way — which I never did — but as if I were content and at peace, as if I'd won a lifetime achievement award, as if I'd really moved on and away from dark thoughts and unhappy memories and reached a place where I could rest and be at ease. I wanted to bottle that feeling and hold it tight forever.

So much of what I'd taken for granted I saw in sharper glorious detail, including my parents' home. A collector to his core, Dad had an eye for the eclectic. As a result, we sat in a gracious space filled with all his favourite pieces, including an early Lowry life drawing, sculptures and displays of rare coins. On the other side of the hall was the dining room, used for more formal entertainment, or if Mum and Dad were hosting a big party as they'd done often when we were kids. Here you could find a dazzling collection of snuffboxes, including a much-loved King Emmanuel III of Italy tabatière, in sleek silver and embossed enamel. Saskia once joked it would make a perfect container for passing cocaine around the table, a suggestion that was met with strong disapproval by my parents. Bohemians at heart, they'd never so much as smoked a joint, preferring good wine and whisky in the company of interesting people to whom they'd regularly throw open their home. Growing up, we were surrounded by itinerant artists, sculptors, the odd writer; creatives that Dad trumpeted.

In the big drawing room upstairs there was a medieval German black suit of armour, with fluting (according to my dad's description). It skulked in the corner near a large fireplace alongside a baby grand Challen piano, on which Dad sometimes thumped out a tune. In other rooms there were various glass-fronted cabinets, containing ancient manuscripts and first editions. Delicate Chinese bowls and plates of eye-watering value were displayed in specialist air-conditioned compartments, and every painting, of which there were a number, was appropriately illuminated. Despite the tilt towards old and vintage, my mother's taste in modern furnishings had created a comfortable and stylish home that doubled as a repository and showroom for Dad's treasures. God alone knew what the insurance was for the place. I had a sudden queasy thought: how could we toddler-proof it when Rufus was older?

'Top up, Faith?' Dad asked, brandishing the bottle. Mum had barely touched her drink and shook her head. I reckon it was Dad's sneaky excuse to freshen his own glass.

'Want a hand, Mum?' I asked.

'Thanks, but everything is under control, Sophie.'

Which came as no surprise. Cool without trying, Mum kept my eccentric dad grounded. The mainstay of our family, it was my mum everyone went to for practical advice. My hero, I aspired to be more like her, although I never thought I'd have my mother's natural grace.

At the sound of roaring laughter, I glanced in the direction of my father who seemed highly amused by something Ben had said. I caught the tail end of the conversation. 'Filming's to take place in Salford, Manchester, *Meeja City*,' Dad explained irreverently.

And he would fit in so well, I thought. Anthony Knox, not Ant, Tony or Tone, as he was quick to point out when someone became too familiar, was a man who unashamedly courted the spotlight. His dark hair, slightly long over his shirt collar and silvered at the temple, exposed a wide forehead that made him look brainy. Coal-black eyebrows, like arrowheads, framed his brown eyes. His sideburns were perfectly sculpted and gave him a rakish appearance. He had what could be described as a generous nose and his smile revealed the shiniest white teeth, courtesy of expensive dentistry. I never thought of him as vain yet knew that he was. He dressed the part of celebrity with a tendency towards the flamboyant. For a man in his late sixties, he didn't go overboard on keeping himself in shape — the extra inch or two around his waist told its own story — but, according to him (and my loyal mother), he 'ran a bit' in the winter and continued to enjoy playing tennis in the summer; forms of exercise to ensure that the well-cut suits and shirts he favoured looked good. He was often to be seen with a scarf, expensive and stylishly tied. Today was no exception: Italian silk, black with an orange geometric pattern. He wore it draped around a crisp white collarless shirt and navy trousers.

At the signal 'lunch is ready', I checked on Rufus, and we all moved through to the informal dining area in the kitchen. It had a lovely view of the walled garden. Taking a seat, as if it were yesterday, I vividly remembered Saskia playing outside with a watering can and child-sized spade, determinedly digging up weeds. Unlike me, she'd never been one for dolls.

During roast pork, home-made apple sauce, lashings of gravy, vegetables, and against a soothing background piece from Ralph Vaughan Williams, conversation ranged from Dad's TV gig, developments at Cake That, including the setting up of a third unit outside Cirencester in the village of South Cerney, and similar to the one we'd opened up in Tetbury eighteen months before, to the kitchen extension Ben and I had designed for our rapidly expanding cottage.

'We had to change the layout of the extension to fit in with planning,' Ben said, helping himself to more broccoli.

'I was never keen on floor-to-ceiling glass anyway,' I remarked, 'not with a small boy roaring around.'

'It was hi-spec safety glazing,' Ben pointed out. 'Not your average.'

'Even so,' Mum said. 'I think Sophie's right. I'd have been terrified with you two.' She exchanged a grin with Saskia. If anyone got into trouble in our family, it was always my little sister. I suspected there was a bit of Saskia that would never grow up. She definitely did not look thirty-six years of age. Once, mortifyingly, I'd been mistaken for her mother.

'What a nuisance,' Dad said. 'Costly, too.' He glanced at me, knowing that 'cost' was my area of expertise, unnecessary expense something that would rankle. Before I'd got into cakes, I'd worked in banking, first in Jersey and then in London. I'd had a glittering career ahead of me before I ditched it overnight. For the second time that day a dark thought hovered at the edges of my mind before mercifully flitting away.

'Couldn't be helped if we wanted to get the planning application through,' I remarked.

'If it's not too rude, how much is the spend?'

Ben looked to me. 'Around ninety K, possibly a little more,' I answered.

'Bloody hell,' Saskia burst out. I knew what she was thinking. That kind of money could be ploughed into the business.

'Is it strictly necessary?' Mum asked kindly.

'We'd rather do it now than wait and have the disruption later.'

'And it will make a massive difference,' Ben said, backing me up.

At the sound of Rufus squeaking from next door, I pushed the last piece of roast potato into my mouth and sped off to grab him.

'Bring him in here,' Mum called after me, desperate for a cuddle with her only grandchild.

The living room smelt of baby scent: warm milk and vanilla. Rufus's clear blue eyes were wide open, and he watched me in wonderment — or at least I liked to think he did. I grabbed my bag, unearthed everything I needed to change his

13

nappy, bent down, slipped my hands underneath, careful to support his head, and popped him onto the changing mat. Rufus didn't much care for being undressed so I talked to him softly, told him it wouldn't take long. He kicked a bit as I popped open his stripy sleepsuit. Working quickly, I removed his soiled nappy, dropped it into a nappy bag, cleaned him up, applied cream and, putting on a fresh nappy, gently positioned his legs back into his sleepsuit, fastening it back up.

'Good boy,' I crooned, holding him tightly against me.

Aided and abetted by several glasses of claret, Dad was in full flow when I returned, rattling on about the psychology that governed the purchase of antiques, a subject he trotted out regularly to anyone who would listen, Ben his latest unfortunate victim.

'The most discerning customers are attracted to the intrinsic beauty of a particular piece. For others, it's the possession of something unique, of quality and value. Then there are those who, for more sentimental reasons, desire to bridge the gap between past and present . . .'

I read Saskia's pleading expression: *let's catch up in the garden where I can have a cigarette*. I grinned back, handed Rufus to Mum, who couldn't have been more delighted and, grabbing cardigans and sweaters, we sped outside to the terrace.

'Poor Ben,' Saskia said, producing a lighter and cigarettes, shaking one out, plugging it between her lips and lighting it.

'He'll live.'

'I swear he's heard it all before. Oh, I forget,' Saskia said with a grin, 'Ben likes old people. Fuck,' she said, when I immediately bristled. 'I didn't mean you, silly.' My wild child younger sister possessed a mean streak; nobody was safe from her more acerbic observations.

'It sounded like it.' To be honest, I was a teensy bit sensitive about the age gap between me and Ben, and Saskia knew it. Oh, I'd combed through articles in the media about the joys of middle-aged women dating younger men — *so liberating, so subversive* — but I'd also encountered enough of the raised eyebrow and 'how did you pull him?' to feel a little undermined and not one hundred per cent confident.

'I was referring to his job, Sophs.'

As a junior doctor, Ben had been introduced to lots of different specialties yet developed a passion for geriatrics, which many people regarded as inexplicable. I found it easy enough to understand: his father had died after a long illness. Ben always regretted that more could not have been done to save him. Despite Saskia's explanation I wasn't entirely certain I believed her, and she knew it.

'When did you become so thin-skinned?' Saskia puffed out a cloud of smoke that made me cough.

'I'm not.'

'You are so.'

'Well, possibly,' I said, drumming my fingers on my chin. 'It has . . . oh, I don't know . . . something to do with me being knackered after having a baby?' I flashed a grin.

Saskia playfully punched my arm, sisterly spat over.

'And how is it all *really* going, the whole motherhood thing?' She tipped her head to one side, deep brown eyes locking onto mine. She took after Dad: dark hair, olive colouring and sharp cheekbones that gave her a dangerous edge. Her beautifully styled hair made me even more conscious of my unruly locks. The days when I wouldn't go out without an up-to-the-second cut, full make-up, painted nails, killer heels and sassy suits were long gone.

'Mostly pretty good,' I said easily.

'Apart from terminal exhaustion.'

'I'm luckier than some.' It was true. Rufus was a champion sleeper, although I still hadn't really got the hang of the big and sudden changes in my life. Two years before, I hadn't known Ben and then, in the space of months, there were three of us to consider.

'And you and Ben . . . ?' Saskia let the question delicately drift and hang.

On alert, I knew she was fishing even after all these years. Saskia wasn't asking: *Are you happy? Will you marry him?* What my nosy sister really wanted to know: *Will you dump him for no good reason, like you did with Leo days before the wedding?* Nobody knew the answer to that one. Only me and with me it would stay.

'We're good,' I answered, businesslike. Swerving the subject, I asked, 'How's Luke settling in?' Our latest employee was charged with downloading daily, weekly and monthly checks to meet food preparation and hygiene standards at our kitchens. You'd never know that this tall, good-looking man had had his arm broken in three places by a vengeful partner with a baseball bat. When I started the business I'd made it my mission to help survivors of domestic abuse. We mostly employed women; Luke and Ron, our sanitation man, the exceptions. Once again, an ominous thought surged out of nowhere.

'Luke the Abused?' Saskia said, with a grin.

'That's not remotely funny, Sash.'

'I thought it quite a witty literary twist,' Saskia shot back. My cool expression told her I was singularly unimpressed. She huffed a sigh. 'He's doing really well.'

'Fitting in all right with the others?'

'Like a dream.'

'Great.'

'Luke's appointment definitely gives me more time to concentrate on social media,' Saskia said. 'Tomorrow you can judge for yourself.' I was scheduled to drop into a meeting with a new packaging engineer. A professional could present our cakes more elegantly while saving us a lot of waste. 'Still reckon you'll be good to return to work on schedule in a couple of months?' Saskia pressed.

'As long as Rufus is weaned, and Mum is still happy to have him.'

Saskia chuckled. 'Mum will tear your arm off.' Narrowing her eyes, she blew out another plume of smoke. 'You know, everything is running smoothly. I'm quite capable of handling things. It wouldn't matter if you needed more time.'

'No,' I said firmly.

'Control freak,' Saskia teased.

'Well, if the cap fits,' I said, with an easy smile. 'Now you can put that thing out, wash your hands and go and dish up the puds.'

No, I said firmly.

Honestly, Saskia teased.

Well, if she say he'd said with an easy smile. Now
you can put that thing away, way [...] used, and point to and dab
up the mud.

CHAPTER THREE

Layers of moist lemony-yellow light sponge, raspberries, buttercream and raspberry jelly topped with meringue — pudding was my take on Eton Mess. It never failed to please and
was one of our most popular bakes. Apart from our Diehard
Chocolate cake, created by Saskia, it was Ben's favourite so I
was surprised he was nowhere to be seen. Must have popped
to the loo.

As Saskia plated up, Dad worried he wouldn't look good
on TV. 'It adds at least ten pounds, apparently,' he fretted.

'Better dust off your game show host jacket, Dad,' Saskia
teased to collective groans from Mum and me and embarrassment from my father. Dark navy with a garish paisley red and
gold design, the jacket suggested that Dad had gone colour blind.
To be fair, it had been an impulse buy some years ago to accom-
modate his then fuller figure. Fortunately, he no longer needed
it. I'd no idea why such a horrible item of clothing remained in
his wardrobe — I thought my mother would have chucked it
out. Maybe she'd hung on to it to serve as a salutary lesson.

Still no Ben, I asked where he was.

Mum glanced up from baby-gazing. 'Went outside to
take a phone call.'

'Seemed urgent,' Dad remarked.

I couldn't think why. Ben wasn't on call.

I walked out into the hallway and into the living room to better look out of the window. Ben was striding up and down, pale-faced, intensity in his expression. Instinctively, I thought it spelt trouble.

There is a moment in a person's life when the unpredictable phone call will bring the walls crashing down. The death of a loved one; a worrying diagnosis resulting in a terrifying prognosis; the realisation that the person you've been living with is not the person you should end your days with. Each is high on the 'this is going to screw you' chart. With a sudden stab of anxiety, I believed that what I was witnessing on a cold wet March afternoon was a game changer for Ben and possibly for me. And the reason I thought this? Not because I was in full-on protective tigress mode. Not because my brain was awash with happy hormones and I was afraid, eventually, they'd go into terminal decline, but because I had received a similar life-changing phone call eight years before.

Please, please let me be wrong, I thought, stealing back to the rest of my family.

'I think your little man is hungry,' Mum said, handing Rufus to me. Luckily, it was easy enough to feed him while demolishing a large helping of pudding, although, weirdly, my normally monstrous appetite had deserted me. Nursing a funny curdled sensation in the pit of my stomach, I requested a glass of water from Mum.

My gaze shot up as Ben returned and, scraping back his chair, resumed his seat next to Dad. 'Oh good,' he said with a grin, eyeing up dessert.

'Everything okay?' I asked casually.

'It is, if a little astounding.'

Saskia's eyes glinted with curiosity. 'Ooh, what's that?'

'Do tell,' Dad chimed in.

'My brother, Adam, is back in the country,' Ben said. 'He wants to reconnect.'

19

The mysterious brother Ben barely mentioned, I registered. 'But that's lovely,' I said. Frankly, I felt relief.

Happy to share my family with Ben, and they were genuinely keen to welcome him, I'd sometimes catch a slightly lost expression in his eyes when we were all together. I knew how much Ben had loved his father because he talked about him with affection, especially the times his dad had taken him fishing as a boy. Ben spoke less of his mother, but when he did it was always with fond regard. Adam barely featured. 'Have you arranged to meet?' I asked.

'Tomorrow, late afternoon, after surgery.'

'He's visiting Cirencester?'

'He's staying.'

'Fabulous, where?'

Ben twitched a smile, cleared his throat. 'Actually, I said they could stay with us. It seemed the brotherly thing to offer.'

Before I could respond, Saskia blundered in and beat me to it.

'They?'

'He's bringing his girlfriend, Brooke.'

I wasn't good with surprises at the best of times. The thought of people I didn't know staying with us, particularly when I was still in the early stages of navigating motherhood, was dismaying. I glued my expression to my son, knowing full well that Ben was desperately trying to catch my eye.

Failing to make contact, Ben asked, 'Is that all right, Sophs?'

Not wishing to be the voice of dissent, I took a breath. 'The house is in disarray. With a tiny baby the last thing we need are house guests. Rufus is into a routine. I don't want it disturbed . . .'

'Perish the thought,' Saskia said, a facetious lilt to her voice.

'Saskia, darling, do shut up,' Dad intervened good-naturedly.

I flashed him a grateful smile. 'If you'd let me finish,' I said, eyeballing Saskia, 'Ben hasn't seen his brother in an age and I'm happy to host, cook dinner and do whatever to make his stay as nice as possible, but,' I said, appealing to Ben, 'wouldn't it be easier all round if they stay in town?'

'I think money's a little tight,' he replied, pained.

'Fair enough,' I said, snookered.

Keen to smooth things over, Mum offered to pop over, tidy the house and make up the bed in the spare room. She had a key to our home and had spoiled me rotten when I'd come out of hospital. She'd often drop in so that I could nap and when she did, I'd invariably find the cooker had been cleaned or the laundry done.

'That would be marvellous,' I said, 'but remember you're having Rufus for a couple of hours in the morning while I'm at work tomorrow.' I didn't want to put on her too much.

'I haven't forgotten,' she said breezily. 'It will be so nice for Ben and his brother.'

'Absolutely,' I agreed, a little too heartily.

I glanced across at Ben. I wanted him to look totally made up, delighted and excited even if he felt a little apprehensive. He looked none of those things. The smile stretched tight across his handsome face didn't fool anyone, least of all me.

CHAPTER FOUR

Ben was reassuring as we drove the short journey home. 'It's only a flying visit.'

'Does he have any other plans?' From what I'd gathered from Ben in fleeting conversations, Adam was nomadic, always on the move, leapfrogging from one country to another.

Ben changed gear. 'I gather he intends to relocate to the UK.'

'The Cotswolds?'

'Don't think he could afford it. He'll probably return to the Midlands.'

'Home ground,' I said, feeling unaccountably relieved. 'What's he going to do jobwise?'

'Didn't say. He's always been a free spirit.'

'He must have some skills.'

'He's quite musical.'

I had images of late nights with badly played guitar. 'Would you like to give me a steer?'

'Plays the piano a bit.'

'"Chopsticks" or Chopin?'

Ben glanced across with a grin.

'I'm serious. You've barely mentioned his name since we met. I have absolutely no handle on him.' And I was suspecting that Ben didn't have one either.

'Okay,' Ben said, all brass tacks and factual, which I appreciated. 'He's four years older than me.'

'Thirty-eight.'

'Glad to see your skill at mathematics kicking in.'

'Ha-ha. Carry on.'

'He's highly intelligent — smarter than me.'

I found that hard to believe. Free spirit. Muso. Approaching the big life crisis. Definitely flaky or, as Dad would say, a layabout; shame on me.

'So he makes a living?'

'I guess so. It was a pretty short conversation, Sophie. I wasn't going to quiz him about what he has in his bank account after we'd lost touch for so long.' Ben had the war-weary tone of a long-suffering, long-married spouse. 'Satisfied?' he said, glancing across.

I'm a numbers girl so not really. But I wasn't about to argue and instead feverishly planned a strategy for the following day. After visiting Cake That, and if Mum was amenable, I could fit in a supermarket dash, pick Rufus up, pop into the estate agents to check on progress on the sale of my flat, speed home and make a start on preparing dinner.

'Don't suppose you asked whether they're vegan or vegetarian?'

'Or coeliac, or gluten intolerant,' Ben said, with dry humour. 'Relax. It will be fine, might even be fun.'

'You'll certainly have a ton to catch up on. When was the last time you actually clapped eyes on each other?'

Ben took his time answering. 'Twelve years, or thereabouts.' He fixed his eyes on the road. Good job I wasn't driving.

'*Twelve*?' I spluttered. 'Did you two fall out?'

'We drifted apart after our parents died,' Ben said, a nerve in the side of his jaw pulsing. 'It happens in families.'

Feeling shallow and insensitive and kicking myself for being negative, I said I was sorry and touched Ben's thigh affectionately.

He briefly rested one hand on mine and, without another word spoken, we left it at that.

CHAPTER FIVE

With gables and mullion windows and walls the colour of warm butter, Lamb's Leap was the epitome of a Cotswold stone cottage. Dating back to the late nineteenth century, it had two wings: one we currently lived in, the other we were doing up. The one destined for renovation comprised a main bedroom that led into a smaller bedroom, typical of old Cotswold houses, together with a bathroom. Easy on the eye, the interior tumbled with natural light — a rarity, in my book.

Leaving Ben to unpack the car, I went inside with Rufus and placed him in his crib upstairs. We hadn't wanted to know the gender of our baby, so I'd deliberately kept the room neutral. Nonetheless, Ben had insisted on erecting a mobile with bright blue airplanes over Rufus's sleeping area. Nothing unusual about women flying aircraft, he'd said in answer to my protest.

Reckoning I had a couple of hours, at least, before Rufus woke again, I slipped downstairs and found Ben in the kitchen. We didn't keep wine in the house, but there were leftover spirits from Christmas and, partial to bourbon, Saskia often brought her own booze. Astonishingly, she'd left a bottle behind. To my surprise, if not quite consternation, Ben had poured a couple of fingers of Jack Daniels into a tumbler.

'Are you okay?' I asked.

Ben raised the glass to his lips and took a long swallow. 'Perfectly.'

I hopped up onto the bar stool next to him.

'Don't suppose you want one?' His smile was lop-sided.

'Better not.' I sounded as if I would if I could but couldn't — no judgement here — and what my mother would deem a pragmatic response.

He took another swig.

'Ben, I appreciate this is a big deal with your brother.'

He nodded slowly, stared out of the French windows, shortly to be replaced by an extension and bi-fold doors. Ben had seemed relatively relaxed in the car. Had it all been show, for my benefit? Deep down did he entertain concerns? And if he did, should I have them too? I didn't say anything and listened to the slow tick of the clock on the wall and the blackbirds singing their mellow evening song. Eventually, Ben broke off from what had apparently caught his attention and trained his soulful eyes on mine. I thought he was about to say something profound then changed his mind.

Lightening the mood, I said, 'Think you'll recognise him?'

Ben frowned. 'How do you mean?'

'Maybe he's gone bald, or grown a double chin, or a beard.'

He flicked a smile. 'That, I very much doubt, but it's always a possibility.'

I raised my eyebrows. 'Will *he* recognise *you*?'

'I haven't changed that much.'

'Not if your graduation photo is anything to go by.' About the only one I'd seen of Ben in his twenties. He looked solemn, I recalled, less carefree than the man I knew, which was only to be expected after losing both his parents so close together during his studies.

'You said you last saw each other over a decade ago.'

'Yep.'

'Do you remember where?'

'Pub, where else?' he replied, without missing a beat. It sounded as if Ben was a regular pubgoer, which he wasn't.

'Which pub?'

'God's sake, Sophie, Cock and Magpies on the Hagley Road, Birmingham. Do you want the website address to check out the menus?'

I pulled a sorry face. Sometimes, my need to know got the better of me; this was one of those moments.

But Ben wasn't finished. 'Adam went travelling shortly afterwards, Sweden first, if you're interested, and I later took my finals.'

'I apologise, unreservedly,' I said. 'I didn't mean to read anything sinister into it.'

Ben set down his drink, tipped forward and kissed me long and slow. I tasted the sweet and peaty flavour of neat whisky on my tongue.

'What was that for?' I asked, smiling.

'Do I need a reason?'

'Never.'

We kissed again. As he pulled away, Ben took both my hands in his and, once more, gazed into my eyes. 'Promise me something.'

'What?'

'Don't believe everything that Adam tells you.'

'Ri-ight.'

'I love my brother,' Ben said quickly, 'but sometimes he has a loose grasp on the truth.'

I frowned, not really understanding.

'He's wired differently.'

I wondered if he meant autistic, or on the spectrum, and said as much.

'No, no, he just has . . .' Ben broke off, struggling to find the right description, the *fair* description, I intuited. 'He's cursed with a vivid imagination.'

Cursed?

Spotting my alarm, Ben said, 'Wrong word. He's a little bit full-on, theatrical, you know.'

I thought about that. To be fair, Saskia was similarly inclined, although I never viewed it as an affliction. Growing up in the same family we often regarded events from completely different perspectives. Saskia's usually contained a highly dramatic flavour; mine tended to be more cerebral, factual, down the line. It was simply the difference between our personalities. One wasn't right or wrong. Yet I didn't believe that this was what Ben was getting at.

'Is he going to tell me all the appalling things you did as a small boy?' I said, humouring him.

'Something like that,' Ben replied uneasily. He could have instantly made light of it, but he didn't.

'He's a liar, you mean?' I was pushing it, but Ben's response wasn't exactly reassuring. It took him an age to answer.

He viewed me with the kind of sage, listening expression I bet he used in the surgery. Except I didn't think he was hearing me. 'Too strong,' he said eventually.

'Whatever has happened between you two, it's for the pair of you to sort out,' I said. 'It has naff all to do with me.'

'I'm simply letting you know that Adam isn't like other people.'

And then I tumbled to it: Ben was giving me fair warning. I jolted forward.

'What about Rufus?'

'What about him?'

'He will be safe with Adam here, won't he?' Did paranoia come with motherhood?

Ben's face relaxed into a smile. 'Of course, Sophs.'

'You're sure?' How could he claim to know after all this time? Ben was not making me feel any better and I said so.

'Sophie,' Ben said sternly, 'give me some credit. I would never put our child in danger.'

As my gaze locked onto his I realised a fundamental truth: given a choice between protecting my partner and protecting my child, Rufus would win. Always.

'Forget it,' Ben said, patting my knee. 'I'm basing my thoughts on the Adam I knew back then when we were in our twenties. I daresay I've changed a fair bit too.'

'But . . .'

'You and Rufus will be perfectly fine and, like I said, it's probably only a flying visit.'

I watched Ben lift the glass of bourbon to his lips and wondered why the hand of the father of my child was shaking.

CHAPTER SIX

The next morning Ben was his usual sunny self. I thought he might have a hangover. If he did, he didn't admit to it.

'I'm going to pop into the estate agents before I head back home later,' I said.

'Good luck with that,' Ben remarked ruefully.

'The flat has to sell sooner or later.'

A penthouse in Cheltenham's Pittville Circus Road, my apartment had been on the market for months and months. We needed to sell it so that I could put money back into the household budget to cover my share of renovation costs, including the extension. As lovely as my old home was, it wasn't my wisest purchase. A penthouse is fine as long as there's a lift. It didn't have one. The ground charge for communal gardens and service rent for the building were extortionate. Even so, I needed to shift it. I'd already dropped the price once.

Ben grabbed his jacket, ready to head out. 'Have you spoken to Louise recently?' he asked randomly.

'No, why? She and Elliott have only just got back from the Maldives, remember?'

'Oh yeah.' Ben picked up his keys. 'Hopefully, a nice, relaxing holiday will have helped things along.'

'Sometimes you can be so coy,' I teased him. 'You mean she'll get pregnant.'

'I hope so for Elliott's sake. I gather things are getting slightly regimented in the bedroom.'

'Sounds grim,' I said.

'He thinks so, poor chap.'

'Every time Rufus makes a sound I feel as if I'm rubbing Louise's nose in it.'

Ben expressed acute surprise. 'Is that why you've seen less of her lately?'

'Subconsciously, perhaps.' I felt bad. Louise was a bit younger than me and worked in the charity sector, helping victims of domestic abuse. It's how we'd first met. When I'd wanted to get involved, she'd helped to facilitate it, talked to the right people, ensured that what I was offering — a job, security and respectful environment — was real and not some publicity stunt. We'd been firm friends ever since. The hurt in her eyes when I'd announced my unplanned pregnancy was fleeting, yet unmistakable, and although she'd never made a deal of it, I was sure that she felt I'd gained instant access to the parents' club from which she was denied. I explained this to Ben.

'I'm sure Louise doesn't view it like that.'

'It can't be easy for her. I mean look at us. We barely knew each other and—'

'Result!' Ben boomed, his smile wide. 'Talking of which, where is little man?'

'In the kitchen doing the washing-up,' I said, straight-faced. 'Where do you think he is?'

Ben slipped his arm around my waist. 'You're very skittish this morning.'

I didn't know what to say to that. I suppose I was putting on a positive front after our slightly unnerving conversation the night before. I walked with Ben to the door. 'You won't be late tonight, will you?'

'Not unless someone's leg drops off.'

I grinned and stood in the porch while he crossed the drive to his car, and disconnected his Audi Q4 e-tron from the charging point. After watching its silent passage out, I went back inside, making a mental note to phone Louise and write a shopping list. As soon as Rufus woke, I'd change his nappy, feed him and then we were good to go.

CHAPTER SEVEN

Running late — I was always running late these days — I bundled Rufus into Mum's arms, gave her hurried instructions about how to warm up expressed milk — never in the microwave — and fled.

It took me twenty minutes to cut through traffic from leafy Painswick Road, on which my parents lived, to the main unit on Kingsditch Trading Estate. I parked my Honda Jazz in between Saskia's baby-blue Fiat and the former ice-cream van that had been kitted out in Cake That decal — Saskia's brainchild — then headed to our offices at the back.

All clatter and thrum, Saskia was on the phone to a supplier, and Luke, six foot three of him and looking mildly comical in his white overalls, a hairnet covering his blond hair, and gloves — remarkably similar to a scenes of crime officer — was making an impassioned call to a maintenance engineer about a faulty fridge. Not an impressive start to the morning.

I looked to Saskia, who'd done something different with her make-up — new eyeliner, I suspected — and mouthed, 'Is he here yet?' Meeting with Misha, a potential new packaging engineer was my main reason for calling into work.

'Hang on a sec, Kirsty.' Then to me: 'He's had to postpone.'

'What?'

'His kid's been knocked off his bike.'

'God,' I exclaimed. 'Is it serious?'

Saskia shrugged. 'He's been taken to Cheltenham General.'

I dropped Misha a quick supportive email, reassuring him that we would reschedule, baulked at a recent notification regarding the increased price of sugar and, double-whammy, electricity and, while Saskia and Luke were otherwise engaged, slipped on an apron, gloves and hat and headed through the door to the cooking area.

We employed six cooks, all part-time to fit in with life-styles and school holidays, one full-time driver and two full-time counter staff. It was a similar set-up in our unit in Tetbury. We sold primarily online but more recently direct to customers. Opening at ten, we had a reliable retail trade from people who worked on the trading estate. As word spread, customers came from further afield. We were able to reach locals who couldn't travel with our delivery service, courtesy of our converted ice-cream van.

A wall of heat enveloped me. On a chilly March day it was welcome. In the summer, it could be sweltering.

There is something unique about a bakery. It's not only the spicy aroma of cakes and warm flour and icing sugar; it's the memories those fragrances evoke. My earliest was standing on a stool next to my mother, helping her beat eggs, cream-ing butter, adding sugar and, best of all, licking out the bowl afterwards. It was about birthday parties and friendship, cel-ebration and comfort. Most of all, it was about sharing and community. I reckoned this was what we were really selling to our customers; it wasn't all about the cake.

A single glance told me that everything was running fairly smoothly, despite the fridge issue, which I mentioned to Vanessa our most experienced and longest-serving employee. She'd been with us from the beginning of the enterprise when we were still working out of my mum's kitchen. Taking out a batch of golden-brown almond croissants from an oven, Vanessa flashed me a ready smile.

'Fortunately, we had spare capacity in one of the other refrigerators,' she said.

'Wastage?'

Vanessa wrinkled her nose. 'We rescued most of the stock, maybe ten per cent lost, but don't quote me. Saskia will have a better handle on it.'

I chatted to Lisa, another baker, admiring a tray of glossy-topped meringues, and spoke to our youngest recruit, Maeve, who was icing cupcakes. Poor girl was required by Hygiene Standards to either cover up her piercings or remove them entirely. Plastered in blue stickers, she glanced up briefly and nodded.

We switched off the ovens around three in the afternoon, allowing for heavy-duty cleaning but there was always plenty of food debris to clear up during the day. Roy, a former retiree, was our man in charge of sanitation. As such, he would have a close working relationship with Luke.

'Everything okay, Roy?' I asked.

A man of few words, Roy replied, 'Yep.'

'All good with Luke?'

'Yep.'

I moved on to the counter section where Andrea and Sharon, two women who'd come to me directly through Louise, were laying up patisserie in the display counters.

'Looking great,' I commented.

Sharon grinned. 'Not looking so bad yourself.'

I grinned back.

'She's been like that all morning,' Andrea said.

'All what?' Sharon said, still with the wide smile.

'Dead cheeky. How's your little one?' Andrea said, addressing me.

'Doing well.'

'Doesn't seem that long ago you announced you were pregnant. You looking forward to coming back?'

It was a good question. I missed the cut and thrust of work. There were days when time slipped by, and I had no idea what I'd done to fill them. Routine by nature, it sometimes felt alarming, as if I were on a runaway train, with no clear idea of the destination, yet the idea of leaving Rufus, even in good hands, wasn't that appealing. Saskia was very capable, but my staff saw me as their cheerleader as well as their boss and the woman who held the purse strings. I responded to Andrea with the answer she needed to hear, an unequivocal 'yes'.

'Right,' I said, noting the long line of customers waiting outside, 'I'd better leave you to open up.'

I returned to the office, peeled off my hat and work clobber, spoke briefly to Luke who, a man on a mission, was keen to get back to the kitchen and, after a visit to the loo, accepted a cup of coffee from Saskia who was now off the phone.

'Will you still be available for appraisals at the end of the week?' Saskia asked.

We had regular one-to-ones with staff to allow a safe space for niggles to be aired, encouragement given and to check up on any welfare issues. Nine times out of ten I'd be asked for a pay rise.

'Why wouldn't I be?'

'You have guests, remember.'

'Good grief, they'll be gone by then.'

Saskia elevated an eyebrow, leant back expansively in a chair and parked her stilettos on the desk. 'And if they aren't?'

I wasn't keen to consider it. 'They'll have to amuse themselves.'

Saskia's expression was one of barbed amusement. 'All set then?'

'I will be. Why so interested?'

'Just curious.'

Curious translates as *interested* in Saskia's book. Loud and party-loving, my younger sister had a track record with men that made D-list celebrities look like slouches. Not to put too fine a point on it, the streets of Cheltenham were paved with Saskia's casualties. What Saskia wants Saskia gets in that department and when she's finished, she discards. Mum's shoulders were permanently damp due to the number of broken hearts that have cried all over her. I couldn't bear the idea of Saskia muscling in on a man who hadn't even arrived and, according to Ben, was arriving with a shedload of baggage. I went full older sister. 'Adam is spoken for and will be staying all of five minutes.'

'Says who?'

'Says Ben.'

I thought that was the end of it, but no.

'Do you think he'll be as good looking and charming?'

'You are incorrigible,' I said, laughing despite myself.

Saskia eyed me over the rim of the coffee cup. 'Has Ben told you anything about him?'

So unsubtle. 'He's a musician apparently.'

'Explains why he hasn't got a dime.'

'You were listening hard.'

'Always,' Saskia said with a wink. 'Think we'll get to meet him?'

'We?'

'Me and Mum?'

'Doubt it.'

Saskia looked thoughtful. 'You have to admit it's strange him turning up out of the blue.'

Nothing wrong with a brother wanting to reconnect with a brother, I told my sister. I didn't reveal that he had an 'extremely vivid imagination' or that he 'saw things differently'.

CHAPTER EIGHT

It's never a good idea to shop for food when you're hungry and definitely never great to panic buy. I did both, hurtling around the supermarket in record time. Adding several bottles of wine, red and white, and beers, I sped off to Mum's and got snarled in traffic. I phoned her on my hands-free.

'Everything okay?' I asked anxiously.

'He's been a little poppet. Taken his milk and gone back to sleep.'

Thank God. 'I should be with you in fifteen, quicker if I can.'

'Sophie, darling, relax. Take a breath.'

I needed to take several. I think I was more worried about Adam's visit than Ben, which was daft.

With immaculate timing, my mother had the kettle on the second I walked through the door.

'Not sure I can stop.' I explained I needed to drop into the estate agents in town.

'Can't you call them?'

I could but feared I'd be fobbed off on the phone. Turn up in person and you're less likely to be given the runaround. I outlined my thinking.

My mother gave me a wry look. 'You can't control everything, Sophie. Sometimes you have to let life find its own level. Half an hour will make very little difference.'

She was right. Suitably chastened, I relented and accepted a cup of tea.

'Sandwich?' she asked.

'Only if you're having one.'

She was and I watched as she prepared cheese and tomato on sourdough.

'Did Dad get off all right this morning?'

'After a lot of faffing about, he did.'

Typical, Dad. 'It's good though, isn't it?'

'I guess.'

'You're not keen?'

'Only about the timing. I was rather hoping that he'd slow down, and we'd have more time together.'

'It's only a one-off, isn't it?'

'Who knows where it might lead.'

The thought had never occurred to me. I didn't think Hollywood beckoned and made a joke of it. Slow on the uptake, there was something halting in her expression. I suddenly noticed how tired she looked. Perhaps yesterday had taken it out of her. God forbid Rufus was responsible.

'Are you okay, Mum?'

Her head snapped up. 'Why do you ask?'

'You look a little . . .'

'I had a bad night. Always do when your father has to get up early. Anyway, enough of me.' Mum planted a plate on the island unit with such deliberation the matter was definitely closed. 'Is there anything you need me to do this afternoon, other than make up the bed?'

'Honestly, you don't need to come over. I can manage.'

'I know,' she said, with a firm smile. 'But I'd like to.'

'As long as you're sure.'

Another smile convinced me that it was no trouble at all.

'I'm so pleased for Ben,' she said, nibbling at a crust.

I nodded agreement. I confided in my mum about many things. This wasn't one of them. And what would I tell her? That Ben thought his brother a little tricky to handle? I knew what she would say: *Chill out, Sophie.*

We spoke of nothing consequential, other than me establishing that Mum could have Rufus again towards the end of the week while I conducted one-to-ones at work.

'Same sort of time?' she asked, setting her sandwich aside.

'Around ten thirty a.m. Aren't you hungry?'

'I'll eat it later. Ten thirty it is,' she said, smiling warmly at Rufus. 'I'll be ready.'

Taking Mum's advice, I phoned the estate agent and, predictably, received the response to which I was accustomed: *trade is a bit slow at the moment; it's a buyer's market; if we tweak the price it would provide traction.*

The price already 'tweaked', i.e. dropped by ten thousand pounds four weeks ago, I wasn't keen. I ended the call, demoralised.

'It will happen,' Mum said soothingly.

Rufus remained spark out when I loaded him into his car seat. Fingers crossed he stayed that way until we were home.

CHAPTER NINE

Rufus was fed and sleeping. Mum had been and gone. Before I did anything else I put my big girl pants on and phoned Louise.

'Hey,' she said, happy to hear from me.

'How was the holiday?' I asked.

'Blissful. We had such a lovely time, and it was *so* hot.'

'Must be a jolt to come back to the cold and wet.'

'I had to dig out my thickest, warmest sweaters. My tan will wear off in no time.'

'Don't expect sympathy,' I said with a laugh.

'Have I missed anything?'

Did Adam's impending arrival constitute an event? Not one for drama, it somehow felt auspicious. Sticking to the simple facts, I told Louise.

'I don't think I've ever heard Ben mention a brother.'

'No,' I confirmed.

'And you say they're staying at yours?'

'Ben assured me it's a flying visit.'

'You believe him?' Louise chuckled.

I was banking on it. Skidding past her question, I said, 'I'm planning to be in town on Thursday, hopefully they'll

41

be gone by then. I wondered if you were free, say around lunchtime?'

'I'm working from home all week, but I should be all caught up. How about we have a quick bite here?'

'I don't want to put you to any trouble.'

'No trouble at all and it will be easier for you to feed Rufus.'

Touched by her thoughtfulness, I said I'd bring a tray bake from work.

'Special request for banoffee?'

'You got it.' I ended the call thinking Ben would be pleased I'd acted on his advice.

I spent the rest of the afternoon cooking minced beef, onion, garlic and red peppers for moussaka. Letting it cool, I roasted aubergines in the oven and let them rest. I got everything ready for making a béchamel sauce and knocked up a green salad and put it in the fridge. Mum had always advised me to lay a table when having guests, so it looks as if you're prepared even if you aren't. I followed her advice. I was as ready as I'd ever be and found myself nervously eyeing the clock as it passed five thirty. Ben was not home, and Adam and Brooke hadn't arrived. I had wine chilling in the fridge and was tempted to pour a glass.

At the sound of tyres on gravel, I flew to Ben's study at the front of the house and, through the window, watched a taxi draw up on the drive. It knocked me back a bit, if I were honest. I stupidly thought Adam would have his own set of wheels. The fact they'd cabbed it meant they wouldn't be independent. But then Ben had said 'flying visit' so maybe this was a good sign. Deep in conversation with the driver in what seemed an amusing exchange, the passengers showed little sign of getting out. What to do? Stay put, go to the door, or step out and bound across with my game face on? The decision was magically taken out of my hands when both car doors opened, and the occupants stepped out. *Action*, I thought, as a tall figure in a hoodie, face obscured and giving the appearance of a Benedictine monk, was followed by an equally tall figure; a young woman, no more than a girl. Her thick coat finished below her knees. She wore a long purple dress and Doc Martens in a matching colour. Her flaxen-coloured hair was in plaits. They both disappeared behind the car, to the boot, no doubt, to collect their luggage. Good grief, I thought, as several bags were manhandled out of the cab. They looked as if they were coming for a fortnight, at least. I was about to cross the hallway, preparing to greet them, when Rufus let out a cry.

I hurried to the front door and flung it open, sprinted back upstairs, picked up Rufus, flew down the staircase and, out of breath, was met by the man I presumed was Adam at the bottom. 'Hi,' he said, setting down two enormous travel bags and pushing back the hood from a face that, I wasn't kidding, blew my socks off. Silky smooth black hair fell from a middle parting. It shone like satin, its sheen curiously reminding me of an undertaker's top hat. I swear he'd done something with his eyebrows, which were dark and well defined, no scar. Eyeliner framed eyes that were deep-set, dark and appraising. He had several studs in his ears; his cheekbones were sharper than Saskia's. His mouth quirked at the edges in an amused smile that I suspected was his resting expression. He looked as if he needed a shave but had no intention of doing so. His black shirt, which clung to his wiry physique, was open to reveal tanned skin and a silver St Christopher necklace. Below: a tattoo with wording I couldn't read without seeming intrusive. His jeans were black and ripped above the knee. Slim-hipped, he wore three chains that were clipped to the waistband. He wore sneakers on his feet. Whatever cologne he was wearing was exotic and spicy and intoxicating. Everything about him spelt louche muso and my first impression was that he was seductively attractive; my second: I must not let Saskia anywhere near him.

'You must be Sophie. At least I bloody hope so otherwise we've come to the wrong house.' His voice was deep with a salty edge; a smoker, I thought. He stared at me intently as if it were his home we were standing in and I'd strayed in.

43

'No, you've come to the right place.' Nervous, I let out a giddy laugh that didn't quite sound like mine. Mercifully, Adam joined in, breaking the proverbial ice in our stilted introduction.

'And this must be Rufus,' he said, soft-eyed, reaching out and resting his hand on my baby's back, in a way very similar to Ben. Unlike Ben, Adam wore tan fingerless leather gloves. I caught a surprising flash of navy-blue nail varnish. I couldn't help but think a cuckoo had flown into the Taylor family nest; Adam was nothing like Ben in looks and bearing. I was so mesmerised I barely noticed Brooke until she peered over his shoulder, her thin build making her seem even taller. As if at his command, she stepped forward out of a sea of belongings. With a rucksack on her back, she held a bouquet of flowers in her tiny, bird-like hand.

'These are for you.' Visibly shy, she spoke in a voice I strained to hear.

Close-up, she looked even younger than she'd first appeared. Her smooth skin was exceptionally pale, the colour of white icing. Her eyes were sea green and curved down at the edges, highlighting her vulnerability because I had no doubt that this girl-woman, barely out of her teens, if that, was very much in thrall to Adam, a confident, extraordinary-looking older man.

'That's so sweet, thank you,' I said. 'Leave your luggage and come on through.' I ushered them down the hall to the kitchen. With my hands full, I motioned Brooke to pop the flowers in the sink, which she did.

'You've got quite a place here,' Adam said, heading straight for the view of the garden.

'It's very pretty,' Brooke said, 'and so light.' Now that she'd spoken more loudly, I deduced an east London accent.

'We think so. This is all coming out,' I said, indicating the French windows. 'We want to create a large diner extension and terrace with a running water feature from harvested rainwater.'

'Awesome,' Brooke said, admiringly. 'Are you doing all the work yourself?'

'No way,' I said, smiling. 'We've got an architect who's advised us on experienced local builders. All done by the book.'

'That's Ben for you,' Adam said, twisting round. 'And where is the old man?'

'On his way home.' At least, I hoped so.

Silence erupted as if nobody quite knew what to do or say next. I took the lead. Sounding hopelessly like a concierge in a three-star hotel, I said, 'Would you like to see your room?'

'That would be great,' Brooke said. 'I'd love to freshen up.'

With Rufus still in my arms, I led them back out into the hall, through the main living room to a door that led up a second narrow staircase. It would take them at least two trips to transport their belongings, I thought ruefully.

'The west wing,' Adam exclaimed, trooping up behind us.

'You'll be quite private,' I said. 'Apologies if it's a little rough and ready, but you have your own bathroom.'

Mum, I noticed, had thoughtfully put out tissues and body lotion, as well as fresh fluffy towels and soap. She'd also placed a bowl of fruit on the window ledge in the bedroom.

'This is so lit,' Brooke said admiringly.

I think she meant 'perfect' or 'exactly right'. We'd had a couple of interns the summer before, and they seemed to speak a different language.

'We hope to connect it to the main part of the house one day.'

'You could let it out as an Airbnb and make a shedload of cash,' Brooke said, the thought obviously exciting her.

'Maybe.' *Not on your life*, I thought.

Adam softly dropped his gaze on me. 'It's too perfect to hand over to strangers.' His expression was slightly unnerving, as if he were looking right into my mind.

Nervous, I smiled agreement and wondered when the hell Ben would be home.

CHAPTER TEN

'Where have you been?' I hissed as Ben finally walked through the door almost two hours later. In that time, Brooke had taken a bath and changed into a flimsy diaphanous number that accentuated her bony build. I'd fished out an individual portion of vegetarian lasagne from the depths of the freezer on discovering that Brooke was a committed vegetarian, fed Rufus and, while Adam cuddled him, lit the log burner and made final preparations for dinner. Initially, I was reluctant to hand Rufus over and yet Adam was a natural. Often men, my father included, were so scared of 'breaking' a baby they almost came to grief.

'God's sake,' I once regrettably snapped at Dad for his clumsy handling. 'You have to support Rufus's head.' How Saskia and I made it to adulthood remained a mystery.

Adam wasn't the least bit scared of Rufus and Rufus, mesmerised by his uncle's shiny jewellery, responded accordingly. Adam rattled away and told me about his travels through Europe and beyond. Was there a country he hadn't been to? I'd joked. But his real enthusiasm lay in the big music hotspots in the US: New Orleans, Memphis, L.A., Detroit and Chicago. He talked knowledgeably about blues, jazz, gospel and R & B and about his passion for the piano. Relaxed and at ease, he proved interested and engaging even when I blithered on about swatches and paint colours. Offering his own suggestions, he showed no sign of boredom. I couldn't help but like him, especially after the bad press he'd received from Ben.

'Sorry, sorry,' Ben said, kissing me on the cheek. 'I got held up. All good?'

'Well, we haven't died of hunger,' I said, with a reproving smile. 'To be honest, your brother is nothing short of charming. He has a terrific eye for colour and is excellent with Rufus.'

'I'm so pleased,' Ben said with a flat stare.

'Don't know what all the fuss was about.'

Ben's answering smile was brittle.

I followed him into the kitchen where Adam and Brooke were sipping wine at the island unit. Adam slipped off his stool and, a couple of inches taller than his brother, enveloped Ben in a man hug, which Ben stiffly accepted. Perhaps, as a man who dressed conservatively, Ben was blindsided by his brother's appearance. There were a lot of 'good to see you' and 'you haven't changed a bit', which was a downright lie, I suspected, on both sides. Ben peeled off his jacket and, unusually, helped himself to a beer from the fridge. Before dinner was completely ruined, I suggested we eat. Ben offered to dish up and I was glad to sit down. I could tell Ben was keen for a conversational diversion because the second we had plates of food in front of us he turned the spotlight on me.

'Has Sophie told you about her brilliant online cake business, Cake That?'

'She has not.' Adam raised his eyebrows in exaggerated surprise. 'You're a dark horse. I thought there had to be more to this woman than home interiors.'

I flicked a polite smile.

'Have you always baked?' Brooke asked.

I shook my head. 'I'm a latecomer. My background is in economics and banking.'

'Handy,' Adam said with a shrewd expression.

'It certainly helped.'

'Costing out capital, cash flow and pricing strategy is key to starting any business.'

'Yes,' I said, surprised that Adam had the remotest grasp. 'I'm guessing you must have boned up on hygiene and environmental health too.'

'It's central to what we do.'

'So what gave you the idea?' Adam helped himself to green salad.

'Not a clue,' I said breezily. 'I guess I fancied a change.'

Adam shook his head and theatrically waggled a finger. 'Oh no, you don't get off that easily. Has to be more to it than that,' he said, eyes glinting with intrigue.

Sensing danger, I adopted a neutral expression. 'Not really.'

It didn't deter Adam who seemed to be on a merciless roll. 'Why on earth leave a well-paid job with career and pension prospects to take a punt on cakes?'

'It wasn't a punt,' I declared firmly. 'The bakery business is a massive and growing market, raking in five billion a year in the UK alone. Globally, it's considerably more.'

'But it was still a risk.'

'A calculated one.'

'I like this woman,' Adam said, smiling from me to Ben, in a way that was vaguely unsettling. 'So when did you start the business?'

My heart pounded. 'Six years ago.'

'And it's a success?'

'We've progressed to a couple of retail units and are planning a third, although our hardcore sales are online.'

'Extraordinarily good going in a short space of time.'

'Sophie is a pretty determined individual,' Ben said admiringly.

'Must be to make that sort of career leap.' Adam met and held my gaze in way I found challenging.

Deflecting, I said, 'I simply wanted a reason to get up in the morning, to do something practical that was people-centric rather than number-centric.'

'And help the community,' Ben chipped in. 'Tell them about your charitable work.'

Colour flamed my cheeks. I glanced down at Rufus who'd fallen asleep. I'd only just recovered from Adam questioning my motivation and here was Ben unwittingly pressing another of my buttons.

'It's behind the scenes really.'

'It is so not.' Ben grinned and dug into another mouthful of moussaka.

'Oh?' Brooke interjected, eager. Adam leant forward, keen to hear, too.

'I wanted to help victims of domestic violence by teaching them skills some women might not have and give them the confidence to seek out new employment opportunities.'

'She's passionate about it,' Ben said, chewing vigorously.

'It started off with me giving workshops,' I explained. 'Now a number of those women are Cake That employees.'

'Wow,' Brooke exclaimed. 'That's so so cool.'

Not how I'd describe it.

'Is that how you two met?' Adam asked, forking in a mouthful of salad.

I frowned, slow to catch on.

'Ben being a doctor,' Adam explained. 'Bust noses, broken arms etc. Sorry,' he interrupted himself, catching my shocked expression, 'that sounded crass.'

Taking a swig of wine, Ben came to the rescue. 'We met on a blind date.'

'Get you, dude.'

'Glad I can still surprise you,' Ben said, uncharacteristically hearty.

'Doctor and community worker, quite the golden couple.' Adam tilted his glass to his lips and took a deep swallow of wine.

In the spirit of acting the perfect host, I chose to ignore the touch of sarcasm in Adam's voice. Not so Ben, his narked expression plain to see.

49

Before brotherly blood was spilt, I changed the subject.

'And you two? How did you meet?' In a pub or club, I wagered.

Brooke glanced at Adam as if asking for permission to speak. At an unspoken signal, she answered, 'I was in New York for a school reunion.'

'You went to school there?' Ben asked, obviously surprised.

'No,' she said, with a timid smile, 'it was a kind of cool place for us to all meet up.'

'Wish our school reunions were in such exotic places,' Adam said. 'Ever go back, Ben?'

Ben shook his head, coldly polite.

'It's okay, little brother. I'm not going to blow your cover.'

Ben looked straight through him. I dry swallowed, wondering where the hell we were all travelling with this. Spotting my consternation, Adam burst out, 'Joke!'

'Funny,' Ben said, deadpan, then to Brooke: 'You were saying?'

Flicking a grateful little smile at being remembered and included, she said, 'I was having a horrible time.'

'Oh?' I questioned.

'It was nobody's fault,' she said, big-eyed. 'I didn't fit in. Never had really. Don't know why I went. Know what I mean?'

I didn't but pretended I did and nodded sympathetically.

'When I sloped off to the bar to escape, who should I bump into but . . .'

'*Me*,' Adam said, with a flourish. 'We totally hit it off, didn't we, babe?'

Brooke glowed. 'Best day of my life.'

'For both of us,' Adam said, stroking her bare arm.

Ben topped up glasses and I cleared away the plates. As soon as I sat back down, Adam turned his attention once more to his brother.

'So how did you wind up here? Last thing I knew, you were studying at Nottingham.'

Composed again, Ben nodded. 'After I qualified, I completed my GP training in Swindon, so it was a natural progression to join a practice in Cirencester.'

'You forgot your stint in palliative care,' I chipped in. Ben blinked and seemed to go blank. 'At the hospice,' I reminded him, smiling.

'Oh, yeah,' he said, 'in Minchinhampton.'

'Savage.' Brooke reached for her glass with a shudder.

'On the contrary,' Adam said, 'must be fascinating to watch people on the edge of life.'

Spooked by the keen note in Adam's voice, I was equally surprised that Ben, who was clasping the back of his neck, didn't respond. 'Who'd like pudding?' I said, desperate, once more, to change the mood.

Brooke pushed an awkward smile. 'I don't do desserts.'

'All the more for me.' Adam chuckled.

CHAPTER ELEVEN

Three portions of chocolate paradise pudding later and after the dodgy bit earlier, conversation, thank God, found a natural rhythm. Ben was more solicitous and made every effort to be warm to which Adam appeared to respond. I sat back and watched as the shadows lengthened and thought I saw a glimmer of what the brothers had been like once, before their family was shattered. They spoke intently to one another, as if the women in the room weren't really there. I now saw that they shared similar mannerisms, the way they stroked the stubble on their chins when they were thinking and smoothed the backs of their heads in a nervous displacement habit. They had the same deep note when they laughed. This could work, I realised, hopelessly optimistic. After the initial awkwardness, I decided that Ben had nothing to fear from Adam's arrival. Consequently, I had nothing to angst about either.

When Ben asked Adam about settling back in the home country, Adam replied, 'It feels like the right time. Through a mate of a mate, an opportunity has come up in Birmingham with a recording studio.'

'Doing what?' I asked.

'Session work. Keyboards.'

'He's so on point,' Brooke said, admiringly, which I interpreted as pretty good.

'I'm pleased for you, mate.' Ben glanced at me. *Who'd have thought it?* his expression said.

'Hey, remember Uncle Larry?' Adam said, performing a quick gear change in conversation.

Ben gave a startled blink. 'Who?'

'I didn't know you had an uncle,' I said, perplexed.

Ben opened his mouth to speak and closed it again.

'An *honorary* uncle,' Adam said, shooting Ben a look. '*You* remember.'

Ben shook his head and reached for more wine.

'Lived in Harborne.' Adam smiled encouragement, like a carer encouraging a dementia patient to recall the unreachable.

'Not far from your parents then,' I said to Adam. 'Ben took me to the former family home when we first met.' I'd been pushy because I knew so little about Ben's life and longed for landmarks.

'Of course,' Ben exclaimed, flattening the palm of his hand against his forehead. 'Larry lived down the road from Mum and Dad. Haven't thought about him in years.'

'I expect he's dead now,' Adam said, his gaze never shifting from Ben.

'Why do you ask?' Ben sounded like a workman speaking with a mouthful of nails.

'No reason.' Adam drained his glass. 'Oh, before I forget, I've got you this.' He leapt up, sped lithely over to where one of his bags was parked, unzipped it and produced a half bottle of Japanese whisky. He deposited it in front of Ben as if he were a serious player going all in in a game of poker. 'Never one to turn down a drink, our Ben.'

Ben was virtually teetotal or, at least he was until Adam's announced arrival. Maybe Adam was referring to a silly passing phase when Ben was a medical student. I'd heard horror stories of young junior doctors hooking themselves up to IVs after a heavy night out.

Embarrassed and responding with a stupid smile, Ben thanked him.

'Well, what are you waiting for?' Adam said. 'Let's crack it open.'

'I've got an early start tomorrow,' Ben said.

'A nightcap then.'

Before Ben could protest further, Adam twisted the cap on the bottle and, swiping two tumblers intended for water off the table, poured out two stiff measures. I watched, mystified.

When Brooke said she was tired and was going to bed, I followed her lead. 'I'll leave you boys to chat about old times,' I said, desperate to escape.

It was only later when up in the night, feeding Rufus, I remembered the smug expression on Adam's face and the look of frozen fear on Ben's.

CHAPTER TWELVE

'What time did you come to bed?'

It was the next morning. Ben had made me a cup of tea, sweetly gone to Rufus when he stirred, given him a cuddle and changed his nappy before plonking him on me.

'Far too late.'

'I guess you had a lot to catch up on.' I had to admit the second my head hit the pillow I had absolutely no problem sleeping, my only complaint I could never get enough of it. If they'd talked until dawn, I'd be none the wiser.

Glum, Ben downed two painkillers with a glass of water. I was sympathetic. He had that slightly green hue and sweaty pallor associated with an overload of booze. 'That bad?'

'Horrific. Put it this way I won't be asking my patients how many units they consume in a week.'

I gave a snort of laughter. 'Don't breathe on them, whatever you do.'

With a wan smile he gazed at Rufus. 'I envy him his uncomplicated life.'

Forcing myself to sound casual, I said, 'Is Adam a complication?'

'You saw how he was.'

I did and didn't know what to make of it. 'After the initial awkwardness you seemed to be getting on reasonably well.'

'*Reasonably*?'

'Well enough then.'

'He certainly rates you.'

'Really?'

'Went on and on about how smart you are.'

'The man has taste,' I said with a grin.

'On this we can agree,' Ben said, smiling. 'I thought his
clothes style was a little . . .' He tailed off, struggling to find
the right words.

'Out there?' I offered.

'That's charitable.'

'Has he always dressed like that?'

'In a milder form.'

'What did you think of Brooke?'

'Impossibly young and easily manipulated.'

'Ouch,' I said.

'You know what I mean.'

I did. 'She barely touched dinner.'

'Closet anorexic?'

'Search me, you're the doc.'

Ben tilted his hand. 'Maybe she was nervous, although
I reckon her BMI would tell its own story. The big question:
what is she doing with him and he with her?'

'That's two questions.'

'Smarty pants.'

I continued, undeterred. 'Music is the connecting factor,
I guess.'

'Music?'

'He was telling me about the music venues he'd visited
in the States and places he'd gigged in. You never said he was
that talented.'

'I didn't know.'

And that felt odd. 'Can you really become that gifted in
the space of a decade?'

'Depends if he's telling the truth.'

'Ben,' I exclaimed, 'why would he lie? More to the point, why would Brooke lie?'

Ben clasped the back of his neck, like I'd seen him do the night before. Did he know something I didn't?

'They seem quite affectionate towards each other,' I said, attempting to sound more positive.

'It can't last.'

He sounded like my dad after I'd announced my whirl-wind romance and unscheduled pregnancy, not that I'd ever let on to Ben.

I swapped Rufus to the other boob. 'Adam's relationship with Brooke is not your problem.'

'True.' Ben bent down to kiss me. I reached out, caught his hand and looked into his eyes.

'Are you okay?'

'Yes.'

'Only . . .'

'Only what?'

Big breath, I thought. 'You should be proud of the work you do.'

'I am.'

'Why were you so reluctant to speak about your stint at the hospice?'

'Honestly, Sophie,' Ben responded, with a loose smile, 'it's hardly a great dinner party topic of conversation and you saw Adam's reaction. "Fascinating", for God's sake.'

'It *was* strange,' I admitted.

'Adam didn't cope well with our dad's death,' Ben said. 'He could barely go near him towards the end.'

'I'm so sorry I brought the subject up. I should have thought before I spoke.'

'It's fine.' Ben deposited a dry kiss on my cheek. 'You'll be okay then today?'

I nodded. 'I'll drive them around, show them the sights.'

'And before you know it Adam and Brooke will be on the road to Brum,' he said, brightly.

'Want me to find out when they intend to leave?'

'You can do that?'

'I can,' I said.

He didn't need to say 'can't wait'. His expression spoke volumes.

CHAPTER THIRTEEN

After Ben left, I popped Rufus into his crib, showered and dressed. With no sign of Adam and Brooke, I fixed myself a poached egg on toast, washed down with another cup of tea and found two WhatsApp messages on my phone from our family group chat. The first was from Saskia.

How's it going? What's Adam like?

The second from Mum: *Do you need a hand with anything? How are you getting on with Ben's brother?*

The tag team in action, I pictured the feverish conversations taking place at Knox Central. Unable to give a definitive answer, I replied with a bland *Fine* and hoped my less than forthcoming response would not be swiftly followed by a phone call.

Wrong. Saskia called before I'd had a chance to breathe out.

'I can only assume Adam is not quite what you expected,' she blasted in.

'Correct.'

'So? Give us the gory deets.'

'He seems nice.'

'*Nice?*'

'Warm, friendly . . .' Weird.

'Does he look like Ben?'

'Nope, Adam is taller.'

'Is he fair, dark, has a limp?'

I had to smile.

'God, Sophie, you can be so buttoned-up. Is he hot?'

My smile cleared off. Saskia could be far too direct on occasion. 'I couldn't say.' I didn't want to say, more like. 'He's a little alternative.' Shit, I shouldn't have said that.

'Magnificent. How alternative?'

Wears nail varnish, eyeliner and chains. 'Dresses like a muso.'

'Bare-chested and leather trousers?'

'Isn't that passé? Interesting you haven't asked a single question about his girlfriend.'

'What's she like then? And don't say *nice*.'

'Pleasant,' I said, tit for tat. I'd exchanged no more than a few paragraphs with them and Saskia was expecting an essay.

'And is Ben pleased to see his brother?'

Honest answer: not particularly. If I told Saskia this she would dig and dig. 'I believe so.'

'How long are they staying?'

'No idea.'

'If they're here at the weekend, Mum says you can all come for supper.'

I put a hand to the side of my head to tame the beginnings of a headache. 'Did you put her up to this?'

'No-oh.' Meaning Ye-es. 'You know how she feels about the importance of family. She wants Ben to feel accepted.'

'He *is* accepted.'

'And so is his brother. I don't know why you're making such a deal of it. Dad will be home, and it will give you a break from entertaining.'

'It's irrelevant. They won't be here,' I said. 'And now I really have to go.'

I didn't know which fazed me more: a week with house guests I barely knew or an extended family dinner at my parents with house guests I barely knew.

I was clearing away when Brooke poked her head around the door. I didn't ask how she'd slept; it was evident in the blue-grey shadows under her eyes.

'Breakfast,' I said cheerily. 'There's toast, eggs, croissants, fresh fruit . . .'

'Fruit would be great and coffee, black, if that's okay.'

I took fresh strawberries and raspberries from the fridge, piled them into a bowl, set it on the table and made a cafetière of Columbian coffee. 'What about Adam?'

'He won't be up yet.' Brooke picked at a strawberry.

I flashed a 'no problem' and sat down.

There's silence that's easy and silence that's awkward. This was the latter. She looked at me and I looked at her and, as the older woman and woman of the house, no less, I did my best to break the impasse.

'So where are you from originally?'

'London.' Brooke nibbled at another strawberry.

'Which bit?'

'Barking. My parents run a riding stables.'

I expressed surprise. If she'd mentioned Surrey or Hertfordshire, I wouldn't have given it another thought. Picking up on my reaction, Brooke became defensive. 'It's not all poverty and urban decay. There are country parks and plenty of nice places.'

'I don't doubt it,' I said mildly. 'Must have been fun when you were growing up. You ride?'

'Not anymore.' She hiked a bony shoulder. 'I left home when I was seventeen.'

'But you still see them?'

'Never felt the need to go back.'

'You're not in communication at all?'

'Nope.'

'That's sad.'

'Not really.'

I wondered what had orchestrated such a situation. 'Won't they worry?' I was genuinely anxious on Brooke's parents' behalf and, to be fair, hers too.

'Doubt it.'

Conversationally without direction, I headed towards what was safer ground.

'So how long have you and Adam been together?'

'Couple of years, something like that,' Brooke replied, narrowing her eyes.

'Do you mind me asking how old you are?'

Brooke grinned. 'Everyone asks me that. I'm twenty-three.'

'Goodness, I'd never have guessed. I want whatever you're on,' I said, in an effort to please, but also because I was genuinely impressed.

'Can be a hassle. I take ID with me everywhere.'

'I think it's a lovely problem to have.'

'You're older than Ben, aren't you?'

'I am.'

'Is that difficult?'

It amazed me how often women remarked on age difference when men, in the same situation, were cut a ton of slack. Before Brooke could pursue it, I said, 'I'm nine years older than Ben, not nineteen and, even then, what the hell?' My smile was big and wide to underline I didn't consider talking about it a problem. (Not true.)

It had to be said Brooke looked unconvinced.

'Before you met Adam,' I said hastily deflecting, 'did you work, have a job?'

'Marketing, yeah.'

A broad subject, I was none the wiser regarding specifics. 'For a company?'

'Uh-huh, devising social media campaigns.'

'Interesting,' I said, thinking how banal I sounded.

'It was all right. I don't really get on with people,' Brooke said, without expanding.

Seemed a popular refrain. Goodness, this was hard work. I glanced at the clock and prayed Rufus would wake soon so that I could escape.

'I guess it's tough to market dirty food,' Brooke said. Without a hint of guile, her sea-green eyes fastened on to mine.

'Dirty food?' I repeated, a phrase I detested.

'Sugar, fats,' she said, 'not exactly clean living, is it?'

An honest enough question, I was astounded Brooke was bold enough to ask it.

'Depends on your point of view. Obviously, if cakes are your primary food source, that's not ideal. Our aim is to produce deliciously healthy products from ingredients that are carefully sourced.' I winced at how much I sounded like a walking mission statement. 'More coffee?'

'Please.'

I topped up her mug. 'Adam must be very talented to make a living from music.'

Her face lit up. 'He hasn't had his big break yet, but he will.'

Knowing zilch about the music industry, I believed it was largely driven by youth, not that I said so. Was thirty-eight considered over the hill? Now who was being ageist? 'Even so it must be a challenge financially.' The banker in me still lived.

Brooke shook her head. 'Not with a well-paid side hustle.' She gave a nervous glance over her shoulder. The big question was what? I offered a reassuring smile, thinking, God help me, *drugs*.

In a small voice, almost a whisper, Brooke said, 'He does escort work.' In answer to my astonished expression, she cut in: 'It's always with professional older women.'

Gigolo, I thought. Crikey. 'Don't you mind?'

Her eyes shot wide. 'There's never any sex involved.'

'Course not,' I said, not believing a word of it.

'Please don't tell Adam I told you,' Brooke hurried on, pale and strained. 'He's not particularly proud of it and it's only until he gets his big break.'

I held a straight finger against my lips. 'I'm an excellent secret-keeper.' The best. 'Hopefully, the recording studio in Birmingham will provide an alternative work opportunity.'

Brooke looked momentarily blank. 'Oh, yeah,' she said, at last.

Before I had a chance to chase it up, Adam loped in. He wore a tee over tartan trousers tucked into black lace-up leather commando boots, his chains rattling like Marley's ghost.

'So, people,' he said, with a louche grin, 'what's the itinerary for the day?'

CHAPTER FOURTEEN

Squashing flat all thought of Adam's novel side hustle, I suggested we go into town for a walk around before wending our way back through a couple of pretty villages. I planned for us to finish up for a late lunch at the Mason's Arms in Meysey Hampton, roughly seven miles east of Cirencester, before returning to home turf in Poulton.

The weather unsettled and cold, I dressed Rufus in his warmest Babygro, clobbered him up with a hat, jacket and mittens and made sure I had his baby sling. Brooke sat in the back next to Rufus's baby carrier; Adam, with his long legs, next to me in the front passenger seat.

We parked in the central car park and headed up the main street to the market square. A chilly breeze had picked up and, after a brief respite in the Corn Hall where market traders sold anything from jewellery, paintings, handmade cardigans and sweaters to chocolates and Indian food, we cut through to Cricklade Street. Adam had missed out on coffee that morning and, intent on rectifying the situation — 'can't function without my caffeine hit' — he'd insisted we went into Sam and Jak's. Brooke suggested a window seat so she could 'people watch'. Adam pointed out it wasn't ideal for me to sit on a high stool with a baby and we sat at a nearby table instead. I couldn't fault his attentiveness. After we'd ordered Americanos (decaffeinated for me), Adam asked about my family. I described how close we were, that my sister, Saskia, and me had grown up in the same family home my parents still shared with Saskia. Brooke was gauchely smitten by stardom when I mentioned, in passing, my father's fledgling TV career.

'See,' she said to Adam, 'it can happen at any age.'

'Not sure what you're getting at. How old is your dad, Sophie?'

'Late sixties.'

Visibly rattled, Adam turned back to Brooke. 'Thanks a lot.'

Her little face fell. His petulance was so unnecessary. This chink in their blissful relationship told me two things: Adam was vain, and he wasn't averse to embarrassing his girlfriend in front of other people. I swallowed, tamping down a memory I'd tried to suppress. Another time, another woman, someone I'd spectacularly failed.

Attempting to take the heat out of the conversation, I said, 'I think Brooke only meant that if you keep at something long enough, good things will eventually happen.'

'Exactly,' Brooke said, wide-eyed and apologetic.

Adam pasted on a smile, slipped his arm around Brooke's narrow shoulders and gave her a hug. 'All good,' he said.

I swallowed. This is now. This is not the same. Not remotely similar.

Our drinks arrived. The emotional temperature reset to normal, I chatted about Cake That, and Saskia's role as my right-hand woman.

'She deals with the marketing and social media side,' I told Brooke, believing she'd be interested. When she didn't comment, Adam appeared to dive in on her behalf.

'Vitally important,' Adam said.

'Do you cater for diabetics and vegans?' Brooke asked, scratching her chin.

'We do, and folk with gluten intolerance.'

She nodded appreciation.

There is only so much stuff you can talk about to strangers and, after I'd done the weather, the property market in the UK, (pros and cons of renting and buying) and resisting the urge to bore on about babies, I was fast running out of road. Circling back to my family, Adam's gaze locked on to mine over the rim of his coffee cup. 'How much has Ben told you about us?'

The atmosphere felt suddenly heightened. Was Adam about to make some dreadful revelation that would upend my life? What was it Ben had said?

I love my brother, but sometimes he has a loose grasp on the truth.

Whose truth?

The bigger issue was that Ben and I had been together for a relatively short time. Perhaps I didn't know as much about him as I should have done.

The same could be said for you, a little voice whispered.

'I was so sorry to hear what happened to your parents,' I stumbled.

Deep frown lines appeared at the corners of Adam's eyes as if I'd made an enormous gaffe at a pitch to a client.

'And *what* did he tell you?'

On sensitive, potentially dangerous ground, I cleared my throat. 'That your father passed away after a long battle with illness and your mum was killed in a road accident not long afterwards.' Saying it aloud made me feel desperately unsettled, as if I was straying from a safe and narrow route into untamed wilderness.

Adam nodded, dark-eyed. 'That's about the size of it.'

The overwhelming relief I expected to feel was mitigated by the tumbling thought that I was missing something vital, which would change my view of Ben, not Adam.

Aiming for a more factual and less emotional note, I said, 'I gather your dad worked in accountancy and your mother was his secretary.'

Adam silently nodded, neither confirming nor denying.

'Like I mentioned last night, Ben took me to visit the big house when we first got together.' Stretching it a bit. We stood outside on a freezing cold day. The roof was covered in frost, I remembered.

'You did mention it, yeah,' Brooke spoke, as if on Adam's behalf.

'Looked quite grand.'

Adam agreed with his eyes. He'd talked incessantly the evening before and now he was virtually monosyllabic.

'Ben seemed to be quite close to your father.'

Adam tilted his head. Not yes, not no.

'I'm sure he was as close to your mum,' I said, fearing I'd unwittingly dissed her.

'No, that was me,' Adam said.

'One each,' Brooke chimed cheerily. 'Lucky you, I had to pit myself against several siblings for my mother's attention.'

Adam shifted from his slouched position and sat up straight. 'I wouldn't call losing my parents in my twenties lucky.'

Crushed, Brooke chewed her lip.

'Don't look like that, babe,' Adam said, pushing a smile.

'Like what?'

'Wounded, like I hit you.' Adam's gaze turned to me.

It took all I had to mask a reaction. Would he see the remnants of guilt I'd tried so hard to shed lurking inside me? Dry swallowing a response, I requested the bill.

CHAPTER FIFTEEN

Adam picked up the tab. We had a quick stride around town and, with me forced to take a pit stop for Rufus to feed in the King's Head, Brooke and Adam expressed a desire to check out estate agents.

'You're thinking of buying here?' I wondered if by trying to keep the conversation going, I'd unwittingly put the stupid idea into their heads. It certainly flew in the face of Ben's conviction that they couldn't afford it.

'I'd love to,' Brooke said with enthusiasm. 'The town is so amazing.'

'Need to see how much bang we get for our buck first,' Adam said.

Very little, I could have told him, but he'd discover that for himself. Hang on a moment, I thought. 'How would that fit with the job offer in Birmingham?'

'Nothing's been signed and sealed yet. Pays to keep your options open.' Adam appeared a lot more dismissive of his chances than he'd sounded the night before.

'Always good to have a Plan B.' Brooke backed him up in what sounded suspiciously like a rehearsed script.

'Shall I drop you a text when I've finished,' I asked.

They looked at each other. 'We don't use phones.'

'Oh,' I said, taken aback. What else could I say other than: How, in God's name, do you manage to function without them?

'Back in an hour?' Brooke suggested.

'Great,' I said.

Bemused, I watched them saunter out, hand in hand, unable to get my brain around the 'no phone' thing. Brooke was of an age when life was lived through instant and immediate communication. If Adam was in the thick of the music biz, how could he signal his availability for gigs? Or was this all part of his shtick? I'd read somewhere about highly successful music moguls, the Simon Cowells of this world no less, never using mobile devices.

I hated to admit that it was bliss to be left alone with my own thoughts, or it would have been if my thoughts hadn't clattered around inside my brain like a heavy metal band. The odd vibe radiating off Adam in the café puzzled me. Although I could have framed the conversation with greater sensitivity regarding Adam and Ben's parents, my need to know was based on a genuine desire to understand what had happened between the brothers. A forward-facing man, Ben didn't talk about his past very much, so I didn't exactly have a benchmark. All those dark, moody looks and unspoken words, courtesy of Adam, were exhausting.

'Come on, little chap,' I said, collecting my stuff together, wondering when Adam and Brooke would rock up. The thought of them brandishing details with viewings already booked made me flutter with alarm. God knew what it would do to Ben.

Eventually, they returned wreathed in smiles — no details, thank goodness. 'Success?' I said, falsely bright and encouraging.

'Given us a few ideas,' Adam replied.

I made some mild remark and, trudging back to the car through a fine mizzle of rain, drove us back through the Ampneys. For Brooke's benefit I pointed out a highly-acclaimed riding stables at Ampney St Peter.

'They're expert in dressage, apparently,' I said.

Nobody commented, although there was a lot of oohing and aahing at the lush scenery and numerous Cotswold stone houses, glowing orange in the wet light, much of which I shamefully took for granted.

Driving through Poulton we arrived at the next village and the Mason's Arms, a seventeenth-century pub with rooms. Set on a green with an old village pump, it was a popular place to dine outside in the warmer summer months, particularly with the London set. Early in the week it was quiet and the perfect place for a light, informal lunch. We were taken up a short flight of steps to a no-frills restaurant with wooden floorboards and two cosy alcoves off the main dining area.

'I'm not really hungry,' Brooke said.

'But you haven't eaten anything.' Unless a couple of strawberries constituted a meal. I recalled Ben's remark about potential eating disorder. Poor kid.

She shifted her weight, such as it was, from one foot to the other, her face tight and scared. 'I'm tired,' Brooke complained, in answer to Adam's exasperated expression. 'Could I go back to the house? You two can stay here.'

I stood up. 'I'll drive you.'

'Can't I walk?'

'It's almost two miles along a busy main road and it's raining.'

'I like walking in the rain, and I'll be careful.'

I looked to Adam who looked to Brooke. 'That's super disappointing.' He spoke as if she'd somehow let the side down.

'I know, I'm sorry.' Her small hands tightened into fists.

'Are you sure?' I said, kindly. 'Why don't you stay? You don't have to eat very much.'

She cast Adam an apologetic expression to which he responded with a shrug.

I wasn't keen on someone I'd only met yesterday having free run of my home. I really didn't like the idea of Brooke walking along the road either, but she seemed so determined and it would give me a chance to find out more about Ben's brother. Rifling in my bag I slipped the front door key off my key ring and handed it over.

'Thanks so much,' Brooke said, giving an audible sigh of relief.

'Is she okay?' I said to Adam, as she disappeared.

'Eats like a bird.'

'It's not terribly healthy.' I sounded like my mum, I realised.

'And she's almost run out of her meds.'

'What meds?'

'Anxiety pills. Good thing we have a doctor in the house.'

Not really. Although writing prescriptions for family and friends was widespread, particularly opiates and the very pills Brooke quite possibly needed, it wasn't considered either legal or ethical for doctors to prescribe to mates or mates of mates. Ben would rather stick pins in his eyes than break rules. I explained this to Adam who looked quite affronted.

'Surely, he could make an exception. We're not asking for speed or heroin.'

'It's more than his job's worth, I'm afraid.' I decided to leave Ben to expand on that thorny little issue.

We ordered drinks and food, and I settled into a chair with Rufus who was now wide awake. After the mild run-in earlier, I was keen to avoid emotive subjects and definitely didn't want to alight on Adam's side hustle, by accident. I opted to find out when our house guests were intending to leave so I could plan the rest of my week. Psyching myself up to enquire, (not easy after they'd only just arrived) I was outplayed.

'You're not at all what I imagined,' Adam said.

'And what did you imagine?' Someone younger and beautiful perhaps? 'Someone in a similar profession?' I said hopefully.

Adam sipped his beer. Wrong answer, obviously. 'You're not Ben's usual type.'

I didn't know what that amounted to. On the cusp of making a joke of it, it struck me that Adam, who had not seen his brother in over a decade, would have no greater clue about Ben's taste in women than me.

'I don't mean to cause offence,' Adam said, misconstruing my silence.

'None taken,' I said with a smile.

'We are so appreciative of what you've done,' Adam gushed, companionably touching my arm, in a way I bet he did with his older female clients, 'putting us up, driving us around and making us so welcome. No shit, you've been a marvellous host. I can see why Ben chose you.'

'Well, I . . .'

'And it's amazing to be in a real home, with people who genuinely care for us and believe in me.'

Bit OTT, yet the way he looked into my eyes from underneath insanely dark lashes was so trusting I found myself nodding like one of those toy dogs you see on the back parcel shelf of a car. This boy is good, I thought. He knows exactly how to win people over.

'Obvs, we don't want to outstay our welcome.'

Hallelujah.

'So,' he said, pausing for dramatic effect, 'to give you some space we've been looking at all the local attractions, places we'd like to visit like the Wildlife Park. Would it be easy for us to travel to it by bus tomorrow?'

Disappointed that he didn't take 'outstaying a welcome' more seriously, I told him I hadn't a clue, but didn't think so. 'Tell you what,' I said, 'I'll run you there and collect you at closing time.' Around four, I recalled, my heart lifting at the thought of a visitor-free day and time for me to mentally regroup.

Adam frowned in concern. 'You're sure?'

'Fifty minutes there and back, no problem.'

'Ben really landed on his feet with you,' Adam said, smiling warmly.

I shook my head. 'I'm the lucky one.'

Adam nodded, the smile on his lips unnervingly slipping from his eyes.

CHAPTER SIXTEEN

Brooke was still resting when we returned home. I'd hoped Adam would join her. He didn't.

I made a big deal of faffing about: unloading the machine, folding laundry, and attending to Rufus in the sitting room. *Go and do something useful, be with your girlfriend, shoo.* Adam appreciated the art on the wall as if he were a high-end collector, picked up a paperback from the bookcase, flicked through it with his long fingers, sat down, stood up and finally, grabbing a dark grey trench coat, headed outside to vape. Through the window I caught sight of him, collar up, prowling across the terrace like a leopard about to slay antelope. When he returned, his olive features were tinged blue with cold. In the intolerable silence I found myself counting the hours before Ben came home. Seemed we each had Ben on our minds.

'It's great to see my little brother again after all this time,' Adam enthused, sitting at the island unit. 'He really is one of the good guys.' His face searched mine for approval.

Self-consciously, I agreed.

'I'm relieved we've been able to put the past behind us, especially after the last time.'

I raised an enquiring eyebrow. Rootling around in my brain, I remembered Ben had mentioned the Cock and Magpies, high emotion and booze never a good combo, although Ben never mentioned any discord.

'Wasn't the best,' Adam said, clicking his tongue. 'As soon as legal beagles get involved in anything it all goes to rat shit.'

'I'm sorry,' I said. What legal beagles? 'In a pub?'

'What pub?'

I told Adam what Ben had told me.

Adam shook his head. 'Last time we spoke was at a solicitors in Birmingham.'

'Not sure I follow.'

'Probate. Inheritance shit.'

I didn't know what to say. It didn't sound like the kind of meeting that slipped your mind. How come Ben had forgotten? It would be indelible, wouldn't it?

'O-kay,' I said, extremely uncomfortable. Was Adam hinting he'd been hard done by? Ben had been left a sizeable sum of money, which he'd told me he'd invested wisely. Later he'd paid off his grant and put almost all of it into the purchase of Lamb's Leap. He never mentioned Adam's share, but then why would he?

'Trauma doesn't always unite, Sophie,' Adam said, his expression horribly intense. 'It can blow up in your face.'

And his was very close to mine. It felt as if all the furniture in the room had shrunk into the background, and it was just he and I in a big white space. In the brief time I'd known Adam I witnessed his talent for mixing it under the guise of being playful and amusing. Did he harbour a grudge? Did he have a capacity for resentment? Had he burnt through his inheritance or had he, in fact, been disinherited? I hated to imagine the fallout if it involved money.

'But you're reconciled now?' My voice was scratchy.

He raised a fist and punched the air. 'We're all good, yeah.' A wide grin cracked his face, as if the joke were on me.

I forced a nervous smile. Talking to Ben's brother was akin to being in labour. Just when things quietened down, and you could breathe easy, another eye-watering contraction came along.

'Fancy a cuppa?' I said, desperate to be doing rather than talking. Adam declined but offered to make it for me. I wasn't keen because, a kitchen bore, I deeply dislike people messing about in it. Churlish to decline and keen to please, I agreed. After a lot of 'teabags are up there, the pot is in there and the kettle . . . um . . . is right there' I was hugely glad when Brooke re-joined the party. She definitely seemed more rested.

'Good sleep?' I asked.

'Brilliant,' she replied.

Afterwards, I prepared the evening meal. Keeping it simple, I popped a chicken in the oven, peeled vegetables and hunted through the freezer for another vegetarian bake I kept for emergencies, in the hope of tempting Brooke.

Armed with wine and beers, Ben arrived earlier than I'd anticipated. I greeted him as if he'd scaled the Alps through appalling weather to rescue me.

During dinner, conversation centred on the nuts and bolts of the day. Adam didn't mention family, didn't share his thoughts on moving and didn't flag up contradicting recollections. It didn't prevent me from feeling on edge. Picking up on my mood, Rufus became unsettled. I spent most of the meal pacing up and down and stealing the odd forkful of food.

'Here, give him to me,' Adam said.

'You haven't finished.'

'You haven't really started,' Adam retorted with a loose grin. 'Come on, you need to eat.'

'It's okay, Adam, I'll take him.' Ben started to get up.

'Rufus likes his uncle Adam, don't you, buddy?' Adam outstretched his arms.

In a bind and ignoring Ben's pained expression, I handed my baby over to his brother. Magically, Rufus quietened down.

'You have quite the touch,' Ben observed, a little acerbically, I thought.

Afterwards, with Rufus back in my arms, Adam and Brooke cleared away and nobly offered to stack the dishwasher. They wouldn't do it the way I liked but it gave Ben and me an opportunity to catch up. As soon as the door closed, Ben said, 'Sorry.'

'For what?'

'I was rude but, bloody hell, *buddy*? Rufus is a baby.'

I couldn't help but laugh. 'Be fair, it was nice of Adam to offer.'

'And does that girl ever eat?'

'She's genuinely got a problem, I think. Adam mentioned she's nearly run out of medication for anxiety.'

'Not surprised living with him.' Ben flicked up his palms at my disappointed expression.

'I think Adam intends to lobby you for a prescription.'

Ben shook his head. 'No way. I could probably get her an appointment with one of the GP's at the practice.'

'Only if she registers as a temporary resident at our address.'

Ben looked crestfallen. 'I'll think of something. Did you manage to find out when they're leaving?'

I shook my head. 'Your brother is exceedingly difficult to pin down.'

'That's Adam, the master shapeshifter,' Ben said, suddenly glum. I briefly wondered whether to tell him about Adam's part-time occupation as an escort before hastily dismissing it.

'A couple of things came up, actually.' I waited a beat.

'Yeah?'

This was going to be awkward. 'Adam alluded to the last time you met.'

'*Alluded*, huh?'

'All right, he spoke about it. He implied you had a row that involved lawyers.'

Ben's gaze darkened. He topped up his drink.

'Well, are you going to tell me?'

'There's no mystery, Sophie. Everything from my parent's estate was split down the middle. Nothing dodgy about it. Nothing underhand. Fair and square.' Ben took a large swallow of wine. 'Did he mention Mum and Dad at all?'

'Well, yes.'

'And?' Ben looked at me intently.

'I probably said the wrong thing.'

'*You* said the wrong thing?' Ben blinked slowly. 'How so?'

'I don't know exactly. Used the wrong words. Picked the wrong time. He sort of closed down. Obviously still raw for him. I—'

The door opened and Adam and Brooke burst in with a 'ta-dah'.

'We'd like to return your hospitality, guys, by cooking a meal for you here, not tomorrow, obviously, with us being out all day, but we thought Friday night, or whenever you want really.'

I stared in astonishment. Friday night meant that they would be here on Saturday. God, they'd probably still be here on Sunday. Worse: my kitchen is my kingdom. Everything in it has been selected with care. I am possessive about every ludicrously expensive pan, piece of equipment and utensil in it. The idea of ruined cookware, blunted blades and burnt offerings was abhorrent, but I can lie like a politician when the need arises. 'That's a terribly kind thought, but I wouldn't dream of putting you to that much trouble.' The realisation that the 'flying' visit was to extend to four days and counting was almost incidental by comparison.

'We'd like to, and it would give you a break,' Brooke said earnestly. 'Adam is *such* a good cook.'

Ben hiked an eyebrow. I sensed what he was thinking: *is there no end to his talents?*

'I'm sure he is but it's not necessary. You are our guests.' Not my best move. It sounded as if I expected them to be with us for the equivalent of three weeks' holiday in Majorca.

'We absolutely insist,' Adam said, casting Ben a flinty look that had a strangely transformative effect.

Ben bit his lip, averted his gaze from mine, and leapt up to fiddle with the dimmer switch on the lights. 'It *would* give you a break, Sophs.'

Sick of people telling me what was good for me, I would have stood my ground if it hadn't been for Ben, astoundingly, caving in. What had got into him? Ben knew how much I hated anyone, even my mother, messing about in my domain. And what had happened to his stated desire for our house guests to leave as fast as possible? Had Adam pulled older-brother rank?

'We won't burn your kitchen down,' Brooke said, the thought almost inducing a panic attack in me.

'I know and I'm honoured and . . .'

'Say *yes*,' Adam said, bullish.

Outgunned, on my own, with great reluctance and less than good grace, I agreed, but I was going to kill Ben later.

CHAPTER SEVENTEEN

'What were you thinking, Ben? You know how I feel about my kitchen.' We were lying in bed, trawling through the evening. I sounded precious and parochial but couldn't help the level of annoyance I felt.

'Is it such a big deal?'

'You *know* it is.' I truly didn't understand why Ben had given in to Adam's request. One sharp glance from his brother was all it took. I hadn't realised that Adam had that much power.

I would not have described myself as a woman with recognisable hang-ups yet, on this score, I admit to a significant issue. Baking had saved my life at a time when I thought I would never be able to live with myself. Not that Ben knew the real story. Nobody did.

'It would have been pissy to refuse,' Ben countered.

For the life of me I couldn't understand the step change in his attitude. 'I don't understand you. Seconds before the MasterChef incident, you were gagging for them to leave and then one biting look from your brother and you completely folded.'

'That's not quite—'

'And do they show any sign of leaving, do they hell? They are digging in, I swear. At this rate, they'll be booking in for Christmas.'

'Not like you to exaggerate.'

'It's an exaggerated situation,' I said huffily. 'You know they're house-hunting here.'

Ben flinched and punched his pillow. 'All talk.'

'And Adam obviously has some grievance against you.'

'I don't see why. Are you sure you're not making too much of a meal of it?'

'Is that supposed to be amusing?'

'No,' Ben said, with a tired sigh. 'Look, Sophs, I admit the situation isn't ideal. I want them to go as much if not more than you. I wish I could be at home to ease the burden. However, I'm not in a job where I can take time off without notice.'

'And I'm not asking you to,' I said, running my fingers distractedly through my hair.

'They *have* only been here a couple of days.'

'Feels longer.' I'd thought the whole point of the visit was for Ben and his brother to spend time together, to bond and heal. This evening Ben had hoofed off to bed, leaving Brooke and Adam to finish the wine.

'That's because you're understandably exhausted.'

Why is it that when people shove 'understandably' into a sentence, they think it makes them sound empathetic? I took a breath. I *was* tired. It didn't excuse Ben from entirely missing the point. It didn't explain his entire psychological volte-face. Anyone would think he'd been taken outside and threatened with a big fist to his head.

I reached for a glass from the bedside table and swallowed some water. Great for indigestion and 'taking a moment' so I'd been told, and utter horseshit. 'Do you think deep down Adam's jealous?'

'Where did that come from?' Strain tugged at Ben's mouth.

'That *golden couple* remark.' I sounded petty and vindictive, as if I stored up perceived slights, which I did not. Come to think of it, Ben had seemed peeved at the time.

'A throwaway line days ago.'

'You didn't answer my question,' I said, pushing it.

'Which one?'

'Adam being jealous of you.'

'Shouldn't think so. He seems comfortable enough in his own skin, tats and all.'

Not buying it, I shook my head. 'One moment he's lovable and on the level, the next, temperamental and inconsistent.'

'I warned you the architecture of his mind is a little flaky.'

'Can you translate that without scaring the hell out of me?'

'He had a few mental health issues in his youth.'

'What sort of issues?' I sat up straighter, my turn to punch the pillow to make a point. 'And why didn't you mention it before?'

'Because it's nothing serious. It comes and goes and doesn't impact on his ability to function in daily life.'

'Good to hear.' My tone of voice won me a disappointed look from Ben. Didn't sound very scientific to me but, hey, what did I know?

To be scrupulously fair, a mental health problem went some way to explain Adam's capricious behaviour. It also explained why Ben cut him slack. I only wished he'd explained it in greater depth first.

Eager for an easy life, I did what I always do and apologised.

'Don't. It's a lot to take on board and you are doing a magnificent job.'

Ignoring the fact Adam had said something similar that very afternoon, I snuggled back down. 'Charmer.'

Slipping his arms around me, Ben drew me close and kissed the top of my head. 'Soon it will be just you, me and Rufus,' he said dreamily.

We stayed like that for a little bit, lost in our own cosy world. It didn't take long for a disturbing thought to intrude.

'Mum looked pretty tired when I saw her yesterday.'

'Seemed all right on Sunday.'

'What if she isn't up to having Rufus when I go back to work?'

'Did she say that?'

'No.'

'Then it isn't a problem.'

'But what if it is?' I literally had no Plan B.

'Then we'll find another way.'

'I'm not keen on a stranger looking after him.'

'You're only going back part-time, aren't you?'

'Even so, Ben.'

He squeezed my arm. 'Don't worry so much.'

But I did and it felt as if time were trickling through my fingers.

'Ben,' I said, looking up into his eyes.

'Yeah?'

'Can't you have a discreet word with Adam about when he intends to leave?'

Ben loosened his grasp. His open, honest features suddenly clouded with anxiety.

'It would be better coming from you, brother to brother.'

Ben grunted a reply, to the effect that he would see what he could do, kissed me goodnight and rolled over.

Not exactly stated with conviction, I thought. Sinking into the pillows, I closed my eyes.

CHAPTER EIGHTEEN

Adam and Brooke were late getting up. Watching the clock tick, I was as frustrated as a racehorse waiting for the starting gate to open. By the time they surfaced, around ten, I'd sorted out Rufus, planned dinner, run around with a vacuum cleaner (Rufus peculiarly enjoyed the noise), dumped a shedload of empty bottles in the recycling bag, and had even found the time to apply mascara and lipstick; a major achievement in my new mum world.

'Can I use your washing machine?' Brooke asked.

My mind immediately flipped to the bags of luggage they'd brought with them. Were these crammed with dirty laundry?

'If you bring it down, I'll sort it.'

'Thanks,' she said, dull-eyed.

Disappearing, she reappeared with a huge stash of mixed clothing. I sorted white from colours, put on a load, calculating it would take four washes to get through the lot and then, with the weather being iffy, I'd have to tumble dry. I hoped she didn't expect me to iron.

At least Brooke's aversion to food meant I didn't need to provide a big breakfast. Adam settled for black coffee and a vape outside in the garden. When he returned, I said, not exactly pushing them out through the door, but not far off, 'We'll have to go soon to fit in with Rufus's feeds.'

Finally, good to go, the drive was uneventful and silent. I didn't know Adam, yet sensed he was in a mood about something, possibly connected to Brooke who sat wan and pale in the back, staring out of the window.

With roadworks and heavy traffic, it took longer than expected and I spent the last couple of miles anxiously checking my rear-view. Dropping them at the gates, I stressed when Rufus started to cry and bawled lustily until I reached the very pretty Cotswold town of Burford, a couple of miles away. In pre-baby days, my ideal would be to park and head to one of the many hostelries for a drink and pit stop. Rufus, red-faced and hungry, had other plans; I fed him discreetly in the car park and changed his nappy. Smiling at him, he smiled straight back.

'We ought to head home,' I told him, nattering away as I tended to do. Domestic jobs had piled up since Adam and Brooke's arrival and now I had their mountain of washing to wade through. 'But the weather isn't bad at the moment so let's catch a few rays.'

I popped him in his baby carrier and, locking the car, walked over the little bridge into town and ambled up and down the High Street. There, I bought a vegetable quiche for Brooke, bacon and cheese for the meat eaters, eventually finding a cosy corner in a café to grab a coffee. Tempted by a slice of cake — coffee and walnut — I ordered that too and ate and drank in record time. Happy and high at the sudden sugar rush I headed back to the car and home.

I stuck a load of washing in the tumble dryer, planted another load in the machine, and took a mango and passion fruit cheesecake from the freezer to defrost. That was pretty much it as my previously uplifted mood dissipated. Aimless and unsettled, I drifted from one room to another, considering whether Ben and I would have our home back any time

soon. When my mobile rang, I thought it was Adam sum-
moning me for collection, until I remembered he didn't have
a phone. It was Hugh Gemmel, our architect.

'Sophie, great news, planning has been passed. We're on.'

My heart gave a little leap of pleasure. 'Terrific, when
can we start?'

'I've assembled a team who reckon they can begin in a
couple of weeks.'

'Tell them to schedule us in. I'm thrilled and I know Ben
will be too. Thanks, Hugh.'

I finished the call. Adam and Brooke would have to be
gone by then.

* * *

In a celebratory mood I broke the good news the moment we
sat down to dinner. Ben beamed. Adam, catching the mood,
congratulated us. Brooke glanced at him shiftily. Either Ben's
brother hadn't factored in the logistics, or didn't see it posing
a problem. Surely, Adam recognised we couldn't entertain
guests with builders tramping through the place? I was just
getting my head around that one when Adam announced he
and Brooke wanted to take a run out the following day. 'We'll
cab it,' he assured me, placing a warm hand over mine. 'You've
done quite enough driving for us already.'

Unexpectedly, things were looking up. 'Actually, that
will fit in well because I've got to be in work tomorrow for
appraisals.'

Adam's eyes sparked. 'In Cheltenham?'

'Um . . . yes.'

'But that's marvellous. We had plans to visit Cheltenham
too. We could all go together.'

'I'm sorry but I've arranged to see a friend for lunch afterwards.' Thank goodness for Louise, I thought.

'That's fine. We can amuse ourselves and we'd really love
to see your little cake outfit.'

Did I detect a patronising note or was I being pissy? 'There's very little to see, a couple of offices and bakery and that's it.'

'I've never visited a bakery before,' Brooke chipped in.

There's a surprise, I thought waspishly. I pulled an apologetic face. 'It will be running at full tilt, not really suitable for visitors and the unit's rather out of the way.' *It wasn't.* 'Not central to town at all.' *Trueish.*

'Couldn't we catch a bus from there back into town?'

'Well, yes, but I still don't think—'

'I'd so love to see where the magic happens,' Adam said.

'That's sweet of you to say, but—'

'And maybe we could get to meet your sister. Didn't you say she works there?'

Ignoring the perturbed expression on Ben's face, I replied, 'I did.' Regrettably. The thought of Saskia meeting Adam filled me with dismay. Adam was exactly her type: good looking, alternative and sexy.

'There you go. Perfect,' Adam concluded with a grin.

My answering smile was weak. This was *such* a bad idea.

Making an excuse to visit the bathroom, I put a call through to Saskia to forewarn her about Adam and Brooke tagging along the following morning.

'Only popping in,' I warned before she got too enthused, although it didn't prevent her from making a crack about them getting their feet under the table.

'Very funny,' I said, without mirth.

'You know your problem?' Saskia said, positively buoyant.

'No, but I'm sure you're going to tell me.'

'You're too much like Mum. You make everything look deceptively easy. If I had my own place, I'd keep the fridge empty and give them a lumpy mattress.'

'I'll bear it in mind,' I said, ending the call.

Re-joining the party at the kitchen table, I was appalled to see a flashpoint had ignited in my absence.

'Why are you looking like that?' Adam angrily demanded of Ben.

87

'Like what?'

Who knew two words could express such irritation? My stomach tightened. I had a nasty taste in my mouth.

'Like I've just pissed on your chips. Sorry, Sophie,' Adam said, glancing at me with a tepid smile.

Eager to avoid conflict and, about to intervene, I was beaten to it by Ben. 'Being in steady work and solvent beats the hell out of drifting around.'

'And your point?' Adam bridled.

Ben fixed his brother with a laser-like stare. Adam put down his knife and fork, dabbed at his mouth with a serviette and leant back expansively. 'Come on, out with it.'

'Okay,' Ben said, rising to the challenge. 'How do you make a living?'

'We pay our way,' Brooke interjected. Pushing the food around her plate; she'd hardly eaten a thing.

'Doing what?' Ben's eyes thinned to slits.

'I don't *do*,' Adam fired back. 'I create.'

'We gig and entertain,' Brooke said, glancing at Adam, his very own spokesperson, not that he needed one.

'That's right,' Adam said, acknowledging her in a show of solidarity. 'Not all of us can help the sick but we do our bit in our own way, just like Sophie here.'

I didn't care for being dragged into Adam's argument, especially on his side. 'I'm guessing obtaining work permits and visas to work abroad can't be easy,' I said mildly.

'We have sponsors,' Adam explained.

I gave Ben a 'case closed' look.

The rest of the meal passed in stilted silence. It was like the dead time between Christmas and New Year when, bloated and bored, nobody knows what to do with themselves, or each other, or what to talk about. Adam drank prodigiously. Brooke nibbled. Ben kept his head down and ate. And me? Greedy for comfort, I ate two slices of cheesecake. Sod it.

CHAPTER NINETEEN

At Rufus's anguished cry, I stumbled out of bed and, keen not to disturb Ben, slipped next door to the other bedroom. A marathon sleeper, it was the first time Rufus had got me up in weeks; sensitive to the change in dynamics, no doubt about it.

I picked him up, gave him a cuddle and settled him down to feed. Barely awake, my mind meandered. What was Adam doing here? What did he hope to gain? Did he honestly seek reconciliation and, if his feelings were genuine, how did he intend to bridge a twelve-year gap? If Adam had really put the past behind him why engineer a conversation about a long-ago row and foist it onto me? Was he looking for an ally? Surely, Adam must know that my loyalty was to the brother I knew and loved and not the one who, with strutting bravado, parachuted out of the clear blue into our settled lives one rainy Monday?

It came back to the same question: what was Adam's agenda? Sure as hell, he had one.

Which didn't mean to say that his intentions were flat out, no messing, bad. I had to stop judging characters in the present by characters in my past. The Adam I'd met was disarming, keen to please and amuse. The cynical voice inside my head asked 'what about the other Adam?'. The sharp-tongued. The manipulator. The man who didn't ask questions, but posed them?

Eyes gritty through lack of sleep, I set my thoughts aside and, finally, settling Rufus back down in his cot, crept out to the landing on tiptoe. About to enter our bedroom I heard a noise. Someone was walking around downstairs. The sound was coming, not from the sitting room beneath Adam and Brooke's bedroom, or the kitchen below ours; it was coming from the hallway.

I glanced at my watch: 3.45 a.m.

A shiver rolled up my spine, setting the hairs on the back of my neck to attention. Had Adam gone outside for a late-night smoke after we'd gone to bed and forgotten to lock the front door?

I glanced back at Ben: on his back, one arm dangling out of bed, sleeping soundly. It would not be prudent to wake him.

Then another thought journeyed through my mind. What if Adam was sneaking around downstairs and I could discover his true intentions?

Drawing my dressing gown close around me, I tiptoed down the stairs. I didn't turn right into the kitchen but went left down the hall to Ben's study. The door was ajar. A thin light seeped out from the notary lamp on Ben's desk.

I stepped inside and switched on the main light and was met with a startled cry and frightened gaze.

'Brooke,' I gasped. 'What on earth are you doing?'

CHAPTER TWENTY

I am not heartless but I'm not great with 'caught red-handed' tears and there were a lot of them.

'I thought Ben might keep pills in his desk,' Brooke wailed.

'He's a doctor, not a drug dealer.'

'I'm desperate,' she cried.

I could see. She'd virtually turned the place upside down. The drawer in his desk was pulled out, papers strewn on the carpet. A chair had been overturned, no doubt in her anxiety. Books had been unearthed from the shelves that lined one wall. God alone knew what she hoped to find. It looked as if we'd been burgled.

'Adam said that Ben wouldn't give me a prescription,' Brooke said, as if this were a defence for her appalling actions.

'He can't,' I said, deliberately short with it. 'Your best bet is to register with a GP when you're settled.' I didn't tell her about temporary residency. I was too annoyed and, if I were honest, mildly frustrated I'd caught Brooke and not Adam. 'Does Adam know you're sneaking around?'

Her eyes widened. 'He'd kill me. You won't say anything, will you?' Two confidences in two days was starting to grate. She cast her eyes around the room, as if surprised by the wreckage. 'I can tidy this up.'

'Don't touch a thing.'

'But.'

'I won't tell Adam, but I will have to tell Ben.'

A hand flew to her mouth, and she cried some more. Great heaving breaths and strangled sobs. I willed myself to be sympathetic. I wanted to be kind and compassionate. Living with a doctor, I had a cursory knowledge of mental health issues and recognised how debilitating they were, yet I was hugely annoyed that our hospitality had been abused and couldn't help think that Brooke stood a better chance of recovery if she took time out from a man like Adam and reconnected with her own family.

'You can't go on like this,' I said more gently, sneaking into the gap between the next torrent of tears. 'Why don't you give your mum a ring?'

'I can't,' she said feebly.

'Why not?'

'She threw me out.'

Normally, I'd ask why, but it was after four in the morning. I feared an answer that would take until the middle of next week. 'Would you like me to make you a warm drink? It might help to calm you.'

She nodded vacantly and followed me into the kitchen where I handed her a box of tissues. I warmed milk in a pan, slipping in a spoonful of Manuka honey when she wasn't looking. She'd probably chuck the drink into the nearest plant pot, but my conscience was clear. Packing her off to bed, I went back upstairs to our room, reflecting uneasily on how I was going to break the news to Ben as I slipped in beside him.

Tired and wired, I should have dropped off quickly; sleep proved maddeningly elusive. Lying there in the dark, thinking about Brooke, her very obvious pain, which did not escape me, I realised that I was not cut out to be a shoulder to cry on. Emotionally self-reliant, *controlling*, according to my sister,

I was adept at coping mechanisms and blocking out experiences that hurt me.

Mostly.

It was not always so.

When I ripped up my life, fled London and dumped banking, I didn't seek counselling. I didn't join a gym; take up running marathons or extreme sports. I didn't travel, although I could have done, or learn a new language. I rented a flat, which, later, I bought and, safe inside, spent an entire year baking.

I never believed I had an addictive personality, but I am a perfectionist. I'd cook at all hours of the day and night, sometimes *through* the night. I didn't sleep. I didn't venture out or socialise. I saw little of my family — apart from when Mum came round to check I was still alive — and I regularly forgot to eat proper meals. Tasting recipes didn't count.

I'd picked up basic cooking skills from my mother but what I set out to achieve in that peculiarly awful period of my life was next level. On a mission for the perfect sponge, I studied every aspect of cake-making and researched how to source only the very finest ingredients: French flour, high quality granulated and caster sugar and unsalted butter. I learnt the differences between Genoise and joconde and I revelled as much in the science as the art. Entire days were spent analysing the right proportions to create the lightest, most moist, fluffiest or biscuity delicacies. The zesty flavours I had in my head did not always translate to my tongue. I practiced, obsessed, threw away and practiced more until success was guaranteed. Visually, and this took a surprising amount of effort, everything had to look sensational. A lot came down to mastering the art of icing: buttercream, ganache, fondant and frosting; glacé and, bastard of all bastards, Italian meringue buttercream, which lived or died by the sugar syrup reaching the correct temperature for melding with whipped egg whites without them splitting. Tray bakes and cupcakes, muffins and sponge cakes, cookies and perfect pavlovas spilt out of the kitchen in my flat and into the living room. With the entire street smelling of delicious warm dried fruit and spices, word got round. I gave a lot away to food banks and local charitable organisations. But, seized by a sort of mania, I wasn't done and moved on to viennoiserie — Danish pastries and croissants. Next, patisserie: millefeuille, tuile, sfogliatelle and that magic amalgamation of custard with pastry. I experimented with combinations of booze and fruit steeped in vanilla sugar. Aside from mastering the creation of syrups, I manually learnt to spin sugar and gained inspiration from Mum's old *A La Carte* magazines, circa 1980s, with adaptations of favourite confections like brandy snaps and roulades. I could have enrolled on a Cordon Bleu course, but this wasn't my purpose. I had no vision of turning my skills into a business; that came later. The truth was that I was on the run: from the life I thought I wanted, from the man I thought I loved, but most of all, from me.

Turning over, I draped my arm over Ben's body and snuggled in tight and realised how little he really knew me and wondered how he would feel if he did. And then I had another more compelling thought: how much do I know you, my love?

CHAPTER TWENTY-ONE

In a day measured by feeds I can practically tell the time by the size of my boobs. Swollen and leaking, they told me that it was way past Rufus's normal feed time. Fearing something was wrong, I shot out of bed to his room and bent over his crib. Softly breathing, his little tummy moving up and down, he was sound asleep. Strung out, I could have cried with relief.

I never knew the terror a baby could induce before I'd had one of my own. It was as if all my senses were more highly attuned to danger. I sparked with anxiety at the thought of Rufus choking, or not breathing, and regularly thanked God that we literally had a doctor in the house. Since having my baby, I couldn't bear to read awful news reports about children. With wars raging and news articles reporting the mind-blowing cruelty of individuals to their own offspring, the possibilities seemed endless.

Slipping downstairs for a soothing cuppa, silence wrapped itself around me. I put the kettle on to boil, chucked a teabag into a mug and took milk from the fridge. As if surfacing from a strange dream I recalled the night's bizarre events. As annoying as it was, the incident provided me with leverage to ensure that Adam and Brooke hit the road faster than they probably intended. All I had to do was threaten to break Brooke's confidence if they weren't gone in the next twenty-four hours. How she persuaded Adam to leave was not my problem. While Ben was at work I would tidy up and he would be none the wiser. *Result.*

The tea brewing, I padded down the hall to the study. Opening the door, I stood, brain fried. Everything was magically back in its place: books on the shelves, the chair righted, the desk tidy, papers off the floor and returned to their resting place in the drawer. Ben must have popped into the room earlier on his way out to work and discovered the chaos. Furious, he would have cleared up and, wrongly deducing that his brother was to blame, confronted Adam, which was a bit awkward for Brooke and, actually, a bit awkward for me. I wished I'd got to Ben first to tell him what I'd witnessed. On the upside, if this wasn't a case of house guests outstaying their welcome, I didn't know what was. Maybe that's why our home was so extraordinarily quiet, I thought, grimly telling myself Adam and Brooke were silently packing. Things hadn't been the same since their arrival and now I simply wanted them gone.

I never phoned Ben during surgery hours unless in an exceptional circumstance like when I went into labour. I dropped him a text.

Are you okay? So sorry you had to find the study in such a mess. I didn't want to wake you last night. No doubt you've already spoken to the culprit.

If Ben was seeing a patient, he could come back to me in ten minutes. If he was flat out it could be a couple of hours. I'd barely made it to the top of the staircase with my mug of tea when I received an incoming message.

I'm fine, sweetie. Are you?! Haven't the faintest clue what you're on about.

Shit, I bristled. Despite my insistence that she leave everything alone, Brooke must have crept back afterwards or risen early. Like a fool, I'd made the wrong assumption. I texted Ben back.

No worries. Will explain when you get home. Have a good day.

Out of sorts, I went into Rufus's room where he quickly stirred. Scooping him up, I held him close and fed him. I tried not to feel angry with Brooke, a scared young woman disconnected from her family and in deep with a man who was not easy to define. I wondered what had transpired between her and Adam while I'd been out for the count, and whether Brooke had come clean or whether, too afraid, she'd hoped that Adam would take the blame for something he hadn't instigated. The ensuing argument would have been loud and heated. I was surprised I hadn't heard them.

After I'd changed Rufus, I took him downstairs, fully expecting Adam and Brooke to slip into the kitchen, profuse with apologies, bags packed, keen to say goodbye.

Helping myself to breakfast, I braced at the sound of footsteps outside the door. There was no point in me being brittle. About to have Ben returned to his normal easy-going self, my routine back and the kitchen unmolested, I could afford to be magnanimous. I wasn't going to go so far as 'nice to see you and hope to see you again', but I could do 'no hard feelings'.

Imagine my shock when the pair of them bowled in smiling, dressed as if they were delegates at the World Confectionery Conference. Adam wore a beautifully cut tan suit that, without his chains and tattoos on display, gave him a more conventional appearance; Brooke, a blue linen trouser suit with a burnt orange tee underneath. No longer in plaits, her hair fell around her shoulders in soft curls. Lip balm tinged her lips. Mascara framed her eyes.

I gaped from one to the other.

'Something wrong, Sophie?' Adam's dark eyebrows drew together in concern. 'You look as if you've seen a ghost.'

I cleared my throat and thrust Brooke a meaningful look, which she ignored. No, it was more than that, as if I were sheet glass. To hell with my promise to keep my mouth shut.

'I hadn't expected you,' I said, pointedly, 'not after last night.'

97

Adam frowned and looking puzzled. He turned to Brooke for an explanation. 'What happened last night?'

I tipped my chin in Brooke's direction. 'Why don't you tell him?'

She pressed a finger to the side of her mouth and gave it a little scratch. 'Don't know what you're on about.'

'Ben's study. *You* in it. Going through his things, turning it upside down at three in the morning.' My voice rose louder with each accusation. My cheeks scorched with anger. This was ridiculous.

She stared at me blankly, then shook her head slowly.

'I made you a drink afterwards because you were so upset.' I looked to where I'd left the milk pan in the sink. It wasn't there. Had Brooke been thorough and removed all evidence, but why?

'Maybe you dreamt it.'

'That's not *true*.' I shouted so loud Rufus gave a start and began to cry.

'Hey, hey,' Adam said, 'let's all calm down, shall we?'

'I am calm,' I said through gritted teeth, clutching Rufus and trying to soothe him. 'Your girlfriend is a liar.'

'I am so not,' Brooke said, with wounded eyes.

'You really want to double down?' I yelled, exasperated.

'Okay,' Adam said, patting the air, trying to suppress the emotional temperature. 'Show me what she did.'

And there he had me. There was nothing to see. Defeat sat heavy on my shoulders. 'I can't.' My voice barely rose above a whisper. I couldn't bring myself to look at Brooke. God help her when Ben got home.

'Let's take a moment, huh, to figure this out,' Adam said.

'I don't need a moment,' I said, standing up. 'I'm going to take my baby and get showered and dressed. Best you make alternative arrangements.' Not my brightest idea. I didn't want the pair of them skulking around at home while I was out of the house. 'I'll call you a cab,' I added, to make my position clear. And with that, I walked out, head held high and marched upstairs.

CHAPTER TWENTY-TWO

My composure disintegrated the second I was in Rufus's bedroom. Brooke's denial was so convincing, a part of me wondered if I really had dreamt the whole incident. *Could I? Did I?* I'd only ever once experienced that same sensation of being out of control, as if events were driving me to take one bad decision after another. Throughout those dark and dismal days, I'd never been subject to hallucinations, despite being told that I was 'imagining things, getting the wrong idea, didn't understand' and 'there's an alternative point of view'.

Never would I allow anyone to subject me to that type of persuasion again.

I changed Rufus out of his sleep suit, took him to the main bedroom, placed him on the bed and surrounded him with pillows so he wouldn't wriggle off. He gazed up at me adoringly and my heart instantly melted. 'Who's a gorgeous boy?' I said, chucking him under his little chin, my reward a gummy smile and a ton of dribble. Putting my hands over my eyes, I swept them away and cried, 'Peekaboo!' Rufus gurgled with delight and kicked with his little legs. It was such a simple and uncomplicated moment I felt instantly calm and clear. I *knew* what had happened the night before. I did *not* dream it. Brooke was lying.

I had a little think about that. Ben denied all knowledge and that left Brooke and, potentially, Adam in the know. To be fair, he'd looked clueless; it didn't mean he was. The big question was why the deceit? What did anyone hope to achieve? Was Brooke mentally ill, an addict, malevolent, or plain manipulative, and why the hell pick on me?

Taking Rufus with me into the bathroom and laying him down on a play mat, I had a quick shower, towelled myself dry and smoothed body oil over my skin to reduce the criss-cross pattern of stretch marks on my thighs and stomach. Clouded by steam, my blurred reflection revealed brown eyes, the colour of chocolate drops, Ben had once told me. My honey-coloured skin was not as smooth and taut as it once was. Frown lines creased my forehead, and I had two straight short indentations between my pale eyebrows. Emotional war wounds, I conceded. Picking up Rufus, I grimly pushed away memories of the long-ago battle that had caused them.

I'd just about dressed when the sound of a floorboard creaking outside the bedroom caught my attention. As soon as I heard the tap-tapping on the door, I knew what was coming: an appeal to my better nature. Tough. Right now, I didn't have one.

'Yes?' I said, a snap in my voice.

'Sophie, it's me, Adam.' I heaved a sigh. Better than Brooke, I supposed. 'Are you decent?' Sounded like my mother wanting a quiet chat in my bedroom when I was a bashful teen-ager. I assured him I was. 'Can I come in?' he asked.

I opened the door. Time-consuming, conversation start-ers and conversation stoppers, babies have surprising uses. I stood with Rufus clutched against me like a shield and gestured for Adam to sit down on the Lloyd Loom chair I sometimes used for nursing. He moved swiftly and silently, lynx-like, and sat, legs splayed, easy and relaxed, still with the smile. Hopefully, Brooke had come clean, and he was on a mission to make peace. I didn't say a word. Let the man speak and don't concede a thing, I thought, yet his mesmerising gaze fixed on me in such a way it had the effect of loosening my resolve. I felt instantly uncertain and less sure of my ground.

'Are you okay?' He spoke softly, his expression sympathetic and uncomfortably intrusive. I did not know this man and yet I felt as if he knew me.

'No, I'm not,' I replied.

'I'll level with you.' Adam sounded like a hostage negotiator trying to persuade a kidnapper that their demands were reasonable and understood. 'I don't know what the hell happened between you . . .'

'Let me stop you right there,' I said. 'This isn't some girly falling out. Events took place in the small hours, which your girlfriend now denies. She was snooping, looking for pills after I explicitly made it clear that Ben would not give her a random prescription. When I caught her . . .'

'She was with *me*, Sophie. All night. You've met her. She's a sweet kid. She wouldn't have the balls to do what you suggest, or, frankly, the guile.'

My gaze narrowed. 'You're saying I imagined it?'

'I'm not saying that, no.' Still with the warm smile, he seemed keen to appear neutral. 'Clearly, it's real to you.'

'Because it *really* happened!' I was damned if I were going to concede.

'For argument's sake,' Adam said, changing tack, 'say she did.'

'She did,' I said stonily.

'Well, have you ever done something you're ashamed of?'

The room swam. A white-hot pain lanced the inside of my chest. 'Irrelevant,' I stuttered, under his weighty gaze.

Adam tipped his head, apparently weighing up whether he agreed with me or not. He seemed to conclude that he did.

'And she made a mess, you said.'

'Yes.'

'So someone tidied up?'

'*Yes*, Brooke.'

'How do you know it was her?'

Fizzing with frustration, I kept my voice rock steady. 'Isn't that perfectly obvious?'

'*I* didn't put things straight, *you* didn't, Brooke says she didn't, what about Ben?'

'I messaged him this morning. He knew nothing about it.'

Adam drummed his fingers on his chin. 'Must be one of those great inexplicable mysteries then.' He spoke with finality, as if the matter were closed.

Not a chance. 'According to you, there are two narratives: mine and Brooke's. I have news for you: there's another. It's called the facts, and the facts are your girlfriend was in Ben's study when she should have been asleep in the guest bedroom. This is *our* house,' I said, on a roll. 'I will not have us living here as if it belongs to someone else.' God knows where that came from. I try to be precise and unemotional. As Saskia was fond of telling me at work: *when you speak people sit up and listen.* Well, I hoped Adam was listening now.

The smile on Adam's face didn't slip; it fell. His hands shot to his head in consternation. 'Oh my God, Sophie. I'm so *so* sorry we've upset you.' And he genuinely looked dismayed. 'I see how this must make you feel. Can you forgive me?' With sudden emotion in his voice, his dark brooding eyes searched mine.

Uncomfortable with the question, I mumbled, 'There's nothing to forgive.' In fairness, Adam had done nothing wrong.

'Please let's not fall out,' Adam said, beseeching. 'I understand this hasn't been easy for you. Me turning up out of the blue, but Ben *is* the only family I have.'

I sheepishly remembered my mother's advice.

'Give us a chance to make this right,' Adam pleaded.

My thoughts fled to the dreaded cookery evening scheduled for the following night. It took all of me not to let out a deep groan.

'Can we be friends?' Adam pressed. 'I swear to God I'll keep my eye on Brooke.'

Buckling under the weight of such an emotional onslaught, how could I refuse? 'Sure,' I said, exhausted.

CHAPTER TWENTY-THREE

But I wasn't that much of a pushover.

Ignoring Brooke, who stood as if someone had forced foie gras down her throat, I set out the ground rules: *brief* visit to Mum's to drop off Rufus and even *briefer* visit to Cake That after which they could catch a bus into town for the day and bugger off. (I didn't say the last bit). There was plenty to occupy them in Cheltenham, I told them, sounding and feeling like Head Girl at school again.

'I'll meet you at the car at two thirty p.m. in the main car park in Rodney Road. It's central and near the shops.'

'Cool,' Adam said.

Brooke concurred, studying the floor.

That sorted, we set off.

Mid-March, it was a pretty nice day: little wind, streaks of blue sky and puffy clouds.

It's a lovely drive from Cirencester to Cheltenham, along a leafy road that runs past a tiddly tributary of the River Chelt. It's fast and it's quiet. To block out the need for conversation, I put the radio on and tuned it to Radio 2. I'd wager it was a million miles away from the music Adam and Brooke enjoyed. Glancing at the rear-view mirror, I could see Brooke hunched down, staring out of the window, thunderous. I hoped Rufus didn't catch on to the bad vibes radiating off her. Fortunately, he'd dropped off for a snooze.

Nearing Mum's, I switched off Soft Cell's 'Tainted Love' and finally turned into the drive and parked. Adam's chin tilted up, as if taking stock of his surroundings.

'Won't be a second,' I said.

'Want a hand?' Alarmingly, he was already reaching for the door.

'No, thanks.' I was eager to release Rufus from his car seat and pass him into my mother's safekeeping with a minimum of fuss. Unfortunately, Mum had other ideas. I'd barely climbed out when she was crunching across the gravel, smiling broadly.

'We're in rather a hurry, Mum,' I said, attempting to cut her off.

'Five minutes won't hurt,' she said, sailing past.

Next, Adam was out of the car, shaking her hand and smothering her in compliments about her dress, how young she looked to have a daughter my age — thanks, very much — and about the visual appeal of her home. *Creep*. Determined to block him out, I thumped my way to the rear door to unstrap Rufus. Snatches of conversation clattered my ears. I didn't need to look to see how beguiled Mum was. I could hear it in her voice.

'How wonderful for you after all this time.'

'I can't tell you how fond we are of Ben.'

'Are you staying long?'

At this I pinned my ears back.

'It's not yet been decided,' Adam replied, swivelling his gaze towards me.

Before Mum issued an invite, I stood up straight and banged my head on the ceiling liner. Nobody other than Brooke noticed.

'You okay?' she asked, smirking.

'Perfect,' I said, eyes watering.

Staggering back to my mother and parking Rufus in her arms, I said, 'Sorry, Mum, but I do need to get going.'

She gave me one of those looks that told me I was spoiling her fun. She had no idea what I was saving her from.

'Nice to meet you,' Mum trilled to Adam as he climbed back into my car.

'Hope to see you again,' he called back.

Not if I had anything to do with it, I thought sourly.

'What a lovely woman your mother is,' Adam said, as we pulled out of the drive. 'She would have got on well with my mum.' Feeling momentarily mean-spirited, I agreed with a nod. 'Mum was always so welcoming to my friends,' Adam continued. No mention of Ben's, I noted.

'What about Ben? Were your friends his friends too?'

'We moved in different circles. Ben was too much of a swot to have mates.'

I glanced across, surprised by the ugly twist in Adam's voice.

Realising his mask had slipped, Adam snapped a smile. 'And boy has it paid off. Smart guy, he's done *way* better than me.'

CHAPTER TWENTY-FOUR

We arrived at Cake That and piled out of the car.

Crossing the parking area to the back of the office, Adam's gaze travelled to the sign on the wall. It symbolised an empty cupcake paper case with a few crumbs sprinkled around it, the message: these are too good not to eat.

'Is that the company logo?' he asked.

'It is.'

'And it appears on your website?'

I confirmed it did.

'Have you had it long?'

'A few years now, why?'

'The logo is okay but the name's not cutting-edge enough, too boy band, if you don't mind me saying.'

I did mind him saying. It had taken Saskia and me an enormous amount of time to come up with a name for the business that wasn't used by hundreds of other cake companies in the UK. We'd jettisoned Cake on a Plate, Cake or Death, Cakes in the Kitchen, and dozens more before landing on Cake That. 'I'm always open to constructive criticism,' I said with a polite smile.

'Branding is vital,' Adam continued loftily. 'Might be worth a refresh.'

'I'll bear it in mind,' I said sprightly, not so sprightly leading the way. Brooke kept her distance — a wise move — and trailed along behind Adam.

In honour of the royal visit, Saskia's office was barely recognisable. Normally chaotic and littered with anything from cake wrappers and half-drunk mugs of coffee to make-up and magazines, her desk was a vision of fastidiousness and order. The screen on her computer was clean. A new keyboard plugged in, and its grubby predecessor ditched. More surprising still, her demure appearance: papal white collarless shirt with all the buttons done up over straight leg navy trousers and flats. She had seriously dialled down her make-up to girl next door. My sister is predatory by nature, and I'd have put good money on her vamping it up. Perhaps she'd broken the habit of a lifetime and paid attention to what I said.

Who was I kidding?

The second we were inside her smile skidded over my face and landed with a thump on Adam. She stared. He stared. I'd never believed in all that love at first sight stuff, having witnessed this routine countless times before but, alarmingly, I sensed the feeling was mutual. You could have powered several generators from the electricity in the room. I detested the way Brooke had behaved towards me yet couldn't help but feel sorry for her.

Luke ambled in and, needing to crack on, I suggested he, rather than Saskia, gave our visitors a whistle-stop tour.

'I can do it,' Saskia piped up.

'I need you to man the phone,' I said, ignoring the pointy expression on my sister's face.

'Sorry but you'll need these,' Luke said, handing coveralls and hairnets to Adam and Brooke.

'I'm not wearing those,' Brooke baulked. 'They're gross.'

'Then you'll have to stay in the office with Saskia,' I said.

'Your choice,' Saskia cut in with an equally cutting smile.

'C'mon, Brooke, babe, it'll be a laugh.' Adam dropped a hand to her shoulder.

'Buses leave from the top of the road every fifteen minutes,' I said sharply, disappearing into my office and virtually dragging Saskia with me.

'You are such a spoilsport,' Saskia exclaimed. 'Bloody hell, where did you find him?' She fanned her face with a hand.

'He found us, remember? And for God's sake, did you have to make it so obvious you fancied him in front of his girlfriend?'

'If she's his girlfriend I'm Dua Lipa.'

My sister always amazes me with her direct manner. Sometimes I'm taken back by her perspicacity. Yes, Adam called Brooke 'babe'. Yes, he was tactile with her, seemingly unconsciously so in the way couples are but, with neither lust nor love in his expression, it felt for show. In hindsight the story of how they met felt contrived. Drifting off into an internal monologue, I thought, why?

Saskia had to virtually shake me for a response. Eventually, I admitted, 'It's all slightly strange.'

'Strange intriguing or strange weird?'

I told Saskia about the study incident. Her eyes widened. 'Christ, think she's a junkie?'

'Why do you say that?'

'Junkies always lie. It runs through their DNA.'

'How come you know so much about it?'

'How do you think?' Saskia's smile was worryingly naughty. 'An old boyfriend,' she said in exasperation.

That figured. Now was not the time to mention Adam's side hustle. 'Brooke confessed she'd been thrown out of home by her parents.'

'There you go then. Fits the profile. Parents can stand a lot of shit, but drugs, not so much. Awks for you.'

'Adam appealed to me to draw a line underneath it.'

'I guess no harm done.'

'Apart from the fact Brooke made me out to be a fantasist.'

Saskia took a moment to consider. 'Maybe Adam knows she's kinked and was trying to do the decent thing and protect her.'

'Not very fair on me.'

'Oh, you're a big girl. You can take care of yourself.'

'Thanks very much.'

Saskia shrugged her shoulders. 'What does Ben say?'

'He doesn't know.'

'You should tell him.'

'Trust me, I will. But do me a favour, yeah?'

'What's that?'

'Please don't worry Mum with it.'

'Something up with her?'

'She looks tired, seems to be off her food.'

'I haven't noticed.'

'You wouldn't spot an earthquake unless you were standing at its epicentre.'

Saskia responded with a loud tut.

'You promise then?'

Saskia crossed a finger over her heart in a hope-to-die gesture, like we'd done as kids. 'I promise,' she swore.

CHAPTER TWENTY-FIVE

After finishing with Lisa, my last one-to-one, I glanced at the list of requests: shorter working hours/increased pay/more generous holidays together with a few interesting ideas for improvements. Frazzled, I was relieved to see Adam and Brooke were nowhere to be seen when I finally surfaced for air. I asked Saskia when they'd left.

'About an hour ago.'

Which meant they'd stayed for at least an hour. 'Surprised you weren't hotfooting after them.'

Saskia stuck out her tongue. 'You have to admit he's very charming.'

I translated this as bloody gorgeous. 'Almost too good to be true,' I said with a dry smile.

'Yes, well,' Saskia huffed, not keen to have her Adam-shaped bubble burst. 'Before I forget, Adam asked me to tell you not to worry about picking them up later.'

'Oh?'

'They're going to bus it back and spend the evening in Cirencester.'

Maybe, they'd got the message at last. 'Miracles will never cease.'

Strangely, their absence did not reduce my stress levels; I knew that, sooner or later, they would be back and then what?

Remembering Louise's banoffee tray bake I helped myself to one from the counter and, in need of an illicit energy lift, snaffled a ginger cookie, gobbling it down under the auspices of conducting a random quality check. Wiping cookie crumbs from my lips, I wasn't quick enough to avoid Saskia's critical gaze.

'Thought you were out for lunch.'

'I am.'

Saskia elevated an eyebrow.

'I'm stressed as hell, if you want the truth.'

'You? Stressed?' Saskia snorted. 'Nothing ever gets to you.'

Except it did. 'Poor old Sophie,' Saskia said, trying to cheer me up. 'Go with the flow is my advice.'

Picking up my bag, I gave her a hug.

'Before you leave,' Saskia said, in a tone that left me in no doubt going with the flow was about to become a necessity, 'it might not be anything,' she qualified, shifting her slender weight from one foot to the other.

'Spit it out, Sash.' Had the new manager at our Tetbury branch given in her notice? Was there a hitch with the refit at the South Cerney unit?

'Brooke asked me where she could find the nearest chemist.'

Not exactly startling news. She probably needed toiletries. 'And?'

'She waved a prescription in front of my nose.'

I was certain my eyebrows met my hairline. Ben kept prescription pads in his study securely locked away for obvious reasons. I told Saskia this. 'The audacity,' I exploded. 'It's practically an admission of theft.'

'Unless she got the prescription from another doctor.'

'Then why hunt through Ben's things for pills?'

'Desperation? You're absolutely certain you didn't dream it? Baby brain and all that.'

Frustration didn't billow out of me; it surged on a great tidal wave of indignation. 'I may be tired. I may be a little scratchy. But there is nothing wrong with my brain. In fact, it's functioning fully. The only other explanation for Brooke rootling through Ben's study is that she was, in fact, searching for something else; the whole pill story nothing more than a detour.'

With that thought thundering through my mind, I waved my dumbstruck sister goodbye and drove to Mum's.

'Rufus was a little fractious.' Mum handed him over, worry in her expression. 'Fussed over his milk and wouldn't settle at all. I wonder if he's coming down with something.'

'I'll check his temperature.'

'Already done,' Mum said. 'Seems cool enough. It's probably something and nothing.' She watched me as I soothed my son and smiled. 'He'll be okay now he's got his mummy.'

'Let's hope so.'

She gathered up Rufus's toys and handed me his bag. 'I must say I thought Ben's brother was lovely.'

'Everyone says so,' I murmured, head down.

Mum was no fool. 'Am I missing something?'

Just a bit, I thought, but I didn't want to regale her with stories I couldn't yet prove. 'No, I'm tired, that's all.' Although not as tired as my mother. Dark shadows, like bruises, lurked beneath her eyes.

'You do seem a little out of sorts, darling.'

'It will pass.'

'And that's why I'd like to help,' she said, gathering steam. 'As they're still here—'

'You want us to come for supper at the weekend,' I cut in. 'Saskia mentioned it,' I said in answer to her surprised expression.

'Can't keep anything secret in this family.'

I'd managed it, I thought, my smile warm, my heart cold. If only Mum knew. I'd lost count of the times I'd wanted to tell her and almost did. With the passage of years, the guilt had receded, not quite gone away but it was containable. Nobody delved. They'd wrongly assumed I'd simply had cold feet and changed my mind about marriage. To sell it to Ben, I confessed I wasn't cut out to live with the constant threat faced by police officers and, by default, their wives; the long hours spent alone, worrying; the obsessive nature of a job that demanded so much. I painted it that it was *my* failing. *I* was the one at fault. Nobody knew I'd had my mind changed for me.

'You'll come?' Mum said, expectant.

'Let me talk to Ben, first.' I popped Rufus into his baby carrier. 'All right if I leave my car here and pick it up later?' Louise and Elliott lived in a house only thirteen minutes away on foot from my parents, and parking in Moorend Road was a nightmare.

'Of course,' she said. 'Give lovely Louise my love.'

CHAPTER TWENTY-SIX

And I did.

'Your mum's a treasure,' Louise said.

She was. I didn't know what I'd do without her.

We were sitting in the dining room of Louise's period terraced property: all dado rails, high ceilings and cornices. Louise had made sandwiches — smoked salmon and cream cheese — 'because they're easier to eat with baby in tow,' she remarked, parking me on a comfy seat with a view of an immaculately cultivated garden and a lawn that was cut to within an inch of its life. All that would change when she fell pregnant and had a little one of her own, I thought wryly.

Physically, Louise was the epitome of who she was as a person: strong and capable with a wide brow, clear eyes the colour of faded wisteria, and a square chin. Nothing got past her. She'd trained in social work, specialising in child protection, before entering the charity sector. You needed compassion and robust mental muscles to deal with victims of domestic abuse; Louise had both. Saskia's remark about nothing ever troubling me could more honestly be ascribed to my friend.

Initially, we chatted about her holiday, and I viewed snaps on her phone. I asked after Elliott, a conveyancing solicitor, and Louise said that he'd returned to a full workload and a list of stressed-out clients in various stages of moving.

'Can't tell you the number of times sales have fallen through,' Louise said. 'Sorry,' she added, dropping a hand on my arm. 'Not what you want to hear.'

'Must be stressful for him.'

'He takes it in his stride,' Louise remarked with a warm smile. 'Unlike the vast majority of his clients. Any movement on the flat?'

'None,' I said.

We demolished two chunks of tray bake and I suggested Louise keep the rest for Elliott. She held Rufus, dreamy-eyed, while I went to the loo and only then did she mention the possibility of IVF. My heart went out to my friend because I sensed it wasn't what she wanted.

'We're going to give it a few more months before we travel down that route,' Louise said mournfully. 'A single cycle can cost five grand and there's no guarantee it will work.'

'I'm sure it won't come to that,' I said, sympathetic.

'Elliott mentioned adoption.'

'How do you feel about that?'

'Not sure.' She stroked Rufus's cheek. 'It would be a lovely thing to give a needy child a warm and loving home.'

'But it's not quite the same?'

'Selfish of me, I suppose.'

'Rubbish,' I said. 'You can't help the way you feel.'

She looked up with a grin. 'Talking of giving someone a loving home, how's it going with Ben's brother? You didn't mention it so I assume he's gone.'

'I wish,' I said.

'Oh dear. What's he like?'

'Clever.' I delivered similar shout lines to the ones I'd given Saskia. Unlike my sister, Louise did not question my account of the study incident.

'Does Ben keep drugs there?'

'In his bag, yes, although it's not extensive — emergency stuff like adrenalin, opiates and penicillin. Ben would have raised the alarm if anything were missing. Since Shipman, the serial killer doctor,' I explained, 'there are more checks and balances. It's all subject to strict protocols.'

'Sounds as if the girlfriend is more of a problem than Adam.'

'I can't make her out. At first, I felt rather sorry for her. Besotted with Ben's brother she's young and naïve, cut off from her parents and vulnerable. Now I actively dislike her.'

'And you say there's no sign of them actually leaving?'

'It gets worse.' I regaled Louise with Adam's insistence on cooking a meal for us in my kitchen plus my mother's invitation to entertain us all at the weekend. 'I shouldn't be so ungrateful, but it feels, I don't know, as if Adam is burrowing into our lives.'

Louise smiled. 'After a few days? Do you think you're being a little harsh, dare I say overreacting?'

'Probably.' I wanted to be fair, but already I was sick of tidying up, buying extra food, and generally having to be on my best behaviour. 'Thing is, Adam is charming and engaging and quite likeable and yet he's unpredictably sharp with his girlfriend and can be double-edged with Ben.'

'How do you mean?'

I struggled to pin it down. 'It's as if Adam is looking for pressure points and ways to trip him up.'

'That's quite some statement. What does Ben think?'

I took a moment to consider before answering. 'It's difficult. He seems oddly reluctant to nail them down on their plans to leave but wants them to go as much as me.'

'He's actually said that?'

I lowered my head. 'Not so much lately.'

'Do you think you're in danger of superimposing your view on Ben? After all, he must be pleased to see his brother after all this time.'

'That's the point, Louise, I'm not sure he is.'

We left it at that. Time was ticking. Louise needed to get back to work and I wanted to get back to make things nice for Ben when he got home.

'Don't worry,' Louise said, squeezing my shoulder as I left. 'In my experience things are never as good as you think they are and never as bad either.'

How I wanted to believe her.

* * *

Popping into the house to inform Mum I was picking up the car, my heart missed a beat at the sound of familiar voices. To remove any element of doubt, I marched into the sitting room where my eyes swivelled from Adam and Brooke to the cafetière and three mugs on the coffee table. Adam's twinkling smile should have cheered me. I was not cheered.

Spotting my consternation, Mum did her best to put me in the picture and smooth things over.

'Adam and Brooke had lunch at the Norwood.' Our nearest local. In answer to my so what expression, Adam picked up the conversational slack.

'As we were close by and didn't really have a chance to speak to Ben's mother-in-law . . .'

'We're not married,' I said in a cool voice.

Mum snatched a nervous laugh and looked to Brooke who sat with her hands folded tightly in her lap, silent and wary. I addressed Adam. 'Are you still planning on doing your own thing today?' Sure as hell, I was not going to offer them a lift back.

'Absolutely. We have a table booked at a tapas restaurant for dinner tonight.'

'Oooh — off Blackjack Street?' Mum interjected, desperately trying to recover some ground and jolly the conversation along.

'It won't be a patch on your cooking, I'm certain, Faith,' Adam said with an oily smile. 'I'm so looking forward to

Saturday,' he added, daring me to challenge my mother's invitation. Worse, Mum sat entranced, wide-eyed and girlish. Defeated, I said I should get going.

'Before you leave, Sophie,' Adam said, 'might be an idea to leave a key in a secure place, save you the bother of waiting up.'

'It's no bother.' I kept my voice light.

'Next time then.'

There would be no next time. I icily forced a smile.

Mum pursued me down the hall to the front door. 'Sophie, don't be cross.'

'I'm not.' The heat spreading from my neck to my cheeks told a different story. 'I wished you'd let me talk to Ben first, that's all, before inviting them.'

'Surely, he won't object?' Until now, the mortifying thought he might not be thrilled had eluded her. 'Have I done the wrong thing?' she asked, anxious and strained.

No, Adam had done the wrong thing. Keen to make her feel better, I patted her arm. 'It's a kind thought, well-intentioned.'

'You're certain? I could always say I've double-booked.'

'No, no, it's fine. Honest,' I said, with a smile.

Mum's soft features flooded with relief. My mother could never bear to be at odds with her children. Dad was less choosey. I wondered what he'd make of Adam and Brooke.

Before I drove home, I messaged Ben to let him know that we had a glorious evening alone. He messaged me back with a thumbs up.

CHAPTER TWENTY-SEVEN

'Hey!' Ben strode through the door and dropped a kiss on my cheek. 'And hey, little man.' He rested his warm hand tenderly on the top of Rufus's head. 'Is the coast clear?'

'It is.'

'There is a god,' Ben enthused. 'Give me five minutes to change, Sophs, and then I'll take him.'

It was so lovely to be the three of us again, my heart swelled with happiness. I felt lighter than I had in days.

While Ben peeled off his work clothes and got into more casual wear, I took a bottle of Viognier from the fridge and poured a large glass for Ben and small one for me.

Reappearing in jeans and a loose-fitting blue shirt, the same colour as his eyes, Ben took Rufus in his arms and cradled him on his lap. At the sight of me drinking, he asked, 'Are we celebrating?'

'I believe we are.'

'Here's to us.' He chinked his glass with mine.

I thought he'd mention my seemingly mysterious message that morning, but instead he talked about a new initiative to ensure an improved multi-agency approach to treating people with mental health issues. 'We need a better framework for how police and health care professionals work together.'

'Police?' My mind automatically flew to Leo, my ex-fiancé. Was the initiative specific to Gloucestershire or had it extended to the Met? God only knew, it needed to.

'That's right,' Ben confirmed.

My mouth suddenly dry, I deliberately tuned out as Ben rattled on while I threw together a stir-fry.

'Sophs, are you listening?'

'Yes.' I plastered on a smile. 'Sounds great,' I said, smoothly telling Ben about my lunch with Louise.

'She looked really well,' I said, dishing up. 'Want me to take Rufus?'

'Nope, he's fine.'

'Mum said he wasn't his usual sunny self earlier.'

'How was she?' Ben pushed a forkful of food into his mouth.

'Seemed a bit run-down, if I'm honest. Why do you ask?'

'No reason.' Ben dug into another forkful.

'Thing is, she's invited us all for dinner on Saturday.'

Ben's fork hovered midway. 'All?'

'Adam and Brooke and—'

Ben's fork clattered to the plate. Rufus gave a startled cry. Ben lifted him up and kissed his cheek. It did not stop Ben from letting out an expletive.

'Ben, she was being nice,' I said, instantly protective of my mum, even though I was far from keen on the idea myself.

'She doesn't understand.' He reached for his drink. Alarmingly, I felt his knee jink with anxiety from beneath the table.

'And neither do I, not really. Here, let me take Rufus.'

Ben glowered as he handed him over, his suddenly warm mood evaporating. 'The more Adam is made welcome, the harder it will be for him to leave. He embeds himself with people.'

Glumly, I remembered Adam's request for a key to be left for 'next time'.

'Then you have to level with him,' I said. 'You don't have to be horrible, simply let him know that it's inconvenient to stay because of the building work. I'm sure he'll more than understand.'

Ben ran a finger around the rim of his glass.

I took a sip. 'Why is it so difficult?'

Ben shot me a look. 'It isn't.'

I shook my head and then, for the third time that day, recounted the story about Brooke. I was waiting for a strong reaction. I thought he'd be shocked. When I finished, I said, 'Well, say something.'

'She's ill.'

'We both know that. Aren't you bothered she was going through your things?'

'I am but no harm was done.'

'She forged a prescription, Ben.'

'What are you talking about?'

'Bold as brass, she waved it in front of Saskia this morning. She must have stolen it from your study.'

Ben looked down. 'I wrote it for her.'

'*You*?' I struggled to conceal my blind astonishment. 'But you said you wouldn't do it.'

'I know,' he agreed with a sigh.

'What the hell did you prescribe?'

'A combination of anti-depressants and anti-anxiety meds.'

Temporarily speechless, I opened my mouth and closed it like a flailing goldfish scooped out of its bowl by a cat. When I finally recovered my senses, I wasn't nice. 'What the hell made you abandon a deeply held principle?'

'She begged me.'

'So what? You get begged at work all the time. Doesn't mean you comply.'

Ben lowered his gaze. 'This is different. I was only giving her what she'd already been prescribed.'

'*Only*?' I stuttered. 'I presume she can drink while she's on this stuff, otherwise you might be in danger of killing her.'

Ben's answering expression was as cool as a shady graveyard. 'I do know what I'm doing, Sophie. I don't need reminders.'

I stroked Rufus's cheek and made big eyes at him; my reward a dribbly grin. 'When did all this come about?' I asked, dialling down my voice.

'Before I left for work this morning. You were asleep.'

'And they were up? They're never awake before nine.'

'They were in the kitchen.'

'After they'd put everything back in its rightful place,' I said, fired up again. Maybe Adam had given Brooke a hand so he could have a snoop too. This, I did not say.

Ben's failure to comment was designed to cool hearts and minds; it irritated the hell out of me.

'That's *great*,' I said, testy. 'You might have mentioned it. No wonder she looked so damn smug. All the time that she was disputing my story in front of your brother who, incidentally, claimed not to believe a word of what I said — she already had her Get Out of Jail Free pass.'

'Sophie, I . . .'

'And, bloody hell, Adam never breathed a word. Just stood over me, letting me rave on, then begged my forgiveness because I was a bit upset.'

Ben gave a start. 'Forgiveness?'

I stood up and, one-handed, ostentatiously started to clear the plates and load the dishwasher. Lots of clatter and lots of bang.

'I'm sorry,' he said, glancing up at me with haunted eyes. 'But I was put in a difficult position.'

'Who by?'

Sheepish, Ben didn't answer.

'Do you do everything your brother says?' I snapped, swept along by a current of unreasonable indignation.

'Of course not.'

At least that got a reaction. 'Then you can tell him he's not cooking in my kitchen tomorrow night.'

And with that, I stamped upstairs to bathe Rufus and settle him for bed.

CHAPTER TWENTY-EIGHT

I deliberately took my time, then seriously wished I hadn't. Regretting my flash of bad temper, I wanted to make amends and apologise. It was ridiculous us falling out, especially on our precious evening together without our 'guests'.

Creeping along the landing and downstairs, I found the sitting room empty, the lights switched off. Disappointed, I returned upstairs. Poking my head around the door of our bedroom confirmed that Ben had turned in for the night and was fast asleep.

It was past ten. I'd have to stay up to let Adam and Brooke back into the house. Unless they hoofed off to ReVA or Seventeen Black, I doubted they'd be making a night of it. I sincerely hoped not.

Silently slipping out of my clothes and into my PJs, doubt wormed its way into my mind. What had transpired between the three of them that morning? All I had was Ben's account. I didn't know how the conversation rolled, what pressure had been applied or, God help me for giving the malign thought houseroom, what threat had been made. I don't know what I expected when Adam stepped back into his brother's life, but it wasn't this. There was too much edge, too many hidden and

123

indecipherable conversational codes and non sequiturs; reluctance on Ben's part to deal with his brother and determination on Adam's part to not only stay, but also, as Ben maintained, *embed* himself. I kept coming back to the why of it.

Downstairs, I crossed the sitting room and opened the door to the staircase that led to the guest quarters. Fair was fair, I thought, pushing aside inconvenient reservations about what I was about to do. You go through our stuff. I'll go through yours.

Upstairs, I walked straight into a sea of scattered clothes, empty vape cartridges, beer bottles and a collection of dirty plates and mugs that I hadn't even realised had made their journey there. The bed was unmade, half the duvet tumbling onto the carpet. Make-up smeared the sink, (possibly Adam's) in the en suite, the loo wasn't flushed and shower gel cascaded down the tiles in the shower unit. Irritatingly, the clothes I'd recently laundered lay dumped in a pile on the floor alongside two damp towels. A quick hunt through wash bags revealed nothing unusual. I noted that Brooke was prescribed the same contraceptive pills as me.

Nobody would notice a little extra vandalism to a room that already looked as if it had been burgled. I determined that Brooke slept on the right-hand side of the bed, next to a pink four-wheel suitcase, and Adam on the left, nearest the door.

I started with Brooke's belongings, rummaging through underwear, skirts and shirts, a thick green sweater, a pair of denim dungarees, a box of tampons and two pairs of pumps. A theatre programme for a play in the West End. Feeling decidedly grubby and my heart racing at the thought of Ben suddenly waking up and walking in, I was about to bail when my fingers hit the outline of a solid object in a side pocket of the case. Unzipping it revealed a pristine Samsung Galaxy mobile phone. I stared at it for a full five seconds. My first thought: they'd lied. My second: why make the mistake of leaving the phone where it could be found? Was Brooke that careless?

Confounded, pulse pumping, I turned my attention to the other side of the bed and a big black holdall, open and with its contents spilling out like an urban fox disembowelled by a car on an A road.

I liberated loose change from the pocket of a pair of black ripped jeans and found a tatty-looking business card for a pub called the Pig's Snout, Bromyard, a place I'd never heard of in Herefordshire. Socks, underwear, T-shirts and a black hoodie flew out. Digging deeper, my fingers bumped against the smooth surface of plastic. Quick examination revealed a tablet in a protective cover. Nobody had asked me for a password for our Wi-Fi. I guessed Brooke had made a note from the modem when searching Ben's study. I opened the tablet and, password protected, hit a digital brick wall. It did, however, confirm one thing: they had communication with the outside world. In a way it reassured me that they weren't completely peculiar and isolated until I considered the reason for secrecy.

More searching, then, right at the bottom, I unearthed a passport. Nobody looks good in a passport picture. Without make-up, Adam resembled a hologram of himself. This was not the reason for my lips parting and my gaze sharpening. The photograph belonged to Adam, but the name inside was different. This was for Adam Joshua Hall, not Taylor. Was he really Ben's brother and, if he wasn't, why was Ben pretending he was? I stared at it for a few seconds and, shoving it back together with the clothes I'd thrown out, sped out of the room and down the stairs, my heart skipping at the sound of a mewling Rufus.

Emerging from the door into the sitting room, I bowled straight into Ben. No doubt about it I had a lot of explaining to do.

'I looked everywhere for you,' Ben said, annoyed and dishevelled. 'Rufus refuses to settle. Where were you and what the hell were you doing?'

I took Rufus from him. Ben was right about our son. Rufus fretted and squeaked; his little face screwed up, red and unhappy.

'Shush,' I said.

'It's no use,' Ben said. 'He's really upset.'

'I think we'd better sit down.'

Ben followed my lead and plumped down on one sofa, me on the other. It felt like a high-noon moment.

'I was going through their things,' I blurted out, watching Ben's face pale. 'It's not something I'm particularly proud of,' I rushed on hastily, 'but before you get cross, I found certain items that prove beyond reasonable doubt they've been lying to us from the start.' That was a tad dramatic for me, but I wanted to find out who Adam really was and ram the message home that Ben should get rid of this man and his girlfriend sooner rather than later.

By the hard, uncompromising expression on his face, Ben would be hard to persuade. 'What items?' He crossed his arms, peeved.

I started with the phone. 'They maintain they never use them.'

'God, Sophie, perhaps they recently bought it.'

'When? They've been glued to my side for the past four days.'

'Okay, but I expect there's a perfectly reasonable explanation.'

'The same explanation they used for why Brooke couldn't possibly have been in your study in the early hours?' I sounded snarky because I *was* snarky. 'And then there's Adam's passport. His name is not Taylor.'

'No, it's Hall,' Ben said, not missing a beat.

Astonished, I said, 'You have different surnames?'

'Adam changed his by deed poll.'

Holy crap, I thought, embarrassed. 'Why?'

'He wanted a fresh start, I guess, after our parents died.'

'I wish you'd told me.'

'I didn't think it would be necessary,' Ben complained, exasperated. 'What the hell were you thinking? Was it payback?' Visibly cross, he glared at me.

'No, it wasn't,' I said, ashamed. 'And I'm sorry.'

Silence wrapped around us like razor wire.

I lowered my gaze, focused on Rufus and shrank into the cushions.

'You look exhausted,' Ben said, softening at last. It was true. My head ached with fatigue and the incipient fear of things slipping through my grasp. 'Take Rufus up with you,' he said, 'and I'll hang around to let Adam and Brooke in.'

'But they might be ages.'

'Doesn't matter.'

I started to protest. Ben was having none of it. His expression was stern. 'Go to bed. Get some sleep. And put all this paranoid stuff about my brother out of your mind.'

It was as good as telling me that Ben had taken his brother's side. Catching my dismay, he stood and crossed to me, slipping his arm around my shoulder and drawing me in. 'Sweetie, I'm not having a go at you.'

It felt like it.

'Adam is not the easiest person to have around,' Ben admitted. 'What are you doing tomorrow with them?'

'No plans.' I wanted to go to South Cerney to check up on our new outlet. I didn't fancy taking Adam and his opinions on my business with me.

'Then do what you want to do. They'll probably be knackered after a night out.'

'But the dinner,' I began.

'I'll square that. Focus on you and Rufus. A good night's sleep and things will look better in the morning, promise. Trust me, I'm a doctor,' he said, smiling searchingly into my eyes.

I'd heard something similar before. Then it had been 'Trust me, I'm a police officer'. I nodded a smile and, crushed, took Rufus up to bed.

CHAPTER TWENTY-NINE

The next morning, bog-eyed, I didn't hang around to find out whether Ben had spoken to Adam. After scribbling a note — *Back later* — I fled to South Cerney to check on the refit. Electrics were in; cold storage fridges had arrived; the eye-wateringly expensive Italian rotary ovens looked gorgeous. Satisfied that we were on schedule, I phoned Saskia to give her the glad tidings.

'See you tomorrow night,' she said, unable to resist a playful dig.

I trotted off with Rufus to the stone bridge close to the Eliot Arms and ambled along Bow Wow, a narrow tree-lined path that follows the course of the River Churn. If you want a taste of the Cotswolds this is it: amber-coloured, dry stone walls, a manor and a mill house, fast flowing river, silence and privacy. I was glad to step out of my chaotic world into a more peaceful and tranquil environment, however briefly.

When I returned home, I found Adam, semi-dressed, pottering around the kitchen making toast. The full rack of plates and cutlery at the side of the sink suggested that either he or Brooke had decided to clear the guest bedroom of debris. I guiltily prayed it was not a knee-jerk reaction to discovering someone had been in their quarters the night before. Having established evidence of deceit, I could argue that the ends justified the means. However, my snooping would play against me if it were ever to come out. Somehow, I had to expose their lies by using a different method.

Adam's enormous, welcoming smile assured me that we were good and that I had nothing to fear. 'Hey,' he said, 'hope you don't mind.' His gaze glanced from the jar of marmalade on the table back to me.

'It's fine,' I said, meeting his eye, eager to avoid the charge of being pernickety. 'Did you have a nice evening?'

'Sure did. Some lovely pubs in town if a tad expensive — almost as pricey as London. Couldn't believe what they charged for a pint.'

I made sympathetic noises and took Rufus upstairs for his nap. Adam was still in the kitchen when I came down to make coffee. Sitting at the table, leaning back, he said, 'Thought we'd have a quiet one today. Brooke's not feeling too good.'

'Oh?' Hangover, I thought. You couldn't be that thin, take pills and drink like a witch.

'Yeah, she'll feel better once the meds kick in.'

I swear the quirk at the corner of his mouth was designed to challenge. Conversing with Adam was like doing ten rounds in a boxing match, a sport for which I had no skill and little liking. Any minute now he'd deliver a knockout blow.

'Good of Ben to break the rules for us,' he said, twitching another smile.

There you go, I thought. Round one to Adam. 'It was,' I agreed stiffly.

'You don't like having his principles overturned, do you?' Adam's sunny manner failed to disguise the point he was making.

'I don't like seeing anyone having their principles overturned,' I said evenly.

'Nah, I can see that.'

'See what?'

'You're a woman with standards.'

His gaze locked onto mine. There it was again: that intimate sense of him drawing me out, getting me to confirm or deny characteristics about myself.

I popped on the kettle, took out a cafetière and a tin of ground coffee, warmed milk in a pan and resisted the strong temptation to reach for a cookie from the biscuit tin. The silence was as cloying as a supermarket-bought salted-caramel brownie with white icing. How could I kick off a conversation that wouldn't invite questions I didn't want to answer, or lead me to doubt Ben's narrative about his past? How was it that Adam thought he could sit in our home, casually believing he could undermine, manipulate and create doubt? For that was how I felt. I didn't care what Ben had said about his brother's name change and desire for a fresh start. Adam Hall was on the run from something; I didn't know what it was. I could hardly ask him without admitting how I'd found out that, in name alone, he wasn't who he said he was.

Distracted, I plunged my hand into the Belfast sink, full of dirty water. About to yank out the plug, I jumped back with a yelp.

Blood streamed from my right hand and dripped onto the floor. Raising my arm up in a doomed attempt to staunch the flow, I saw a deep cut along the pads of three of my fingers. My God, it hurt.

'Jesus,' Adam exclaimed, leaping to his feet. Swiping a tea towel from a worktop, he wrapped it around my hand and held it tight. 'Sit down,' he said, frowning with concern.

I didn't need an invitation. My vision swam and my legs virtually gave way. 'Shit,' I said, feeling sick, 'who on earth left a blade in the sink?'

Adam shook his head. 'Wasn't me. Where do you keep your first aid kit?'

'In the bathroom cupboard,' I replied, eyes watering. I'd suffered minor burns and scalds. This was next level. How come cuts from blades hurt so much? And why wouldn't it stop bleeding? Because I kept my knives razor sharp, *stupid*.

I listened as Adam's feet pounded up the stairs. Seconds later, he was back down, armed with gauze and sterile dressings.

'I don't want to see it,' I said, shaky.

'You don't have to. Look at the clock, or something,' he said, peering into the sink, gingerly removing the offending blade — a boning knife — and pulling out the plug to empty the water. Next, he vigorously washed his hands to the elbow, like a surgeon preparing to operate.

I did what he said and, bracing myself, let Adam peel away the tea towel. He dropped it on the floor, a sodden, bloodied pile.

'Okay, keep your palm up,' he said.

'Is it bad?' I asked in a quavering voice.

'One's quite nasty and you might need stitches.'

'Oh God,' I groaned.

'At least you're in the right place. No queues for you to see a doctor.'

'No,' I agreed with a limp smile.

'That's better,' Adam said. 'You've got more colour in your cheeks. Think I should give Ben a ring?'

I shook my head. 'Patch me up and he can take a look later.'

'You're sure?'

'Certain.' Ben had more important medical matters to attend to.

'Okay,' Adam said, calm and in control. 'Hold tight.'

Having the wounds cleaned made me want to scream. Afterwards, Adam meticulously dressed each finger and insisted I took a couple of painkillers. 'Tea with sugar, is what you need,' he said authoritatively, moving around the kitchen as if it was his domain.

He couldn't have been more solicitous, and I couldn't have felt more grateful and less sure. Had he left the knife in the water, or was it a simple accident? Had the blade slipped, somehow, from the rack into the sink?

Brooke appeared once the drama had died down. 'Looks like we'll be cooking this evening after all,' she said, her eyes as hard as stone.

131

CHAPTER THIRTY

Chills down my spine, I desperately tried not to think I'd been set up. It was an accident, I told myself. Nobody in his or her right mind would deliberately hurt me simply to score a point. It was a ridiculous idea. Once I'd mentally scaled that hurdle, I allowed Adam to make us sandwiches for lunch and, put out of action, reluctantly warmed to his offer to cook dinner.

'Under your instruction,' he said, emphatic, without a hint of sarcasm.

Brooke drifted around, absenting herself from food preparation and, indeed, food, declaring that she wasn't hungry after the enormous meal she'd eaten the night before. 'Did she?' I questioned Adam. His reply was to tilt his hand *so-so*.

'Doesn't it bother you?'

'What?'

'Brooke not eating.' Wasting her life, I was tempted to say.

'I'm kind of used to it.'

'What about the fact she's estranged from her family?'

'She's an adult old enough to make her own decisions. Do you want chutney with your cheese?' Adam asked, closing down the conversation.

Rufus provided the afternoon entertainment. Letting me strip him off, without protest, he babbled, kicked his legs with glee and sucked his toes. I was in love.

'He's a little yogi.' Adam viewed him warmly.

Later, Adam donned an apron and, under my nervous gaze, prepared the evening meal. It quickly became clear he knew how to slice and dice, (without cutting his fingers off) and was adept at creating a white wine sauce for the chicken breasts already in the fridge. He whipped up a dressing to pour over steamed green beans and he knocked up a tasty-looking bake with spinach, peppers, sweet potato and ricotta, which I was as sure as I could be, Brooke would pick at. When he offered me a mouthful to taste, I put my fingers to my lips in a chef's kiss.

By the time Ben arrived home, the table was laid, wine opened and dinner bubbled in the oven. I should have felt secure; I was anything but. I swear Ben was more taken aback by the seemingly new accord than he was with my heavily bandaged throbbing fingers, which he examined straightaway.

'It's not pretty,' Adam commented.

'You did well,' Ben said, genuinely amazed.

'Think it needs stitching?' I asked tentatively.

'We might get away with it,' Ben said. 'Must be sore. On a scale of one to ten, how does it feel?'

'Around five,' I said, thinking it felt more like eight.

'How on earth did it happen? You're normally so careful.' Ben's gaze was searching. Did he suspect foul play?

I didn't look at Adam. I looked at Brooke. 'A boning knife was left in the washing-up.'

She met my gaze with a glassy stare.

'An accident,' Adam said, handing Ben a glass of Provence rosé, subject closed.

* * *

The evening should have been a success. Dinner was excellent. Thanks to Ben, my kitchen was left spotless. The trouble

133

started when we were sitting in the living room and the 'boys', as I thought of them, were on the second bottle of wine. With everyone mellow I thought I'd insinuate the subject of the extension.

'If you don't mind my asking,' Adam said, his bare feet parked on our coffee table, 'how much is it costing?'

I told him.

'I could get you a better deal.'

'*You?*' Ben snorted.

Adam's lips thinned. 'I've got friends who had something similar done for a fraction of the price.'

'Where?'

'In London.'

'When?'

'Last year.'

'But you weren't here last year.'

'We flew back for a month,' Brooke cut in.

'Materials have increased substantially since last year,' Ben pointed out, impressively bullish. Must be the wine, I thought.

'Tell you what,' Adam said, scratching at the corner of his mouth. 'Why don't you let me talk to your architectural guy? See if I can drive the price down for you.'

I had a fleeting vision of Adam taking Hugh to task to which Hugh, a big man, would not take kindly. From the corner of my eye, I saw Ben's nostrils flare and his hands clench.

'That's a kind offer,' I jumped in, keen to avert a stand-up row. 'But honestly, we have total faith in our guy.'

Adam shrugged a shoulder. 'If you're sure.'

'Positive,' I said, 'Besides, we've agreed everything now but thank you anyway.'

'Your call,' Adam said, unsmiling.

'It is,' Ben said. 'If you really want to help, you could vacate the room.'

Stunned, I thrilled. Adam flashed surprise. I didn't bother gauging Brooke's reaction.

'With Sophie out of action,' Adam said, 'thought we'd stick around to lend a hand.'

'Not necessary,' Ben said bluntly. 'We have plenty of family support, thanks.'

I held my breath, waiting for a weasel-worded response designed to make us feel like we were the bad guys. It didn't happen.

Taking the opportunity to check on Rufus, I almost skipped upstairs where, outside his room, I pumped the air with my good fist in anticipation of the day they were finally leaving. I couldn't have been prouder of Ben for making a difficult stand.

Exhausted by his afternoon activities, Rufus was out for the count. Tempted to turn in, I wasn't keen for Ben to be left without backup. I didn't want Adam and Brooke bamboozling him with fresh ideas in a cunning bid to either extend their stay or return the second the extension was completed.

Noise and bluster greeted me. Walking back into the living room was like straying into a conflict zone.

'It's bloody well opening Pandora's box,' Adam insisted, red streaking the tops of his high cheekbones.

'What is?' I said, sitting down next to a very unhappy-looking Ben.

'Ask him.' Ben tossed his chin in Adam's direction. 'He's the one who brought up the subject.'

'Assisted dying,' Brooke answered on Adam's behalf.

God, I thought, my heart sinking. As the only person in the room not drinking, I reckoned I had the best chance of steering everyone off a highly emotive subject. 'Bump off your granny,' I said, hoping to strike an amusing note that visibly missed by a mile.

'Because she's a nuisance or a burden,' Brooke said earnestly.

'To whom?' Adam said, still with the ugly expression.

Before we got into moral mazes, I asked mildly, 'I think it's good there's been a proper rational debate and consensus on the subject.'

'What's rational about killing people?' Adam countered.

'Trust you to be dramatic,' Ben said, snatching at his drink.

Before Adam could pile in, which from the rabid expression on his face, he was about to, I said, 'Surely, if someone is in agony and really doesn't want to live anymore, and it's the patient's decision,' I said emphatically, 'there's an argument for putting them out of his or her misery?'

'Play God, you mean.' Adam shot Ben a spiteful look.

'No, I did not mean.' I resented the way Adam was twisting my words.

'It's a practice wide open to abuse,' Adam countered.

I mentally counted to ten before I opened my mouth. 'If I was terminally ill and couldn't hack it anymore, I wouldn't want my only option to be a one-way flight to Switzerland. I'd like to think I could die with dignity in the country I was born in.'

'Dignity?' Adam blustered.

'What about people who don't like life?' Brooke's whispering voice gusted through the room like a winter breeze in summer. Was she talking about herself?

'That's called depression,' I said, admittedly sounding a bit no-nonsense.

'In Holland, you can be euthanised for feeling down,' Brooke said bleakly.

'I don't think that's quite right.' Not terribly sure of my ground, I needed Ben to help me out. Better equipped to talk on the subject, he hunkered further down into the sofa, his chin dropped to his chest. It took me a walloping amount of willpower not to nudge him in the ribs with my elbow. *Don't just sit there frozen and wounded — say something, for God's sake.*

'You doctors are all the same,' Adam said, spying another opportunity to take a verbal swing at his brother. 'Know what your problem is?' Adam didn't wait for a reply. 'You medical people have Messiah complex.'

I wasn't having that. 'That's not fair,' I snapped. 'Every doctor I know is driven by a desire to heal and help people lead healthier lives. What you're suggesting is that they get a kick out of their patients' suffering simply to display how they can control it.'

'I'm suggesting they get a kick out of finishing them off.'

Ben's head snapped up. 'You really want to push it?' His voice was low and dangerous. His hands trembled. I'd never seen him so angry. This wasn't a general debate. This was personal and specific.

When Adam didn't reply, Ben stood up. 'I'm not going to stay and listen to this shit. You're entitled to your point of view, Adam,' Ben railed, staring down at his brother. 'But don't think you can come into my home and attack me because you're pissed off with the way your miserable life turned out.'

Then he strode across the floor and slammed the living room door on his way out.

I glanced across at Adam. I thought he'd either be furious or deeply hurt. He sat, rock-still, massively satisfied, like a murderer knocking his victim down in his car then smiling while he ran him over.

CHAPTER THIRTY-ONE

'Come here,' I said, opening my arms.

I'd found Ben standing silent and hurt, gazing out of our bedroom window into a night sprayed with stars.

He rested his chin on the top of my head and slipped his arms around me. 'They have to be gone soon,' I murmured into his neck.

He grunted a muffled reply.

'Why is Adam so vicious?'

Ben drew back. 'It's the booze talking.'

'It didn't help,' I conceded, 'but what's going on?'

'Nothing is *going on*.'

I shook my head. 'He's definitely got it in for you.' Had done from the moment he'd walked through the door. 'It's not normal, Ben.'

'There's screwed-up and screw-loose. Adam is the latter.'

I never remembered Ben putting it that way, and we'd still got tomorrow night to get through. My spirits hadn't sunk; they were flat out, comatose on the floor. And to be honest, I was afraid.

'How's the hand?' Ben cupped his palm gently underneath. 'Throbs.'

'Hmm. I'm still not clear how it happened.'

I held his enquiring gaze. 'You want my honest opinion?'

'Honest opinions always worry me. Nine times out of ten they're not what you want to hear, but go on, surprise me.' Ben's smile was tepid.

'Brooke.'

Ben looked peculiarly relieved. Had he got his brother down for number one suspect? Then I had another more unpleasant thought: what if Adam was pulling her strings?

'I worry about that girl,' Ben said.

'Not surprised after all that stuff about euthanasia for people having a bad day.'

'She didn't quite put it like that.'

Sometimes Ben's desire to be unscrupulously fair irked me. 'Near enough,' I countered. 'Do they really do that in Holland?'

'People with intractable mental health conditions can seek assistance for ending their lives.'

'Not sure I can get my head around that.' I hoped Brooke wasn't getting any funny ideas.

'It's not as simple as it's made out,' Ben assured me. 'There are checks and balances.'

'Which favour the patient?'

He agreed.

'What do you think?'

'Me?' Ben stiffened.

'From a personal viewpoint.'

'I think it's sad.'

'But do you think it just? What about palliative care?'

'Doesn't always work,' Ben said bleakly. 'Despite the tools we have at our disposal and the best care, some people die slow, horrible deaths in shrieking pain.'

The lost expression was back in his eye. He was thinking of his father, I realised, and so was Adam. Was this the reason for the enmity between them? I thought of Ben away at university, out the picture, having a good time, leaving his mother, and possibly his older brother, to carry the load. For this was what he had told me. Then I recalled Ben saying that Adam hadn't been able to hack it and had kept his distance.

'Whatever anyone says, when a doctor ends a life, legally or illegally,' Ben continued, 'it's an admission of failure, as if the medical profession has run out of road. The stupid irony is that it's a game we all ultimately lose in the end, Sophie. There are no winners.'

CHAPTER THIRTY-TWO

In shorts, a sweatshirt and trainers, Ben went out for a run the following morning. He never goes for a run. In response to my baffled expression, he waffled on about getting rid of toxins from his bloodstream.

Nobody stirred on the other side of the house, and I spent the morning seriously toying with cancelling dinner. My parents wouldn't understand but they'd respect a decision if they thought Ben had made it. There were three problems with this: I hadn't had a chance to run it past Ben and, if we bailed, we were lumbered with Adam and Brooke for another night of not-so-happy families. I didn't think I could take any more aggro. Thirdly, Ben, bless him, was a lousy cook and I still couldn't fully function with my right hand out of action.

I cared for Rufus, played with him and decided, like all new mothers, that I had a genius child. Ben returned hot and sweaty and while he showered and Rufus slept, I locked the door to our bedroom, stripped off and lay invitingly on the bed. When Ben smiled and we made love it was as if all our problems melted away.

'Ben,' I said, running the fingers of my good hand lightly across his chest.

'Uh-huh?'

'I can't do this evening, not after what happened last night.'
Ben angled himself up on one elbow. 'But your parents...'

'I know, but they'd understand if you spoke to them.'

I'd love to say that Ben looked convinced. He didn't.
'And Adam and Brooke?'

'Give them their marching orders. I don't care. I refuse
not to feel safe in my own home.' I'd given this some thought.
Rather than making Adam my target, Brooke was an easier
and more logical candidate. 'That blade was left deliberately.'

'You can't prove that,' Ben said.

I raised my damaged hand. 'Isn't this proof enough?' Not
quite answering his question it had the right dramatic effect
and, God help me, I felt dramatic about it. 'What if she steps
it up?'

'By doing what?' Agitated, Ben slid out of bed and reached
for his boxers.

'I don't know. Powdered glass? An accidental push down
the stairs.'

'You're starting to sound like your sister,' Ben said, trying
to make light of it.

'I'm serious, Ben. I can't take much more.' I am not one
of life's natural worriers. The worst that could happen to me
had already happened. But Adam and Brooke were threatening the foundations on which our little family stood. We'd
done our bit. It was time for them to move on. The thought
of them staying without a departure date did me in.

Ben ran his fingers through his hair and scrubbed at his
face. I never had him down for a man who lacked courage. It
frightened me that Adam and his sidekick appeared to wield
that level of power.

'Okay,' Ben said, shrinking under my hurt gaze. 'As soon
as they're up and about, I'll give them the memo.'

I hissed with heartfelt relief. 'Thank you.'

'And your parents?'

'*We* can still go for dinner,' I said with a relieved smile.

Later, we ate a light lunch and read the newspapers. With still no sign of Adam and Brooke, I suggested he went and checked on them.

Ben raised his head above the parapet of a Saturday supplement. 'Is that a good idea?'

'While we've been sitting here, they might have cleared out.'

'Wishful thinking and we'd have heard a taxi.'

'Possibly not.' I raised an eyebrow and pointed with my good hand towards the ceiling and our bedroom above.

'Ah — yes, I see.' Ben smiled at remembered intimacy.

'Reckon they could have gone?' The thought of liberation had a weird, dizzying effect as potent as any sugar rush.

'Maybe.' Ben went back to his newspaper. I got up and loaded the dishwasher — again.

Mildly frustrated, I tried a different approach. 'Thought I'd take Rufus for his afternoon spin around the block.'

'Grand idea,' Ben said, without looking up.

'So would you check on them?'

The newspaper was swept aside. The coffee cup went down with a rattle.

'Please, Ben. It's what we agreed.'

He issued a similar sigh to the one I'd witnessed with my dad when my mother was expressing an opinion with which he was forced to concur.

Ben lumbered to his feet. Honestly, you'd think he was about to undergo a root canal without anaesthetic.

'Thanks,' I said, tipping up on my toes and dropping a dry kiss on his cheek. 'If you get any smart remarks, remember how you stood up to him last night.' That was my final advice and, before Ben bottled, I put Rufus flat on his back in his stroller, grabbed a warm jacket and keys and tore out of the house.

CHAPTER THIRTY-THREE

There is nothing worse than socialising with friends or family after a steaming row. But this was what we did.

'What do you mean they're not fucking ready?' I'd probably only ever sworn in front of Ben once or twice, the last time when I was in labour and in extremis. This was as *extremis* as it got.

'Adam needs a few extra days.'

'Are we talking until Wednesday, or what?'

'I don't know.'

I could have left it at that. I should have. Disappointed and angry, I didn't. 'When the hell are you going to grow a backbone?'

'Sophie,' Ben exclaimed, as if I'd plunged his bare feet into scalding water. 'That's not fair.'

What wasn't fair was heading off to my parents with people I wanted gone. It was intolerable. I took a breath. Actually, I took several. '*Will* they be leaving next week?'

'I'd say so.'

Not indubitably *yes*. In the absence of a more forthright response, I fired a fresh salvo. 'And what did Adam have to say about last night's performance?'

'He's very sorry.'

'He apologised to you?'

'He did, yes.'

I didn't believe that either.

We drove to my parents in stony silence after Adam, all dressed up in the suit he'd worn to Cake That, attempted to explain his rotten behaviour. I cut him off at the pass with a dismissive 'not interested'.

Mum picked up the bad feeling the second we stepped over the threshold. Looking from Ben to me, she said, 'You two, okay?'

'Perfect,' we snapped in unison.

Mum gaped at my bandaged hand. 'What on earth did you do?'

'Slipped with a knife,' I said.

'Goodness, that's not like you.'

Because I wasn't like me; not anymore.

With Rufus spark out, I seized the opportunity to take him upstairs to my old bedroom. Resisting the urge to curl up on the bed and sleep the night away, I put on the baby monitor and returned downstairs.

Full of bonhomie and totally oblivious to the spiky atmospherics, Dad made Brooke and Adam welcome and pushed drinks into their greedy hands. Brooke stayed closer to Adam than a Just Stop Oil protester glued to a motorway. Probably wise as Saskia had abandoned the demure look she'd adopted at work and gone all out in a low-neck sleeveless jumpsuit, cinched in at the waist in navy polka dot print. All I saw were firm boobs, toned arms and narrow waist; the polar opposite to what childbirth had done to my body.

Fresh from his stint in the studio, Dad was buzzing. Adam homed in and they were soon chatting about Dad's pride and joy, his 1973 mimosa yellow Triumph Stag. I watched only slightly less astonished than Ben as Adam talked knowledgeably about 'inherent overheating problems leading to a blown head gasket' and the 'mechanical upgrades and modifications required to rectify the problem'.

'It has the best sounding V8 on the planet,' Dad enthused, in his element.

'Beats the hell out of all those electric vehicles,' Adam said. 'They might look the business — they sound anything but.'

Gas guzzler, I thought. If Adam's remark was designed to take a sly dig at his brother, Ben didn't show it.

All around me micro conversations were taking place.

'Saskia, did you take the puddings out of the freezer?'

'That's a jolly nice part of the world,' Dad to Brooke.

'Nice threads,' Saskia to Adam.

It wasn't long before my predatory sister sidled up to Brooke, ostensibly to ask her about New York, in reality on a fishing trip designed to wipe out the opposition.

I wandered back upstairs, away from the noise and clatter, half hoping Rufus would wake and, when he didn't, took my time to re-enter the family fray. With no sign of Ben or Mum, I beat it to the kitchen where I found them deep in conversation. They sprang apart shiftily, as if I'd caught them having a quiet fag. I assumed Ben was confiding in Mum about our spat.

'Do you need help dishing up?' Ben asked, breezily.

'That would be wonderful,' Mum said overenthusiastically. 'Could I leave you to rally the troops, Sophie, and get them seated?'

Saskia wasn't the only one who'd gone all out for the evening. For a start we weren't eating in the kitchen diner but the little used dining room, reserved for high days, Christmas, Easter and wakes. From a glance at the seating arrangement, I suspected Saskia had taken a firm hand in it. Adam was opposite her and Brooke posted to the farthest end of the table, next to Dad.

Mum had prepared individual Parmesan and wild garlic tarts, followed by bouillabaisse packed with monkfish, bream, cod, gurnard and shellfish. A proper party dish with crusty bread and with the additional option of a fiery version of rouille, it was designed for people to muck in, get messy and be brought together. Knowing my mother, I thought it deliberate. A help yourself dinner, it gave Brooke the perfect cover for eating little while apparently joining in with the rest of us.

As the wine flowed, we got onto the subject of Dad's TV stint. Smiling from ear to ear, he found a ready audience.

'All hell broke loose when one of the runners chipped the edge off a very nice nineteenth-century Chinese vase.'

'How did that happen?' I asked, incredulous.

'A collision with one of the cameras.'

'Short-lived career in TV then,' Adam said, winking at Saskia who smiled seductively. 'Have you got an agent, Anthony?'

'No,' Dad said, as if the idea had never occurred to him. 'I suppose if this takes off, I should consider it.'

'Most definitely,' Adam said. 'I could maybe put you in touch with someone.'

'That would be marvellous,' Dad said. I didn't dare look at Ben who was taking an avid interest in a piece of squid.

Dad yattered on, Mum, barely touching her meal, watched, entranced. With one ear tuned to the baby monitor, I made every effort to loosen up. Not so Ben. He sat silent and brooding and wary.

When we'd finished, I told Mum to stay put while I cleared away.

'I'll help,' Ben said, springing to his feet.

'Anyone fancy a ciggie break?' Saskia announced. *Anyone* being Adam, I thought.

'Do you have to?' Mum said, pained.

'Filthy habit, Sash,' Dad concurred.

Casting an apologetic look in my parents' direction, Adam slipped an e-cigarette from his jacket pocket and, ignoring Brooke's watchful gaze, followed Saskia out into the garden.

'God,' Ben exclaimed when we were alone in the kitchen. I didn't deliver a low 'told you so' blow. Anyone could see that Adam was knocking it out of the park to upstage Ben and ingratiate himself with my parents.

'Were you talking about our quarrel to Mum?'

Ben frowned. 'When?'

'In the kitchen.'

'Oh, *that*,' he said. 'You don't mind, do you?'

I shrugged. 'Not especially.'

'Am I forgiven?' His shy smile was one I could never resist.

'Mostly.' I hated it when we fell out.

Dumping the plates on the side, he wrapped his arms around me.

'Think Saskia's safe?' Ben whispered in my ear.

'It's Adam you should be worried about. There are grown men in Cheltenham with emotional scars inches deep. If anyone can knock your brother into touch, she can.'

'Bring it on,' Ben said.

Not very fair on Brooke, I thought, before thinking she bloody deserved it.

Back in the dining room, Adam and Saskia had returned and Adam was talking to my dad about music.

'But that's marvellous,' Dad said, pink-faced, courtesy of claret. 'You must play for us.'

Ben exchanged glances with me. I knew what he was thinking: let's see how good golden boy is. Catching my eye, Adam broke off, casting me a slow, knowing look that made me instantly uneasy.

After desserts — a selection of Cake That patisserie — we decamped to the living room upstairs. Fortunately, it was on the other side of the house to my bedroom, so Rufus would be undisturbed by the noise from the piano.

With a tremendous flourish, Dad launched into a rendition of 'Autumn Leaves', followed by a medley of film music by 'the two Johns', as Dad put it: John Williams and John Barry.

'He's good,' Adam said to nobody in particular. Dad was okay and not bad in his more sober moments. Under the influence, he got carried away and bum notes appeared thick and fast.

'I haven't got my glasses,' Dad complained when he whacked a stridently wrong note, a standard Dad excuse to which we all took the piss. 'Come on, Adam,' Dad said, untroubled. 'Let's see what you got.'

The room fell quiet. Adam removed his jacket. He sat down. If he'd had shirtsleeves he would have adjusted the cuffs. He placed his slender right hand over the keys then, one-fingered, played 'The Grand Old Duke of York'. Loudly. Painstakingly. Excruciatingly. Bewildered, Dad's jaw was on the floor; Mum's blush of awkwardness only superseded by Saskia's. (I bet she was rapidly rethinking her charm offensive.) Ben's expression was one of pure triumph with no room for sympathy or magnanimity. I couldn't blame him. Me? I was shocked and embarrassed but then my gaze shifted to Brooke. Unnervingly still, hands folded lightly in her lap, her green eyes fixed on Adam's muscular back, her thin top lip tilted in a sly smile. That's when I knew this was theatre. This was showmanship. This was deception and diversion, a game at which she and Adam were expert.

Suddenly raising his left hand and bringing it down with a resounding crash, he burst into a boogie-woogie stomp, fingers pounding the keys, tripping up and down the keyboard before segueing straight into 'Bad Case of Loving You (Doctor, Doctor)', 'Cry Me A River', and a host of songs that I recognised but couldn't name. I only identified 'Three O'Clock Blues' because it was one of Dad's favourites and then, just when I thought Adam would wrap it up, he finished with a sublime piano arrangement of 'Make You Feel My Love'. My heart hitched in my chest. My breath caught in my throat. I swear to God Adam's lingering expression over the keys was aimed at me. How could he know that it was the song Leo and I had chosen for the first dance at our wedding?

'Bloody hell,' Saskia exclaimed, eyes alight, Mum and Dad equally effusive. I turned to look at Ben who stood as if the ground from beneath his feet was comprehensively swept away and he'd fallen into the deep dark hole carved out beneath.

I found myself tumbling into the darkness alongside him.

CHAPTER THIRTY-FOUR

I fed Rufus after which Ben drove us home shortly before one in the morning. Dad begged Adam for an encore even as we were reaching for our coats. Thankfully, Mum came to the rescue.

'Leave these good people to get to their beds, Anthony.'

'You must come again,' Dad said, giving Adam a proper man hug. '*Soon.*'

'Will you be all right, Sophie?'

I assured Mum I'd be fine, and she asked me to drop a text to let her know we'd arrived safely home.

On the way back, Adam was full of praise for my parents. 'They're great,' he said. 'Not at all what I expected.'

I didn't ask in what way they defied his expectations, or why he had any preconceptions; I was too spun out. Ben stared straight ahead, back rigid, concentrating on the road. Brooke fell asleep, her head on Adam's shoulder. I looked out of the passenger window into a thick and starless night.

Arriving at the cottage, it no longer felt like home or sanctuary. It felt like a trap.

Having slept like the dead at Mum's, Rufus was wide awake and not at all happy. Chucking his head, his little body went rigid when I tried to soothe him.

Later, after finally getting him off to sleep, I crawled into bed beside Ben and was astonished to find him lying with his hands behind his head, staring straight up at the bedroom ceiling.

'This is what he does,' Ben said grimly. 'Pretending to be this great guy, he inserts himself like a maggot and doesn't let go until he's wreaked total and utter destruction.'

It was after four in the morning. I really couldn't do this now. 'You can't argue the guy can play,' I said mildly.

Ben gave a snort of derision and turned over.

I had no trouble falling asleep. Two hours later, Rufus had me up again. We weren't the only ones feeling the heat.

* * *

Sunday morning assumed a natural rhythm. Ben took over with Rufus, allowing me a couple of hours of extra sleep, after which he changed the dressing on my hand. Bleary-eyed, I gave him instructions on how to cook breakfast. We had newspapers delivered at the weekend and Ben powered his way through while I tried to get my head around dinner for the evening. Not easy, when you're so tired you can barely string a sentence together. Around noon, Adam emerged briefly, pale and hungover, to collect two mugs of coffee, which he took back wordlessly to the guest quarters. In the afternoon, Ben and I, with Rufus in his baby sling, set out for a muddy walk through nearby farmland. Only when we were well underway and approaching a band of woodland did I raise the thorny issue of 'the problem'. I'd been thinking it over and decided to take Saskia's advice.

'I was thinking that we've made things too comfy for Adam and Brooke,' I said. 'They have free bed and board, booze on tap. I drive them all over the place. If I down tools, so to speak, they'll soon get bored and push off. Plus,' I said, glancing across at Ben to see how he was reacting (not strongly, I had to admit), 'they already know there's a deadline in place due to work starting on the extension.'

'Worth a try, I suppose.'

'Could you be a little more encouraging?'

'How about we pay him off?'

I stopped walking so fast I almost hit a tree. 'With what?' I asked in astonishment. 'You know money's tight right now with the flat failing to sell. And why the hell should we?' I didn't remind Ben that, after the initial down payment, we'd soon have to shell out the next instalment for the garden room.

Ben shrugged. 'Only an idea.'

I was damned if we were going to bail his brother out, let alone the woman he was with. Was this Adam's motive for checking in with his brother after all this time? Had Adam run out of cash and decided to shake Ben down for money? I fumed at the idea.

'Has he approached you?' I asked, accusing.

'Not yet.'

'You think he will?'

'Think about it,' Ben said, matter of fact. 'He's been bumming around for over a decade. Mum and Dad's money was never going to last.'

'But that's hundreds of thousands of pounds he's gone through.'

'Easy to do if you're not working and leading a champagne lifestyle on the equivalent of beer money.'

I recalled how Adam's face had lit up on our first meeting when recounting his travels through Europe and beyond, all the music hotspots he'd visited.

'He has actually been working, Ben.'

'If you say so.'

'Brooke says so.'

'You don't believe a word she says.'

True, but I had no reason to disbelieve her claim regarding Adam's side hustle. And I no longer had a reason to keep my mouth shut. I told Ben.

'Should do well in this part of the world. Plenty of wealthy old ladies.'

'Ben, that's an awful thing to say,' I said, shocked.

'Because my brother *is* awful.'

That did it. The next day, I decided to put my 'siege and starve them out' strategy into action. Sunday dinner was going to be Adam and Brooke's last supper.

CHAPTER THIRTY-FIVE

The following morning, I reminded Ben of my plan and started out as I meant to go on.

We had two bottles of wine left over and I hid them in the garden shed. With the specific intention of letting all but basic supplies run down, I didn't do my normal big weekly shop to stock up. The first day I took off with Rufus and visited Bath, the second we travelled to Marlborough where I treated myself to lunch in a gorgeous French restaurant that I wished would set up in Cirencester. On both evenings I offered beans on toast, tinned soups — it was still cold enough — and cheap supermarket pizzas. Using my bandaged hand as an excuse for the culinary go-slow, I ignored the fact I'd been able to drive and dared anyone to challenge me, which they didn't. Left to fester in solitary confinement at home, Adam and Brooke clearly didn't believe me and I didn't care. I had factored in that they wouldn't starve due to our local pub around the corner. Eating and drinking would be at their expense, however, and not ours. On Wednesday night, I bid them a cheery 'have a nice evening' as I whisked me and Ben and baby off to an Italian restaurant in town where tiny people were welcomed.

'Think it's working?' Ben asked soulfully.

'Definitely,' I said, tucking into linguine con gamberi. 'The clock is ticking.'

'Thank God, not sure I can face the sight of another bowl of Heinz.'

I was wrong. Merrily, stepping back over the threshold, we were enveloped in the pungent whiff of Chicken Biryani and Dhal. The worktops were littered with empty cartons. Dirty plates sat in the sink — no water, no blades, small mercies — and something unspeakable, possibly prawn Balti, dripped down a cupboard and pooled in a sticky mess on the floor. I could barely speak I was so cross. It was like coming home to find squatters had moved in.

'We ordered takeaways,' Brooke said, as if we needed it spelling out.

'Go upstairs, Sophs,' Ben said meekly. 'I'll clear up.'

Inside, I was a hot mess. Outside, I was cold. I detest violence in any form, but I had a chilling insight into myself: I could happily have taken a swing at Brooke standing in front of me or Adam had he chanced to lope through. 'Have a word with your bloody brother,' I muttered under my breath before fleeing upstairs, tears of frustration and anger in my eyes.

I tried and failed to settle Rufus. He cried big fat tears, kicked with his little feet and balled his tiny hands into fists. In the end, I took him into our bed. Once he'd fallen asleep, I'd put him back in his crib. Ben joined me an hour later.

'Well?' I said, Rufus on my shoulder, me patting his back.

'On Sunday they'll be gone.'

'It isn't a wind-up?'

He shook his head, stripped off and climbed into bed. I should have been overjoyed. I felt nothing. 'What did you promise them?'

Ben's face flushed. 'Nothing.'

I breathed out in relief. 'Where are they going?'

'I didn't ask. All I know is that they've made plans.'

I'd believe it when I saw it and took Rufus back to his room.

The next morning, I didn't have the energy to leave the house. A deep part of me worried what would happen if I did. I flung open windows to get rid of the lingering aroma of Southern Indian cooking and scrubbed the kitchen to remove all remnants of the night before, although, I had to admit, Ben had done a forensic job.

Adam loped in at his usual hour — shortly before noon.

'Hey,' he said.

'Hey, yourself,' I said, unsmiling.

'Yeah . . . uh . . . sorry about the mess.' He scratched his armpit, sat down and, producing a pouch of tobacco and Rizlas, started to pack and roll the tobacco with his thumb and forefinger. Designed to provoke, I was provoked.

'I don't want you smoking in here.'

'Not a prob.' His tongue flicked out, licking along the edge of the paper, watching me watching him as he sealed it. Eyes never leaving mine, he said conversationally, 'Saskia was kind enough to do a mercy run for supplies while you were out earlier in the week.'

Saskia, I baulked. My sister often called me a couple of times a day to keep me up to speed on what was happening with the business. Since Adam's arrival, she'd fallen curiously silent.

'What are you really doing here?' I said, point-blank.

Adam narrowed his eyes and smiled. He spoke as if talking to a particularly slow-witted pensioner. '*Sophie, Sophie*, you *know* why I'm here. To see my brother.'

I shook my head. 'It's way more than that. You're on a mission. I haven't worked it out yet but, trust me, I will.' *You barefaced liar.*

'Were you always this paranoid, or is it only since you dumped your fiancé?'

Blindsided, I attempted to splutter an answer; words eluded me.

Adam had this curious way of filling up a room, as if his shape and height and personality could inhabit the entire space and squash everyone and everything in it.

'Saskia told me,' he said, dull-eyed.

'There's nothing to tell.'

'Leo Carpenter, wasn't that his name?' Adam fixed me with a greasy smile and twirled the cigarette between his long fingers.

I didn't answer; too busy trying to control the tight sensation spreading from my throat to my chest.

'A copper, that right?'

'He was,' I stammered. 'So what?'

'A DC. With the Met.'

'Your point?'

'You like men who can provide, don't you, Sophie? Men with professions. Steady stable types with pensions and sparkling careers, not old reprobates like me.' Adam spoke evenly, as if he were reading a factual article about how to make bread, no inflexion, no judgement. 'How odd for you to bail three days before the wedding of the year. All that expense for your folks. All that loss of face for your man. All those awkward questions for you. Quite the mystery.'

Red warning lights banged on inside my head. Stupidly, Saskia had aided and abetted Adam Hall in tilting the lid on a box I thought I'd buried deep enough. Sliding his grubby fingers underneath, Adam had reached in, rummaged through the contents of my past and put them all back in the wrong place. I sensed that what he didn't know he would find out or make up and I was powerless to stop him.

'You stay away from us,' I said, my voice shaking.

Slowly, oh so slowly, Adam slipped a box of matches from his pocket, stood up, and headed for the garden. 'Don't worry, we'll be out of your hair soon enough.'

I stared after him, fear rippling in the back of my throat. Adam hadn't come for Ben. He'd come for me.

CHAPTER THIRTY-SIX

Adam couldn't know.

Could he?

The problem with secrets is that they scream to be let out until inevitably they escape. I could not let that happen. Not now. Not ever.

I fled upstairs and locked myself in the bedroom with Rufus. In spite of the physical barrier, my mind dragged me back to the miserable conversation with my bewildered parents in the wake of my decision to call off my wedding. Once they'd realised it wasn't a mild case of nerves before the big day, they'd set about contacting guests, cancelling the vicar, the church, the cars, the venue, the flowers, the catering, the band. How strange that it was a wedding that had brought me and Leo together originally. My cousin Milo, the only son of my eccentric Auntie Fen, Dad's sister, was getting hitched to a police officer. Leo was a mate of the bride. One of those fortunate people that instantly command the attention of a room, DC Leo Carpenter was surrounded by friends and, as I found out later, colleagues. I'm quite sure he would have passed me by if it hadn't been for Saskia wading into their group and pulling me along with her. Effortlessly entering the conversation, Saskia held court and, at first, I thought the man with the blond hair, brilliant smile and sparkling eyes was interested in my sister — men generally were — until his clean-cut gaze alighted on me. I loved the fact that the funny guy with the sharp features and smart patter found *Sensible Sophie* attractive. Later that evening, when guests were drunk on happiness and joy (me included), he singled me out, then asked me out. Nobody was more surprised and delighted than me. And as Adam had astutely observed, I was into guys with careers, prospects and who, deeply appealing, served the community. That first date in a restaurant in Fulham, Leo talked and I was an attentive listener. He told me about growing up as an only child to parents who were teachers in respectable Hitchin, graduating in criminology at Middlesex University and going straight into the Met where he'd found his feet and acquired a new band of brothers to make up for the siblings he never had. When I'd questioned him about sisters, he'd laughed, and I paid it less attention than I should.

With Leo, there was an extra dimension. Sexually insatiable, he found me thrillingly desirable. I barely got out of bed with him for what felt like weeks in those early mad and heady days. Our relationship was based on obsession and passion, and for a long time it worked, until spectacularly it didn't.

If I'd been less in lust, I might have spotted the signs: the sideswipes that were *only jokes*, the non sequiturs I wanted to follow up but didn't dare because of the crushing put-downs, the subtle taunts and chipping away. I was indestructible, or so I thought. Looking back, it was amazing how quickly my personality changed. Me: clever, positive and assertive Sophie who believed in fairness and justice and equality. It's amazing how principles can slip when the core of who you are is eroded. Guiltily, I remembered how I'd recently attacked Ben for being less than principled. A case of pot, kettle and black, I thought dismally.

Expressing horror at a deeply unpleasant remark made at work about a female police officer and later repeated by Leo, I was informed that I didn't 'understand', that I should 'lighten up', that it was merely 'lads being lads' and 'locker-room talk, having a laugh, Sophie'.

'She didn't hear,' Leo protested when, stumbling across a remnant of the old me, I took him to task.

'That's not the point.'

'Doesn't mean anything,' Leo argued. 'Just our way of letting off steam.'

'It's pure misogyny,' I complained.

'Christ, not that again.'

Yes, that again.

'It's words. Nobody gets hurt. It's how we get by doing a tough job.'

'I understand the nature of your work but . . .'

'While I'm out chasing down hard-bastard criminals, you sit in your swanky office, drinking espressos and pushing money around for the rich.'

Shame on me, I bought it, not because Leo made a fair point, but because, ground down, as much a victim as a bystander, that's what I chose to believe. Easier to think that, in my carefully constructed, no-risk world, with our nice flat, and our nice car, and our nice possessions and pensions, all I had to do was smile and sign up to the 'front it out, believe you're happy and you will be' philosophy. And, for the greater part, Leo was genuinely fun and kind, generous and considerate and I was so grateful and relieved when he was. (I make no excuses, only offering an explanation.) The truth was I should have acted sooner to flag what I knew to be abuses of power, in which women were either 'hysterical, had it coming to them' or 'bossy'. Whether shouting sooner, louder and longer would have made a difference, I would never know.

And that was the tragedy of it.

CHAPTER THIRTY-SEVEN

You would think that after our bruising encounter, Adam would have made himself scarce. Not a bit of it. He spoke pleasantly, without awkwardness, cooed over Rufus and, when I was less than my sunny self, asked politely if he could put on the TV.

'Knock yourself out,' I said.

And he did, settling into Ben's big leather chair as if in for the long haul. Brooke appeared in PJs, although it was well into the afternoon. Parking her bottom on the chair arm, she snuggled up next to Adam in a rare display of affection. With a few days to go until they were allegedly leaving, it didn't look promising.

I retreated to the kitchen — where else? Like a mother of badly behaved teenagers, from time to time I surreptitiously popped my head around the door to check that nobody was smoking, eating or having sex on the sofa.

Ben arrived home. Things already strained between us, we automatically restricted conversation to 'how was your day' platitudes, and Rufus.

After depressingly going back on my word and cooking for what felt like multitudes, I had a feeling of impending disaster. Over an edgy supper of sideways glances and conspiratorial expressions, Adam finally announced their news; it was a slammer.

'We genuinely want to thank you for everything you've done for us, particularly you, Sophie,' Adam said, wrapping me in one of his signature soft-eyed gazes, 'but now we need to move on and we're leaving first thing tomorrow.'

Two whole days early, good grief; let's party! Taken completely by surprise, my little heart soared and roared. Ben could not have looked more shocked if I'd announced I was pregnant again. His expression said 'thank fuck'.

Busy processing the fantastic and long-awaited news (had it only been weeks?), neither of us enquired about their destination.

I was happily putting the last forkful of fish pie into my mouth when Brooke turned to me, bright-eyed. 'Your parents are so sweet, Sophie.'

'They are,' I agreed, perplexed by what seemed a random remark.

'So generous of them to put us up until we get ourselves sorted.'

I almost choked. Coughing and spluttering, I drew a worried glance from Ben who looked ready to pounce and perform the Heimlich manoeuvre. I waved him away and reached for a glass of water.

'Great, isn't it?' A big smile broke over Adam's face, like sun coming up after a rainy night.

Panicked, I plonked Rufus on Ben. 'Won't be a second,' I rasped, heading upstairs.

What I needed was them properly gone, preferably to the farthest end of the universe. Searching for my phone, I found I'd left it in Rufus's room. Sweeping it up, I was horrified to see three missed calls from Mum. She must have phoned while I was preparing dinner.

On speed dial, the line between us connected immediately.

'Sophie,' she said, sounding peeved and relieved in equal measure.

'Sorry I missed your calls but what's this about Adam and Brooke staying with you and Dad?'

'It seemed like the simplest solution.'

'For whom?' I railed. 'Where are they going to sleep?'

'I thought your old room.'

'*My* room?'

'You've barely slept in it for over a decade,' Mum pointed out. 'Where's the problem?'

Where to start? 'Did Saskia put you up to this?' I pictured her wheedling around Mum.

'It was Adam's idea.'

To prevent myself from uttering a full-throated expletive, I screwed my eyes up tight until I saw stars. 'And you're happy with it?'

'With Dad away all week it will be nice to have some company.'

'You've got Sash.'

'Who's at work all day.'

'You do other stuff in the day. What about your Pilates, meeting friends, the film club?'

'I've scaled back.'

'Then scale up.'

'Sophie, I don't have the energy to argue.'

Panic assailed me. 'You're not ill, are you?'

'Don't be daft.'

'You would say if Rufus was too much for you, wouldn't you?'

'Rufus is not a problem at all.'

'But what about all the extra work?'

'What extra work?'

'Washing, cleaning, shopping, cooking.'

'Oh *that*,' Mum trilled. 'Adam said he and Brooke will pitch in. I'm quite looking forward to the help, if I'm honest.'

A vile image of the kind of help Adam offered older women materialised in my overworked brain. 'Mum, I know you mean well but . . .'

'We had such a *lovely* time on Saturday, and it will free you up to spend more time with Ben and Rufus in those last precious weeks before you come off maternity leave.'

'Mum, I really don't think you've thought it through. You have no idea what you're taking on. What about all Dad's precious artefacts and antiques?'

'What about them?'

They're valuable, I wanted to scream. 'They might get damaged or broken.' Or stolen.

'Darling, we haven't had a breakage for years.'

'Adam isn't the nice easy-going guy you think he is.' *He's toxic*, I wanted to yell.

'I do wish you wouldn't judge, Sophie,' Mum said, suddenly sharp. 'It's not an attractive quality.'

Suitably rebuffed, I fell silent. Why was it everyone fell for Adam's easy-on-the-eye looks and oh-so-magnetic personality? Couldn't they see beyond the gloss to the hard-nosed, sponging creep beneath?

'Hello,' Mum said. 'Are you still there?'

'I am,' I replied, 'But you're not hearing me.'

'Sophie, darling,' Mum said, softening her tone. 'I've been on the planet long enough to know what's what when it comes to people.'

I shut my eyes and counted to ten.

'You're cross, I can tell.'

I wasn't cross. I was out of the park desperate. 'Can I ask you something?'

'Of course, sweetheart.'

'When was all this cobbled together?'

Mum hesitated. I pictured her tapping the side of her head. 'Erm . . . we discussed it a few days ago, *I think*, on the phone.' The bloody phone I'd copped in their bedroom. 'Nothing was agreed until this morning,' Mum continued, as if this were a mitigating factor. 'Adam said he'd let you know once Ben was home from the surgery. I assume he did.'

Oh, he did that all right. Couldn't wait to rub our noses in it.

CHAPTER THIRTY-EIGHT

A cab came to collect Adam and Brooke the following morning.

'Catch you guys, later,' Adam threatened cheerily, lugging several bags over the threshold and onto the drive.

'See you around,' Brooke called over her shoulder, similarly weighed down with luggage.

With mixed emotions I watched them leave. Ben had already left for work. The night before, he'd tried to make out that we were now off the hook. I didn't think he believed it any more than I did.

'I'm scared stiff my parents don't know what they're letting themselves in for,' I told him. Trusting people, they were easy prey to someone as unscrupulous as Ben's brother.

'Come on, they're grown-ups, Sophie.'

'*We're* grown-ups but it didn't stop your brother and his girlfriend turning our lives upside down.'

'Frankly, Faith and Anthony are pretty cool, but they aren't Adam's scene at all. He'll soon get bored, you'll see.'

I thought *Adam's scene* was anyone he could ruthlessly rinse for bed and board.

I'd barely gone back inside the house when my mobile rang. Seeing it was Saskia's number, I answered. Like it or not, she worked for me and, at least, she had the balls to phone and not resort to messages.

'Yes,' I said.

'It wasn't me.'

'What wasn't?' I knew full well what she was on about.

'It was Adam's idea to stay here, not mine. I tried to talk Mum out of it.'

'Thought you fancied him.'

'I do, or I did.'

'What made you change your mind?'

She took her time answering. When she spoke, it wasn't especially illuminating. 'A feeling.'

'And did you have this *feeling* when you told him about Leo?' Yep, I was being snarky.

'Sophie, I'm sorry. It fell out, sort of. I know it's a sore subject.'

'Then why the hell mention it?' *Why load him with a weapon to use against me?* 'Did this transpire when you were having your cosy fag break the other night, or when you dashed over with supplies?'

'Please, Sophie, I made a mistake, right?'

'Damn right.'

'He asked a ton of questions. I thought he was genuinely interested in us as a family.'

Been there, I thought, starting to feel a tad sorry for my little sister. 'And now what do you think?'

'He's a parasite.'

'At last, she sees the light.'

'Don't be like that.'

'Can you convey *that* to Mum? And what about Dad?' *No, don't tell me, our ebullient party-loving father was all in favour.*

'I tried.'

'Try harder.'

'If they won't listen to you, they won't listen to me.'

I made a mental note to tackle Dad — if I could get hold of him.

Had my father noticed Mum's constant exhaustion? I guessed it could be age-related. Older than my father by a couple of years, she was nearer to seventy than sixty, yet I'd never seen her like this before. Ben had told me I was worrying unduly, and he would know, but he wasn't her GP. What if she had an underlying condition? I said as much to Saskia.

'Now you mention it, I've noticed she's off her food and dropped a few pounds.'

'Has she made any doctor's appointments?'

'Not that I know of.'

'Can you find out?'

'I guess.' Saskia didn't sound confident.

'You're on the spot. It's down to you to watch everyone's back.'

'Thanks very much.'

'I'm serious, Sash. Adam and his little sidekick are bad news.'

'Any other pearls of wisdom?'

'Make sure Mum and Dad keep a close watch on their possessions and bank accounts. You, too.'

'That won't be difficult seeing as I'm perpetually broke.'

We barely spoke about the business. I finished with the promise of dropping into Cake That some time in the week. It would give me an opportunity to check on Mum, although I didn't fancy coming face to face with Adam so soon after we'd got rid of him.

I phoned Dad and left a message to the effect that I needed his advice (not true, but it would ensure he contacted me sooner than later). Afterwards, I popped Rufus into his portable crib and set about blitzing the house. Starting with the newly-vacated guest quarters, I stripped linen from the bed and, spotting a suspicious-looking stain, was relieved to see, on further inspection, it was fake tan. I threw windows open, emptied two wastepaper baskets, scrubbed the bathroom until it gleamed and, removing a mark from the carpet, vacuumed it, the roar of the motor delighting Rufus.

I'd secretly hoped to find something incriminating stashed under the mattress, like a summons to attend court, or a communication from the police for a serious offence, anything that would prove to every member of my family that Adam was a man you wouldn't want to associate with, let alone offer houseroom.

No such luck.

Closing the door, I picked Rufus up and returned downstairs to the main part of the house. In a week's time we would be in uproar again with groundworkers and builders, but it was *our* mess, *our* uproar and the end result would be well worth it.

I was changing Rufus's nappy when Dad returned my call. Putting him on speakerphone, I shouted, 'Hang on a sec,' as a fountain of fresh baby pee cascaded over the changing mat and over Rufus's legs. Not that Rufus was bothered; he looked exceptionally pleased with himself.

'I can call you back later,' Dad hollered over the din of sirens.

'Where are you?'

'Outside, taking a break, stretching the old legs.'

'Won't be a moment,' I said, cleaning Rufus up in double-quick time. 'This thing with Ben's brother and his girl-friend,' I launched in.

'We've always taken in waifs and strays,' Dad reminded me, a chuckle in his voice.

'Dad, you make them sound like refugees. Trust me, they are not.'

'Adam is as good as family, and we very much liked what we saw when we met him.'

'You don't know him.'

'Then this is our chance to find out.'

'But what about Mum?'

'What about her?'

'It's not fair to impose on her. You must have noticed how tired she looks.'

'That's because of the ridiculous diet she's put herself on.'

'A diet? Is that what she told you?' I took after my mother. We only had to look at a piece of cake to put on weight. Whatever she was doing, however, wasn't good for her.

'She didn't want to make a deal of it.' Dad sighed. 'Now if that's all, I really have to go. I'm being summoned by the producer.' He ended the call.

Frustrated and in deep need of a sugar lift, I reached for the biscuit tin and selected a home-made dark-chocolate-chip cookie. Scratch that, I settled for three.

CHAPTER THIRTY-NINE

The weekend passed idyllically. The final dressing was removed from my hand, which had healed nicely. The weather was kind; it felt as if spring really was on the way after months of rain and cooler temperatures. With the pressure eased I realised how stressed I'd become. Back into his routine, Rufus took regular naps, was easier to please and feed, and wasn't awake for long in the night.

Speaking to Ben about Mum's diet, I said, 'It's not as if she's particularly overweight and, at her age, it's important all the food groups are covered.'

'Which diet is she on?'

'The "starve yourself and see how gaunt it makes me" diet — I don't know. Don't think Dad knows either. Could you offer her some advice?'

Ben frowned. 'Not easily.'

'Maybe drop a hint that she's lost weight?'

He blew out between his lips. 'After Brooke, I'm starting to think eating disorders are catching.'

Saskia dropped me a heartening WhatsApp message on Saturday evening.

*All good. Dad and Adam spent most of the day tinkering under
the bonnet of Dad's motor and nobody has yet made a threat for money
with menaces!*

—*Early days. How's Mum?*'

*In good spirits. Auntie Fen is visiting this week. Did you know
she's split from her latest husband?*

—*The stockbroker?*

The cosmetic surgeon.

—*God, how many is that?*'

Three, by my count. Practically making a career of it.

—*Where is she staying?*

*Nice try — not with us! Where she always stays — hotel. How's
things with you?*

—*Blissfully quiet.*

I wondered what my dotty aunt would make of Adam.

Monday came and I caught up with washing and shopping and spent an adorable time playing with my delighted
baby. Ben called to say he'd be late and didn't roll in until after
eight p.m., full of apologies.

'No problem,' I said, wondering why his breath smelt of
alcohol. 'Heavy day?'

'Uh-huh.'

Assuming a patient had died, I left it.

'Did you remember to pay Hugh?' I asked.

'All done,' Ben said.

We turned in for an early night and the next morning I
drove straight to the unit with Rufus in tow in his car seat.
Parking next to Saskia's car, I bowled into my office, babe in
arms, and skidded to a halt at the sight of Adam sitting in my
chair like a chairman of the board. He didn't jump up like a
startled cat. He stood slowly, leather trousers creaking, and
greeted me as if it were his company, not mine.

'What the hell do you think you're doing?' I demanded.

Unperturbed, he flicked a smile that would have dazzled the
eyes of a blind man. 'Getting a feel for what it's like at the top.'

'Dream on.' I pushed past and, like a keen holidaymaker reserving a deckchair with a towel, stuck my bag on my chair. No amount of offbeat charisma was going to charm me. 'Why are you here?' No point in pussyfooting around.

'Thought I'd tag along.'

'It's a business, Adam, not a gig.'

The smile stretched wider.

'Where's Saskia?' I half expected him to say he'd given her the day off.

'Gone to the loo. Do you want me to hold Rufus while you do what you have to do?'

'No, thank you.' I went to the water cooler, helped myself, moved my bag, sat down, opened my laptop and, one-handed, very ostentatiously pecked at the keyboard, checking through online sales figures for the month, something I'd already done at home. After that I ran through the number of events we'd got lined up for the following weeks, including a tea dance, birthday parties and a wedding tea for an elderly couple getting hitched at a local care home. Ignored, Adam sloped towards the door.

'Popping out for a smoke,' he informed me.

'Not outside the unit,' I said, without looking up. 'Bad look.'

A few minutes, later, Saskia walked into my office. 'Ooh,' she burst out, startled.

'Ooh, indeed. Why is he here?' She didn't need me to draw a picture of which 'he' I was referring to.

'Ah, well,' Saskia stumbled, embarrassed. 'If I'd known you were coming, I'd have let you know.'

'That doesn't answer my question.'

Saskia hesitated, nibbled on the corner of her little finger and perched on the corner of my desk. 'Adam's had a couple of brainwaves.'

I closed the laptop. 'Which bit of watching everyone's back didn't you understand?'

'Yes, I get . . .'

'You called him a parasite.'

'I know but . . .'

'But nothing. Am I the only sane person in this family?'

'Sophie, calm down. You'll make Rufus cry.'

I could have cried. It was if everyone I loved had joined a cult in which charismatic Adam Hall was leader. Fleetingly, I wondered what he had on Saskia to persuade her to change her mind about him. Not trusting myself to speak without saying something I could never take back and would later regret, I said nothing. Siblings have that uncanny ability to read each other's minds. Saskia read mine and backed off.

'Let me explain,' she said meekly.

I took a sip of water and nodded for her to continue.

'Adam suggested we expand into the café market.'

'That's not what we're about. Seventy-five per cent of our business is online sales and ten per cent outside events.'

'Which would continue but cafés . . .'

'Plural?' I said, raising an eyebrow.

'Eventually,' Saskia replied airily. 'A café would give us a strong visible presence. It would enhance the brand. The return on coffee, alone, is phenomenal.'

Which was true. 'I realise that, but we are not in hospitality.'

'Then why not branch out? There are loads of empty units in town.'

'For a reason — rents are too high and competition too fierce. And think of the physical outlay: staff, supplies and insurance. Blunt answer — we can't afford it.'

'We could if we cut back on our suppliers. For example, we don't have to use French flour. We could go for something cheaper.'

I gaped in astonishment. 'Our whole business is based on the very best ingredients.' We didn't use the word 'artisan' to describe our products for nothing.

'Nobody would notice.'

'*I* would notice.'

'I knew that's what you'd say,' Saskia said huffily.

'Then you should have told Adam.'

'Told Adam what?' He'd loped back in and positioned himself like a sentry near the door.

'Sophie has sacked off your café idea.' Saskia petulantly slid off the desk and landed with a small jump on her feet.

'Pity,' Adam said, clipped.

'I've known too many companies expand too quickly and fail,' I said evenly.

'Or wither and die because the owners were too risk-averse,' Saskia countered. 'You used to have such grand ideas.'

'Pre-baby, is that what you mean?'

Saskia stared, not daring to articulate further.

Adam shrugged. Saskia cleared her throat. First round to me.

In the yawning silence that followed, Saskia fiddled with an earring. There was more.

'How about we employ a proper marketing and PR team?' Saskia suggested.

'Better still, hire an influencer,' Adam chipped in.

'I've spoken to Brooke about it,' Saskia said with enthusiasm.

'She's got loads of contacts,' Adam confirmed.

His blatant bid to wiggle his way into our family and now my business triggered my internal alarms. Adam Hall was the human equivalent of a piece of malware disguised to corrupt systems while looking perfectly innocent. I'd heard enough and had enough. Collecting my bag and my baby, I strode towards the door.

'Sophie, where are you going?' Saskia cried.

'To see Mum. I'll leave you two to plot and plan, but let me make it perfectly clear—' I fastened my furious gaze on my sister — *nothing* happens in *my* company without *my* express say so.'

CHAPTER FORTY

I was strung out. I was tired. Deep down, I was afraid.

Mum looked relieved to see me and pleased to see her grandson. She offered me a cuppa that I declined although I trailed her into the kitchen.

'Auntie Fen is coming tomorrow,' Mum said brightly.

'Sash mentioned it. How long is Auntie staying?'

'A couple of weeks. She's booked a suite at No. 131.'

'Blimey. She doesn't do things by halves. Must be costing her a fortune.'

Mum agreed with an indulgent smile. 'Be lovely for you to drop in. I'm sure Fen would love to see her great nephew.'

'Makes her sound ancient.'

Mum suppressed a giggle. 'Please don't say that to your aunt. You know how sensitive she is about her age.'

I made a solemn promise not to mutter a word.

'It's been quite a morning,' Mum said, running a weary hand through her hair.

'Oh?'

'Brooke's gone.'

My lips parted in surprise. 'That's very sudden. Maybe I'll have that cup of tea after all.'

'I definitely need one,' Mum said soulfully.

'Does Adam know?' He never mentioned a word at work.

'Not unless she phoned to tell him.' Mum busied with mugs and teabags. 'They had a massive row this morning.'

'What triggered it?'

Mum rested her top teeth on her bottom lip, filled the kettle and popped it on.

'It's all right,' I said, spotting her reluctance to drop Saskia in it. 'I've just come from Cake That. I know Adam went into work with her.' No way was I going into detail about what had transpired.

'I knew it was a bad idea,' Mum said unhappily, clearly wishing to put distance between what or was not going on. 'Not that there's anything between him and Saskia, but I'm not sure Brooke sees it that way.'

'Did you overhear what was said?'

Mum poured boiling water from the kettle into two mugs, gave the tea a stir and, after fishing out teabags, added a splash of milk, and sugar for me. 'I did,' she said, without offering what. 'Can I have a cuddle with Rufus?'

'Course,' I said, handing him over.

'Lovely boy,' she crooned, smiling at him. Lost in baby land it would take a crowbar to prise her away.

'Mum?'

'Yes.'

'Start from the beginning.'

She kept her eyes down, but the twitch in her mouth told me she was unhappy with being a snitch.

'How did it all kick off?' I pressed.

'Raised voices coming from your room.'

'Must have been pretty loud.'

'Sounded quite contained at first.'

'And then?'

'There was a lot of swearing.'

'You couldn't make out what was said?'

Mum glanced up, two short lines between her eyebrows. 'I didn't want to hear what was said, Sophie.'

176

'I realise that, but you must have caught something other than curses.'

Mum breathed in and out. I think she was either struggling to be accurate without putting a spin on it or didn't want to convey what she thought she'd heard. '"Not part of the deal", Brooke said.'

'She used those exact words?'

Eyes glued back again on my son, Mum nodded.

'You don't know what the deal referred to?'

'No.'

'Do you know where she went after she left?'

'She told me she was going home.'

I expressed surprise. 'I guess that's a good thing.'

'Exactly what I said.'

And displayed the depth of Brooke's desperation. 'You said she was angry, Mum.'

'Very.'

'Was she lucid, or did she lose her temper?' We all say things we don't mean in anger. I should know.

'She wasn't hysterical, if that's what you mean.' Mum paused, taking her time to consider. 'Odd really.'

'How odd?'

'She was quite cold and clinical.'

I lifted the mug to my lips and took a sip. I'd focused on Adam. Maybe I should have concentrated on Brooke the Brittle, the liar and deceiver. Who the hell was she and had her vulnerable act been a charade, or was it a case of, having had enough of Adam, the proverbial worm finally turning after countless put-downs? It was hard to revolt against everything you'd thought and believed about someone. Dark clouds rose up out of the bright blue of my mind, threatening to overshadow me.

'Sophie?'

I gave a start. 'Yes?'

'Where were you?'

Taking a hike through forbidden territory. 'Nowhere,' I said breezily.

'You are such a poor liar,' Mum countered. 'I was saying what a godsend Adam has been. He cooked us a lovely meal on Saturday and mowed the lawn for your dad yesterday.'

Looking into her grateful eyes, I had no choice other than to agree it was a kindness.

'Even ran your father to the station this morning,' Mum said.

'In Dad's Triumph Stag?' I was astounded. Dad didn't lend his car to anyone, let alone someone who'd rocked up days before.

'Adam's borrowing it while Dad's away.'

If someone took a photo of me at that precise moment, I'm sure it would show my eyebrows meeting my hairline. 'Dad gave his permission?'

'Good for the engine, apparently. Why are you looking like that?'

'I'm not.' Heat flushed my cheeks. I didn't say that Dad had never offered to put Ben behind the wheel.

'And Adam brought me breakfast in bed when he got back,' Mum continued happily.

'Mum, I really don't think you should allow Adam that level of intimacy.'

'Sophie,' she said, wide-eyed. 'What are you suggesting?'

'Nothing,' I said, back-pedalling like crazy. 'I simply don't think it healthy that you become too dependent on him.'

Mum didn't say a word. I could see by the set of her jaw she was cross. While she was channelling her irritation by making funny faces at Rufus, I excused myself and, under the guise of visiting the bathroom, I headed to my old bedroom.

Gliding upstairs, crossing the landing, the air felt different. It lacked the distinct scent I'd always associated with home; a distillation of my mother's perfume, the artefacts and old books dotted around the house, and Dad's woody aftershave. Something had replaced it: Adam.

My hand on the doorknob, I paused, wondering what new chaos I'd discover inside. Imagine my surprise when, on pushing the door open, I found a tidy room: bed made, no debris, one side of the wardrobe stripped bare, the other containing a couple of suits, Adam's trademark jeans, sweats and sweaters. I did not rifle through the mostly empty bags parked at the base, as I had done previously at ours.

In the tiny en-suite bathroom, converted from a cupboard thirty years before, I found Adam's toiletries arranged with military precision. The sink and loo were clean. No smears of make-up on the towels or anywhere else. As good impressions went, he'd made one.

I was heading back downstairs when my phone rang from a number I recognised.

'Hugh,' I said, a smile in my voice.

'Sophie . . . um . . . Hi.'

'Hugh, is everything okay? You sound worried.'

'It's slightly delicate,' he said, stilted. 'About the next instalment for the garden room.'

'Yes?'

'It hasn't arrived.'

My heart gave an involuntary bump. 'I'm sure Ben said he'd taken care of it.'

'The money isn't in the account.'

'Are you sure it's not a technical error?'

'Afraid not.'

'I don't know what to say.' I absolutely didn't. Ben had assured me he'd paid.

'The thing is it's quite a sizeable amount and, in all honesty, we can't start on the due date until we have it.'

'I understand,' I said, with a shrinking feeling. 'I'm sure there's a silly explanation. It must have slipped Ben's mind. He's been so busy lately.'

'That's what I thought.' Hugh's obvious relief bore a striking similarity to a man reprieved from a custodial sentence.

'Can you bear to leave it with me? I promise to get back to you by tomorrow morning.'

'Absolutely, although,' Hugh said, apology in his voice, 'there is a degree of urgency about it. Schedules to plan and so on.'

I ended the call with platitudes, sped downstairs and told Mum I had to leave.

'Problem?' she asked.

'I don't know,' I replied. But if it was, it was massive.

CHAPTER FORTY-ONE

All the way home I told myself there was a logical explanation. Ben had been distracted. We all had. Perhaps he'd got confused with the order of staged payments, but he'd said 'all done' when I'd asked him. Feverishly dreaming up a Plan B, I called the estate agents on my hands-free to see if there was any movement on the flat sale. In soothing tones, I was informed that 'the market had gone quiet'. I tuned out when I heard the same spiel repeated about the need for *realistic* prices.

I arrived back at Lamb's Leap in bad shape. My home for the past year, it now felt like a house of mirrors in which images were distorted, and nothing was quite what it had first seemed. I knew then, in my heart, that Ben had lied to me. What else had he lied about?

At a loss, I dropped Ben a text, requesting he call me as a matter of urgency. Two hours passed, although I could see he had read the message. Must be busy, I told myself. When another hour chugged by, I phoned the surgery. It took forever to get through. When Willow, one of the receptionists, finally answered I was told he wasn't at work.

'When did he go out?' I asked, incredulous.

'He hasn't been in all day.'

'Did he say where he was?'

'A family matter. Sophie, I thought . . .'

'Sorry, of course,' I exclaimed, blushing with the lie and recognising that Willow would sense I was covering for him. 'I'll let you get on.'

I hung up. At risk of straying into the danger zone, I tried to close my mind to ugly possibilities: an affair, or a gambling habit. I tried to forget the alcohol on Ben's breath when he'd come home late, the inconsistencies in Ben and Adam's accounts of the past, Ben's general anxiety about his brother and his utter failure to stand up to Adam when he could and should have done.

A nervous laugh erupted from between my lips. Who was I to question Ben's absence of courage? Who was I to get on my sanctimonious high horse?

In turmoil, I went through the motions, focused on my baby, played with, fed and bathed Rufus. As Ben's home time approached, I glanced anxiously at the clock thinking any moment the front door would open, followed by his soft tread along the hall carpet before he made his way to the kitchen and hub of the house. There had to be a rational explanation for not paying Hugh. Had to be.

But what if Ben was with someone else, an exhausted voice in my head needled? Destabilised by the thought, I went online and bought a ton of cosmetics. Proper hardcore potions steeped in science (but snake oil just the same) in the hope that it would make me more attractive, less mumsy, less *older partner*.

At last, I heard the click of Ben's key in the door and, beside myself with anxiety and frustration, forced a welcome and expectant smile.

'Good day?' I asked mildly.

'Flat-out busy.' Running a hand under his jaw, Ben cast me an apologetic look. 'Sorry about not getting back to you — pig of a day.'

My smile stretched so wide I thought my cheekbones would crack. 'I had Hugh on the phone this morning.'

Ben cleared his throat and muttered about needing a glass of water.

'You need to tell me the truth.' My eyes fixed on his, the resulting expression on his face the same as if I'd punched him hard in the stomach. 'How the hell did you think I wouldn't find out?' I snarled. 'The ground crew are due to start next week. Worse, you damn well lied to me. In fact, you lied to me twice. You might have had a "pig of a day" but it was nothing to do with work because you weren't there due to "a family matter".'

A pulse in his jaw ticked. 'I can explain.' His eyes flicked to the fridge. I knew what he was thinking: beer.

'I think we'll leave the booze until I find out what the hell is going on.' My voice was dark with warning.

He sat down, or rather slumped onto the nearest chair.

'Are you having an affair?'

He sat up. 'God, Sophie, no.'

'Then what have you been doing all day?'

'Raising funds.'

I folded my arms. 'For what?'

'To cover the extension.'

'But it's already saved and good to go from your account.' Eventually, I would be contributing to half of it. It was why I needed to sell my flat with a degree of urgency. I felt suddenly sick inside.

Ben gazed at me with eyes that I'd once believed I could trust. 'Not anymore,' he whispered, pale and wan.

Flat out, I demanded to know where it had gone.

'Adam. He needed a sub so I gave him the money destined for the instalment. I'm so sorry.'

I breathed in hard through my nose, attempting and failing to contain the loud protest bubbling up from my gut. Ben almost fell off his chair as I let rip.

'Sophie, please. He's my brother.'

'And what am I?' I roared.

He stood up, mortified and came towards me. I took a smart step back. I'd never recoiled from him before and read fear in his expression, of what he'd done and how he'd messed things up between us. It wasn't so much the money as the lies that went with it and the reason behind those lies.

'Sophie, you are the most important person in my life.'

'No, I'm not,' I gasped. 'Your brother is.'

'No, no, no.'

I stared at Ben, tears filming my eyes — for him and for me.

My mind reeled with questions: what if Ben's cosy, steady personality and existence was built on deception? What if I'd fallen into the same trap as before but with another man? It led me to draw an obvious conclusion.

'What dirt does Adam have on you?'

CHAPTER FORTY-TWO

Ben denied and denied and denied. 'Babe, you're overthinking the whole thing.'

'Am I?' Pale and sick with fury, I'd heard those blasted words once before and it had cost.

'He's in a hole, Sophie,' Ben repeated for the zillionth time.

'Not deep enough.' Give me a spade and I'd bury him.

'He's my brother.'

'A man who scares the living crap out of you.' And now me.

'And you must think me very stupid.'

'What?'

'Long gone are the days you chatted to your friendly bank manager to request a loan. Now it's all about systems and decisions that take time to process, but you didn't go to a bank today, did you?'

His chin dropped to his chest. His shoulders slumped.

'Christ, Ben.'

'Does it matter where the money came from?'

'Yes, it does. So you've got it? What interest are you paying?'

'Look, it's all legit, right?' Which didn't answer my question.

'How legit? Secured or unsecured?' A secured loan would require an asset as security.

His knee jinked. 'Secured against the house.'

'You *what*?' I was livid. God alone knew from where or who he'd borrowed the money. Frankly, I didn't want to know. It was his damned mess. I'm not a woman who resorts to insults. Didn't mean I didn't think them.

'I suppose you think I should be impressed by your resourcefulness?' I struggled to keep my temper in check.

Eyes fixed on mine he shook his head slowly.

'Did you manage to get a loan to cover all of it?'

He flinched. 'I'm ten grand short.'

'This is madness,' I fumed. 'I assume there's a cooling off period?'

'There is, but if we don't press ahead, we'll lose out and we'll still have to pay Hugh for drawing up plans and the work he's already carried out towards getting the application through.'

I could probably cover the cost from the business. It would lead to a difficult conversation with Saskia, but it had to be done. I wasn't giving up on the extension and I wasn't prepared for our home to be used to secure a loan because Ben's brother was a greedy feckless bastard.

'I'll handle it,' I said in more measured tones. 'Cancel whatever you've agreed. I'll take the money out of the business.'

'You can do that?'

'With difficulty,' I said. 'Leave Hugh to me.'

'One other thing.' Ben glanced down. He did this a lot when he was gearing up to something. I waited, stoic.

'It's a lot to ask,' he said, 'but, please, I'd rather nobody knew about this.'

'About your mind-blowing generosity towards your brother, you mean?' It sounded as icy as I felt. Before he drowned me in more apologies, I grabbed my laptop, sped upstairs and sent an email to Hugh to assure him that the money would be with him by noon the next day. Next, I checked the account we used to set aside money for tax and VAT and called Saskia.

'About this morning,' she began, probably expecting me to chew her ears off.

'Forget it. I need to access funds from the business.' Technically, I could just take it, but I didn't think it fair to extract such a large amount and not tell Saskia.

She gave a little huff of surprise. 'How much?'

I told her.

'Shit.'

'I can pay it straight back once the flat sells.'

'Which might not be any time soon.'

'Correct.'

The line went silent.

'Can I ask what you need it for?' Saskia asked eventually.

'No.' Revealing that Ben had handed over thousands to his brother would result in making Saskia feel a lot less warmly towards Adam — a positive. No fool, she would also be wondering why Ben had felt pressurised to do so — a negative, and one I still hadn't fathomed.

I could almost hear her making connections. 'This is strictly need-to-know basis. Not a whisper of this to Mum and Dad, or anyone else,' I said with emphasis.

'Got it.'

'Good. I need to transfer it straight away.' My sister would be wondering why the emergency.

'I guess that's all right.'

'I guess it is.'

'Sophs?'

'Yes?'

'You don't have to tell me the detail, but are you in some kind of trouble?'

Yes, and it was all Adam Hall's fault. 'Don't stress it,' I said. 'A temporary cash-flow issue. Nothing more serious than that.'

CHAPTER FORTY-THREE

I don't know how Ben and I staggered through the rest of the evening, or the following days and nights. I felt as if I'd been in an accident, as if every muscle in my body had been wrenched. My limbs ached and so did my brain. Coldly polite summed up most of my responses, despite Ben making every effort to be his normal warm and caring self. Like a thick swirling fog sitting over a swamp, I felt a hatred for Adam that I hadn't known I was capable of.

Ben barely reacted when I told him about Brooke breaking up with Adam, something I'd omitted in the wake of the financial disaster. At least, the garden room was going ahead, although how we were going to find the rest of the money was anyone's guess.

'He won't come back for more, will he?' I asked Ben.

'He can't.'

'He can.'

'Then he will be disappointed.'

I responded with a cynical expression.

'I'm so hugely embarrassed and sorry, Sophie.'

Ben did his best to convince me that he had acted from the best of intentions and now deeply regretted it. By Friday,

I was starting to thaw a little. Over the weekend, I felt less uneasy. On Monday, the groundworking team finally arrived to clear the site in readiness for laying the concrete base; it would be another week before the team from the workshop constructed dwarf walls and assembled the oak frame. Confronted by a big thick-set guy in his late sixties who'd been involved in groundworks 'man and boy', he told me, I had no choice other than to get back to normal, if only for the sake of appearances.

'What are you up to today?' Ben enquired over my morning cuppa, the steady drone of a digger in the background.

'Thought I'd escape the ear-splitting noise of men at work and drop into Mum's to see Auntie Fen.' I'd steered clear of Cheltenham following my aunt's arrival, but didn't want to miss catching up with her. As a precaution I'd phoned ahead and discovered from Mum that Adam was wisely removing himself for the day, no doubt swanning around in Dad's car. Although I'd promised Ben I wouldn't take a verbal swing at his brother, I didn't trust myself not to comply.

Ben gave me a dry kiss on the cheek on his way out. I drove to Mum's and parked next to Auntie Fen's Aston Martin, one of her many spoils of marital war.

I found Mum and her sister-in-law in the drawing room upstairs, drinking coffee. Auntie Fen's greeting was effusive.

'God, Sophie, darling, what an absolute sweetheart you have there,' she said, eyeing Rufus as if he were a brand-new Hermès handbag.

'Would you like to hold him?' I asked.

Her nose wrinkled in apology. 'Better not,' she said, stroking the sleeve of a black woollen jacket. 'Ralph Lauren,' she explained in a low voice. 'Besides, unlike your mother here, I'm not very good with babies.'

'Nonsense, Fen,' Mum said sportingly. 'Milo is an absolute credit to you.'

'Darling, that would be his father's influence, nothing to do with me.'

Auntie Fen is very like her brother, my father, not in looks but in personality. Theatrical, irreverent, wildly eccentric and rather good at putting her foot in it, like when she asked one of Saskia's fuller-figured friends if she were pregnant. She was what one might describe as colourful and not simply because she had a mass of chestnut-coloured hair (professionally cut and dyed at one of London's leading salons) and wore acres of make-up. Her private life made Saskia's appear tame. Making a career of marrying and divorcing a string of wealthy men, she had done the impossible by staying on exceptionally good terms with each of them. According to Dad, there had already been some talk about them holidaying together and hiring a villa with their new respective wives and assorted adult children and grandchildren. Different world to the one I inhabited.

While Mum went to fetch another mug for me, Auntie Fen fired questions designed to gauge how I was, how the business was and how Ben was. I lied in two of three answers. 'Ben sends his best,' I told her, which was true.

'Such a darling man,' she enthused. 'We all love him to bits.'

They'd said the same about Leo, I remembered. I nodded and smiled and wondered how long I could pretend everything was fine.

'How did Adam take the news about Brooke?' I asked Mum when she returned.

'Thunderstruck.'

'Upset?'

'Terribly,' Mum said, 'although, apparently, she has gone walkabout before.'

'He thinks she'll come back?'

'She'll be in for a shock if she does,' Auntie Fen interjected with a chuckle. 'Saskia and Adam seem quite cosy, if you get my drift.' What I feared most. Were we ever going to see the back of the man? 'We could do with another wedding in the family,' Auntie Fen said with a wink.

I tensed, firstly because it reminded me of my own flight from the altar and, secondly, because the thought of Adam as Saskia's husband made me feel physically sick.

'Fenella,' Mum chided, pressing a hand to her chest and casting me an anxious look.

Clueless, my aunt gaped from Mum to me and then, catching on, said, 'Oh, Sophie's aborted wedding was ages and ages ago. Sophie doesn't mind, do you, darling? Not now you're all loved up with Ben and baby Rupert.'

'Rufus,' I said.

'Exactly — as I was saying, you're not still hung up on the man whose name we dare not speak?'

'Not a bit,' I stuttered.

'There,' Auntie Fen said, chalking up a point. 'My niece understands the maxim "marry in haste and repent at leisure". Thank God one of us in the family has sense.' She let out a throaty laugh and blithered on. 'I have to say I can't blame Saskia. Ben's brother is sex on legs and *so* interesting. Oh, to be forty years younger,' she trilled.

More excruciating conversation had me reaching for my car keys. As soon as I decently could I made an excuse and left my mother and aunt to it, or so I thought until, about to drive away, Auntie Fen tapped on the car window.

I dropped it, peered out and turned off the engine.

'Faith told me about your little difficulty.'

My eyes shot wide. 'Pardon?'

'Selling the apartment, darling.'

'Oh,' I said, smiling in relief, 'yes, it's proving to be quite tricky.'

'How long has it been on the market?'

'Over a year.'

'Not good.'

I agreed. 'I've dropped the price, and the agents are pressuring me to drop it again.'

'Agents for you.' Auntie Fen's top lip curled with distaste. 'I can see it's taking quite a toll.'

Did I look that bad? If I did, it wasn't because of the flat.

'I'm concerned about my favourite niece,' Auntie Fen said affectionately.

Genuinely touched, I said, 'Are you allowed to have favourites?'

'Definitely, which is why I have the perfect solution — let me buy the apartment from you.'

'You?'

Auntie Fen gave the drive a theatrical glance. 'Don't see anyone else in the offing. I'll give you a fair price, naturally.'

I suddenly saw an answer to a prayer. With the money I could transfer it straight back into the business. Saskia would be pleased. Ben would be relieved. I'd feel more reassured, and nobody would be any the wiser. It was an elegant solution to an issue that was driving me crazy — not as crazy as the Adam problem, admittedly. 'That's extremely generous of you, Aunt. Are you thinking of moving our way?' She was between marriages and Cheltenham had enough high-end shops and restaurants to satisfy her. Mum would be thrilled too.

'Good grief, no.' Auntie Fen twitched her nose, the idea obviously repellent. 'The apartment is *far* too poky. Where would I put my clothes, darling? No, I was thinking of letting it out.'

'Is that wise? The buy-to-let market has all but collapsed.' I thought it only fair to warn her.

'Darling, I'm not going to let any old Tom, Dick or Harriet move in. I was rather wondering whether Saskia might consider it. High time she flew the family nest and gave your parents a little P&Q.' Peace and quiet, was what she meant.

Alarm flickered inside me. If Saskia left, my parents would be stuck with Adam. A more troubling thought: was Saskia really getting close to Adam? What if it wasn't a fling — an abhorrent thought — what if it were serious? Had Adam craftily seeded the thought into my sister's mind and then my aunt's? I pictured him dropping hints, squirming his way into my aunt's affections. The thought of Adam moving into my old place filled me with abject horror. Not wishing to squash my aunt's magnanimity, I said I'd think about it.

'Well, don't leave it too long,' Auntie Fen said briskly. 'From what your mother told me the situation requires radical action.'

Couldn't have put it better myself.

CHAPTER FORTY-FOUR

Like a walker finding a nice piece of pasture to stroll through towards open country and freedom, I found myself suddenly presented with a solid rock face.

Determined to discover a logical solution, I scribbled a pros and cons list in my head. The cons were easy and could be summed up in one word: Adam. If he hooked up with my sister, was it a given he'd move in with her? Surely, Saskia would want her own space and independence after all these years? She might be genuinely averse to living with someone after such a short acquaintance. You weren't, my conscience reminded me. Annoyingly, I wondered whether I'd have acted with such haste had I not fallen pregnant with Ben's child. The thought rocked me. Where on earth had that come from? I'd never once doubted my decision — until Adam's arrival.

As soon as I reached home, I checked on progress. I expected the ground to look a mess to start with but hadn't quite bargained on it looking as if a meteorite had hit it. I quickly scuttled back indoors to settle Rufus. Once he was asleep on the other side of the house, away from the penetrating noise of a digger, I made tea for the workers and called Saskia, relaying the gist of my conversation with Auntie Fen.

'She's intent on winkling me out of the family home,' Saskia said, laughing.

'About time too. And Adam?'

'Whatever do you mean?'

'Don't treat me like a fool, Sash.'

The gale of a sigh issuing down the phone line almost blew me over. 'Who said there's anything between us?'

'Auntie Fen.'

'She has a vivid imagination.'

'And Mum.' Which was rather dropping her in it, I admit.

This provoked a defensive response from my sister. 'Not my fault if his girlfriend cleared off.'

'It is if she cleared off because of you.'

'Funnily enough, she didn't say,' Saskia sniped back. 'Adam was incredibly cut up about it, if you must know.'

I could picture it all: upset boyfriend, consoling, attractive woman (my predatory little sister) next thing you know, they're sleeping together.

'Anyway, it's none of your business,' Saskia said.

'So you *are* sleeping with him?'

The line went very quiet. I didn't know what to say and neither did she: stalemate.

Recovering with unruly speed, Saskia said, 'What's your response to Auntie Fen bailing you out?'

'God, you didn't tell her about me borrowing from the business, did you?' I loved my Auntie Fen, but her mouth was even bigger than her wallet.

'Course not,' Saskia said, sounding hurt. 'I made a promise, remember?'

'Fair enough.'

'So?'

'I said I'd think about it.'

'What's there to think about? It's a genius idea.'

'Was it Adam's?' No way could I put it any less straightforwardly.

'Sophie — don't be so paranoid. I might even share your place with Meadow.'

195

'Meadow Fortescue, gossip and ghoul?' With her nose into everyone's business, WhatsApp was redundant.

'She's not that bad.'

'She is.'

'All right, she is.'

'As I was saying,' I said loftily, 'if you're intent on moving Adam in, make sure he contributes financially with a very healthy deposit on the rental.'

'Awks. He's a bit strapped for cash right now.'

I didn't see red. I saw fire and it was crimson. 'He told you that?'

Saskia gave a nervous laugh. 'Sophs, what the hell are you implying?'

'He has money, a lot of it. If he tells you he hasn't, he's lying.'

'How do you know?'

Keen to undermine Adam in any way I could, I'd given too much away. Saskia wasn't daft. She'd soon put it together. Fortunately, she was too annoyed to put it together quite yet.

'Why do you always have to spoil things?' she bawled.

'I'm trying to protect you.' And me, and Ben and everyone.

'I don't need protecting. You're jealous — that's your problem.'

'Of *you with him*? Hardly. Adam is a creep who . . .'

The line went dead. In a sisterly stew, I swore I wouldn't do what I usually do: phone her back. My resolve lasted all of thirty seconds, and I was mightily pissed off when I got her voicemail, the equivalent of: screw you.

By the time Ben came home, late as usual, my brain was ready to explode. I became even more rattled and maddened when Ben avoided conversation by demanding to inspect the building site outside before he'd got his jacket off.

'Looks a bit of a mess,' he observed.

And the garden wasn't the only mess. Like a croupier shuffling cards in a game of baccarat, I considered which piece of news to drop on him first: Saskia taking up with Adam, or Auntie Fen's generous offer. I started with the easy bit.

'Wow!' Ben exclaimed. 'You're going to accept?' His expression blared: go for it.

'It's not that easy.' I wondered if this should be inscribed on my tombstone.

Spotting my hesitation, Ben pressed. I explained precisely where the complication lay.

'Dear God, Saskia didn't waste any time. What the hell is she thinking shacking up with my brother? No, don't tell me, it's too gross.'

There's a weird thing with families. It was fine for me to slate my sister. God help anyone else who dared, including Ben.

'Don't you take a pop at Sash. It's your blasted brother you should be gunning for.'

'Oh, come on, Sash is no angel.'

'And what does that make your brother?'

'Jesus, Sophie, he's a bad apple. What more do you want me to say and do?'

'You're a doctor, for Chrissakes,' I yelled in frustration. '*Think* of something.'

'I'm not God.'

'No, you're a father and my partner and, right now, I see very little evidence of you taking either of those responsibilities seriously.' I flinched at how much I sounded like a Victorian schoolteacher.

Ben's skin drained to the colour of old stone. Turning on his heel, he swept down the hall, swiped his car keys from the drawer and headed for the front door.

'Ben, I'm sorry, come back,' I called after him, mortified.

'Don't bother waiting up,' he snapped back.

CHAPTER FORTY-FIVE

Ben returned well after midnight. He didn't come straight up, and I pretended to be asleep when he slunk into bed, stinking of whisky.

At seven thirty, we were woken by the return of the ground-works team and noise from a cement mixer. On waking, my first thought was Rufus, my next the awful argument the night before; it sat there like a lead weight on my chest.

We both got up and moved around in silence. Eventually, I spoke, 'Ben, I'm so very . . .'

'No,' he said sadly. 'You were right. I've let you and Rufus down. It's me who should be apologising.' He reached out and I fell gratefully into his arms. 'It's a mess, isn't it?' He sounded so bereft.

'But one we'll recover from.' *We would, wouldn't we?*

Ben drew away, half-smiling. 'Is there any way you could put a clause in the condition of sale to your aunt?'

'Nobody named Adam allowed to rent?' I smiled back.

'That would be something, wouldn't it?'

Further discussion was cut off by a babbling sound in the next-door room. We crept inside together and watched Rufus making cooing noises at his mobile.

'See, at least we got something right,' Ben said.

We stood like that for a little bit, watching our boy in wonder.

'I won't be late tonight, promise,' Ben said, kissing me.

Glad we'd made up, I told him I'd cook something special.

When Louise called mid-morning and asked how things were, I told her they were better.

'And Ben's brother?'

'He moved out.' Excluding Ben's sub to Adam, I gave Louise a potted version of events.

'Crikey,' she exclaimed, which was strong coming from Louise. 'You say Saskia and Adam are an item?'

'Unfortunately.'

'The guy's like Teflon.'

'One way of putting it. How's things with you?'

Louise paused, as if weighing up whether to answer. 'I'm pregnant.'

'Fantastic news!' I was so made up for her.

'I'm trying not to get my hopes up. It's not the reason for the call by the way,' Louise said, with a nervous laugh. 'We wondered if you're free to meet up for lunch on Saturday, the four of us, or I guess I should say six,' she added shyly.

'That would be lovely.'

'Do you mind driving to the Bell?'

'At Sapperton?'

'We're dog-sitting at Elliott's parents for the weekend.'

'Sure the pooches won't mind?'

'Ancient Labradors, they probably won't even notice we're missing.'

I'd barely finished the call when Auntie Fen phoned, a rare event in her non-techie world. Her aversion to anything remotely digital meant her phones never worked properly, largely because she never read instructions or took an interest in setting them up correctly.

'Darling,' she gushed. 'Have you given my offer consideration?'

'I have.'

'And?'

I cleared my throat. 'It's a marvellous opportunity but—'

'How about you take it off the market with the agents and we negotiate a private sale? That way, you could save on estate agency fees.'

'I'd have to check the contract.' I was pretty sure there would be a catch.

'You sound very reluctant, darling. Is Saskia the problem?'

'No.'

'Then?'

'I'm worried she'll move Adam in.'

'Ah.'

I was sure I could hear Auntie Fen fumbling with the rings on her jewelled fingers as she planned her next move. 'What does Ben say?'

'It's caused a certain amount of tension. No, I lie,' I continued boldly, 'Adam is responsible for making life difficult for us.'

She didn't sound remotely shocked and, wisely, didn't question in what way Adam was a problem. 'Are you open to advice, sweetheart?'

'Always.'

'It would not be speaking out of turn to say that Saskia takes after her aunt in certain respects. She's wilful, wily, fun-loving and has an eye for bad boys, and I think we can agree that Adam can be classed as such.' She spoke with dry humour. 'But,' she continued, 'Adam will soon be toast like all Saskia's conquests. It would be a pity to pass up an opportunity that addresses a dire financial need.'

'I understand but . . .'

'Ben is a very nice boy, Sophie. Don't get caught in the crossfire because of bad feelings between the brothers.'

I expressed surprise. 'How did you know?'

'I listen, darling.'

To Adam, possibly. I could imagine him pouring out some sob story. Mum would also have formed an opinion after the bad press I'd given her about Ben's brother so that could also be a contributory factor. How strange that a man who turned up just weeks ago had become the centre of all our conversations. Worn down, I asked my aunt when she needed a decision.

'Come to your mum's tonight for a pre-prandial drink and we can discuss it then.'

The prospect of bumping into Adam for the first time since Ben had handed over thousands of pounds was deeply unappealing. 'Not if Adam's there.'

'Darling, I can hardly chain him to his bed.'

'He'd probably like that,' I said, making her laugh.

'You'll come?' she said, practically clapping her hands.

'With Ben, yes.'

'Excellent. One thing you don't know about me.'

'What's that?'

'I'm an excellent referee.'

CHAPTER FORTY-SIX

Pre-prandial in my parents' house meant drinks served any time between five and seven o'clock. I didn't warn Ben. I simply whisked him away before his feet crossed the threshold of our home. He grumbled all the way to Cheltenham. I didn't blame him.

'Why the theatrics?' Ben complained.

'This is Auntie Fen, remember?'

'Why you can't simply phone or drop her a text is beyond me.'

'You know how hopeless she is with technology.'

'I take it you've made a decision?'

'I'm going to accept,' I said, putting my foot down.

That shut him up.

I left Ben to gather up Rufus from the car and, shoulders back, rang the doorbell. Much to my surprise, Dad answered. 'My presence in the studio is not required again until Friday. Who am I to question schedules?' he announced, obviously put out.

'That's a bore.' I tipped up on my toes and dropped a kiss on his cheek. 'On the plus side, you get to spend more time with Mum and your sister.'

'And I get to sleep in a decent bed,' Dad said with a spry smile.

'Where shall I put little man?' Ben asked, trundling in behind me.

'I have instructions to direct you to our bedroom,' Dad said, with a kindly flourish. 'Faith has made up the cot for Rufus. The monitor is on.' Dad winked at me.

While Ben disappeared, Dad hung back. 'I gather we have a delicate situation.'

There must have been an awful lot of chatter behind closed doors for him to arrive at that conclusion. I nodded slowly.

'Brothers don't always get on,' Dad observed, 'no more than sisters.'

Ben and Adam were way beyond 'not getting on'. 'Is Adam here?' I asked.

'Upstairs with the others. Unfortunately, your aunt has already had a few.'

'Oh God.'

'Don't you worry, dear girl, I will escort you.' Dad very sweetly linked his arm through mine. Wrapping me in a smile, he said, 'Think of it as backup.' Curiously, I felt like a bride escorted down the aisle on the arm of her father.

We entered together. Ben was standing next to Mum and as far away from Adam and Saskia as humanly possible. Turning her warm gaze on me, Mum and I exchanged glances. Auntie Fen nattered on about the weather, the number of empty shops in Cheltenham since she'd last visited and the 'state of the country', as she put it, while dispensing strong gin and tonics with seasoned finesse. I accepted a weaker version and averted my eyes from the soon-to-be renters of my old flat.

All set, Auntie Fen took up a position next to the suit of armour and made some half-arsed speech about the importance of family and the need for greater tolerance and understanding. I'd always said she'd missed her calling as a thespian. Upstaged by his elder sister, Dad joined in like a leading man demoted to stagehand. Ben and I, standing close to each other, exchanged wary glances. Thankfully, Auntie Fen petered out and, before she got any more gin down her neck, I went over and told her that I'd gladly accept her offer.

'Fabulous, darling. How does the full asking price sound?'

Obviously tipsier than I thought. I agreed with alacrity.

'Now do go and make up with your sister.' Auntie Fen directed her stewed gaze to Saskia who stood quite lost and alone, Adam nowhere to be seen.

'All right?' I said, approaching Saskia.

'I'm all right. How are you?'

'All right.'

She grinned. I grinned. Sisterly relations restored if not exactly fully functioning. I took a sip of gin. 'A toast to your new home.'

Saskia looked at me with big eyes. 'You don't mind?'

'Just don't go and paint over the floorboards I so lovingly stripped.' I glanced across at Ben talking to Mum. I hoped he was warning her about her gimmicky diet. Angling my head in Mum's direction, I asked Saskia how she seemed.

'Tired all the time. I questioned her about a doctor's appointment the other day. She said it was her annual MOT.'

'You believe her?'

Saskia shrugged. 'Hopefully Ben will sort her out.' Skilfully avoiding any conversation connected to Cake That, Saskia asked after her nephew.

'Well and growing, talking of which I'd better go and check on him.' I put my glass down. 'Don't let Auntie Fen fill it up.'

'Easier said than done,' Saskia retorted.

Treading softly, I went upstairs and crossed the landing. Ben had left the door of my parents' room ajar. Not a peep although the absence of sound from my child always bothered me. I tucked myself inside and my heart shot into my mouth.

'Jesus, you gave me a shock,' Adam said, wheeling round.

'What the hell do you think you're doing?' I pushed past and bent over Rufus's crib. Snoring softly, Rufus was flat on his back, palms up, trusting and vulnerable. Snatching him up, I could have cried with relief and fury.

'I'll only ask this one more time, Adam,' I snarled. 'What were you doing?'

Adam's cool expression relaxed into a flinty smile. 'I thought I heard him crying.'

'Liar.'

Adam shrugged. 'You don't like me very much, do you?'

'I don't like you at all.'

'Is this about the money my brother gave me?'

'It wasn't his to give.'

'Then thank you very much, Sophie,' he said, with a swaggering bow.

'Take your blood money and piss off.' If my hands had been free I think I might have hit him.

'In case you've forgotten, I'm with Saskia now.'

'Don't get too comfortable.'

'Or what?' Adam jibed.

Before I could answer, the doorbell rang. It was followed by heavy footsteps on the stairs. Spotting an opportunity for a fast exit, Adam's eyes flicked to the door. Not yet finished with him, I stalled at the sound of a voice I hadn't heard in years, one that made my heart hammer and stole my breath away.

What, in God's name, was Leo Carpenter doing in my parents' home?

CHAPTER FORTY-SEVEN

Clutching Rufus tightly to my chest, I stumbled out of the room and downstairs to the kitchen where I found Dad and Leo with another man.

'Sophie,' Leo exclaimed. His blue-eyed gaze darted from my face to my baby son and back to me. Awkward didn't cover it. Leo had always wanted a large family. Was he shocked to see that I was now a mother? Was he recalling angry words and furious accusations? Or was he remembering his tears and desperate phone calls begging me to stay? Physically, I'd changed so much when he had changed so little. A few more laughter lines around the eyes, same shock of thick blond hair, receding a little at the edges maybe; same generous lips that had once smothered me in kisses. There was no beer gut to distort his rangy, athletic build. I must have looked as if I'd accidentally walked into a wall of sheet glass because Leo viewed me with concern and asked if I needed to sit down.

I shook my head. 'What are you doing here?' I could barely get the words out.

'Official business,' Dad answered. 'Leo's a DI now.' No idea why Dad chucked that in.

'But this is Gloucestershire,' I said, bewildered. 'You work for the Met.' I looked to Leo.

'And still do,' Leo explained smoothly. 'We're investigating an incident in London.'

In which case the Met would retain the investigation and ask Gloucestershire police to carry out enquiries on their behalf. All came down to cost, Leo had once told me.

Unless it was something serious.

I nodded dumbly.

'This is DC Jared Hicks,' he continued, introducing his colleague.

Hicks nodded a polite greeting. Built like a rugby player, his suit jacket barely stretched across his shoulders. Thick-necked with oversized ears, he had wide facial features and deep-set brown eyes in a heavy brow. His hair was razor short, so it was difficult to tell what colour it was.

'I still don't understand,' I said.

'We want to speak to Adam Hall.'

It felt like the answer to a prayer. Carried away, I counted off a mental list in my head: fraud, demanding money with menaces, extortion, theft. They'd be carting him off and Adam's reputation would be so comprehensively trashed he would never return. *Result.*

Dad flinched in alarm. 'Has he done something?'

Leo pushed a smile that neither affirmed nor denied. 'We need to speak to him about Brooke Gentry.'

'Brooke? Is she all right?' I asked.

'She went missing five days ago.'

My pulse tripped. I feverishly tried to nail down the time-line. Right now, I was struggling to recall what happened five minutes ago. Then I remembered: Adam in a room, alone, with my son.

Leo cut into my thoughts. 'Has Brooke been in touch?' He looked from me to Dad. We both shook our heads.

'She was only here for a weekend,' Dad said, frantically putting distance between our family and Brooke's missing status. *Nothing to do with us.*

'And before that?' Leo elevated an eyebrow.

I answered. 'She and Adam Hall stayed at ours.'

Leo asked for how long.

'A couple of weeks,' I answered.

'Ben Taylor is Adam Hall's brother, correct?' Leo's expression was so penetrating I feared confirming it.

'How on earth did you know about Ben?' Dad asked, perplexed. I wanted to say 'Dad, it's his job to do his homework'. Before Leo and Hicks had crossed the threshold they already knew where we lived, who Ben was, what he did for a living, what I now do for a living.

Leo flashed a smile. 'Brooke's parents filled in background information.'

So Brooke really had gone home. I remembered that she said her parents lived in Barking. If she'd travelled there straightaway, she hadn't stayed for very long, which raised a question: Brooke's parents were accustomed to their daughter going walkabout. Why report her missing so quickly? It told me this was more serious than Leo was letting on.

Dad scratched his head. 'I'm not sure I'm following this.'

The door to the kitchen swung open. Adam sloped in, took one look at the men in our midst and, instead of offering one of his 'hi, guys' trademark smiles, recoiled in a way that I'd never witnessed before. He didn't say I *smell* the law; his body language did the job for him. A trickle of fear slid down between my shoulder blades. *What had he done?*

'Are you Adam Hall?' Leo asked, issuing a direct look.

'Who wants to know?' Adam said, surly.

'Police,' Leo replied, running through the introductions and flashing a warrant card that had a distinctly sobering effect on Adam. I'd never seen him look so perturbed. Like a man with something to hide.

'What's this all about?' Adam asked, obviously nervous.

Dad opened his mouth to reply. Leo smoothly cut him off. 'We'd like to ask you a few questions about Brooke Gentry.'

Adam's face fell. 'Why, what's she done?'

Leo inclined his head. I knew what he was thinking: *That's a funny question.*

'Nothing. We're concerned for her welfare.'

Adam adopted an expression of concern and surprise.

'We hoped you could assist in our investigation to find her,' Leo continued.

Before Adam could get his head around that one, Leo turned to Dad with an enquiring look. 'Is there somewhere private we can talk to Mr Hall?'

Dad indicated the small sitting room and, without another word, off they trooped.

'Dear God,' Dad exclaimed, briefly sinking onto a chair in the hall. 'What do you think of that?'

I didn't know but, for the police to act this decisively, it couldn't be anything good.

CHAPTER FORTY-EIGHT

We were back upstairs in the big sitting room with the others. A natural orator, my father is not a man easily lost for words. Shock rendered him incoherent. In no particular order he muttered 'Brooke, Adam, disappeared' and, the grand finale, 'police'. It was down to me to interpret and present a clearer narrative, or one that wasn't steeped in speculation. The hardest part was the revelation that Leo was the investigating officer.

Ben looked as if he'd fallen down a lift shaft.

Bleary-eyed, Auntie Fen poured more gin.

'Holy crap,' Saskia burst out.

Mum gaped at Dad. *Leo?*' she whispered under her breath.

'And he's a detective inspector,' Dad said admiringly.

'Out of all the DIs don't the police have someone else to cover Brooke's disappearance?' Mum asked.

I privately agreed. It seemed too much like a horrible coincidence. Then another thought struck me: had Leo deliberately signed up for it? Was that even possible? The answer came flying back: no, it *shouldn't* happen, but, yes, it *could* happen.

Saskia was first to come to Adam's defence. 'I bet attention-seeking Brooke did this deliberately to cause trouble.'

'I think that's unlikely,' Dad said.

'A guy with rock-star chic and tats, the cops are bound to take a view,' Saskia chuntered on.

'Surely, Leo can't think there's a sinister connection,' Mum said.

'She's gone missing, Mum. She's not dead,' I said gently. 'The police are in information-gathering mode. The more they know about Brooke, the greater the chance of locating her.'

'Exactly, Sophie,' Saskia said, relieved to perceive an ally.

I didn't say that they would already know when Brooke was last seen, courtesy of CCTV, although I'd heard recently, again due to issues with resources, examination of footage was restricted to around thirty minutes for anything other than emergencies. If Brooke had carried out a financial transaction with a credit card, or phone, the time and possible location of where she last used either might offer a more precise timeline.

'So where are the police now?' Mum asked, not entirely convinced that it was as straightforward as I'd claimed.

'I've put them in the snug,' Dad said. 'I really don't think we should worry,' he added.

'Ben,' I said softly, sidling up to him. Throughout the entire conversation he hadn't uttered a word.

'What the fuck has he done now?' Ben muttered under his breath.

We stood around, waiting, the atmosphere turbocharged until the low grumble of approaching male voices alerted us that the police had finished. Saskia flew out of the room, her feet pounding the stairs. I pushed Rufus into Ben's arms and hung around the top of the landing.

'Long time, no see, Saskia,' I heard Leo say, warmth in his voice, sounding genuinely pleased to see her.

Nervous, I went downstairs and hovered on the bottom step as Leo was shaking Adam's hand in the lobby.

'Thank you very much, Mr Hall. You've been most helpful.'

'Anything else you need,' Adam said, earnest and servile, 'you know where to find me.'

It all seemed alarmingly convivial. Once again, I detected that Adam had smarmed his way out of a tricky situation. Leo would be thinking he was a stand-up regular guy and, in another life, a man to share a beer with in the local.

With lots to discuss, Adam and Saskia retreated to the kitchen.

Leo glanced over and smiled. Considering I'd taken a wrecking ball to his life I thought him remarkably magnanimous.

'Could I have a word, Leo?'

'Sure.' He indicated the snug with the palm of his hand. Hicks went to join us.

'Alone,' I said.

Leo twisted round. 'Wait in the car, Jared. I'll give you a shout when we're done.'

Leo followed me into the room, shutting the door behind him. The tension in the air fizzed. Without a word of a lie, I trembled not because of the blaze of Leo's smile or the proximity of standing near a man I'd lusted for and loved, but because of the stirred-up memories I'd spent the past eight years trying to bury deep. The question that haunted me most was why I, a capable, intelligent woman, could have been so deaf, so blind, so stubborn and so stupid. I still had no real answers.

'You're looking well, Sophie.' A warm smile tugged at the corner of his mouth.

I was looking fat and tired but let it go. A persuasive charmer, appealing to men and women, irrespective of age and status, Leo Carpenter had always displayed a lovely common touch.

'And your business is going great, I hear. Cake That,' he said, rolling the name on his tongue appreciatively. 'Terrific name. Always knew you'd succeed.'

'And you a DI now,' I said, my voice thick and sluggish.

The smile faded a little, sudden sadness in his eyes. 'I won't lie. It's taken a while.'

Because I'd so badly wounded him, privately and publicly. No doubt it was enough to severely dent any man's pride, even somebody as confident as Leo Carpenter. And I hadn't only left him; I'd abandoned the entire police family, many of whom had been our friends. I understood how much that hurt and I felt sorry on one level. On several others, I didn't feel sorry at all.

'After you left it was . . .' He paused, a shadow passing behind the back of his blue eyes. '. . . painfully difficult.'

And it should have been. If there was any upside, Leo seemed to have reformed. People did. *I did.*

'I'm sorry, Sophie. You didn't ask me in here to talk of old times. How can I help?'

'I don't want to know about the investigation.'

'That's a relief,' he said with a grin.

I smiled nervously back. 'I know very well you can't discuss it, but it strikes me that Brooke's parents wasted no time in contacting the police.'

'And your point?'

'They must have been worried about her for another reason.'

'She was classed as vulnerable.'

'That figures.'

'You knew?'

'Anyone could see — including Adam Hall.'

'What are you suggesting?'

'What type of man hooks up with a young woman like Brooke? It was quite clear she had mental health issues.'

Leo shrugged a shoulder, not wishing to be drawn.

'An exploitative person,' I declared. 'Did Adam reveal the row he had with Brooke before she left?'

Leo blinked. 'I'm not at liberty to say.'

'Five days ago, you say Brooke went missing.'

'Correct.'

'Day or night?'

'Early hours.'

'And you have no record of where she went.'

Leo blinked again.

'You do, but you're not saying.'

'Not at this point in time.'

'Did Adam deny meeting her?'

Leo's gaze sharpened. 'Are you alleging he did?'

'No, I'm telling you that, however charming and convincing you find Adam Hall, he's a liar and thief and someone who messes with people's lives and minds for the hell of it.'

'Those are pretty strong allegations.'

I blanched. Leo had spoken the same words years before. Then, it had been in an effort to refute and deflect the blame from him and other colleagues in a case that should have got the lot of them dismissed.

'I'm giving you a head's-up, Leo.'

'Thank you for your candour,' he said.

'Thank you for listening.'

'Could you ask Dr Taylor to come downstairs, please?'

'What?' I was stupefied.

'We'd like a word.'

'With Ben?'

'Please.'

'But . . .'

Leo's gaze hardened. 'If there's a problem, I could ask DC Hicks to fetch him.'

'No problem,' I stammered, dizzy with confusion. 'I'll get him now. Right away.'

I fled and found Ben on his knees, changing Rufus's nappy. He glanced up and saw the fear in my eyes. The relaxed expression on his face instantly froze. 'What's wrong?'

'The police,' I said. 'They want to talk to you.'

Me?

'Downstairs.'

'That's absurd,' Dad burst out.

'Whatever for?' Mum said.

I didn't know but had a rough idea and it scared the life out of me.

CHAPTER FORTY-NINE

Adam and Saskia joined my parents and aunt upstairs. Everyone clustered around them for the low-down. Not me. I loitered in the hall, waiting for Ben to emerge, which he did half an hour later, followed by Leo and Hicks. Leo nodded a curt goodbye to Ben and avoided my questioning gaze. Almost out of the door, Leo turned and said, 'Send my best to your parents, Sophie,' and that was it. The front door opened and closed, and they were gone.

'Let's get out of here.' Clipped, Ben's expression was tight.

'What happened in there?' I asked, aghast.

'Just get Rufus,' Ben said, fury in his eyes.

I fled upstairs, gathered up our baby and maddeningly woke Rufus in the process, then addressed my parents. 'We're off now,' I said. 'Ben's had a long day.'

Dismay darkened Mum's eyes to the colour of Dorset blue. 'But what did the police say?'

'Routine stuff, covering all the bases, you know.' I was wittering and she knew it. Studiously fixing my eyes on Mum and aware everyone else in the room was sifting through my every word, I blanked them out. 'I'll give you a call tomorrow.'

Dad got up, took my go-to bag and followed me downstairs to the front door. Ben was already in the car, engine running.

Dad gave me a clumsy hug on the threshold, not like him at all. Dad was a good hugger. 'Darling, will you be okay?'

'Fine, don't worry, honest. I'm sure Brooke will turn up and then we can all get back to normal.'

'Absolutely,' he said, with less conviction than I'd hoped.

I cut across to the car, put Rufus in the back and climbed in next to him. Ostensibly, it was to keep him amused. In reality, I needed the distance.

Dad opened the passenger door and put the bag inside. 'Everything all right, Ben?'

'Sure,' Ben said.

The briefest of silences followed before Dad decided to retreat. 'I'll let you go then,' he said, slamming the door shut.

Ben eased out of the drive and into Cheltenham traffic. He didn't speak and I didn't engage. Whatever had transpired needed to be discussed in a proper environment where I could see his face and listen to what he said. I hadn't forgotten his thunderous expression, one I'd never witnessed before.

It was after ten before Rufus was fed and settled. Neither of us was hungry. I thought Ben would be necking into the Japanese whisky Adam had brought. Instead, he'd made a good old-fashioned pot of tea — a crisis beverage befitting a crisis situation — and had taken it on a tray into the sitting room. We sat opposite each other.

'This is about the medication you prescribed, isn't it?'

Ben nodded slowly. 'Brooke told her parents that she'd seen a doctor — me.'

Shit. 'What exactly did Brooke tell them?'

He viewed me with haunted eyes. 'God knows. The truth is I shouldn't have done it, Sophie. You know it and I know it.' Shame glanced across his cheekbones and he looked down.

'You didn't prescribe anything lethal, did you?'

Ben's gaze snapped up. 'Of course not.'

'Sorry, but I had to ask.' I had to know. 'She didn't take anything from your bag, or anything like that, did she?' I was thinking of when she'd ransacked Ben's study. He would have said if any drugs had gone missing, wouldn't he?

Ben scratched the side of his head with one hand. 'I probably didn't take as much care with her medical history as I should have done.'

'That's not like you,' I murmured. I reached for the sugar bowl. Alarmingly, my hand trembled as I stirred a spoonful into my cup.

Ben agreed. 'Neither of us have been ourselves lately.'

'And Leo questioned you about it?'

Ben's eyes hardened. '*DI Carpenter* did.'

I shifted in my seat uncomfortably.

'According to what the parents told the police, Brooke had a long history of drug abuse.'

'Then how did she manage to enter the US?'

Ben's eyes widened. 'You're right. They're hot as hell on drug-taking. You only need to be pulled up for smoking weed during Freshers week to be turned down by Customs and Border Protection officers.'

My mind flipped back to a conversation with Adam. *We're not asking for speed or heroin.*

My gaze narrowed. 'Think she was lying?'

'You mean think *they* were lying?'

Suddenly, the picture looked quite different to the one with which we'd been presented. 'We both assumed that Adam and Brooke were telling the truth about their American adventures. What if it was fabrication?'

'We should have twigged something wasn't right when she turned my study upside down,' Ben said.

I didn't remind Ben that he hadn't taken me seriously enough at the time.

'I explained I'd acted under duress,' Ben continued, as if it were a mitigating factor, which it wasn't and certainly wouldn't cut it with Leo.

'I get you shouldn't have done it, Ben, but I don't entirely understand the police angle. How is your prescription a factor in Brooke going missing?'

'Depends on whether they find her alive, or dead.'

My nerve endings flared in panic. 'Oh my God, they seriously think she might have overdosed?'

'That's what I read into it.'

I shook my head vigorously. 'That's really jumping ahead. She'll probably pop up out of nowhere, hoping to make it up with Adam. You saw how crazy she was about him.'

'I never thought I'd say it, but I'd be overjoyed if she did. I'd bloody welcome her back with open arms.' Ben's expression was washed out.

I raised the cup to my lips, took a sip. He'd be on his own if that happened. But I got his point.

'What was it like seeing Leo after all this time?'

A perfectly reasonable question asked in a perfectly neutral tone, it did not temper my reaction. It had me wanting to reach for a large gin and tonic. 'Strange,' I answered.

'No regrets?' Ben sounded one thing and looked another, the keen light in his blue eyes transparent and needy.

'None,' I said truthfully. 'Like I told you, I wasn't cut out to be a police officer's wife.'

Ben held my gaze. Now he'd met Leo, I don't think he believed me. 'Did he give you a hard time?' I was concerned Leo might.

'No, he was professional and solicitous. Scribbled down a log number and contact details. I couldn't fault him in that regard.'

'And in what regard could you fault him?' I leant forward, all ears.

Ben hiked a shoulder. 'He was trying too hard.'

'To do what?'

'To like me, to be fair.'

I let out a breath.

'Unfortunate *him* running the investigation,' Ben said spitefully.

It wasn't just unfortunate; it was an extraordinary coincidence.

CHAPTER FIFTY

Liam, the site manager and lead carpenter, was a wiry man in his forties; his employees, Burt and Oscar, exceptionally strong-looking individuals, in their twenties. After inspecting the base and declaring it a fine piece of work, vans were divested of bricks, tools, a cement mixer and creature comforts, including a radio. After establishing which loo they could use, they set about erecting the dwarf wall, which would provide the foundation for the oak frame. To the sound of Bruno Mars, I took out my laptop and banged *Adam Hall musician* into Google. I found a trumpeter based in Perth, Australia, nothing relating to a British pianist. Next, I sped through newsfeeds searching for information on the missing Brooke Gentry. Deemed vulnerable by the police, she was bound to appear somewhere online. Trawling through the big news websites, I drew a digital blank.

I sat back. Was Brooke's disappearance another of her deceptions? Whatever she was up to it spelt trouble and I very much worried that Ben was about to become embroiled in it.

Disconnected and out of sorts, I fell back on tried and tested old ways to relieve my anxiety and decided to bake a roulade, something I hadn't done in years. In the middle of a hunt through the cupboard for finest quality dark chocolate, the phone rang. I hadn't called Mum so she called me.

The conversation was as stilted as the conversations I'd ever encountered during the misery months, eight years before. When she asked after Ben I told her he was unconcerned and fobbed her off with spiel I'd delivered the previous evening, throwing in 'background information' for good measure.

'I don't understand why the police want to speak to him,' she said.

I took a tremulous breath. Better come out with it now than later. 'He prescribed anti-anxiety pills for Brooke.'

'Well, that's all right then. Poor girl was obviously not quite right,' Mum said, failing to see a potential issue with it.

'Did Adam tell you what the police said?' I asked.

'Bits and pieces. Brooke had apparently been welcomed back and was in good spirits before she inexplicably disappeared. I think the parents were concerned she'd done something silly.'

I frowned. Ben maintained that individuals who topped themselves often seemed calm and together to the casual observer. Even close family and friends could be fooled. Refusing to be negative, I told myself *no body, no problem*. It brought me up short. I would never be thinking this way if it weren't for the Adam factor. It seemed that his manipulative presence and involvement in our lives had skewed and changed the way I thought about anything and everything.

'They spoke to Adam for *context*,' Mum continued.

'He actually said that?'

'He did. How long he'd known Brooke, how long they'd been together as a couple, where they'd travelled, when he last saw her, how she was, that type of thing.'

'And Adam came clean about their row before she left?'

Mum took her time answering. 'I've no reason to believe he wasn't truthful.'

I frowned again. 'Did Adam mention Brooke's history of drug abuse?'

'Abuse?' Mum was shocked.

'According to the police, she's a long-term user.'

'Good grief. I'd no idea.'

'And neither did Ben.'

'Oh, I see,' Mum said, catching on. She wouldn't only be concerned about the implications for Ben. She'd be worrying about Saskia and the man she'd suddenly taken up with. Wouldn't be the first time. Poor Mum was thinking that Adam had been aware of his previous girlfriend's addiction and had possibly condoned it. Perhaps Adam's shiny and glamorous image was about to receive a big dent. *Hurrah*.

'Brooke must have lied to Adam, too,' Mum said conclusively.

I shut my jaw tight and shivered with frustration. How was it that Adam Hall managed to hoodwink everyone, including my incredibly discerning mother?

'Sophie, darling?'

'Yes?'

Mum cleared her throat. 'It must have been awkward for you with Leo, awkward for Ben, too.'

Excruciating would have been a better description. 'It was perfectly civil,' I said, a little too briskly. 'We've each moved on. Sorry, Mum, but I must go. Rufus has woken up.' He hadn't but I was keen to wrap up the call. We said goodbye and Mum's final remark was to tell me that Auntie Fen sent her love. Poor woman must be wondering what she'd wandered into. The flat sale suddenly seemed inconsequential.

Desperate to mentally escape, I whisked egg whites, melted plain and continental dark chocolate and lined a greaseproof tin with silicone paper. Activity didn't make a bit of difference. My thoughts refused to shut up. Should I phone Leo? I'd blocked his number years ago and he'd probably changed his phone in any case, but Ben had left Leo's scribbled contact details upstairs. Was there something I could say that would take the heat out of the situation and exonerate Ben? Would Leo believe me if I told him that Ben had only acted out of compassion? Or would my call be viewed as interference? Would it draw attention and make it worse? How many times had I heard those words spill from Leo's lips? *Don't say anything. It will sort itself out. Never come between a husband and wife.* No, I told myself firmly, this was different, but maybe it was better to delay.

The thing about roulades is that they take around fifteen minutes to cook and need several hours to cool right down, overnight if possible. With more thinking time to burn, I began to knock up a Mississippi mud pie. First, I made the dough which I wrapped in cling film and popped into the fridge. About to make the filling, the doorbell rang. I discounted it being the obvious candidate, Mum, because we'd already spoken. It could be Saskia, but Sash would be at work. My next, more ominous, thought: Leo, in which case I should probably answer. More ominous still: Adam. Sneaking into the study, I peeped out behind the curtain. I was surprised to see Saskia on the doorstep. Very importantly, she was alone.

Speeding into the hall, I swept open the door and enveloped her in an enormous hug.

'I'd ask for booze,' she said, squeezing me back, 'but as I'm driving, best not.'

'Come on through,' I said, dragging her inside.

'Blimey,' she said, eyeing the culinary mess. 'Throwing a party?'

'Thought I'd keep my hand in.'

'And your legs and feet by the look of it. How is Ben?'

I told her what I'd told Mum. Saskia got it straightaway. 'Holy crap, the police can't think that Ben loaded Brooke up with drugs, can they?'

I shrugged, dismissive.

'To be honest, Sophie, I don't think Brooke's gone walkabout. I think it's all a big thing designed to get attention.'

While I thought Saskia had a point, the words ripped into me. *Attention-seeking* only ever seemed to be applied to women. Sometimes they had every right to. A line from a poem coursed through my mind: *Not waving but drowning.*

Never one to shy away from difficult subjects, Saskia said, 'Must have felt crazy seeing Leo after all this time.'

I agreed. 'Park yourself while I check on Rufus.'

Adorably, he was awake; little arms up, trying to take a swipe at his mobile. He turned his head at my approach and gave me a massive grin. I picked him up, dropped a soft kiss on his cheek and told him he was going to see his auntie Saskia.

'Swear to God he's grown overnight,' Saskia said.

'Want to hold him?'

'Doesn't he need you?'

'He'll be okay while I make us a drink.'

While Saskia chatted amiably to Rufus, I made a cafetière of coffee. 'I've left Vanessa in charge, by the way,' Saskia informed me.

'Work is rather off my radar.' I poured out for both of us and relieved her of Rufus to feed him. 'I don't need to be an Einstein to work out the reason for the visit.'

Saskia shook her head, suddenly sad.

'It's Adam, isn't it?'

'No,' Saskia said, incredulous. 'It's Mum.'

CHAPTER FIFTY-ONE

I instinctively shrank inside. Chill swept over me. 'Mum?'

Saskia opened her mouth, closed it and fluttered her fingers, as if trying to net words she couldn't say. I reached across, caught her hand in mine. She viewed me with scared eyes. 'You were right, Sophie,' she blurted out. 'She's ill.'

'What sort of ill?' I knew but needed to hear it in black and white.

'The sort where you go through a battery of tests.'

I tried to take easy breaths in through my nose, out through my mouth. 'How long have you known?'

'Adam overheard a conversation with Auntie Fen a few days ago.'

'Adam?' I exclaimed.

'Don't be like that, Sophie.'

'Like what? What the hell was he doing earwigging?' If Saskia had overheard, I'd be all right with that. Adam was the last person I wanted to hear something so personal and private. Somehow, it made awful news that much worse.

'Can we stay on point?' Saskia said, uncharacteristically snippy.

'Yes, of course,' I said, chastened. 'Sorry.' I took a moment to swallow down the pain and shock. 'Does Dad know?' I saw now how a diet was Mum's ruse. Either that, or Dad was trying to knock me off the scent.

'Hasn't a clue.'

'You're certain?'

'Sophie, you know he's a terrible liar.'

Unlike Ben, I realised. His private conversations with my mother suddenly made sense. He knew and hadn't told me. While I could get my head around the need for sensitivity and discretion — almost — I didn't think it should exclude my mum's own flesh and blood. It wasn't as if my mother was Ben's patient with all the associated issues of breaches in patient confidentiality. It rattled me that, when I'd mentioned her weight loss, Ben had gone along with my theory, never once pointing out that it might be something more serious. My eyes filmed with hot tears.

'So typical of Mum to try to protect him, to protect all of us,' Saskia murmured. She picked up her coffee and put it back down again, untouched. 'What are we going to do, Sophie?'

Everything was a mess. It could only be resolved in bite-sized pieces.

'I'll talk to Ben.'

'Think he knows?'

'It's more than possible.'

'You'll tell me what he says.'

I agreed I would. 'Handling Mum will be more tricky.'

'You have to convince her to share whatever it is with Dad.'

'It might not be as serious as we imagine,' I said.

Saskia swallowed and ran a manicured nail round the rim of her cup. 'You're going to drop Adam in it, aren't you?'

I raised my eyebrows and gave her a square sisterly look over the rim of my cup.

'Please, Sophie.'

'I won't mention Adam, though Lord knows why you're so into him.'

'Because I'm a sucker for cool sexy guys.' She flicked a smile I did not return.

'I'm serious, Sash. Cool or not, don't let that man distort your judgement.' Too late, I thought; he already had.

She briefly held my gaze, a searching expression in her eyes. 'I'd best be getting back,' she said, downing her drink, spilling some on the worktop. 'Damn,' she said, swiping a cloth from the sink and mopping it up.

After she left, I wondered what else she'd meant to say.

CHAPTER FIFTY-TWO

Courtesy of Google, I stressed about what type of illness my mother had and then, sincerely, wished I hadn't. There were so many vile variations on how people's bodies can let them down. Like it or not, I could do nothing for my mum until I'd talked to Ben.

Baking provided temporary solace. Once again, I toyed with calling Leo. How Brooke had managed to travel to the States remained a mystery.

Unless it was a lie.

And if it was a lie, it meant it was another one of Adam's.

Spurred on, I retrieved Leo's contact details and phoned. After a series of digital bleeps and transfers, I eventually got through. Sounding initially surprised, Leo quickly recovered. 'Sophie, what can I do for you?'

'I have information which may, or may not, have a bearing on Brooke Gentry's disappearance.'

'I'm listening.'

I told him about the anomaly concerning Brooke's alleged trip to the States. I'd hoped he'd react strongly. He didn't. *Because it's already been established*, I thought. And that paints Adam as the liar he is.

'It's possible to have a history of drug-taking without ever coming into contact with the police, Sophie.'

'You mean she never got caught?'

'She never came under our radar.'

And that blew a hole in my theory. 'I know you think I have it in for Adam Hall,' I continued bullishly, 'but he's not a good person and it's not right that Ben is in the firing line for a perfectly innocent mistake.' I bit my lip. I was doing well to get my view across in a rational and reasonable manner and now I sounded like Ben's mother.

'I understand where you're coming from, but you'll appreciate I have to follow all lines of investigation.'

Pushing it, I asked, 'Don't suppose you have a lead on Brooke? There must be some evidence regarding her whereabouts.'

A stranger would never have spotted the fractional hesitation. I'd learnt the hard way to distinguish between a natural dip in conversation, a dramatic pause and a gap in which thoughts and words were dissembled.

'You know I can't discuss it.'

Precisely the answer I expected. 'Daft question,' I said.

'Worth a try.' Making light of it to make me feel better, I surmised. 'You okay, Sophie?'

The warmth in his voice made me unsteady. 'I'm good,' I said curtly.

'You were always strong.'

Not strong enough.

Silence lingered. I had an uncontrollable impulse to fill it. Desperate for an answer, if I didn't ask the question quickly, I knew I never would.

'Do you ever think of Caron, Leo?' Instantly, I recalled an astonishingly pretty woman, with pale green eyes, a mop of blonde hair, slim yet shapely, with a tendency to get wasted — and no wonder. It struck me then that I hadn't phoned to talk about Ben or even Adam.

Leo let out a long painful sigh. 'Every day.'

'We let her down.'

'There is no *we*. *I* screwed up. *Others* screwed up. An entire department screwed up. An appallingly mishandled situation, *you* did nothing wrong.'

'I didn't listen. I didn't believe her. I didn't trust her. I could have saved her.' My voice cracked.

'No, you couldn't. Lester was a clever, conniving charmer who fooled the lot of us. We believed he was a decent copper.'

A sob caught in my throat. 'Until he killed her. She had two kids, Leo.' I reached for a tissue to catch a tear coursing down my cheek. Too late, it dropped onto Rufus's Babygro.

'Sophie, Sophie, we did all our talking years ago.'

Did we? I didn't recall. There were a ton of angry words. Mostly mine.

'Why the hell are you still beating yourself up?' Leo sounded exasperated.

Because Caron had come to me as a last resort, believing that I, of all people, as she'd said, was someone she could trust. My problem was that I hadn't trusted her. She was flaky. She'd agree to meet and then wouldn't show. When she did, she was often drunk and an angry drunk at that. There were never any marks on her face. Bruising on her body could as easily have been the result of a fall or from bouncing off a wall, which I'd seen her do. I'd believed the clamour of competing voices, Lester's included: *attention-seeking; drama queen; an exaggerator; I love her so why would I hurt her?*

'You have a new life now,' Leo said, smashing through bad memories, 'a baby, Ben, a loving family. You have to move on.'

I didn't think I ever could. Guilt is as corrosive on the mind as sulphuric acid on skin. 'Have you?'

'I don't know how to answer that.'

Please try, I thought, please let me into the secret of how you live a life that is full, how you survive.

Leo took a moment. 'Things have changed.'

'What things?'

'The culture in the police, the way we deal with domestic violence. Our entire approach and mindset has had a complete

229

recalibration — and thank God for that. You may not believe me, but I've changed, too, in every way imaginable. The way I think, how I react. I'm a different person now. Not that this excuses my failures with Caron. But, for God's sake, Sophie, my part and yours, if you must insist on it, was small by comparison to others who failed her.'

Deep down, I knew Leo was right and yet something in my make-up wouldn't allow me to shake it off. Maybe I was the one with the Messiah complex.

'How do you cope with the shame?' I asked him.

He took his time answering. 'I embrace it.'

'Embrace?'

'It's good, makes me a better person.'

No longer the brash young man I used to know, I was glad for him.

'You take care, Sophie.'

'You, too, Leo.'

'One other thing.' Leo altered the note in his voice, embarrassed I believed, that he'd strayed from the professional to the personal.

'Yes?'

'Probably best, in the circumstances, you address any other concerns regarding Brooke Gentry to DC Hicks.'

'I understand,' I said, finishing the call.

In a reflective mood, I stared out of the window and looked beyond the earthworks at a neat line of trees behind. Leo was right to draw a big red line between us, yet I was surprised how much it stung. I should have been the one setting boundaries, not him. Worn down and worn out with thinking, I longed for Ben to come home.

After clearing up the culinary debris, I played with Rufus and gave him a bath, cuddled and fed him, then prepared dinner. At the sound of a car entering the drive, I slipped out into the hall, eager to greet Ben and talk to him about Mum.

Opening the door, I found Adam on the doorstep with an elastic smile that could stretch across the Atlantic. *Shit.*

'I'm busy,' I said, not allowing him a single step over the threshold.

'I imagine you are. This won't take long.'

I crossed my arms.

'Are you going to invite me in?'

'No.'

'That's not very friendly.'

'I'm no friend of yours. I dislike people who listen in on private conversations.'

The corner of his mouth squirmed into a smile. It did not disguise the cold as stone expression in his eyes. 'Ever heard the phrase, don't shoot the messenger?'

'What do you want, Adam?'

'Ben not home yet?' He glanced over my shoulder as if his brother might pop out of the panelling.

'No.'

'You might want to check out where he is and who he's with.'

'Another of your tall tales?'

'Only looking out for you, Sophie. I'd hate to see you getting hurt.'

I rippled with misgiving. Somehow, I kept my face a mask of unconcern. Inside I sparked with heat and anxiety. 'I don't need your brand of help.'

'You will, you'll see.'

'Sounds like a threat.'

'Nothing could be further from my mind,' he said, dismissive. 'I understand you're upset. This Brooke business has got to us all.'

He paused, leaving me room to agree or disagree. I did neither. 'In a spirit of honesty, I thought you should know that, while it was my duty to mention Ben's prescription to your old squeeze, I knew nothing of any illegal drug-taking. Brooke was clean, as far as I was concerned.'

'That it?'

I was about to close the door on him when Adam shot a booted foot out. 'Not quite.' He tweaked another smile. 'It wouldn't be the first time Ben has dished out drugs.'

'Liar,' I said.

'Not that I let on.'

'Fuck off, Adam.' To make my point, I crushed the edge of the door as hard as I could against his instep. He didn't flinch.

Eyes sparkling with malice, he said, 'How much do you really know about the father of your child?'

My arm went slack. With the pressure off, Adam finally moved his foot, crunched back across the gravel and climbed into my dad's Triumph Stag. Crashing out of the drive, he sped away.

CHAPTER FIFTY-THREE

By the time Ben eventually walked in shortly before nine, I was hitting a ten on the emotional Richter scale and ready to flip.

'Don't insult my intelligence by telling me you got delayed at work,' I exploded.

'Can I get my jacket off before you launch in?' Ben said, darkly defensive.

I waited and watched and trailed him from the kitchen into the sitting room. 'I've had a horrible day,' I raged, conscious I sounded borderline pathetic.

Ben ran a hand underneath his jaw. 'Is Rufus okay?'

'Rufus is just fine,' I snapped. 'First, Saskia tells me that Mum's seriously ill . . .'

'Who told her that?'

'Your brother.'

'How did he arrive at that conclusion?'

'Are you saying it isn't true?'

'I'm saying this is the first I've heard of it.'

I studied Ben for signs of deception, all those non-verbal signals and tics. He stood ruler straight and stared back. I felt as if I were mentally slipping and losing my ability to distinguish between truth and lies. 'What about all those quiet conversations you've been having with Mum?'

'Quiet? Uh . . . *screw it* . . . your birthday. You were so under the weather last year your mother wanted to plan something special this year.'

It was true. I'd been super rough for the entire pregnancy and then contracted influenza. With everything going on, I'd barely given a thought to my birthday in a couple of weeks' time.

'Now I feel as if I've ruined it,' Ben said, irritated.

'I'll act surprised, promise.'

More relaxed, Ben reached for the decanter of whisky we kept on the sideboard.

'Aren't you hungry?' I asked.

'I ate a sandwich on the way home.' He poured himself a healthy slug of booze and retreated to the sofa. 'What gave Adam the impression your mum was ill?'

'An overheard conversation between Mum and Auntie Fen.'

'And Saskia believed him?'

'Why wouldn't she? And if it isn't true, why would Adam say such a thing?'

Ben elevated an eyebrow. 'You really want me to spell it out?'

I was starting to feel incredibly stupid. Adam's whole purpose in life was to keep everyone off balance. Well, he'd certainly achieved his goal. 'It's so pointlessly nasty.'

'Which is how he rolls.' Ben clicked his tongue. 'I can't believe neither of you spoke to your mother first.'

It felt like criticism. But I was too relieved to complain plus I had another reason to speak to Ben. 'Adam came to the cottage this afternoon.'

Ben took a deep swallow of whisky, the bridge of his nose twitching with the first flush of neat spirit. 'What did he want?'

'To make serious allegations about you.'

'What sort of allegations?'

'About who you were with this evening.'

Ben's mouth dropped open. 'I haven't been with anyone.'

234

'Then why are you late home?'

'I went for a walk.'

'For hours?'

'I needed to think.'

I slumped down next to him. Unsurprisingly, he had a lot on his mind. We all did. 'More seriously, Adam claimed it wasn't the first time you'd handed out drugs illicitly.'

'Ben Taylor, the doctor turned drug dealer. Adam's been reading too many lurid stories in the press.' The facetious smile on Ben's face was alarmingly hard and cold.

'It's not funny, Ben. It's serious.'

'God's sake, of course it's bloody serious. How do you think it makes me feel when he's shooting his mouth off like that?'

'It isn't true then.'

Ben twisted round, pale with sudden anger. 'You believed him?'

I recoiled. 'No, of course not.'

'You did,' he said. 'I can see it in your eyes.'

The truth was I didn't know who to believe anymore.

CHAPTER FIFTY-FOUR

After a strained night in which we quarrelled royally, the carpenters arrived in full force around eight, shortly before Ben left for work the next morning. I watched as Liam and his men effortlessly unloaded great beams of wood and set up an awning so that they could continue to work even if it poured with rain. Ben chatted, all smooth and glad-handing, sharing a joke with Liam. I asked myself, How can you detach yourself and behave as if you didn't have a care in the world after what we've been through?

Depositing a cool kiss on my cheek, Ben told me he'd try to get back early. I swallowed down the 'don't bother' on the tip of my tongue, offered a smile and made all the right noises.

Finding a quiet spot in Ben's study, I phoned Saskia at work. I prayed Adam wasn't with her — probably too early.

'Sophie.' She sounded edgy, as if I were the last person she wanted to speak to.

I got straight to the point. 'Ben has no knowledge of Mum being sick and trust me, he would if it were true.' More charitably than he deserved, I suggested that Adam had picked up the fag end of a conversation and drawn the wrong conclusion. 'That's what happens when you eavesdrop,' I said, with biting precision.

I expected a spirited defence and interruption. Nothing of the sort.

'You've gone quiet,' I said.

'I'm relieved.'

'Any news from the police?' I asked tentatively. Saskia, of all people, would know.

'Nothing.'

'How are things at home?'

'Tense. You?'

'Same.'

Fearing another development that I couldn't handle, I ended the call and soothed myself by pouring vats of tea and coffee down the throats of our workers and feeding them trays of home-made biscuits and cakes.

Stilted evenings, patchy days in which Rufus provided the only joyful highlight, it seemed to take an age for Saturday to come around. Pragmatically, Ben and I pre-agreed that, rather than trying to hush it up, we'd come clean with our friends about Brooke's disappearance. 'Let's get it out of the way first,' Ben said.

The Bell at Sapperton is a proper 'dogs and kids welcome' pub. It's the kind of place where in the summer men in striped sweatshirts, collars up, and foreign-holiday tans, congregate with their wives and families. Inside, it's low ceilings and bare stone, log burners and quarry tiles.

We strolled down steps along a lavender-flanked path to the main entrance. Turning left towards the dining rooms, we were accompanied by an old-school playlist that included 'I'm a Believer' by The Monkees, a pop band popular in the dinosaur years, with a fan club, of which hilariously, according to Mum, she'd once been a fully signed-up member.

Louise and Elliott were already seated and studying menus. Elliott looked to be a third of the way down his first pint. He was a lean, bespectacled man with messy brown hair, a stoop and shy smile that concealed a fierce intellect. In his tweed jacket and corduroys the colour of old mustard, he resembled a geography teacher. Louise, I noticed, drank orange juice, not her usual alcoholic tipple of dry white wine. As we clattered in with baby paraphernalia, they stood; Ben greeted Elliott, and I gave Louise a clumsy hug, nearly crushing Rufus in the process. When I asked how she was she gave a warm smile and said, 'All good. Fingers crossed.'

After drinks were ordered — G&T for me — just the one due to me breastfeeding — and a pint of Budding Premium Pale Ale from a brewery in Stroud for Ben — and before we all got chatting, Ben revealed the latest with his brother, including Brooke's disappearance.

Elliott is a man accustomed to managing clients' expectations at a torrid time in their lives. Immensely calm, little fazes him. Same went for Louise. Now they were fazed all right.

'Good God,' Elliott burst out. 'Do they think something horrible has happened to her?'

'I suppose it's a possibility,' Ben answered.

I swallowed hard. Why would he say that? Louise seemed equally dismayed. Turning her full attention to Ben, she said, 'And the police questioned you, you say?'

I nudged Ben under the table. They didn't need to know about the prescription fiasco. 'Simply to get a handle on her state of mind, from a medical standpoint, that type of thing,' he replied smoothly.

'Makes sense,' Elliott concurred.

'Slightly awkward,' Ben continued. 'Sophie's ex is running the investigation.'

This we had not agreed to reveal. I flushed as Louise and Elliott's gaze swivelled to me. 'The guy you stood up at the altar?' Louise was incredulous.

'Leo Carpenter,' Ben confirmed, eliciting a sharp smack from my boot against his ankle.

Louise raised her eyes to me for confirmation. 'True,' I said. Horribly so.

When Ben also revealed that Saskia had taken up with Adam, Elliott stared goggle-eyed. 'Beggars belief,' he said, suggesting that this was not the first time he'd heard about Adam's reputation. I wondered if Ben had already spoken to him about his brother until I remembered that I'd told Louise about Adam, and she had probably discussed him with Elliott.

Our drinks arrived. I fell upon mine and took a long solid swallow of gin and tonic. Appetite squashed, I ordered a starter as a main and signalled to Louise that I was going to the loo. Passing Rufus to Ben, I shot off with Louise falling in behind. Fortunately, we were alone.

'Is there anything we can do?' Louise said, sympathetic.

'Other than find Brooke safe and sound, no.'

'God, Sophie. You look absolutely shattered if you don't mind me saying.'

I shrugged and caught sight of myself in the mirror. Grey-skinned and gaunt, I had a vision of me in thirty years' time. 'Ben's brother is doing my head in. Things really don't seem to have been the same since Adam crashed back into Ben's life.' I gave Louise edited highlights. With each revelation, she looked more shocked.

'The other night I caught him alone in the dark, staring at Rufus in his cot.'

Louise paled. 'I don't like the sound of that.'

'In all the commotion I haven't even told Ben.' Brittle, I gave a giddy laugh.

'But you guys are all right, aren't you?' Worry lines appeared on Louise's brow.

'I don't know.' My voice was small.

Louise put her arm around me. 'This isn't connected to Leo, is it?'

'Course not.'

'You're sure?'

'Don't look at me like that,' I protested.

'Sweetheart, it was bound to be difficult seeing him again after all this time. Nobody would blame you for feeling confused.'

'I'm not confused,' I said, stifling a massive desire to weep.

'Poor you,' she said softly, giving me a squeeze. 'Come on, let's go and kick back for a few hours, let the world take a couple of turns.'

And I would have done had it not been for the sound of heated voices coming from the bar.

CHAPTER FIFTY-FIVE

'Take it outside, you two.'

I never thought I'd hear those words from mild-man-nered Elliott. Somehow, he'd got between Ben and Adam and was struggling to keep them apart. In panic, I swivelled round and saw a woman on a nearby table holding Rufus with a startled expression on her face.

'He's mine,' I said, reaching out, and muttering my thanks while Louise tried to intervene between Ben and Adam.

'Stay back, madam.' A tall man in a white shirt and dark tailored trousers gently nudged her out of the way. Grabbing first Ben and then Adam deftly by the collar, he propelled them, one in each hand, to the door where he pushed them outside.

'Christ,' Elliott cursed, searching for his spectacles which had become dislodged in the scuffle. 'That man is seriously kinked.'

'Here,' Louise said, pushing them gently back onto his face.

'This is what Adam does,' I said.

'Sophie, it was Ben who kicked off,' Elliott exclaimed. 'I don't know what got into him. Soon as his brother blasted inside, he was up out of his seat and laying in.'

I couldn't believe it. Ben wasn't a violent man.

'Where's Saskia?' Louise asked.

Elliott shook his head. 'She wasn't with Adam. I suppose she might be in the car park.'

'I'll go and check.'

Louise shot me a stern look. 'Not with Rufus, Sophie.'

I handed him over, thinking this was no way to bring up a baby, and ran outside, past the seating area and up a short drive into the car park where Ben and Adam were now slugging it out.

'Murderous bastard,' Adam screamed. 'Call yourself a doctor? You're a killer!'

I stood frozen, Adam's words running me through as surely as if it had been a seven-inch kitchen knife.

Catching sight of me, Ben wheeled round. Wild-eyed, blood trickled from a cut lip down his chin and there was a livid mark under his right eye. Adam dropped his fists, panting.

Three things happened in quick succession: Adam fled to Dad's Stag, started the engine and tore out of the car park; Louise came up behind me, clutching a bawling Rufus; Elliott, somehow, manhandled Ben to his old Morgan where he pushed him into the passenger seat.

'Come on,' Louise hollered over Rufus's cries, 'we've settled the drinks bill and cancelled the booking. Let's sit quietly while Elliott talks to Ben.'

Dazed, I took Rufus and, stiff-limbed, stumbled to Ben's car. Sitting in the rear while Louise climbed into the front passenger seat, I wondered if anyone had heard what I'd heard. Hurled in anger, or did Adam know something I didn't? *Only looking out for you, Sophie. I'd hate to see you getting hurt.* I swallowed the hard pebble of fear that lodged in the back of my throat and rocked Rufus until he quietened down.

Louise twisted round to face me. 'You can't go on like this, Sophie.'

Too shocked to cry, I nodded blindly.

'Tell me to mind my own business,' Louise said, 'but what's the elephant in the room with the brothers?'

More like a mammoth. 'I don't know.'

'Their parents passed in quick succession. Cancer and road accident, wasn't it?'

'You've got a good memory.'

'Only for dark details.' Louise briefly smiled, trying to cheer me. Didn't work. 'Were Ben and Adam ever close?'

'I believe they each retreated into their own worlds after their parents died.'

'That's not healthy. Retreat can become a dangerous breeding ground for resentment.'

'Do you think?' I wanted to grasp at anything that made logical sense, anything that pushed Adam's wilder claims out of the picture. But what if Adam wasn't lying? What if he was telling the truth? What if I was allowing my judgement to be clouded because it suited me? Fallible, it wouldn't be the first time I'd made the wrong call.

Louise shifted in her seat. I followed her gaze through the window. Elliott and Ben were crossing the car park. Elliott's serious expression suddenly brightened at seeing his wife. They would make good parents, I thought. Better than us.

Louise pushed open the passenger door, letting a flood of cold, wet air in. She muttered something to Ben I couldn't catch before he scooted round to the driver's side.

Needing distance and space, in no mood for rushed apologies and broken promises, I stayed where I was and strapped Rufus into his car seat beside me. Ben glanced in the rear-view mirror and, catching my numb expression, without a word started the car and drove us slowly home.

CHAPTER FIFTY-SIX

Ben was contrite. I was unforgiving. My concern for his injuries, self-inflicted in my opinion, was grudging. *You're a doctor so you fix them.*

He disappeared to the bathroom for an unfeasibly long time. I practically pounced on him the moment he sloped into the sitting room and sat down.

'I heard what Adam said, Ben.'

'Angry words designed to get a rise out of me.'

'It was more than that and you know it.'

Closed down and with little expression, he wouldn't meet my eye. Chill assailed me.

'He called you a murderer, Ben. What's that all about?'

'Why don't you ask him?'

'Because I'm asking you.'

'How should I know what trips through his ugly mind?' He shifted position, crossed and uncrossed his legs. Some might say *squirmed.*

'You're his brother so you'd have a better handle than most,' I fired back. 'The night you had a blazing row.'

'There were so many. Which night would that be?'

I didn't think he was being cute with me but couldn't swear to it. 'The one when he ranted about assisted dying.'

Ben stretched his arms above his head, feigning unconcern. His right leg was the giveaway; it juddered.

'This is about your father and his terminal illness, isn't it?'

'In Adam's head, perhaps.' Ben's eyes flared with sudden realisation. 'Oh. My. God. You think because I'm a doctor, I had something to do with my father's death.'

Shame ballooned inside me. I couldn't hide the fact that the hideous thought had crossed my mind. Colour flushed my neck and spread to my cheeks. It would be pointless to lie.

'Might I damn well remind you, I was a young medical student at the time, living miles away?' Ben said.

'I hadn't forgotten.' But I wasn't there and didn't know what had happened. So much of what I knew was taken on trust.

Ben's expression darkened; his voice rose. 'How could you think that of me? How could you accept the word of a liar over mine?'

'I'm not. I'm simply trying to understand.'

'This is bollocks,' Ben burst out. 'Everyone knew I loved and respected my dad more than anyone else in the world. Adam knew it too.'

'Then why is he making such terrible allegations?'

'Because he enjoys it.'

A narrative I couldn't challenge, I busied myself with Rufus. Ben retreated to his study 'to catch up on admin'. Saskia messaged a WTF about the fight and I messaged back, relaying a similar level of surprise and irritation without the rude reference. Ben and I slept in separate rooms, the first time we'd ever been away from each other apart from my one-night stay in hospital after giving birth. Disturbingly, I didn't recognise the father of my child, the man I believed I'd spend the rest of my life with. Déjà vu assailed me. I'd harboured the same thoughts about Leo once upon a time. Different circumstances, I told myself firmly; potentially similar outcome, a nasty little voice in my head reminded me. Exhausted, overtired and overwrought, I didn't sleep. Rufus was equally unsettled. I think I finally drifted off some time after five.

At first, I thought the loud clamour of noise at the front door was in a dream. Ben's bare feet thudding down the other staircase persuaded me that we had company. Fearing an action replay, I squinted at the bedside clock. Seven in the morning; Adam never surfaced before noon.

I dragged myself out of bed and, padding across the carpet to the window, peered blearily through the glass onto the drive and let out an involuntary gasp. First, I saw an unmarked BMW. Next, Leo and Hicks standing outside our front door. A visit this early on a Sunday morning could only spell trouble — Adam-sized trouble. The bastard must have reported the fight with the intention of pressing charges against Ben.

Wrapping a robe around me, I sped, barefoot, downstairs as Ben and Hicks disappeared into the study. Seeing me, Leo hung back.

'What's this all about?' I asked, although I had a pretty good idea.

'We've found Brooke Gentry's body.'

Speechless, I felt as if I'd been smacked across the back of my neck with the edge of a spade. A silent soundtrack in my mind asked, *Why are you talking to Ben, Leo?*

Finally getting it together, I stammered, 'My God, her poor parents, her brothers and sisters.'

'An appalling tragedy for them,' Leo solemnly agreed.

And for Adam. My parents and Saskia would be devastated too.

'You've spoken to Adam Hall?'

'He has been informed.'

I had a vivid picture of Adam wailing and beating his bared chest. 'Can I ask how Brooke died?'

'Drowned in Barking creek. It's a waterway near where she was last seen. We're treating it as suicide.'

I literally felt the colour drain from my face. We'd all been worried about her, and we'd all ignored the signs. But, if the police were treating it as suicide, it was an open and shut case. 'Then what are you doing here?'

Leo's eyes never shifted from mine. 'Toxicology reports showed a significant amount of opiates in her system.'

'Jesus, Leo, you can't think Ben had anything to do with her death?'

'It's why we need to speak to him.' Sympathetic, he reached towards me and touched my arm. I felt as if I'd strayed into an electric fence. 'I know this is difficult for you.'

No, no, no. This was agonising.

'Hold on,' I said, 'when was Brooke found?'

'Her body was retrieved a few days ago. Her family were informed and there were issues with identification.' Leo viewed me quizzically. 'Do you know how Ben got those injuries to his face?'

'He got into a fight with his brother yesterday,' I replied, horrified by the way in which Leo's mind was tilting.

'Adam Hall?'

'Yes.'

'Must have been heated. What was it about?'

Murder and killing. I shook my head as much to try to shake some sense into my confounded brain. 'I've no idea. I didn't witness what sparked it.'

'Fair enough.' Leo shrugged, seeming to accept my account.

'So it's just a chat with Ben?' I said, hopeful.

'We'll be taking a statement from him.'

Routine. Standard procedure. To be expected. I should be grateful that it was being conducted at home and not at a police station or, God forbid, work. It didn't preclude the possibility that a statement could be used as evidence in court. If that came out what would happen to Ben, his reputation, his career, more selfishly, our life?

As if reading my mind, Leo said, 'We're not arresting, or cautioning him, Sophie.'

'I should think not.' The words felt thick and tangled in my mouth.

Leo smiled, as if to say he'd heard a similar defence from any number of mothers, wives and girlfriends.

'How long will you be?' I asked.

'As long as it takes. Why don't you make yourself a cuppa?'

Nerves as taut as piano wire, I anxiously watched Leo head into the study. My heart gave an involuntary thud as the door closed. Standing there, dismayed and unsure, I returned upstairs to retrieve my son. Before I'd reached the landing, my phone rang and didn't stop. First, Mum: to break news that had already been broken; then Saskia, acting on information from Mum, demanding to know what the police were doing at our home, to which I dribbled on about standard procedure; next, bewilderingly, Meadow, Saskia's fair-weather mate who took a ghoulish interest in the misfortunes of others; finally Dad.

'Sophie, my darling, Mum and Saskia say the police are with you.'

Clearly, my sister wasn't buying the standard procedure line. 'That's right.'

'Is there a problem?'

Dozens. I told Dad about the 'silly slip-up' with the prescription Ben gave to Brooke.

'Mum said. And he didn't prescribe anything else?'

Weeks ago, I would have squashed the idea flat. Weeks ago, I thought our money was safe. Weeks ago, I would never have believed that Ben would throw a punch. 'Dad, I don't know.' I waited for him to remind me of the stupidity of moving in with Ben so fast. My lovely dad didn't utter a single critical word.

'Call me when you know,' he said, ending the call.

Holding Rufus close, I whispered in his ear, 'What do we do?'

I didn't make a cup of tea. I dressed and packed a bag.

CHAPTER FIFTY-SEVEN

I couldn't read the metaphorical writing on the wall because it was plastered in graffiti. Leo and Hicks had gone, leaving behind a trail of misery.

I'd learnt a thing or three when I'd lived with Leo. Interviews generally started wide and casual to put a witness or suspect at ease before zeroing in on the nitty-gritty. As predicted and according to Ben, he was told that oxycodone, a major opiate for pain, and phenobarbital, had been found in Brooke's blood stream, both drugs subject to special prescription requirements. If Ben hadn't willingly written an illicit prescription for anti-depressants, he would have been off the hook, the assumption that Brooke had obtained the stronger drugs from a dealer. As things stood, suspicion remained.

'Did they allege you'd supplied them?' I asked.

'Which I categorically denied.'

'And?'

'They said I was in the "drugs business".'

'That's crap.'

Ben shook his head in frustration. 'I even pointed out that the specific antidepressant I'd prescribed to Brooke was associated with a substantial *decrease* in suicide risk. I also flagged that it would be impossible to overdose on it.'

'What did they say to that?'

'They're so bloody tin-eared,' Ben complained grimly, 'they told me I had unique access to the type of drugs that killed her. Under pressure, I'd displayed a willingness to break rules, apparently. Wanting Brooke and Adam gone from our home, I had motivation.'

My eyebrows shot up at that one.

'Male GPs are more inclined to prescribe for friends and family members than female GPs,' Ben recited gloomily.

'But they weren't talking about prescriptions, were they?'

Ben shook his head.

'Who actually said this?'

'Carpenter's sidekick. Carpenter barely uttered a word.'

I could see how the police side of the story ran. 'You contested it?'

'Of course, I did.'

But was Ben telling the truth?

Packed, the car loaded up and me ready to go, now came the hard part. It was no consolation that I'd run out on Leo years before.

'You can't leave me,' Ben said, hurt and shock in his eyes.

I stayed still, clutching Rufus.

'I need you. Both of you.' Ben reached out and rested a hand on his son. 'More than ever.'

'I know and I'm sorry, but I have to get away.' To think clear thoughts, to get my head straight, away from the madness Adam had visited upon us and away from the confusion Ben's strange behaviour had cast. By any standards, his constant denial that there was a particular issue with Adam was peculiar.

'Is this about last night?' Ben's hands were on top of his head, as if, stricken and knowing the game was up, he was surrendering.

'It's about Adam.'

'But he's gone.'

'He hasn't though, has he? He's still here in our faces. He haunts your every waking moment and now mine.' And you repeatedly swerve the reason your lying duplicitous brother has such a hold on you. You refuse to see him off.

'Stay. We can work it out.'

I shook my head sadly. 'You know that's not possible.'

'But Sophie . . .'

'Please, don't make this any more difficult. You cannot style your way out of this one. Not anymore.' Oh God, I had said those words to Leo all those years before.

Ben's hands flopped to his sides. 'Okay, okay. I didn't visit my father when he was dying. I bugged out,' he said, anguished. 'I chose not to see him, not to help him. Me, the man training to be a doctor abandoned his own dad when he most needed me.'

I stayed stock-still. 'Why? You loved him.'

'I did, Sophie, I really did, but I couldn't bear to see him screaming in agony.'

'I still don't understand Adam's beef with you.'

'Adam thought I should have done more to help at home during my father's final illness. Instead, I stayed away, buried myself in my studies and made every excuse not to go back. Adam accused me of hastening Dad's death. Basically, I failed my father when he needed me most. Adam was right.'

I recognised guilt in Ben's eyes because I'd seen it in my own. Willing me to believe him he implored me once again to stay.

'Why are you telling me this now? Why didn't you say so before? Didn't you trust me to understand?'

'I was ashamed, Sophie.'

It sounded plausible apart from one obvious anomaly. The stuff of family feuds and fallings-out, Ben's failure to do his duty, as a son, didn't explain why he'd allowed Adam to blackmail him. I was getting part of a story. Beneath, I was convinced lay a deeper truth.

'You are not a bad person, Ben. We all react differently to situations . . .'

'You'll change your mind?' His eyes brightened with hope.

'I still need space.'

'Sophie . . .'

'If you want us to work you have to let me leave.'

His face fell in defeat. 'Where will you go?'

'The flat.' I'd never felt so glad it hadn't sold.

'What about your aunt?'

'I'll talk to her.' Least of my worries.

Before I changed my mind, before I took the easy decision, the one that would offer short-term respite and long-term pain, I walked out of the cottage, across the drive and, loading Rufus into the back of my car, climbed inside and drove away. I remembered nothing of the journey.

My old apartment was on the top floor of a period conversion in Pittville Circus Road, a chic part of Cheltenham with easy access to town. I drove into the single allocated parking space and, with Rufus in my arms, walked up three flights of stairs to the front door. Key in the lock and stepping inside, the emotional weight I'd carried instantly shifted from my shoulders. This had once been my sanctuary and would be again. I stood for a few moments, breathing in musty air and silence.

Years before, I'd chosen the place for the kitchen alone. Open plan, it was both living and dining room. The working area housed two single ovens, an induction hob, a combination microwave, dishwasher and integrated fridge-freezer. The surface on a central island was quartz, perfect for pastry and keeping ingredients at the correct temperature. There was also a wine cooler and a fancy tap that dispensed boiling hot and ice-cold water.

I walked into the main bedroom and opened a window. A large Jack and Jill bathroom, with bath and walk-in shower, serviced both bedrooms, the smaller of the two rooms Rufus's new home. In order to make it as attractive as possible to sell the property, I'd deliberately left furniture in place, including a bed. Thank goodness for my forward thinking.

Shipping Rufus's kit into my old flat took several laborious trips up and down the stairs. Afterwards, I drove to the nearest supermarket and stocked up on groceries. Feeling a greater sense of control than I had in weeks, I was methodical and thorough, no random or impulse buys, only items that were necessary to Rufus's existence and mine.

Suspecting my phone would be crammed with messages, I kept it switched off. If Mum got wind of me walking out and into the flat, she would assume I had serious commitment issues and be straight round to give me a solid talking to; Dad right behind her. I hated to think of Ben alone, steeped in misery, yet if I was to help him, I had to break free.

And with that realisation I had a sudden flash of inspiration, and it was all down to Adam. The only person I could think of who could throw light on the real reason for the deep-seated enmity between the brothers was long-lost Uncle Larry — *if* he was alive.

On a countdown, I maintained radio silence. Nobody came, nobody bothered me. In less than twenty-four hours, me and Rufus would hit the road. To unravel the present, I needed to take a trip into the past.

CHAPTER FIFTY-EIGHT

Rufus fretted and fussed, fed badly and howled the apartment down when I changed his nappy the next morning. It was pelting with rain as I set off later than intended for the Midlands. I'd taken the precaution of packing an overnight bag and a portable cot. I wasn't coming back until I had the answers I craved.

Straight up the M5, I arrived in Birmingham an hour and a quarter later. Beyond a wine warehouse, I hung a left into Hamilton Avenue, a classy tree-lined street with grass verges and big houses. Ben and Adam's old home lay behind a gated entrance. Built in the latter part of the nineteenth century, it was a 'captain of Midlands industry' type property, befitting a well-heeled accountant and his family.

I parked a little way from the entrance and, bundling Rufus into my arms, hurried through pouring rain and open gates towards a part-glazed solid oak front door. Huddling beneath a timber gabled storm porch, I pulled an old-fashioned doorbell that made a whimsical chime and waited. Rufus squirmed and began to make funny noises that I recognised as 'I'm ravenous'. I jiggled him from side to side, hoping he'd lose interest while knowing there wasn't a chance in hell.

By the time a woman my mother's age, dressed in a thick sweater and jeans, answered the door, Rufus was in full cry.

'Goodness, he's got a fine set of lungs.' She had close-cut iron-grey hair — you could practically see her scalp — and large hooped earrings that swung as she dipped her head to stare at the squalling bundle in my arms.

'I'm so sorry,' I said, flustered.

'Sounds hungry to me, dear.'

'We've driven a fair way.' I felt like a totally crap mother. Blundering on, I said, 'I was hoping you could help me with information about a local man, Larry Taylor. He knew the previous owners of your home.'

'I see,' she said briskly. 'Well, you can't stand there in the rain with a hungry little boy. You'd best come in.'

'If it's no trouble.' I stepped into a vast hall with tiled flooring and went to take off my shoes. The woman gestured for me to keep them on and directed me to a generous sitting room at the front of the house with a bay window.

'Sit yourself down,' she said. 'Do you feed him yourself?'

'I do,' I said.

'Thought so. You'll need a big glass of water then. I used to be a midwife,' she said as I sank into a deep chair and unbuttoned my coat.

'That's how you could tell he was a boy.'

'The blue jacket was the giveaway,' she said, with a twin-kly smile.

Mercifully, Rufus settled down. While she was gone, I looked around the room and wondered how much it had changed since two little boys had lived here. The coal effect gas fire in the cast iron and brass fireplace was probably original. I couldn't swear to the busily patterned carpet. Coincidentally, an upright piano sat in an alcove although I doubted it was the same instrument Adam had played as a child.

'There you go,' she said, placing a glass on an occasional table next to me. 'I'm sorry but I didn't catch your name.' She sat down near the fireplace and gave me a sharp, penetrating look as if she'd suddenly realised the perils of inviting a stranger into her home. I told her.

'Jennifer Critchley,' she said in exchange. 'I'd extend a hand, but you're otherwise engaged.'

I returned her easy smile and asked, 'Have you lived here long?'

'Around sixteen years. Our girls are flown so it's me and Jerry, although we have five grandchildren who visit often.'

'You must have bought your house from the Taylors.'

Mrs Critchley frowned and shook her head. 'Hall,' she said.

'Hall?' I repeated. Ben had said that Adam had changed his name from Taylor to Hall.

'That's what was so confusing about your question. We bought our home from *Lawrence* Hall. Everyone called him Larry. Do you think it's the same man you're looking for, or an odd coincidence?'

I shook my head. To hide my consternation, I reached for my glass.

'Lovely man,' Mrs Critchley enthused, oblivious. 'Lifelong bachelor and lived here all his life, apparently. Getting on a bit when we met him. Why he was rattling around in a place like this, goodness only knows. I suppose it being the family home, with all those sentimental connections and, obviously, a retired accountant, he could afford it.'

I reeled. My mind journeyed back to the day Ben had brought me here, *his* former family home, he'd announced with pride. Revealed now to be a lie, it didn't mean the place was without significance. Adam had exploited that when he'd brought up Larry in conversation with Ben and in front of me. I recalled how Ben had, initially, seemed confused. The fact remained: the house and Larry mattered to him.

'I don't suppose you know where I could find Larry?' I asked.

'He's dead. A stroke, I believe.'

Furiously wondering how Larry Hall fitted precisely into Ben and Adam's story, I wasn't quick enough to fend off Mrs Critchley's question. 'Might I ask what your interest is?'

I could lie. I could dissemble. But there had already been too many lies and deceptions in my life, so I looked into Mrs Critchley's sharp eyes, the colour of blue fountain pen ink, and told her as much as I believed to be true.

It wasn't very much, and it didn't take very long.

CHAPTER FIFTY-NINE

'What a frightful mess,' Mrs Critchley exclaimed.

She didn't castigate me for walking out on the father of my child, didn't pull a face when I told her about poor Brooke and the trouble Ben was in with the police.

'I've known doctors do a lot worse than that, I can tell you.'

I didn't like to think what that might entail. 'I can see the pickle you're in. And you say the boys' parents were Taylors?'

'It's what I was given to understand.'

'Unless your Ben is telling fibs,' Mrs Critchley said, suddenly censorious. 'Do you know the Christian names of his parents?'

'Graham and Phyllis.'

She scratched the side of her mouth. 'Come to think of it, Larry mentioned a brother. Can't recall his name, but Jerry might know. I'll give him a ring. Now where's my phone,' she said, standing up and patting down her jeans.

'Honestly, I don't want to put you to any unnecessary trouble.' Truly, I wasn't sure I could stand any more revelations although, having come this far, I couldn't turn back now.

'Nonsense, I love a good old-fashioned mystery.'

From the spring in Mrs Critchley's step, I very much got the impression that this delicious piece of news might be shared at her next coffee morning with friends. I listened as her feet clack-clacked across the tiled floor.

In the horrible silence I had plenty of time to think. The sobering fact that Adam could be telling the truth was like a bucket of ice-cold water chucked over my head. Had I mis-judged as much as I'd maligned him? What if Ben, the father of my son, was the real liar?

'Seems to me that neither of the brothers is reading from the gospel,' Mrs Critchley announced, returning with the energy of a cyclone.

I braced myself.

'According to Jerry, Larry had two nephews. They were in their twenties, I gather.'

My heart rate shot up. 'Did your husband recall their names?'

'Afraid not, but Jerry remembered that Larry had a brother called Graham. Graham Hall, that is.' Her intrepid gaze fixed on me like a history teacher urging a pupil to remember the date of the Fire of London. It didn't take long to reach a conclusion, and it slayed me. '*Ben* changed his name by deed poll, *not* Adam.'

My mind rolled back to an early stilted conversation in a café. Adam had been virtually monosyllabic when I'd told him what I thought to be true about his parents. I saw now that he went along with it, ostensibly for Ben's sake, but in reality to threaten Ben later with disclosure. What else had Ben lied about? Christ, was he really a doctor or a con man with a screed of false qualifications?

'*If* they're the aforementioned nephews,' Mrs Critchley said, rather too enthusiastically, 'they're both Halls by birth.'

And the police would discover that fact and want to know why Ben jettisoned his surname. *I* wanted to know the answer to that too. I nibbled on the corner of my little finger. Ben was on the run from his past because he had done something terribly wrong. Adam knew what that was and had used it to blackmail his brother. End of. Deep down I'd always known but was in denial. Was I always destined to follow the same psychological pattern? Was history repeating itself?

'Apparently,' Mrs Critchley enthused, 'Graham and his wife run a public house.'

'That can't be right,' I said. 'They're both dead.'

'That's very possible. It *was* sixteen years ago, dear.'

'Yes, I see,' I said, regretting my need to hammer in a conclusion that fitted.

Mrs Critchley companionably patted my knee, as if to say that it was perfectly all right. I bet she did that a lot when she was counselling mothers-to-be about their raised blood pressure.

'I don't suppose Jerry mentioned where the pub is?'

'Afraid not.' Her eyes glistened, eager and attentive. 'But you have more information now and a possible lead, don't you think?'

I did. In fact, I had rather more than that. Peculiarly, I had Adam to thank for it.

CHAPTER SIXTY

The card I'd found in Adam's belongings was for a pub called the Pig's Snout at Bromyard in Herefordshire. The exact location of the pub didn't exist on satnav so I settled for the market town instead. Once I got there, I could ask around. Taking me well over an hour, I hoped that Rufus would sleep for the journey.

Instead of taking the motorway, I took the scenic route. It meant that I could stop more easily if Rufus kicked off. We got as far as the pretty riverside town of Bewdley when he became restless. I pulled into a car park overlooking the river with swans and ducks and gave Rufus a cuddle. Afterwards, I walked into town to pick up a takeaway cup of Americano, which I drank sitting on a bench, before heading back.

On to Shelsley Walsh, famed for its Hill Climb, and then along a largely rural B-road that took me into Bromyard, where I parked.

My immediate impression was that I'd travelled in a time machine to another era. The main square was sad and run-down and blighted by a large derelict pub or hotel, called the Hop Pole. Off to the right, a central street containing a mishmash of charity outlets, estate agents with properties that were a steal if you longed for rural isolation; junk shops, fruit and veg, a hardware store, which looked more antique than the antique shops, and boutiques with women's clothes that would have appeared dated on the average Fifties housewife. Admittedly, there were odd pockets of modern resistance: a smart wine bar and café, a bakery selling Danish pastries and fresh bread and, right at the end of the street, next to a supermarket, a wonderful farm shop and delicatessen full of fresh and occasionally exotic produce. Rural accents were everywhere with an unexpected smattering of Welsh chucked in.

Doubling back, I headed for a traditional café serving cakes, buns, bacon butties and no-frills tea and coffee. In a dark corner sat two bikers with Midlands accents whose helmets rested on the table like spoils of war. They glanced up and smiled at Rufus. Babies were instant icebreakers, I'd discovered, and I smiled back.

Finding a table, I quickly ran my eyes over the menu. A fresh-faced waitress took my order for a pot of tea and toasted teacake.

'Nice baby,' she said, on her return. 'Do you need me to warm a bottle for him?'

'That's very kind but, no thanks, we're good.' I spooned sugar into my tea. 'Do you live locally?'

'Leominster.'

'Is that far away?'

'Twelve miles, or so, takes twenty minutes in the car. My mum drives me.'

'What would we do without mums, huh?' I said, smiling.

'Yeah, she's good like that. Anything else I can get you?'

'I'm all set, thanks, although there are a couple of things you might be able to help with.'

The waitress gave a willing smile.

'Where would be a good place to stay tonight?' I asked.

'There are a couple of pubs in the High Street that do B & B.'

'Might be noisy.' I glanced at Rufus who was dribbling all over his bib.

'There's Rowden Abbey,' she said. 'Proper posh.' She spoke in a way that suggested it would fit me perfectly.

'Expensive?'

'Probably. If you fancy going off-grid, you could always try Brook House Woods.'

'Sounds appealing, thanks.' It also sounded remote, and I wasn't sure I wanted that when flying solo, without Ben. 'One other thing.' The important thing. The thing I'd left until last.

'Yep?'

'Do you know where I can find the Pig's Snout?'

She repeated the name as if she'd never heard anything so ridiculous in her life.

'It's a pub,' I said.

'Can't say I've heard of it. Is it round here then?'

'Apparently.'

'Not really my stamping ground.'

Cake That and home suddenly felt a long way off my radar. 'Is there someone I could ask in the kitchen?' I tilted my head in the general direction.

'Todor wouldn't have a clue — Bulgarian. Not that I've got anything against foreigners. We've all got to make a living, haven't we? You could try tourist information, I suppose.'

I had visions of people with maps and brochures and a ton of knowledge but not the kind of detailed information I was looking for. I must have looked less than drawn to the idea because she suddenly said, 'Course you could talk to Locky. He runs the ironmongers in town. What he doesn't know you could write on the back of a fag packet. If he can't help, nobody can.'

CHAPTER SIXTY-ONE

Locky was a little man of indeterminate age with big hair and a face the colour of a cooked sausage. He had knuckles like rocks, one of those people that, beneath the affable manner, there's a tricky individual lurking. In full flight to a customer about the merits of a particular door hinge, he acknowledged me with a suspicious tilt of his chin.

I hung around, Rufus thankfully sound asleep in his baby sling, and walked up and down rows of locks, nails, hooks, doorknockers and letter plates, paraphernalia for coal fires and stoves, and an astonishing array of copper-bottomed sauce-pans. The shop had that wonderfully distinctive smell of old metal and WD40. With its dark Dickensian interior, it was a glory hole for all things ancient and not very modern.

Locky finally caught up with me as I was inspecting a candlesnuffer.

'Proper authentic, that one,' he said. 'You'd go a long way to find something this original.'

'How much?'

'To you, forty quid. Anyone else, sixty.'

I beamed and, hoping to sweeten the trade for information, said I'd buy it despite it being absolutely no use to me.

Following Locky to the till I asked if he knew where to find the Pig's Snout. He barely broke stride. 'What's a young woman want with a place like that?'

A place like what, I wondered. 'It's not open then?'

'Hasn't been for years. It's derelict.'

I wondered when exactly it had fallen into disrepair. After Graham had died most likely, *if* that bit of the brothers' story was true. 'And the owners?'

'Long gone,' Locky said, clipped.

'But the place is still standing?'

'Oh aye. Not easy to get to — part of its charm back in the day. I've been in any number of lock-ins there.' He seemed to briefly tune out, as if recalling happier times.

'How do I find it?'

'You know the Downs?'

'I'm not familiar with the area.'

Take the B4203 out of the High Street and eventually you'll see a dog-leg off with a sign for a pig farm. If you take the wrong turning, you'll wind up in Bringsty Common. Follow the road up, steep, mind, past the pig farm and you can't miss the Snout. It's right at the top.'

I thanked him.

'You scouting for a property developer, or what?'

'No, I'm interested in the pub's history.' Not a bad approximation of the truth.

Locky shot me a wary look. 'You know the story then?'

I knew *a* story. I wasn't sure whether Locky and me were on the same page with it. 'A little,' I replied.

'Rum business.' Locky's grey eyebrows contracted. 'Card or cash?'

'Card. Did you know Graham and Phyllis?'

'Everyone knew the Halls. Nice people.' Locky produced a card machine.

'What about family?'

'A couple of sons: Adam and Ben. Like Oasis those two.' Locky chuckled.

'They didn't get on?' They never had.

'I'll say.' Locky puffed out his thin cheeks.

'Why was that?' My hand trembled as I paid.

Locky sucked in through his teeth. 'Different animals. Funny because it was a carbon copy of the relationship Graham had with his big-shot brother, Larry, but that's a whole different story.' Locky leant over the counter. 'Rumour has it that when Larry popped his clogs, he split his considerable fortune between the brothers and a dog charity.'

Which explained how Ben and Adam had come into an inheritance; it had no connection to their parents. I wondered if Larry had been as fair as Ben had made out. What if he'd favoured one nephew over the other? 'You were saying about Adam and Ben,' I said, steering Locky back on track.

'Clever pair,' he said firmly. 'Always knew the youngest would do well. Studying to be a doctor, last I heard.'

'And the other brother, Adam?'

Locky frowned. 'One of those arty-farty types. Ambitious, wanted to make his mark on the world without putting in the graft; something not quite right about him.'

I tried to tamp down the tingling sensation on my skin. 'What makes you say that?'

'Instinct.' Locky tapped the side of his head. 'Want a bag?'

'Thanks.' The encouraging smile on my face felt as if it were stretched to breaking point. 'Were the boys close to their parents?'

Locky handed me my purchase. 'Ben was. Adam idolised his dad, but nothing Adam did sat right with Graham. Consequently, Adam became a proper mummy's boy. In her eyes he could do no wrong. Gave him too much sense of his own importance, if you ask me.'

Locky plunged his hand into a drawer full of washers, extracted several and put them into a separate compartment.

'What became of Graham and Phyllis?'

'For someone studying the history you don't seem to know very much.' Locky's small eyes suddenly turned cold and hard.

With little wriggle room, I said, 'I met the brothers once. They each had a tale to tell. I'm not sure which to believe.'

'That so?' Locky viewed me with a quizzical expression, as if to say he wasn't sure he believed my story either. I think he realised then that I was short on facts.

'It is,' I said, levelling with him.

My forthrightness, if not quite total honesty, appeared to persuade Locky to come to a decision.

'Might as well hear it from me as from anyone else.'

I waited expectantly, hardly daring to breathe.

'Phyllis, the boys' mother, killed Graham, their dad.'

CHAPTER SIXTY-TWO

The breath I'd been holding gusted out of me. I had a terribly strange sensation in my head and clutched poor Rufus to me a little tighter.

Oblivious to my blindsided response, Locky lowered his voice. 'Folk round here don't like to talk about it.'

I wasn't surprised. Was this the secret Ben had nursed for years?

'Tragic, it was,' Locky said. 'Nobody made a fortune running a pub but, my goodness, money was always tight for the Halls, something the older son regularly complained about, if I remember rightly.' Locky spoke as if it was the first time he'd genuinely considered it.

'Old Graham, well, he was a proud man, see? What with all that to-do with his well-heeled brother, Larry. Graham took being skint damned hard. And what do us blokes do when things go tits up, if you'll pardon the expression?' Locky didn't wait for me to express an opinion. 'We *drink*. That's what we do. Reckon it was the booze that did for Graham. Liver cancer.' Locky shook his head sadly. 'His skin was as yellow as one of them old copper taps over there.' His eyes travelled to a shelf above an array of bathroom accessories.

'Skin and bone by the finish. Nasty way to go,' Locky said, with a visible shiver.

Remembering Ben's passionate defence of assisted dying gave me a bad taste in my mouth.

'Anyways, Phyllis, a lovely woman and devoted wife — and don't let anyone tell you different — nursed Graham, day and night until he was in that much pain, she decided to put him out of his misery.'

I imagined a pillow over her beloved husband's face, or, more horribly, a regime of starvation and dehydration. I didn't like to ask Locky for the grisly detail.

'Newspapers made out she was a killer. Nothing could be farther from the truth.' Locky's top lip curled with contempt. 'Surprised you didn't read all about it,' he said, with another of his penetrating looks, 'what with all the media frenzy.'

I was surprised too, but remembered I was so focused on my career at the time it was quite possible that even a high-profile news item would have passed me by. I wondered if it had occurred when I'd been in the middle of negotiations for a new job, transferring from a banking position in Jersey to London.

Thoroughly riled, Locky chuntered, 'She was performing a mercy, that's what it was.'

But not for Adam. And he'd hated his brother for not being there to prevent it. I understood now why Ben had changed his name to protect himself after the unwanted publicity. Jealously, Adam resented Ben's decision to start over and, seeing an opportunity to blackmail his brother, Adam had threatened to dismantle Ben's life by revealing their past.

'What became of Phyllis?' I wondered if she'd served time in prison before the road accident.

'Took her own life.'

Horrified, I clapped a hand over my mouth.

'Got into the family car and drove down the hill, a nasty steep bugger, all right. Came off the road and straight into a tree.'

'After she'd . . .' I couldn't bring myself to say it.

Locky nodded. 'Some said it was remorse. Others that she didn't want to face the consequences. So, there you have it.'

Except, ice cold slithering down my spine, nothing of what I'd heard explained Ben's failure to sit me down, pour me a drink, or make me a cuppa, and simply tell me the plain, honest and unvarnished truth.

CHAPTER SIXTY-THREE

I didn't book into any of the places suggested by the nice waitress at the café and, instead, found an unassuming B & B a short walk from town. Dinner that evening was at a highly recommended Indian restaurant. I was given a warm welcome and nobody appeared to mind I had a baby in tow, mainly because Rufus dropped off halfway through my chicken pathia. When I returned to my room, I took the plunge and switched on my phone. Dozens of messages popped up from Ben, Mum, Saskia and Dad, the general gist:

You're not at the flat. Where are you? (Ben).

We are worried about you, Sophie (Dad).

Ben is devastated. Come back (Mum).

I am devastated. Come back (Ben).

Fuck's sake, answer your phone (Saskia).

Even one from Auntie Fen, nothing short of a technological miracle: *Darling, please don't be a stranger. We all love you.*

Most recently, a message from Louise: *Call me.*

Sensing something was wrong, I phoned her first. I was right.

'I miscarried last night,' Louise said, forlorn.

'Oh God, I'm so sorry.' Instantly, I thought of the fight at the pub, the stress of that day. Had it been a factor? 'Did the doctors offer an explanation?'

'Mother Nature, one of those things, modern life, take your pick.' Louise's voice broke with bitter disappointment. 'Apparently it wasn't my fault.'

'Of course it wasn't your fault.' I shivered inside. Was it Ben's? Was this what Louise and Elliott would be thinking if not quite saying? We hadn't spoken since, but I couldn't blame them if the fight had been a contributory factor in elevating her stress levels. 'How is Elliott?'

'Sweet of you to ask, as well as can be expected. Everyone has been extremely kind to me, but he's hurting terribly too.'

'I'm sure. I'm so sorry, Louise. Are you at home?'

'I am now and taking it easy.'

'Best thing.' Before she asked questions I couldn't answer, I sent her big hugs and finished the call. I had problems but nothing on that level, I reminded myself, looking at my wide-awake child.

Next, I phoned Dad. Although I normally turned to my mother for advice, her brain had gone walkabout under Adam's influence.

'Sophie, we are all worried sick,' Dad said, unusually heated. 'What on earth is going on? Ben is beside himself. He needs you, darling.'

I sensed my father viewed my escape as self-serving. Not knowing what to say or where to begin, I said nothing.

'Sophie?'

'Yes?'

'This business with the boys, it's unfortunate but it's not the end of the world. Neither is the visit from the police. From what Ben says he really isn't—'

'It's more complex than that.'

'Sweetheart, you said exactly the same about the situation with Leo.'

'Leo was different.' Stung, my voice barely rose much more than a whisper.

'You can't keep running away when the going gets tough, Sophie.'

In the background I heard the clamour of voices. I imagined my mother, sister and aunt crowding around my father.

'Mum wants to talk to you,' Dad said, confirming my thoughts.

'Sorry, phone's running out of battery. Catch you later.'

'But—'

'I'll explain everything when I get back.'

Feeling mentally bashed up, I switched off my phone, changed into my PJs, made myself a cup of herbal tea from the welcome tray and played hide the rattle with Rufus until he grew tired and scratchy and then sleepy. Drained, I fell asleep quickly and woke a few hours later angst-ridden. About my parents. About what Locky had told me. About Ben who'd revealed a version of the truth but not the whole truth. In the morning, I was determined to find out what that was.

CHAPTER SIXTY-FOUR

After a full English breakfast, a gallon of tea and a lot of chat about babies, I checked out and, under a deluge of sleety April rain, followed Locky's directions to the Pig's Snout.

The steep hill to the top was exactly as Locky described. The incline started slowly then, gradually and inexorably, became more acute. With one hairpin bend after another I was forced to drop down several gears to coax my car forward. A mad, murderous hill, I could see how you'd be a goner if your brakes failed at the top. Had Phyllis noticed the little chapel as she'd hurtled past, or the entrance to the drive of the pig farm, before she veered off and plunged straight into the dense woodland that flanked one side of the road?

At last, I crested the summit and found the pub, a dilapidated building with decrepit rendering and tiny attic windows. Locky had not exaggerated when he'd said it was derelict. Sheets of metal screens around the perimeter, designed to protect the site, had either blown down or been pulled down. The pub's old brick chimney remained intact by virtue of scaffolding. Part of a tree grew out of the top. Most of the roof tiles had gone. The noble entrance was now covered in metal sheeting. Obvious efforts had been made to break into the boarded-up windows on the ground floor.

Leaving Rufus, snug and warm in his car seat, I stepped outside and viewed Ben and Adam's home with a sadness that crept into my bones. I wondered where they had slept, where they had played, how much their existences were consigned to upstairs, out of the way of smokers and drinkers. I pictured Ben reading a book, Adam dreaming of a better, more exciting life. I thought about his desperation to impress his dad and his jealousy of Ben for the easy relationship he had with their father. Scanning the upstairs windows, I wondered in which room Phyllis had killed her husband. I thought about the desperation she must have felt, the despair in her heart. I thought about Graham. Had he begged for help? Had he known what was coming?

Saddened, I walked away to the side of the pub and car park, a mess of cracked and pitted paving and sprouting weeds. It was littered with piles of rubble, bricks, glass and dirt and what looked suspiciously like sheets of asbestos. On the farthest wall, there was a sign reserving a private parking space, probably for the family car. I pictured Phyllis, distraught and out of her mind, running towards it. Drawing near, I saw that the wall had caved in in the middle, as if someone had taken a great bite out of a sandwich, the upper and lower section of bricks remaining. Peering closer, I saw flecks of red paint adhering to some of the bricks. Embedded in the ground, shards of plastic, possibly from a broken tail light.

Collar up, chilled in the wet and cold, I walked back round to the front, saw that Rufus was dozing and, spotting a sign for a beer garden, followed a red brick path to a narrow entrance carved from a yew hedge. Curious, I crept inside, ducking my head as I passed underneath and found myself in a magical wilderness of grass, weeds and wildflowers. A single track of flattened earth led to a bivouac. Propped next to it: a trail bike with a bright red frame, Canyon logo and big thick wheels. Noise from an accusatory conversation caught on the breeze.

'Wasn't right. But I didn't tell. Not me. I swear.' I listened hard. Male. Youngish. Twenty-something, perhaps. 'Kept my mouth shut.'

Suddenly, a menacing figure dressed entirely in black and wearing heavy-duty boots, plunged out of nowhere. The eyes, visible through a balaclava, blazed at me with a fury that would melt steel. I gaped back, paralysed, all sorts of wrong place, wrong time horrors ripping through my head. I didn't consider what I'd stumbled across. I only thought of reaching Rufus, yet my feet wouldn't budge. Frozen. Vulnerable. I tried to shout out. The words refused to come.

Terrified, my gaze fell on the man's hands; hands that could hit, throttle and choke. Suddenly, the figure grabbed hold of the bike, leapt astride and came straight at me.

Galvanised, I tried to make a run for it. Not quick enough.

I heard the thud before I felt it. A burst of white light crashed across my vision.

Winded, dazed and nauseous, I was flat on my back, mud in my hair, pain in my ribs, terror barrelling through me.

Rufus.

Scrabbling dizzily to my feet, I half ran, half stumbled to my car and to the glorious sound of Rufus crying unhurt in the back. Thank God there was no sign of the stranger or the trail bike.

'Mummy's coming,' I cried, my voice, piping, high and alien to me.

Pain shooting through my back and side, I flung open the door and, liberating Rufus, gathered him into my arms. My face against his wet cheeks, inhaled his soft-as-pure-cotton baby smell. My teeth chattered because of the terrible risk I'd taken with my son. What a stupid fool I'd been to come to this awful godforsaken place — Rufus deserved better.

Terrified of what might have been, I climbed inside the rear and locked the doors. Scratched, bruised, and with a lump swelling on the back of my head, I sat, cuddling my boy. Eventually, coming down from planet fear, I popped Rufus into his carrier and, tunnelling my way between the two front seats, ribs screaming, clambered into the driver's side. Stone cold, I started the engine and banged on the heater. Who was the man on the bike? Was he connected to the Halls, or was it a random person who didn't care for company? And what the hell was he up to? What did he mean about keeping his mouth shut? Although I never saw a phone, did he have one? Was he speaking to someone and, if so, who? Or was he alone and simply raving at the sky?

Shaken and filled with dread, I began the slow descent with every intention of going home. Then I remembered the pig farm and changed my mind.

CHAPTER SIXTY-FIVE

Down a long and pitted drive, the farm looked as if it had gone the same way as the pub. Built of cob walls, in need of renovation, the farmhouse, small by most standards, stood back in the hillside with a vacant stare like it had come to the sudden realisation that it was robbed of its youth, and old age and infirmity had crept up on it, unannounced.

Behind metal railings and a rusty old gate, practically falling off its hinges, was a small recently mown lawn without borders, plants or shrubs. A concrete path ran alongside the front of the house to a muddy orchard. Behind a heavy-duty fence, in among fruit trees, pigs, large and little, rooted about, roaming free, well-fed and happy. On the other side of the building, a scrapyard contained old fridges, tyres, bedsteads and random detritus. Taking pole position in the centre of the garbage, a dilapidated caravan. Next to it: a trail bike identical to the one that had rammed me minutes ago.

The peeling front door of the farmhouse swung open and a sturdy elderly man in wellingtons emerged. A heavy beard obscured most of his face. Carrying a mug in one hand, he cut along the path towards the orchard.

I climbed out of my car stiffly, wincing at the pain in my side, and shut the door loudly. He stopped and I waved.

My appearance was evidently a novelty and he looked surprised, although friendly enough. If he smiled, he could easily double for Father Christmas. He waved back uncertainly, as if he thought he should know me but couldn't remember from where. Abandoning his trip to the pigs, he doubled back and walked along the path and crossed the lawn to the gate.

'Hello,' I said.

'Morning.'

Up close, he seemed older, although his gait and manner suggested a man who was clearly fit for his age.

'That your bike over there?' I jerked my chin in the direction of the caravan.

'Do I look like it's mine?' Amused, he lifted the mug to his lips. It gave me a glimpse of its interior. Stained by decades of use, it resembled the colour of creosote.

'Who does it belong to?' I asked.

'Who wants to know?'

'The woman it knocked down five minutes ago.'

'Ah,' he said, suddenly on the back foot. 'That will be our Cody, my grandson.'

'Does he make a habit of running people over?'

'Only if he's threatened.'

'I didn't threaten him,' I said stonily.

The man coughed and messily cleared his throat. 'Thing is, our Cody, he gets a bit silly sometimes.'

'Silly?'

'Reckless.'

'And menacing. Does Cody normally dress like a ninja?'

'One of his little foibles.' The man laughed good-naturedly and extended an arthritic hand. 'Lloyd Breeze.'

I took and shook. 'Sophie Knox.'

'He doesn't mean anything by it. It's just his way.'

I stood, unimpressed and unappeased.

Lloyd sighed. 'Cody is what they used to call simple or backward in less enlightened times. Learning difficulties, they call it now.'

'Oh,' I said, embarrassed and instantly regretting my hostile stance.

'Did the silly sod hurt you?'

'Scratches and bruises.' An understatement.

'I see your coat's all muddy.'

'It will wash. Do you run the farm single-handed?'

'We manage. Whatever folks say about Cody, he's good with the pigs. That your baby in there?' Lloyd glanced over my shoulder to the car.

'It is.'

'Boy or girl?'

'Boy.'

'Make sure you love him.'

Taken aback by his sudden profundity, I assured him I did, and I would.

'Want a brew?' He raised his mug.

The smart play would be to accept. I didn't want to contract gastro-enteritis. 'Thank you, no.' I smiled. 'Could I talk to Cody, do you think?'

Lloyd took another swig from his mug. 'He wouldn't like that.'

'I don't want to tell him off, or anything. Just chat.'

'About what?'

'I overheard him talking to someone.'

'Nobody to talk to round here, other than me and the pigs.'

'Does he have a phone?'

''Course not.'

'He sounded quite upset.'

A deep frown creased Lloyd's forehead. His manner was suddenly a lot less avuncular. 'Mind me asking where this was?'

As soon as I mentioned the pub, Lloyd raised his chin. His barrel chest puffed out. No longer on the back foot, he was well and truly on the front. 'What in God's name were you doing there?'

I repeated the lie I'd told Locky: researching the history of the place.

'To what purpose?'

'I . . .'

Lloyd took a heavy step forward, his face in mine. 'You a friend of the Halls?'

I feared telling him the truth. I feared telling him a lie more.

Lloyd poked me in the chest. 'Were you sent?'

My eyes narrowed in confusion.

'Because if you were . . .'

'I wasn't. Lloyd, I can assure you. Sent by whom?'

'I'm telling you what I told him: you ever set foot here again, I'll shoot you.'

CHAPTER SIXTY-SIX

Who, I wanted to ask, but Lloyd was already stalking up the path with the gait of a man intent on fetching his shotgun. I didn't hang around.

On the long drive back I was forced to think the unthinkable: what if Lloyd meant Ben? Ben had lied about his past. What else had he lied about? What if he really had given Brooke the drugs she craved? With events seemingly moving at pace with the investigation, it was entirely possible Ben had been arrested and was sitting in an interview room in a police station somewhere. What would I do?

With regular pit stops, it took me until after lunchtime to reach Lamb's Leap. A pop of sunshine broke out over our home. Ben's car was in the drive, alongside two vans belonging to the workmen. I was glad I wouldn't be alone with him.

I pulled in, blocking the entrance to the drive and, before I'd unloaded Rufus, the front door swung open. Ben stood on the threshold, pale, tired and gaunt. The second time in as many weeks, he was not at work when he should have been; it felt significant.

I had no choice other than to take my time. My head throbbed and my ribs barked. From deep in the cottage, I heard an electric planer.

Ben's features relaxed and softened at seeing our son; his expression tightened when he saw me. 'Christ, Sophie, what happened? Are you hurt?'

'I took a tumble.' I swept in as he stood aside. It all felt terribly formal and awkward, as if we were strangers, which I supposed we were.

'Your coat is ruined and there's blood in your hair. Here, let me take a look.'

Before I could respond, I felt his fingers exploring the back of my head. 'Ouch,' I let out.

'There's a degree of swelling.'

'You don't say,' I said frostily.

'Do you feel dizzy?'

I almost laughed. Dizzy with events I couldn't control. Dizzy with revelations I couldn't explain. Yep, I felt dizzy but not in the way Ben meant. 'No,' I replied.

'Let me bathe it.'

'Later.' I walked into the kitchen, to the seat of noise and saw how much progress had been made: the basic structure was up; great thick uprights of oak, sturdy solid and dependable beasts. Oscar was up a ladder fitting insulation for the roof.

'It's coming on, isn't it?' Ben said.

I nodded agreement. If only our lives could be rebuilt with the same solid foundations.

'Sophie.' He dropped a hand on my shoulder and stared beseechingly into my eyes. I flinched. I'd so wanted to believe him, so wanted to trust him and now? 'I'm sorry for what I've put you through.' How sorry, I wondered. Sorry enough to tell me the truth? 'Can I hold Rufus?' he asked.

Whatever I thought of Ben's lies, I didn't believe Rufus was in danger. I passed him over and watched as Ben smiled and stroked our son's cheek.

'I went to the flat this morning,' he began tentatively. 'You weren't there.'

'I went away.'

He glanced up, eyebrows raised, worried. Perhaps he'd thought I'd gone back to Leo. Not a chance.

In my head I said, Sit down. Shut up. And listen. 'Let's get away from the noise,' I said mildly.

He concurred and followed me through to the sitting room.

'Before you say anything,' Ben said, anxious to get in first, 'I admit I haven't been quite straight with you.'

Something of an understatement. I braced and nodded for him to continue. 'My inheritance didn't come from my parents. It came from an uncle. Adam was a beneficiary, but I was given the lion's share.'

'How much?'

'Five point two million.'

'You *what?*'

'It's in trust. I can't get my hands on it until my thirty-fifth birthday in a few months' time.'

'And you didn't think to tell me?' I screeched.

'I know. I know. I thought . . .'

'Thought never came into it. What were you doing, keeping your options open in case we didn't work out?'

'No, no, that's not the case.' He ran his hand through his hair. 'I wanted it to be a surprise.'

'Well, fuck me, it's certainly that.' All the time I'd been running around like a lunatic trying to scrape enough money together, Ben had been nursing his blasted nest egg.

'I'm sorry. I should have told you.'

'Yes, you damn well should. Hang on a moment,' I said, my voice etched with suspicion. 'Your birthday is end of June. How come you can't borrow on the strength of it?'

'There's a specific clause in the trust agreement expressly stating it cannot be used at any time as collateral.'

'Right,' I said, in a rolling up my sleeves voice. 'Adam's problem with you is all about money? A ton of it.' Things didn't fall into place; they tumbled. 'There's nothing else I should know?'

Ben shook his head.

Bum move. 'And this would be from Uncle Larry, the man who lived in the house you told me belonged to your parents?'

284

Ben gawked in surprise. 'How did you know?'

I could have yelled it all out: about the pub, his parents, his mother and what she had done. I could have bored on about Mrs Critchley, Locky the gossip, and Lloyd and his grandson and the anger in Lloyd's voice when he thought I'd been sent, although what I'd been sent to do and by whom I hadn't fathomed. I could have laid out a theory that I hadn't quite nailed and didn't feel remotely close to doing so. Bone-tired and riddled with apprehension, I cut to the chase. 'What really happened on the night your father died, Ben?'

Ben shivered. I wasn't sure whether it was from fear, or relief. His lips parted. His blue eyes darkened. I think he knew then that there was no way out.

'My mother didn't kill my father,' he said. 'And neither did Adam.'

My heart rate shot up and thundered. I literally felt the colour drain from my face. 'How do you know?'

'Because it was me.'

CHAPTER SIXTY-SEVEN

I think I stopped breathing, or it felt like I had. Oh God. Heart banging, pulse racing, I cast my terrified gaze on my son, sleeping peacefully in Ben's arms. Would Ben let him go? Would he fight me if I reached across and snatched him? How quickly could I make it to the door with Rufus? Answer: not fast enough.

'You lied to my face over and over,' I finally gasped, recalling his anger at my suggestion that he'd had some involvement in his father's death.

'I didn't murder my father, Sophie,' Ben said quietly. 'My father and mother begged me to help him die.'

His steady gaze met mine. For the first time in weeks I saw no subterfuge, no shadow darkening his brow, no tightening of his lips as he'd forced out another lie to cover the lie he'd told before that. That's the thing about not telling the truth. It takes guile and energy and persistence to maintain it. There was none of that struggle in his demeanour. The sudden urge to snatch Rufus back receded.

'Dad used to joke that if he was terminally ill, he wanted someone to take him outside and shoot him.'

'Come on, Ben, people say all kinds of stuff when they're healthy and lucid.'

'They do, but in Dad's case, near the end, he genuinely meant it.'

'And you did what he asked?' I had to be really really sure.

'Yes.' No word of a lie in his voice or expression. No dissembling. 'Everything about his death was illegal at the time and would be now. Dad's death was not subject to checks and balances and talking heads and a ton of paperwork. It was not carried out in a controlled environment. Protocols were not observed. I broke the law,' Ben admitted.

Mind racing, I tried to process the enormity of what he'd confessed to. He would have been barely twenty, scarcely into his medical studies. With his strong sense of vocation, was this gentle-natured man capable of taking a life? Caught in a trap, we are all capable, I realised. And who was I to judge?

'I don't know what to say,' I stammered.

'That it's morally indefensible, that people like me open the door to all kinds of abuse?' His tone implied he had no regrets. 'I didn't do it for the inheritance if that's what you're asking because there was none.'

'How on earth did you pull it off?' A hell of a thing, he must have had help.

'It took months to put together and was planned to the last detail.'

That didn't compute. 'You said you didn't visit, that you couldn't bear to see your father.'

'True, but Dad and I spoke every day on the phone and every day he begged for my help. It's why I stayed away. I couldn't bear the pressure of constantly refusing to carry out his wishes.'

'But you changed your mind?'

'When he couldn't talk anymore, I caved in and visited, as much to support Mum as see my dad. I was appalled by the state he was in. Doubly incontinent, couldn't walk, couldn't eat and barely had enough energy to breathe. He was more and more agitated despite being on high doses of morphine. The meds simply weren't controlling his pain.' Ben looked grim. 'I lie. They didn't touch it. There are some unfortunate people who are peculiarly resistant.'

I remembered him telling me that. 'Shouldn't he have been in a hospice?'

'He flatly refused and, to be honest, I'm not sure it would have made a difference.'

'You increased his dosage?'

'It wasn't that simple. A combination of heavy-duty drugs is needed to end a life and in larger doses than are supplied. I don't need to tell you that it's a criminal offence for anyone other than a doctor, dentist or pharmacist to supply drugs under the Misuse of Drugs Act. I was forced to resort to obtaining them illicitly.'

'A dealer?'

'A doctor who'd been struck off and still needed to make a living.'

'You paid him?'

'Yes.'

'What with? You were a student.' And any money flying out of his mother's bank account would be noted.

'Uncle Larry, my father's brother, provided the funds.'

'Larry was in on it?'

'Larry was integral to the plan. We couldn't have done it without him.'

Making a rapid reassessment, I said, 'But Larry and your father didn't get on.'

A thin smile glanced across Ben's lips. 'There had been a difference of opinion between them years before. When Dad got his diagnosis that changed. For the purposes of what we needed to do we kept up the pretence that they were still at loggerheads and, crucially, not in contact. That was Dad's idea, incidentally.'

'He didn't drink himself into an early grave?'

Ben shook his head. 'Not everyone who has liver cancer is an alcoholic. It suited the narrative for people to believe he was.'

And generally speaking, people believed what they wanted to, what suited them, what made their decisions and judgements and actions easier to live with. This, I knew.

'You visited the pub, didn't you? That's where you went,' Ben said.

'I did.'

'Spend much time in the area?'

'Enough.'

'Then you'll recognise news and misinformation travels at lightning speed in that part of the world.'

In any part of the world where there is tragedy and death. 'Back to that night,' I reminded him.

Ben took a breath and seemed to briefly retreat into himself, as if he wasn't really in the room with Rufus and me among all the lovely things we'd put into it to make it our home. He looked like a man with too many thoughts running through his mind.

'Larry drove to Nottingham and picked me up at midnight. We arrived home shortly after two a.m. Larry parked around the back and waited in the car while I went inside.' Ben stopped briefly, visibly struggling at being forced to take a trip into his past. 'Mum was with Dad,' he began again, his voice cracking. 'I asked them both if they still wanted to go ahead. Sophie,' he said, appealing to me, 'I'd have done anything to walk away.'

Laid low and exhausted, his shoulders slumped, bowed with a burden that would never lift, one I understood so well. I could have told him then and there that he was not alone; it wasn't the right time.

My mind shifted back to Graham and Phyllis, Ben's parents. I wondered whether they would have made the same plea if he'd been a farmer, or a fireman. How ironic that Ben's chosen profession had uniquely suited him to what they'd begged him to do. To do no harm had flown out of the window. But wait . . .

'Your mum agreed to take the blame?'

'Yes.'

'She knew she'd be held responsible and accountable?'

'She believed that a court would be compassionate, and any prison sentence would be suspended.'

'And you believed her?'

'No, but she insisted. She was adamant. I didn't know she was going to take her own life, Sophie, if that's what you're asking.'

I wasn't but it felt like an important detail. I urged Ben to continue.

'Mum kissed Dad. Told him how much she loved him and went to sit with Larry in the car.'

'And then?'

Ben viewed me with gentle eyes. 'I spoke to my dad and told him what a great man he was, that I was proud he was my father, and I was his son, and then . . . and then . . . I did the rest.'

I imagined him helping his father to sit up so he could ingest a fatal cocktail.

'He was too weak to do it for himself,' Ben cut into my thoughts. 'I injected into his Hickman line. Technically, I'm a murderer.'

Theory is always easier to accept than practice. Faced with the awful cold clinical truth, I could not condone Ben's actions, although I fully accepted they came from a place of love. But the law was not that accommodating. Ben had resorted to criminality to get his hands on the drugs necessary for his father to die. It would be viewed as taking someone else's life, something Ben, as a doctor, had sworn never to do.

I offered to take Rufus from him. He shook his head. I let him be. Ben needed our son. He needed to hold on to something good. He needed hope.

If it ever came to light, even with big changes in attitude, Ben would go to prison. Every case he'd ever been involved with would be reviewed, particularly his work at the local hospice. It would finish his career. More importantly, it would finish him as a person. No wonder he'd fought so hard to protect his secret. What felt like a lifetime ago I told Brooke that I was a champion at keeping my mouth shut. For Ben's sake, I'd better be sure I was.

'And afterwards?' I asked tentatively.

'I went outside and hugged my mum. Larry was in a panic about getting me back to uni so that I wouldn't be missed. Mum went inside to be with Dad. It was the last time I saw her.' Ben's eyes flared in distress at the memory. 'The next day two police officers came to my hall of residence. I thought they'd come to arrest me. Instead, they came to tell me my mother was dead and a suspect in my father's death.'

'Your mother?'

'As my father's devoted carer, there was an assumption that she, alone, had increased Dad's dose to a lethal level.'

'But . . .'

'An autopsy can prove cause of death, Sophie, but not who is responsible.'

'I assume Larry was questioned, too.'

Ben gave a grim nod.

'And?'

'He stuck by me.' Ben's voice faltered. 'He told the police that my mother was exactly the kind of woman who would take matters into her own hands to prevent my father from suffering.'

'Oh God, Ben.' I reached across, resting my hand on his arm.

His sad gaze fastened on mine. 'Her suicide was never part of the plan. I swear to God, Mum killed herself to steer the guilt in her direction and protect me.'

CHAPTER SIXTY-EIGHT

The afternoon sun fled the sitting room. Dirty shadows cast us into twilight.

'Did your mum leave a note?'

'Nothing.'

If she'd wanted to protect Ben, surely, she'd scribble a confession to remove all doubt? It would have been the simplest way to shoulder the blame and exonerate any third party.

'Had I known what she was intending I'd never have seen it through,' Ben said bitterly.

He fell quiet and brooding. Eventually, he broke. 'You're justifiably angry.'

'I'm not angry.' I wasn't.

'I should have told you before. My shit, you had a right to know.' Ben brimmed with frustration.

And what would I have done if he had? I think we both knew the answer. I would have run and kept on running.

'You don't hate me?'

'No.' I offered a sad smile.

'I don't blame you if you want to walk away. I won't fight you for Rufus.' He chewed his bottom lip and looked down at his son then back at me as if I held his life in my hands. I guess I did.

'I'm not walking.' The decision was simple and took me by surprise. Surely, we could salvage something from this harrowing mess? And that meant telling Ben the truth about me, too. He'd been honest. It was time for me to be honest.

'I think there's—'

'Sophie,' Ben cut in, sad and solemn. 'If you want to report me, I won't deny it. I won't make it difficult.'

'What would be the point? You're a good doctor.'

'Not what the police think,' he said, trying to smile.

'What they think and what they can prove are two different things. Have you heard any more about the investigation into Brooke's suicide?'

'No, thank God.'

'It might go away.' One of us needed to remain hopeful.

'I wish I shared your optimism.' Ben glumly handed a fidgety Rufus back to me. 'What do we do about Adam?'

I'd been considering this. The thought of Ben's brother milking us for money for the rest of our days was terrifying. In normal circumstances and in the spirit of publish and be damned, I'd recommend going public. We couldn't do that. But . . .

'Where was Adam on the night your dad died?'

'God knows. Sofa-surfing somewhere. He used to hang out with all sorts back then. The police had to send out a posse to deliver the news. Adam wasn't best pleased to find out a day after everyone else.'

'The police, the press, people in the local community all believed your mother killed your father, right?'

'Correct.'

'There was an inquest?'

'Yes.'

'And?'

'Coroners aren't permitted to apportion blame. On the balance of evidence, it wasn't clear whether Mum deliberately took her own life, or whether she'd crashed the car while being of unsound mind. Either way, the police took the view that Mum killed my father.'

'Then why does Adam refuse to accept what the police believed?'

Ben blinked. Riddled with guilt, he'd failed to spot the obvious.

'Adam's malicious allegation was purely speculative,' I said, 'unless someone told him the truth.'

'Not possible.' From the set of his jaw, Ben was certain.

'What about your uncle?'

'Larry was complicit. He would never have uttered a word.'

Under Adam's manipulative spell he might have done. But then I thought of a more obvious candidate. 'Then there's only one person left: your mother.'

Ben gaped then shook his head.

'How was she when you left?'

'Emotional.'

'Distraught?'

Ben closed his eyes, picturing the scene, the last scene with his mum, as it turned out. 'Relieved. Glad it was over.'

'Her state of mind was within the normal spectrum of distress after what had taken place?'

Ben thought again. 'Yes, but I can't rule out her falling apart after I left.'

I rolled the story back and tried to imagine the sequence of events. It threw up more questions than answers.

'How long did your father take to die? Sorry to ask,' I said, pulling an apologetic face.

'Dad very quickly slipped into a coma. He died a couple of hours later.'

'What time did you get back to Nottingham?'

'Just before five a.m.'

'And what time of year was this?'

Ben looked at me quizzically, as if the blow to my head was more serious that he thought. 'June, we were approaching end of term.'

'So it was light?'

'Daybreak, why do you ask?'

'Bear with me. What make of car did your mother drive?'

'A Vauxhall Astra.'

'Red?'

'Yeah,' he said astonished. 'How did you know?'

'Educated guess.' *Very* educated guess. 'Did the airbag go off?'

'*What?*'

'Did it?'

'Yes.'

'Which should have given protection.'

'Well, yeah, but . . .'

'It didn't,' I finished. Perhaps Phyllis lost consciousness, and it was this that caused the vehicle to veer off the road. 'When was the car found?'

'Sophie . . .'

'It's important.'

Ben ran a hand through his hair. 'Around midday. It had come off the road and plunged through trees. A pathologist confirmed that Mum had suffered catastrophic injuries and died quickly.'

'She could have crashed any time between you leaving and the car being found?'

Ben shook his head. 'A kid on a bike said he'd seen the car hurtling down the hill around eight in the morning.'

'A kid?'

'From the neighbouring farm.'

'Cody Breeze.'

Ben started forward. 'You met him?'

'He put me flat on my back.'

'*Cody?*' He said in a 'kid wouldn't hurt a soul' way. Apparently, he would.

'He's not the little boy you once knew.' Notwithstanding his difficulties, Cody was big and strong; I had the injuries to prove it.

'Haven't thought about him in years. He'd often hang around the pub. Mum would feed him bars of chocolate and crisps.' There was warmth in Ben's eyes. Surely, Ben was not the brother Lloyd wanted to kill. 'He must be, what, twenty-something?' Ben said, cutting into my thoughts. 'His mother ran off and left Cody with his grandfather to bring him up.'

'I met Lloyd too.'

As if in a moment of clarity, Ben's expression revealed that he was as much in the dark about the mother of his child as I was about him.

'Lloyd told me that Cody had learning difficulties,' I said.

'From a traumatic birth, yes.'

'Any observation Cody made, or testimony he gave and, bearing in mind he was a kid, Cody would not have been taken seriously by the police.'

'I'm not sure he was even questioned.' Ben's eyes narrowed, his gaze sharpened. 'What are you getting at, Sophie?'

I wasn't quite sure and, until I was, I wasn't sharing my thoughts with anyone, not even Ben.

CHAPTER SIXTY-NINE

We ate an early dinner against the clamour of men determined to finish the roof and prepare for the glass to arrive for the windows. The easiest Ben and I had been in each other's company for weeks, I hated to be the bearer of bad news closer to home.

'While I was away, I heard from Louise. She miscarried.'

'God, that's rough. When did it happen?'

I told him. I saw dismay in his eyes. Being a clinician didn't mean he discounted the stress factor. 'Elliott's taken it pretty hard.'

'Think I should drop in?'

'Up to you.'

We finished our meal in silence. Afterwards, while Ben looked after Rufus, I took a long hot bath and gingerly washed my hair. A quick examination by Ben confirmed what I already knew: my head would heal and my ribs, severely bruised, would take longer but I would recover. Later, I spoke to Mum to let her know I was back home. Relief billowed out of her.

'I'm thrilled. Wonderful news,' she enthused.

Too tired to go into detail and not sure which detail to go into anyway, I asked if she could pass on the news to Dad and

Saskia. I couldn't bear the idea of a long-drawn-out post-mortem with my sister.

'Adam still with you?' It nearly killed me to ask after him.

'Off and on.' I was quick to pick up on a definite cooling in Mum's tone.

'He must have taken this whole Brooke business hard.' I wasn't being sympathetic; I was fishing.

My mother made a noise midway between *uh-huh* and *hmm*. Was this the reason for Saskia's impassioned message: *Fuck's sake, answer your phone!* I asked Mum how she was.

'I worry about that girl,' Mum said enigmatically.

'Is she there?'

'Out with Meadow.'

'Not Adam?'

'Apparently not.'

Were cracks appearing in the relationship? I bloody hoped so. 'Are you around tomorrow?'

'I can be. Lunch?'

'Will Auntie Fen be there?' I wanted to talk to Mum alone.

'She has other plans. Mind, she's extended her stay and checked out of No. 131 to a suite at Ellenborough Park.' A luxury five-star hotel midway between Cheltenham and Winchcombe and favoured by A-list celebrities.

I was genuinely surprised on two counts. Even for my aunt, this was the height of extravagance. Secondly, I thought she'd be hotfooting it back to the capital, her more natural environment. Knowing Auntie Fen, she was enjoying the intrigue and drama; made a nice change from engendering her own.

'She wants to know if you want to press ahead with the sale.'

'I'll give her a ring.' If I could get through, which was questionable. First, I needed to speak to Saskia.

My sister is not a person to miss a phone call, still less a WhatsApp message. I tried both and got nowhere. I couldn't rule out the possibility that she was paying me back for not picking up when she wanted me to. This was how we, as sisters, rolled.

I phoned Aunt Fen and, on receiving her voicemail, left a message to the effect that I wanted to go ahead with the sale and we should sit down and iron out the details. Maybe she and my sister were hanging out together. Saskia wouldn't be averse to having a drink with my aunt and indulging in a little famous-people spotting.

Ben and I watched TV, held hands and went to bed where we held each other.

'I love you,' Ben whispered in my ear.

I nestled into his chest. I still didn't know how to process his confession. And I was conflicted. How would Ben react to me telling him about Caron? It is said that it's not the things we do that lead to the greatest regrets, but those things we failed to do. I had failed in a way that Ben had not.

The next morning, the men arrived with great sheets of glass. With them tramping in and out, we told them to leave the front door open despite a gale blowing through.

Ben hovered, anxious about going to work. Perhaps he feared I wouldn't be home when he returned.

'Go,' I said, dropping a kiss on his lips and shooing him out.

I made the first round of teas and coffees for our workers and was about to grab one myself when Saskia strolled into the kitchen. About to launch in with 'I've been trying to get hold of you', I stopped when I saw her pale tear-stained face void of make-up.

'Saskia, whatever's wrong?'

'Can we talk?'

'Of course we can.' I wrapped a sisterly arm around her shoulder and ushered her through to the sitting room.

'Tea?'

'Coffee, please.'

'Sorry to be a bore, but does Luke know where you are?'

'Ever the businesswoman.' Saskia spoke without raising a smile. 'I called him first thing.'

I squeezed her shoulder and belted off to the kitchen. The kettle took an age to boil, the coffee an eternity to brew. Even the blasted milk took its own sweet time to heat up. Rufus cried until I raced back upstairs, scooped him up and dumped him on my sister.

If Mum felt *meh* about Adam, chances were Saskia felt similarly. At last plonking everything onto a tray, I returned to the sitting room where Saskia sat hunched and small. She looked like a person who'd lost her job and been made homeless on the same day.

I handed Saskia a cup. She handed Rufus back as if he were an item of soiled clothing in a jumble sale. I stuck him on a boob and sat back to listen.

It all came out in a blurry hot mess and wasn't what I expected.

'This business with the police,' Saskia began. 'I'm scared there's more to it.'

I sat up a little straighter.

'Adam was behaving oddly before everything kicked off with Brooke. You know he borrows Dad's car?'

I nodded.

'He's done miles and miles in it. I checked,' Saskia said shiftily in answer to my astonished expression. 'God alone knows where he goes. I questioned him and he swears blind he tootles around the Cotswolds. The mileage tells a different story. He could be driving to John O'Groats and back, for all I know.'

I opened my mouth to interject but Saskia was in full flight. 'And he spends a lot of time dashing outside to vape or smoke at the bottom of the garden. I swear he's on a phone, but he doesn't possess one.'

'How do you know? Brooke had one when they swore they didn't use them.'

Saskia didn't so much as blink. 'See, why am I not surprised? He's so predictable in his unpredictability, if that makes sense.' She pulled a funny face. 'One second he's all over me and the next he's cool and detached.'

'Like he was with Brooke.'

Saskia fell silent, an unusual event in my sister's life. 'Crap, you're right,' she said, at last. 'And here's the thing — I don't think he ever missed her. He said he was upset but he was more put out, if I'm honest, and then there's him and me. I was *such* a fool.'

I'd lost count of the times I'd heard Saskia utter those very words over the years. 'Hate to point it out, hon, but you were critical of Adam around five seconds before you slept with him.' I put my cup down. 'I presume you are still sleeping with him?'

'I was. I did.'

'Not now?'

Saskia dropped her gaze. 'Not now.' She looked back up, beseeching. 'How, in God's name, do I get rid of him?'

CHAPTER SEVENTY

I didn't think Saskia meant what she said in the way it sounded. Me? I was up for anything.

'Hell, Saskia, how do you get rid of any and every guy you deem expendable?'

Saskia shook her head. 'It's not that easy.' Coming from the expert ditcher, this was worrying. 'What if he won't leave?'

'That's not his choice. If you say "Go", he goes. He's in our parents' home, for God's sake. Should be simple enough.'

'I'm frightened, Sophie.' Saskia averted her eyes and rested her top teeth on her bottom lip. Tense. 'I think Adam hurt Brooke.'

I gave such a jolt, Rufus broke off from feeding. Horribly, I could believe it. Less horribly, it would put him in prison for a long time. Ben and my problem solved. *Eureka!*

'I know it's dramatic,' Saskia continued, all worked up, 'but I was calculating timelines and the day he took his longest trip was also the day Brooke went missing.'

'You realise what you're actually alleging?' I needed Saskia to be very sure. Get this wrong and it would come back to eat us all alive.

'Maybe.'

Maybe wasn't good enough. 'He's an arch-manipulator, Sash. He makes horrible claims. He's unkind and expert at messing with minds, but I've seen no hard evidence of violence.' I felt like a Michelin-starred chef testing a recipe to destruction.

She stared at me, silent. My ballsy, 'not putting up with shit' sister had fear in her eyes.

'Christ, has he hurt you?'

She looked away. 'Uh-huh.'

I smacked a palm over my mouth to smother the gasp of shock threatening to burst out of my body. I'd been here before. I'd let one woman down. I was never ever going to do that again. This time I'd make the right call.

'Saskia, you're going to have to be more explicit than that.' I was shaking. I could practically feel my eyes blazing hot with conviction.

She lowered her gaze. 'He slapped me.'

Livid, I couldn't speak.

'He apologised straightaway. It was only once, or twice,' Saskia said defensively.

'There's nothing *only* about it and don't you dare make excuses for him.' I used to think I didn't understand how women who protect abusive partners do things they don't want to do; say things they don't want to say and conceal things they should never conceal. That was before Leo, not that he'd ever hit me. Ours was a different story, with violent DCI Lester Street taking the lead role. 'When did he hit you?'

'After Brooke walked out. We'd had a lot to drink, and I asked too many questions. I provoked him.'

'No, you did not and if you did, so what? Hurting a woman is never an excuse.'

Saskia hung her head, as if it was all her fault. Oh. My. God. 'You said there was another occasion.'

She nodded, still looking down.

'Where did he strike you?' I thought she'd point to her face. She slipped a hand protectively around her stomach. 'He *punched* you?' Lester had done the same. He never struck Caron in a place where it could be seen easily.

'Yes,' she said in a small voice.

'How many times?'

'A few.' She chewed her lip. 'A lot.'

'Show me.'

'Sophie . . .'

'Please,' I said softly.

Saskia slowly rolled up her sweater. She looked as if her body was a piece of abstract art. Bruising in blues and greens, yellow and reds spread out from the middle of her abdomen, reaching up to the edges of her bony ribs.

'Bastard,' I burst out. 'That's it. You go to the police.'

Saskia rolled her sweater back down, shook her head, destroyed. 'I can't.'

'You have to, Sash.'

'No.'

'But . . .'

Her face creased in anger. 'God's sake, I'm not like you!' she exploded. 'I'm not strong.'

'It's not about being strong.'

'Yes, it is. Look, I respect what you do,' Saskia said, searching for a more moderate tone. 'I get it, but I'm not prepared to parade my embarrassment and pain to strangers.'

'Is that how you see it?'

'Yes,' she snapped.

'Sash, a woman is dead! If you really think Adam had a hand in it, you have to speak up.'

'No.'

'Before someone else gets hurt.'

She opened her mouth to speak, changed her mind, breathing hard. I saw all the moves on her face: fear, regret, guilt, shame. At last, she said, 'What would I tell Mum and Dad?'

'The truth.'

'No, no, no.'

'If you don't, I will.'

'No, Sophie, please don't do that. I know you have a thing about domestic violence but—'

'Because it's wrong. It's against the law.' I was incredulous. Yes, I had a *thing*, as Saskia put it, and so did any sane individual.

'I'm such a let-down,' Saskia wailed. 'I get myself into all kinds of scrapes. It would be another of 'Saskia's stupid decisions', only this time, it's serious.'

I unlatched Rufus, parked him on the sofa, stood up, fetched my bag, and fished out the keys to my flat. 'Take these.' I pushed them into Saskia's hands. She stared at them and then at me.

'You go back home, pack a bag, drive to the flat and stay there. Want me to come with you as backup?'

Saskia shook her head. 'Adam's gone out. Again.'

'Anything else you need, put to one side and I'll pick it up later and drop it off.'

'But I can't leave Mum on her own with Adam.'

'I can sort that.' Almighty hell was I going to fix it. 'As long as Dad and Auntie Fen are around, she'll be safe.' I wasn't certain but it was imperative to convince Saskia that it was in her best interests to leave home as fast as possible.

'Mum will wonder why I left so suddenly.'

'Leave Mum to me.'

'She can't know he hit me.'

'I can get around that.' God knew how. Truth be told, I didn't think I could. 'Does Adam know where my flat is?'

Saskia nodded, afraid.

'Don't answer the door, not in any circumstances, and block his calls.'

'What if he turns up at work?'

'Call the police.'

'It's so extreme.'

'Because it *is*, Sash. I'll speak to Luke and Ron so they're on their guard.'

My little sister looked at me with pleading eyes. 'Please don't tell Louise.'

'I won't if you don't want me to. I will if you go back to Adam.' Caron had returned to Lester endless times. *He'll be better. He doesn't mean it. I'll be good.* I couldn't let that happen to Saskia.

She eventually gave me her word, although she didn't look happy about it. 'What are you going to do, Sophie?'

'Get rid of him.' And, unlike my sister, I didn't rule anything out.

CHAPTER SEVENTY-ONE

I phoned Cake That and informed Luke that Saskia wouldn't be in for the rest of the week. Afterwards I spoke to Vanessa to explain the reason why.

'Greasy murderous git,' Vanessa exclaimed. 'Has she reported it?'

'Not yet.' Not ever, if I knew my stubborn little sister. For someone who enjoyed the limelight this was a level of attention she disliked. I'd listened to what Saskia had said about fearing my parents' disappointment, but it went deeper. A go-getter, confident and popular with men and women alike, Saskia couldn't understand how she'd lost control and, in her eyes, put herself in the firing line and allowed a terrible situation to happen. It was the song of women the world over.

'How is she?' Vanessa asked.

'Not good. Still in shock.'

Until it dissipated, I stood no chance of persuading Saskia to change her mind, which was maddeningly frustrating. Viewed against the background of Brooke's disappearance and death, however, Adam's violent streak was bound to interest the police. Leo had told me to filter any information through Hicks. Not this.

'Can you man the fort today?' I asked Vanessa.

'No problem.'

'I'll come in tomorrow. And Vanessa?'

'Yes.'

'Keep it under wraps?'

'You got it.'

I scrolled down to Leo's number. Reporting Adam's violence to a man who had once upon a time not taken domestic violence seriously was not lost on me. Leo had changed, he'd said. Here was his chance to prove it. And if he didn't or couldn't, if I came up against a suggestion of a brick wall, I would go over his head to a higher authority, exactly as I'd done years before. Tragically, I was already too late back then.

It took an age to get through and when I did my call connected to voicemail. I left a brief message for Leo to phone me. With still no word from him when I set off for Mum's, I started to worry and sent Ben a message to check the police weren't with him. Almost immediately, I could see he'd received and read it and was typing a message back.

No. All good. Everything okay with you?

I typed a thumb's up. News of Adam's abuse could keep.

Interrupting Liam wrestling with one half of a bi-fold door, I told him I'd be back later.

'Right you are. Bye, Rufus.' Liam smiled kindly. Having recently become a dad, he took more interest than the rest of his crew.

I'd driven to Mum's dozens of times. This time felt different because *I* felt different. It was as if something had clicked inside and I'd found a bit of the old me: the cool, unflappable, purposeful, businesslike Sophie. No way was some sly and violent creep going to push me around or hurt the people I loved.

I was pulling into Mum's drive when Leo phoned me back. As soon as I heard his voice, I plunged in. 'I know you asked me to channel everything though DC Hicks, but this is of vital importance.'

'What's the problem?'

So off I went. I told Leo about Adam's long drive on the day of Brooke's disappearance and finished with Adam abusing Saskia on several occasions.

I couldn't see Leo, but the long pause before he reacted told its own story. This would strike deep and heavy. 'Jesus Christ, Sophie. How bad is it?'

'Bad enough. Her body is black and blue.'

'She's reported it?'

'No.'

'Let me talk to her.'

'She's very reluctant, Leo.'

'You know as well as me that time is of the essence. If she speaks to someone who understands, like me, I could speed things up.'

I heaved a sigh. I knew Leo was right. I also knew that Saskia would rather stick pins in her eyes than make it public.

After a leaden pause, Leo said, 'I could make some calls. Discreetly, of course.'

'I'm not sure.' I didn't like the idea of Leo intervening without Saskia's say-so.

'Can't you persuade her to talk to me?'

'I can try,' I said uncertainly. 'It's a factor though, isn't it, with Brooke? It shows Adam Hall has a history of violence.' Yes, I was laying it on thick.

There was another pause. 'I see where you're coming from,' he conceded. Stating the obvious, I didn't like the sound of that. 'But how would this connect to Brooke exactly?' Leo asked.

'He might have coerced her.'

'Coerced her to do what?'

'Kill herself.'

'O-kay,' Leo said uncertainly. 'You're suggesting that, after the dust-up with his girlfriend, Adam Hall tracks her down.'

'He had access to Dad's car. It's done a ton of mileage since he borrowed it and especially around the time Brooke went missing.'

'How do you know?'

'Because Saskia checked.'

'Saskia?'

'Yes.'

Busy reflecting, he didn't respond straightaway. 'So,' he said, eventually, 'Adam allegedly catches up with Brooke and does what exactly?'

'Maybe he attacked her. Maybe he gave her the pills. You've seen how charming and persuasive he is. Maybe he encouraged her to jump and that's how she wound up in the drink. He's a mind-bender, Leo.'

'Sophie, you don't need me to tell you that's highly speculative.'

I'd been around enough police officers to know that Jo Public wasn't invited to speculate. 'But what if I'm right?'

He was quiet for so long I thought we'd been cut off. 'Hello,' I said.

'There's no easy way to say this, Sophie, and I don't blame you and totally get it, but bad experience doesn't always translate to the present. This isn't Lester Street Mark Two.'

'I know a bad guy when I see one, Leo.' I always did. 'Why would a man stand over a little baby in the dark alone?' I explained how I'd found Adam at my parents. 'God alone knows what he planned but he didn't expect me to find him.'

'Are you sure you read the room right? He's the child's uncle.'

'Leo, if you'd been there, you wouldn't see it as anything other than sinister.'

'Okay,' he said. 'You're saying that Hall had means and opportunity, but what would be his motive?'

I had absolutely no idea. 'That's for you to find out.'

He went quiet again. 'I appreciate your call,' he said, finally. 'Let me look into it.'

'Into *him*,' I insisted.

'Got the memo.' There was a smile in his voice. He spoke with more humour than I deserved.

'Thank you.'

'Although I can confirm that there was nothing to suggest that Brooke was assaulted before she died.'

Water did terrible things to a body, I recalled Leo telling me, although I guessed a pathologist would discover anything out of the ordinary. Absorbed by the thought, I almost missed Leo stressing what was incontrovertible. 'Sadly, there was plenty evidence of opiates in her system.'

'Which isn't uncommon with people who drown themselves.'

'Who told you that?'

'You did.' A long time ago. 'It's the lead cause of suicide with women.'

'Which brings us right around to how Brooke obtained them.'

It did. I couldn't odds it. I was starting to feel nervous. 'A drug user, she could have got them from anyone.'

'Or the doctor who had access.'

'Doctors have access every day.'

'Accepted.'

'Even for prescribed pills doctors are not accountable for how a patient chooses to use them.'

'They are liable if proper protocols are not carried out. Brooke Gentry was not Ben's patient. C'mon, Sophie, you know this as well as me.'

Stumped, I shut up.

'How are you — honestly?' he asked gently.

In the middle of conversational mayhem, the question took me by surprise. 'Me? So-so.'

'Bearing up?'

'Yes.'

'Good. Getting back to Saskia, she's living with Adam at your parents, isn't she?'

'Not anymore.' I told him the steps I'd taken to ensure her safety.

'Well done — and she's agreed to stay away from him?'

'She has.'

'Make sure she keeps her word. If he approaches and lays another finger on her, she *must* phone me. That way it can all be recorded.'

'Thanks, Leo.'

'Only doing my job.'

I stayed on the line, reluctant to hang up.

'Sorry, Sophie, but I've got a call coming through. If I dig anything up, either me or Hicks will be in touch.'

'Yes, of course,' I said briskly. 'Goodbye.'

I regretted that I hadn't achieved what I'd hoped for. In my desire to nail Adam, I'd nailed Ben.

CHAPTER SEVENTY-TWO

Mum looked better than I'd seen her in weeks. I prayed she wasn't going to say it was a result of the Adam-effect.

'You look well,' I said.

'Ah, I've been meaning to talk to you about that.'

I pushed a smile to disguise the sinking sensation in my stomach.

'Let's go into the kitchen,' Mum said briskly.

She'd popped a play mat on the floor for Rufus and laid out a lovely lunch: sourdough bread, smoked salmon and prawns and a big bowl of salad, with asparagus.

I handed her Rufus while I peeled off my jacket.

'I've had a slight medical issue,' Mum began.

For 'slight' I read 'serious'.

'It's nothing to worry about.'

No worries, no problem so why mention?

'It's all sorted now,' Mum said in a 'that's that' tone.

'And does this problem have a name?' I asked.

Mum doesn't care for facetiousness. I was rewarded with a sharp look.

'Hyperthyroidism or overactive thyroid to you and me. It's all quite treatable with beta-blockers and I'm feeling very much better.'

'So the diet . . .'

'Darling, I didn't want to worry anyone, least of all your father. You know how he frets over the slightest thing.'

'And Ben, did he know?'

'Well, he *is* a doctor.'

He lied. Again. Damn it.

'What is it, Sophie? You've gone quite pale.'

'I knew something was wrong. I asked Ben because I thought you might speak to him, and he denied all knowledge.' Denial seeming his default position on any subject one cared to mention.

'Because I made him promise not to tell you.'

'He *should* have told me.' I didn't stamp my foot. My voice did the job instead.

'Sophie, Sophie,' Mum said, seeing how upset and angry I was. She popped Rufus down on the mat and put her arms around me. Pain lanced through my ribs. The tears in my eyes were for real.

'It was a little white lie to stop you from worrying.'

I wasn't concerned so much with the little lies but the whopping big ones.

'Don't be cross with *him*. Be cross with *me*. And look,' Mum said, drawing away, 'see, I'm all better.'

I inhaled sharply, trying to get on top of the white-hot heat spreading through my ribcage. 'Honestly?'

'Cross my heart.'

'Don't say the rest.' I smiled awkwardly.

She ruffled my hair like she used to do when I was little. 'I'm going to be around for a very long time, I assure you. Besides, I have a little grandson to look after.' Her warm gaze fell on Rufus. 'Now, let's eat and you can tell me what on earth is going on with Saskia.'

It was my turn to say, 'Ah.'

* * *

'He hit her?' Mum exploded — and my mother is not an explosive person. Crimson flushed her neck and cheeks. I was glad she was on beta-blockers.

'Several times.' I'd never made promises to Saskia. She would be furious with me and probably wouldn't speak to me for a month. It would pass. Adam had to be outed for who and what he was. 'The police have been made aware.'

'Good for Saskia,' Mum said heartily.

'Saskia didn't report it.'

Mum's face fell. 'Why ever not?'

'She has a hang-up about being a disappointment to you and Dad.'

'What? That's ridiculous.'

'Might be an idea for you to let her know.'

'Silly girl,' Mum fretted. 'It was you who spoke to the local police then?'

I shook my head. 'I spoke to Leo.' I read surprise and curiosity in Mum's expression. 'He can't action anything unless Saskia comes forward and agrees to press charges. I'm not sure she's there yet, although Leo offered to talk to her.'

It was several seconds before Mum responded. 'How is that all working out?'

I took her to mean Ben and the police, not Leo and me. For one thing there was no Leo and me.

'No more developments since Ben gave a statement.'

'Let that be the end of it.'

I genuinely hoped so.

'As for Adam Hall, words fail me,' Mum said. 'To think this went on in our home, under our noses.'

I couldn't swear for sure where it had taken place, but it was a fair possibility.

Mum fiddled with her wedding ring, a sign that she was uncomfortable. 'Sophie, I offer an unreserved apology. You warned us and we took no notice. We should have listened. *I* should have listened. I'm sorry.'

I shrugged. None of it mattered now and I was never one for scoring points and holding grudges.

'Do you forgive me?'

'Nothing to forgive, Mum.'

Her soft expression swiftly switched to anger. 'I will not have that blasted man in my house another moment.' She stood up, went to a drawer next to the sink and took out a roll of black bin liners. Mischief in her eyes, she beckoned for me to follow her upstairs.

We went into Saskia's room, the one she shared with Adam. Sweeping two bags off the top of a cupboard, Mum dumped these on the floor and ordered me to empty all Adam's belongings into them. I parked Rufus on the bed while I emptied drawers of underwear, socks, T-shirts and general crap. Next, I cleared the bathroom of his toiletries. It was strangely exhilarating. Meanwhile, Mum, having flung open the doors of the wardrobe, tore Adam's trademark suit from a hanger, scrumpled it up, together with shirts, jeans and a leather jacket. These all went into bin liners.

'Has he got a key to the house?' I asked.

She gave me a worried nod.

'We'll get it back. Don't worry. I can sort it. What about the car?'

'Fortunately, it's in the garage having new tyres fitted.'

After all the driving Adam had done, I wasn't surprised.

'What shall we do with this lot?' I asked, viewing Adam's earthly possessions.

'Is it raining?' Mum glanced towards the window.

'It is.'

'Chuck the lot outside then.'

CHAPTER SEVENTY-THREE

We did.

Ceremoniously, Mum hurled every bin liner out of the sash window straight onto the gravel below. One of the bags split open and the arm of Adam's prized leather jacket unfurled into a puddle. Not having the strength to lift and heave without enduring untold agonies, I shuffled downstairs with the rest of his stuff, a holdall in each hand, and dumped them in the dirt just as Adam strolled straight into the drive. This was my moment to square up to him, tell him he was a despicable human being and spell out exactly what would happen to him if he dared utter so much as an angry, or belittling word to my sister or, indeed, any woman ever again. I was sure this was written on my face, in my eyes, in the no messing way I stood, my boots planted firmly, my arms crossed, my back ruler straight, despite the pain in my ribs. Everything about me shrieked 'you've been seen for who and what you are'. And Adam wasn't stupid. He would realise it was now public knowledge he thumped women. Anyone else would voice an apology, an excuse. Anyone else would smoulder with humiliation. He looked cool, calm and composed, like a politician who is out on manoeuvres hell-bent on removing a leader from office so he can slide into his place. With a slick supercilious smile, he glanced from me to his worldly possessions and back again. When Adam was on form he could electrify. He could also suck the light and love out of a person. My spine softened. My arms dropped. I felt drained.

'Keys,' I said, boldly holding out my hand. Rain spattered my hair and face. My clothes clung to my skin.

He threw me a vicious look and fumbled inside his raincoat. Dropping them, a sign that he wasn't quite as together as he appeared, he plucked them out of the dirt and walked towards me. I felt the edge of his fingers graze my hand. It wasn't a pleasant sensation. I pictured his fist, knuckles tight, a weapon of war.

'I'll arrange for my stuff to be collected,' he said, as if it was a trifling matter, of no consequence.

Was this it? Was he finally out of our lives and we'd never see him again? Why did I feel as if he held the winning hand and not me?

He turned to go.

'Saskia is fine, by the way,' I called after him, shrill. He continued without a backward glance. 'And she's marked your card with the police.'

He stopped dead and wheeled round. Marching straight up to me, he stood, panting lightly. I surged with satisfaction at witnessing him keen to keep control and yet in danger of losing it. He bent down, angling his long neck, his face in mine. I could smell expensive aftershave. I also smelt fear and anger, and it was feral. 'And the police have marked Ben's card,' he snarled.

'Is that so?' I said, feigning unconcern.

'Oh, yes.' A wide smile split across his face. 'One little word from me—'

'I know what really happened, Adam. Ben told me.'

'Then you know he's . . .'

'I went to where you grew up. I asked around. I saw the pub. I saw *everything*.'

318

He took a step back, as if I'd put a lighted match to his skin.

'I know what you did. You've lost your power, Adam.'

He stayed still, thinking, wondering if I was bluffing. I saw him make some kind of calculation.

'Whatever,' he finally said, stalking away.

That's when I knew for certain he had a Plan B.

CHAPTER SEVENTY-FOUR

If I hadn't been driving with precious cargo, I'd have downed a double Jack. Instead, I settled for a cup of tea and a slab of red velvet cake.

Afterwards, Mum packed up enough food supplies to last Saskia until Christmas and told me to pass on the message that she'd look in later. I left Rufus with Mum, and we agreed that I'd also drop him off in the morning while I went into work.

My sister's belongings jammed into my car, I drove to my old apartment and staggered up the stairs, bags in each hand.

Saskia opened the door as I trundled in and dropped the first load. She greeted me with a sisterly hug that made me want to scream with pain.

'No baby?'

'No room,' I gasped. 'There's a stack of stuff. Mum went a bit mad with goodies.'

'Shit, Sophie, you told her?' Saskia plumped down onto the sofa and thrust me an accusing look.

'It's better this way.'

'For whom?'

'For everyone.' I waited a beat. 'I also told Leo.'

'You did *what*?'

'It's okay. He can't action it unless you agree.'

'I don't agree.' Saskia's voice was full of reproach.

'He'd understand. Where's the harm in talking to him?'

'It harms *me*. I don't want to talk about it to him, or anyone else. I want to forget it.'

I patted the air with my hands. 'Calm down, it's okay, Sash.'

'It is *so* not okay.' Saskia tipped forward, a sketchy look on her face. 'Have you seen Adam?'

'He's gone.'

'Where?' Worry lines appeared on her brow.

'I didn't ask, Sash.'

'Think he's left the country?'

'One can pray.'

'Seriously?'

'I don't know.'

'But he *was* okay? He wasn't angry?'

My breath caught in my chest. Bad memories assailed me. *He's not angry, is he? You didn't threaten him, did you? Lester can't bear to be ticked off.*

'No, he was not angry,' I said, digging my nails into my palms. 'And what do you care? Too bad if he was.' The truth was Adam was scared. And scared people are dangerous.

Trying not to dwell, I told Saskia about the arrangements I'd made at work. 'I'll go in tomorrow.'

'Bloody hell, does everyone know my business?'

'That Adam's a shit? Only the people that matter.'

'Did you have to?'

'Yes, I did. Now can we please unload my car?'

Doing something useful mollified her and gave me a break. To be fair, Saskia didn't respond to what she saw as my betrayal too badly. It could have been a lot worse. I was absolutely finished by the time we'd gone up and down for the fourth time. Awash with expensive and branded clothing, my seemingly big apartment shrank to the size of a shoebox. No wonder my little sister was permanently skint.

'Mum's going to pop round later,' I told her. I didn't tell my sister that Mum had genuinely been poorly. I didn't want to gift Adam that level of credibility.

'Have you spoken to Auntie Fen?' Saskia asked.

In the chaos I'd forgotten about her. I hoped my aunt's silence didn't mean she was having second thoughts. It wouldn't be a disaster for my sister. I could always rent my place to her. It would prove financially challenging for me until Ben got his hands on his trust fund and ensured it stayed out of Adam's malevolent reach. 'I'm waiting for her to get back,' I told Saskia. 'I'll reach out again this evening.'

We stood on the threshold. Odd for me to be on the other side; it felt like I was finally letting go of an old life.

Saskia tipped up on her toes and kissed my cheek. 'Thanks, Sophs.'

'Don't be daft,' I said, embarrassed.

CHAPTER SEVENTY-FIVE

I beefed up security at Cake That. I couldn't prevent Adam from posting vile reviews about our products on social media, but I could take steps to prevent him breaking in and contaminating ingredients with faeces, or importing rats, or using the place for a rave and inviting all his mates (more likely random strangers), or burning the unit to the ground. Yes, I was thinking that wildly. A CCTV system was already in place. What I needed was something more physical: a proper security guard with biceps like pile drivers to patrol at night. I called a company that I'd heard good things about and explained I needed someone on a short-term contract. I was promised a man with a plan (I hoped) would drop into the unit the next day. It would cost; a small price to pay for peace of mind.

I phoned Auntie Fen, left another message, bathed and changed Rufus and was stirring a pot of chilli when she called me back.

'Darling,' she gushed. 'So so sorry. I haven't been ignoring your calls, but I've been so terribly busy.'

Shifting trunks of clothing to Ellenborough Park, I suspected. 'Having fun, I hope.'

'Always. Now about your little flat. You're sure you want me to go through the estate agent?'

'I can't see another way.'

'You know your trouble, my darling? You're far too honourable.'

A depressing thought, that I didn't match the hype. 'I'd feel more comfortable if you went through the appointed channel.'

'Thought you'd say that. But I have a proposal.'

'I'm listening.'

'I'll make an offer below market price. With great reluctance, you accept. The agent gets his pound of flesh based on the price I pay.'

'And you pay me the balance of the sale direct into my account?'

'Clever girl.'

'Clever aunt.' It was shady but not too shady.

'Done. I'll pop into the agent tomorrow. Now I must go. A large gin awaits.'

Bonkers, I thought.

Ben arrived home. He looked dead on his feet.

'Bad day?'

'Elliott put the phone down on me.'

'You're kidding.' This was not like Elliott at all.

'Not before he'd laid in.'

'He blames you for Louise's miscarriage?'

'In short.'

'I'm sorry.'

'Maybe he has a point.'

'He'll come round.'

'You think?' Ben asked, despairing.

'There's nothing you can do. Give it time,' I said.

I waited until he'd poured himself a glass of water and then started with the good stuff — Auntie Fen's clever plan. Then I moved on to the sketchy stuff: *you lied to me about Mum.* I held off the big stuff until after supper. In response to Mum's news, he spread his hands. 'Not so much a white lie as a grey one.'

'She made out it wasn't a big deal.'

'Left untreated, it would have been.'

'I wished you'd told me.'

'*I* wished I'd told you.' Ben ran a hand under his jaw. 'I don't appear to be getting many things right at the moment, but your mum didn't want to worry anyone until she knew what was wrong.'

It sounded plausible.

'Am I forgiven?'

'Mostly.'

Ben snatched a smile, one I returned. 'Mostly is an improvement.'

'Do I still get my birthday treat?' I teased. 'Or was that nothing more than a ruse to deflect me?'

'You do,' he said with another good-natured smile. 'How was the rest of your day?'

I didn't know how to answer that but did my best.

CHAPTER SEVENTY-SIX

'Someone should take my brother down a dark alley and beat the crap out of him,' Ben blasted.

'That would really help. The police would have a field day.'

Ben said nothing for a moment, a worried expression on his face. 'I can't help thinking Adam had something to do with Brooke's death. I don't know how or why but I wouldn't put it past him.'

'You are not alone. Leo is looking into it.'

Ben's eyes darted to mine. 'You spoke to him?'

'It was important he knew.'

'Surely, it was up to Saskia to report it?'

'She's too fragile.'

Leo, a sore subject, Ben stood up and cleared the table.

'It was strictly on a professional basis,' I said sheepishly.

'If you say so.'

'Ben, please . . .'

He stopped what he was doing. 'Can we drop it? I accept what you say.'

From the way he was clattering about I could see that he didn't.

'We have a bigger problem,' I said quietly.

'Jesus, is that even possible?'

I told Ben about my run-in with Adam earlier. 'For a man caught in the act, he was extraordinarily self-possessed.' When Ben didn't react, I said, 'I think he'll go nuclear.'

'Inform the police about me?'

'What he *suspects* about you.'

Ben sat back down. 'The police will investigate my background—'

'And in isolation, it might not matter—'

'But added to their obsession with me prescribing pills to Brooke, it will make me come across as highly dubious.'

About the size of it, I was forced to agree.

Tortured by the prospect, Ben's brow creased in concentration. He knew he could lose everything. I didn't doubt he was wondering if he would lose Rufus and me too.

'You know how I think of Adam?' Ben spoke slowly and softly.

I shook my head.

'He's like one of those thugs you see in conflict zones. Armed to the teeth, hopped up on drugs, waving an AK47 in the air, firing off a volley of shots into the sky.'

I frowned, not really getting it.

'Takes one stray bullet to land badly and kill a random individual — that's what Adam does. He sprays allegations and rumours, hoping and knowing one will stick. Everyone has skeletons in their cupboards and Adam's a genius at giving them a rattle.'

And Adam had rattled mine. My mouth felt dry. Heat flamed my cheeks. I surged with panic. Would Ben be more forgiving than I was of myself? 'Ben, there's—'

'Wouldn't it be easier if I came clean?' He looked grey at the thought.

'What?' I said, confused.

'Turn myself in.'

'And get banged up for two crimes, one you didn't commit?'

'If only the police would look more closely at Adam,' Ben said.

'Leo is.'

Ben's mouth straightened into a grimace. 'Must have been quite some conversation.'

The jealous note in his voice was unmistakable. I said, 'Like I said, it was strictly professional.'

'If highly unorthodox.'

'I was trying to take the heat off you,' I claimed, struggling to defend my actions. 'I was trying to show Leo that you were a good guy. I wanted to cast doubt in his mind about Adam.'

'Then I can only hope you succeeded.' The dry, uncompromising expression on his face set like concrete.

'Please, don't be like this.'

'Like what? How do you expect me to be, Sophie? You were going to marry the man.'

'But I didn't.'

Ben's eyes never left mine. *They* were searching. *He* was thinking. *I* was afraid.

'It wasn't cold feet about being a police officer's wife at all, was it?'

I slowly shook my head, realising that I had absolutely no choice but to tell him the truth about why I'd bailed on the man who once owned my heart.

CHAPTER SEVENTY-SEVEN

'You knew?' Tears pricked my eyes.

'I'd always figured there was more to it. I hoped when the time was right, you'd tell me.'

'This is hardly the right time.' I forced a smile and cast a glance outside the window.

Ben leant forward and crooked a knuckle under my chin, tilting my face up to meet his steady gaze. 'It's *exactly* the right time. What can be so bad after what I've told you?'

Worse than you think. My voice shook a little as I began. 'When Leo was a young and ambitious police officer he had a mentor, a DCI called Lester Street. Street was a skilled detective. Charismatic and charming, he was popular with his team.

'I didn't know him well, not like Leo. I knew his wife, Caron.' I briefly closed my eyes, wanting to do right by her. I pictured Caron at her best: loud and laughing, dark and flashing, beautifully made-up and dressed in the designer clothes she loved to wear. 'Caron was noisy, very sweary, not my cup of tea, if I'm honest. She tended to hang out with more senior officers' wives — Leo was a DC at the time so, in a subtle way, I wasn't one of her crew. Our paths sometimes crossed at dinners and celebrations. I thought she was outgoing and funny, highly irreverent and not a woman to take herself too seriously. That was the lovely side of her personality, but she had a dark side when she drank, and she drank a lot.'

'A dark side?'

'She would turn. You could almost see it. The daft remark would be wilfully misinterpreted. She would taunt and ridicule. She could be quite insulting and crude. Some of the other wives and girlfriends took exception to her.' I paused, catching my breath. 'You couldn't always believe what she said.'

'She was a liar?'

'Too strong, although not according to her enemies.'

'Kids?'

'She and Lester had two children, a boy and a sweet little girl, eighteen months and three years of age. The kids spent a lot of time with their grandparents.'

'Because of her drinking?'

'It got in the way of her parenting. It was so sad because when she was sober, she could be the best, a really nice woman, but on the booze, she was a different animal. It wasn't uncommon for her to go AWOL for weeks at a time. Fact is I didn't know why she drank. I didn't ask and I didn't listen, and I didn't care. I was too busy getting on with my life to get involved in her problems.' A terrible admission, I stalled. Ben patiently waited.

'Do you want some water?'

'No, thank you.' I needed to keep going.

'There were rumours that the marriage was in trouble followed by reports of domestic abuse. Lester persuaded his colleagues that Caron was the abuser, not him.'

'Which was credible because of her drinking?'

'Basically, her optics were bad.'

'And where was Leo in all this?'

'He didn't believe Caron any more than I did. He believed Lester.'

I looked at Ben with sad eyes. 'Without knowing the full story, I took a side, one that didn't want to get involved, didn't want to deal with the unpleasantness in other people's lives. When social services were called in, resulting in both sets of grandparents sharing the load with the children, I thought it a good thing.'

'And wasn't it?'

'Not for Caron. It broke her. Whatever else, she loved her children.' I was going to say that she would have died for them. Too near the truth, the words tangled in my throat.

'What happened?' Ben reached across, took my hand and pressed his thumb against my palm.

'I saw Caron one day in the street. She looked so forlorn that I took her for a coffee. She poured out her heart to me.'

'She was sober?'

'Yes.' I recalled her frightened eyes. I'd never seen someone look that terrified. 'The abuse she'd suffered had been going on for years. She spoke firmly, like you know when someone is telling the truth, without self-pity, giving it to me straight with dates and descriptions of incidents that would make your hair fall out. That's when I started to take her seriously.'

'But Leo continued to convince you that you were wrong?'

'He didn't believe a word of it. Said she was a proven pathological liar. I lost touch with Caron, which wasn't that surprising or unusual until, one day, she doorstepped me at work. I was so shocked by the deterioration in her appearance I invited her into my office.' Her breath was rank with alcohol. Always beautifully turned out, her clothes were creased and smelled unwashed and there was a faint odour of urine. I thought she'd spent the night in a shop doorway. 'Once we were inside, she lifted her sweater.' The bruises on my sister's body bore little relation to what I saw on Caron's that day.

'Was it bad?' Ben's brow was a collection of short straight lines.

'Horrific.'

'Then you were fully on board?'

'I needed to act but nobody else would. A female PC, who attended a call out, told Caron that, as she was intoxicated

— she'd had a single glass of wine, Caron told me — there was insufficient evidence to follow it up. The view was that Caron had injured herself when drunk.' My voice brittle with cynicism, I said, 'It was unconscionable that a fine and decorated police officer could beat his wife.'

'The wife who was a drunk and incapable of looking after her kids,' Ben murmured.

'Exactly what Leo argued. But the abuse was all true, Ben. Caron was many things, but she was no liar when it came to her husband.' Perspiration popped up on my brow. I released my hand from Ben's to wipe it away.

'Surely, a risk assessment would have been carried out, records checked, an investigation mounted?'

'You'd think, but this was over a decade ago.' I recalled Leo's words about changed attitudes and culture. I hoped he was right. I hoped it would be handled differently today.

'What did you do?'

'I couldn't take on an organisation, but I could take practical steps to help. I contacted a refuge that would take her. To this day, I'll never know why Caron didn't get up and leave. Frustrated, I voiced my concerns to a detective superintendent. Unknown to me, the super was a personal friend of Lester Street. There were procedures and protocols to follow, I was told.'

'You were fobbed off?'

I nodded. 'When Leo discovered that I'd "interfered", to use his words, he was furious. We fought tooth and claw. It worried me that Leo was taking life lessons from a man who had used his rank to hide his abuse of his wife.'

'But you didn't leave?'

I tried to recall my state of mind at the time, as if it would offer a path in which I could forgive myself for my cowardice. About to marry a man I thought I loved I was out of my depth. I was wilfully blind. Period. 'No excuse but Leo put it to me that I was destroying a talented officer's career.'

'Bastard.'

'Yes, but I share the blame. Caron had come to me because she saw me as a woman who was steady and fair. I was neither, Ben. I was weak.

'Two weeks before my wedding, Caron came to the flat I shared with Leo. She blasted in, making wild accusations about him.'

Why would you marry someone like him? Soon as he has that ring on your finger, he'll beat the living crap out of you. You'll see.

'Leo had gone to the Street's home after answering a report of a disturbance. Caron claimed he'd humiliated her, despite her wrist being broken.'

'Was it true?'

'When I confronted him, he told me that if Lester had hit her, he was provoked, that she'd driven him to it.'

'Christ Almighty.'

'As if that was somehow a mitigating factor,' I said, as repelled now as I was then. 'The moment he used such a lousy defence we were done. It was over.'

'And Caron?'

I sank into a clutch of horrible memories. If only I'd been stronger. If only I'd acted sooner.

'Sophie,' Ben said gently.

'That same evening, Lester Street beat his wife to death with a claw hammer in front of their children.' Averting my eyes from Ben's, I hung my head in shame. 'I should have done more. I could have done more.'

Ben squeezed my hand.

'The case briefly hit the news cycle,' I continued wearily, 'but it was quickly lost in the great morass of scandals involving the Met. An apology was issued subsequently from the deputy chief constable to the effect that the police had not handled it well, but that Street was a highly manipulative individual. There was the usual line about lessons being learned.'

'Was anyone held to account?'

'Not to my knowledge, although I didn't stick around long enough to find out.'

'So that's when you changed direction?'

'I ripped my life up. If it's any consolation, it also had as profound an effect on Leo. I genuinely believe he's a changed man.'

Ben didn't say anything. I wondered what was travelling through his mind. Would he ditch me like I'd ditched Leo? Eventually, he spoke and, initially, I didn't see where he was going with it.

'All sorts of characters came to my parents' pub,' he said. 'There was this guy, William Bywater. They used to call him Three-Piece Bill because he always dressed in a three-piece suit. A steady drinker, he could shift three quarters of a bottle of Scotch in a night. A quiet, dignified man he once let it slip that his mother was Russian and that he was fluent in the language. He was a translator, or so he said, and he talked about the many times he'd been to Russia and described the time when he'd spent an uncomfortable couple of days questioned by the KGB. Everyone believed he was a fantasist. He got royally ragged and, consequently, never spoke of it again.

'When Bill died my parents went to his funeral. There were hardly any people but they said that two men stood at the back of the church that nobody knew. Spooks in suits, my dad said. Bill, it seemed, had been telling the truth.'

'And you're telling me this why?'

'We all make mistakes about people, Sophie. You got it massively wrong with Caron. But you were right about Lester. Wasn't your fault if nobody was listening.'

CHAPTER SEVENTY-EIGHT

For the remains of the week and into the weekend we were like two survivors of a train derailment, staggering from the wreckage with only minor cuts and bruises.

Solicitous towards one another, we fell into a natural domestic rhythm: sorting out the recycling, planning what we were going to do with the garden now that the garden room consumed a third of it. I coaxed Rufus onto solids: fruit puree a hit, mashed potato a miss, pureed broccoli a definite no-no. I went to work on Monday, slipping into the welcome familiarity of routine and doing something I loved.

A phone call from the estate agent announced I'd received an offer well below market price from a lady who lived in London but had family in Cheltenham. *Thank you, Auntie Fen.* I went through the motions of being less than happy with the price while allowing myself to be persuaded to take it. 'I know it's disappointing,' the estate agent said, no doubt with a furrowed brow, 'but it's the only offer you've received otherwise I'd advise you to hold out. In the current climate however . . .' He trailed off, leaving me to do the maths, which I'd already done. Deal sealed I told him to proceed.

Without contact from either Adam or the police, I began to relax and so did Ben. A pause, while Liam and his crew started another job down the road, enabled us to take our time in choosing the tiling for the floor. We plumped for limestone.

After days of being spoiled by Mum and Dad, Saskia re-joined our crew at Cake That mid-week to save her from 'terminal boredom'. Surrounded by kindness and humour, never pity, she settled back in slowly and gradually and, as one day rolled into another, the fear of a random appearance from Adam lessened, not only for her, but also for the rest of us. Unknown to my sister, I'd asked everyone to put the equivalent of a ring of steel around her. I was certain that if Luke asked her one more time if she wanted a cup of coffee or a bun, she'd scream. She didn't.

Despite the change in tempo, the return to the new normal, I was wary. The strong undercurrent of anxiety I felt, low-level mostly, intense at others, refused to budge. I was plagued with what ifs. Then two events occurred that significantly ramped up my inner tension.

The first happened as I was travelling into town on a beautifully sunny Wednesday after I'd collected Rufus from Mum's. Popping into the High Street to drop in signed papers to my solicitor handling the apartment sale, I decided to use St George's Road car park, next to the Magistrates' Court in Cheltenham. From there it was a short walk onto the Promenade.

Pulling in, I paused to make room for a car pulling out. Not any car: a right-hand drive Chevrolet Corvette in metallic blue, top down. Accustomed to spotting expensive motors in Cheltenham, it didn't strike me as anything out of the ordinary. A casual observer would believe the driver was a man of note and reputation with wealth and connections. Wearing shades and an open-neck white shirt so bright it matched his teeth and hurt my eyes, Adam turned towards me with a wolfish grin. My first thought was: *Shit, he's still here*. My second thought: *What a waste of our money*. My third: *Is this part of the plan because, sure as hell, he has one*.

I offered a tight smile to demonstrate that I was unfazed. I thought he'd drop the window and speak. His mouth contracted in contempt, as if I were a person who, feeling the ship sinking, elbows her way past the elderly and children in search of a lifeboat. Satisfied that he'd made his feelings clear, he shifted his gaze back to the road. Dismissed, I sat inhaling fumes as the Corvette sped into the street with a throaty roar before disappearing down the road to the traffic lights.

The second oddity occurred a day later when Leo phoned and asked if we could meet.

'When?'

'Tomorrow?'

Tomorrow was my birthday, any celebrating to be saved for Saturday. A Friday, Ben would be at work.

'Where?' No way was I travelling to London.

'St Michael's Park at ten.'

I expressed surprise. St Michael's was a small park in Cirencester where little kids played, and it was forbidden to take dogs. The Abbey grounds would have been a more central and obvious choice.

'Is it anything serious, Leo?' Absolutely it was. Why else the cloak and dagger? Maybe he'd found out something about Adam, a history of domestic abuse of partners, for example.

'We'll discuss it tomorrow.'

Leo didn't advise me to keep it a secret and I didn't ask if it was supposed to be private and confidential. Off the record, I suspected, so I didn't tell Ben. I didn't tell Mum. I didn't tell anyone.

CHAPTER SEVENTY-NINE

My day began sleepily at six thirty. Ben got up and, while I fed Rufus, he prepared and brought me tea and buttered toast. I read a ton of birthday messages on my phone and opened several cards.

'Anything from Louise and Elliott?' Ben asked, casually dropping it into conversation and budging up next to me.

'Not yet,' I said.

'I think I've ballsed it up between us.'

'Elliott is cross and embarrassed, but they aren't grudge merchants, Ben.'

He sipped his tea. 'I might as well tell you now — they can't come to the party tomorrow.'

Surprised and disappointed, I didn't show it. 'They're entitled to make other plans.'

'I guess. Here,' Ben said, brightening, 'I got you this.' He reached over the bedside drawer and, taking out a small box wrapped in tissue paper, handed it to me. 'It's not an engagement ring,' he said hurriedly.

I unwrapped and opened it and let out an astonished little cry. 'My God, Ben, it's beautiful.' A single ruby set into a white gold band, I held it up to the light, watching the shade change from deep red to pale pink. 'Must have cost a fortune.'

'After all you've put up with it's no more than you deserve.'

I met Ben's open and trusting gaze and tried not to think of how he'd got the money for such an expensive gift. A wash of guilt crashed over me at the thought of meeting Leo later that morning; it felt dishonest not to mention it to Ben, but I knew how sore he felt about him, maybe more so now that he'd heard about Leo's past behaviour.

I turned my head, my lips softly meeting his. We kissed long and slow. 'Do you mind if I wear it on my left hand?'

A great heart-warming smile broke over his face. It felt like an age since I'd seen him look this happy. 'You may have some explaining to do to your folks.' He had a point. If I didn't put her straight, my mother would be feverishly making wedding plans.

'Before I forget,' Ben said, 'Liam dropped me a message about the tiles. He's delivering them first thing tomorrow morning so Sam the tiler can lay them on Sunday.'

I pulled a face.

'The only time the guy can fit us in,' Ben said. 'It's not a problem, is it? It's not as if we're having the party here.'

'I guess not.'

'Liam said he'd take them through the gate and round the back so as not to disturb us.'

'Goodness, I'll be glad when this is over.'

'It hasn't been that bad.'

No, it was the combination with everything else.

I sat back and watched as Ben got up and, stripping off, headed for a shower. Eventually ready to leave for work, he said, 'See you tonight. Got any plans?'

'This and that. Probably drop in and see Mum.'

'Well, take it easy and have fun — not too much though.'

Fun and Leo were not entirely compatible. Unwilling to spoil Ben's mood or the moment, I gave a mechanical smile and promised I'd see him later.

CHAPTER EIGHTY

I parked outside the gates in King Street and met Leo near the little kiosk inside the entrance to the park. Dressed down in leather jacket, jeans that were loose on his rangy build and desert boots, he bathed me in a smile that once I'd fallen for.

'Happy Birthday. I got you a coffee. Still take sugar?'

'Unfortunately, I do.'

'Good,' Leo said.

Passing the drink to me, his eyes travelled to my left hand. Was he making a comparison with the diamond-studded engagement ring he'd bought me once upon a time? I briefly wondered what had become of it.

'Nice rock,' Leo said, turning away, dismissive. 'Walk and talk? There are some benches up ahead where we can sit.'

I nodded and we ambled along the path past a small football pitch on one side and a children's playground and clock golf on the other. To break the conversational ice, I asked after Leo's parents. I remembered his father as a quiet, reticent soul, possibly because Leo's mum was a dominant woman with strong opinions.

'Mum passed last year,' Leo said, strain in his voice. 'Sudden. A heart attack.'

'I'm sorry.'

'Hell of a shock.'

'And your dad?'

'Curiously energetic.'

I glanced across and caught Leo's bark of a laugh. It sounded strangely off-key. 'Horrible to say but it's as if he has a new lease of life.'

We came to a clearing where there was a table tennis table, to which you brought your own bats and balls, and three benches.

'Shall we?' Leo pointed to a seat underneath a tree. I sat at one end, Leo the other. It didn't feel as if we'd once been lovers, a couple committed to each other and about to embark on the biggest journey of our lives. We were not old friends. We were not colleagues. It wasn't a professional relationship: he the copper and me the witness. What were we? Suddenly nervous, I wished I hadn't come.

'How's Saskia?' Leo began.

I gave him a short précis.

'No more trouble?'

'Not yet.'

'You sound as if you're expecting it.'

'Because I am.'

'Maybe you're looking in the wrong direction.' He turned to me and his cool blue eyes never left mine.

'I don't understand.'

'Ben.'

'You were supposed to be looking into Adam,' I said, bullish.

'I am. I have.'

'And?'

'Nothing additional to report.'

'Other than he smashes up women?'

'Point taken. Has Saskia changed her mind?'

'About reporting the incident? Sadly, not.'

Leo looked at the ground, scuffed the dirt with the side of his boot. 'Sophie, how well do you know Ben Taylor?'

I glared. 'Is that supposed to be funny?'

'Sorry.' Leo grimaced and smiled. 'Obviously, you know him pretty well.' He stole a look at Rufus, the small person I carried in my arms a better barometer of my commitment to Ben than a piece of jewellery on a significant finger.

'Ben is a good man.' I was so angry I insisted through my teeth.

'Means well, I'm sure.'

'What are you driving at, Leo?'

'You're aware of the brothers' family background?' Not a statement. A question.

'You mean their parents?'

'The story goes that their mother murdered their father.'

'I wasn't aware it was a story.' I have a mental traffic light system. The light was shining amber. 'Anyway, it was a mercy killing, not murder in the accepted sense.'

'Depends on your point of view.'

Front it out. 'That is my point of view.'

'Ben told you?'

'He did.'

'You knew about it from the very beginning of your short relationship?'

I ignored his emphasis on the word 'short'. 'What difference does that make?'

Leo shrugged a shoulder. 'Beyond the tragedy, you have to ask yourself how a humble publican's wife got her hands on the kind of heavy-duty drugs required to kill off her hubbie.'

Sweat trickled down my spine. 'I'm not sure what you're implying.' Only I was. 'Did you get your info from Adam Hall?'

Leo viewed me as if he were disappointed that I could make such a snide suggestion. 'I'm a police officer, Sophie, and it's a fair question to ask.'

'It's already been asked. There was a police investigation, remember?'

'By a local force more accustomed to investigating horse theft. And police don't always get it right, as well you know,' he countered.

Feeling mighty uncomfortable, I beat a hasty retreat into silence.

'Putting aside your claim about Adam beating Saskia,' Leo began.

'It's not a claim,' I said stonily. 'And it's not something to be put aside.'

Leo flicked his palms up in a 'hear me out' gesture. 'You still believe Adam Hall is intent on poisoning the well with his brother?'

'I do.'

'Why?'

Stay cool. Stay calm. I trotted out a tried and tested defence. 'Because Adam is jealous of his younger brother's achievements.'

'Achievements — huh?'

I didn't care for the tone. My eyes flicked to another bench. A woman with a rucksack approached but, on seeing us, changed her mind and walked away.

'It's not an unusual scenario for brothers not to get on, Leo.'

'There's not getting on and there's family vendetta.'

As an only child, Leo wouldn't have much direct experience. Waste of time to point it out.

'Ben was a young medic at the time of his father's death, wasn't he?' Leo asked.

'A student in Nottingham.'

'With access to drugs.'

'No.'

'You know that for a fact?'

My heart thundered. 'Do you?'

Leo didn't confirm or deny. I sensed imminent danger. I could smell it on the wind, in the trees and the earth beneath my feet.

CHAPTER EIGHTY-ONE

'For the sake of argument,' Leo continued fluently, 'Ben would certainly know which drugs would do the trick. He'd be knowledgeable about the correct dosage and how best to administer it.'

'Having knowledge is not the same as putting that knowledge to good use,' I retorted.

'I hear you,' Leo said. 'But what if Ben drove from Nottingham and if he, not his mother, administered the fatal dose? You see where I'm going with this.'

I did and I didn't like it one bit. 'Ben didn't drive.'

'Ah, my bad,' Leo said, giving a self-deprecating laugh, 'although it's not beyond the realm of possibility for a man to drive a car without a licence.'

'Isn't that called speculation? Thought the police were entirely evidence-based.'

Leo flicked a touché smile as if he was my teacher and I was his star pupil. 'It's okay to speculate about Adam Hall and what you claim he did to Brooke Gentry — in fact you encouraged it — but not the brother who changed his name, who ran as far away as possible from his roots, who assumed a new identity.'

'It's not a crime to change your name.'

'You're right, but what interests me is the why of it.'

I froze. Leo knew me well. He knew I was protecting Ben. Threats came from the most unexpected quarters, and this was as threatening as it got.

'I'm simply investigating the facts, Sophie.' The set of his jaw was not tight and defiant. He was authoritative and oh so reasonable. It was me who was floundering.

'Ben is not a criminal,' I said as firmly as I could.

Leo searched my face with the kind of concentration Customs officers adopt at Border Control. I stayed perfectly still, my gaze unwavering.

His lips twitched into a dismissive smile. 'A tragic coincidence then.'

I didn't believe him any more than he believed me. I should have thanked him for the coffee and the chat, got up and walked away. Attack the best form of defence I was going nowhere.

'What the hell are we doing here, Leo?'

He frowned.

'Are we off the record, or what?'

'I'm looking out for you, Sophie.'

'You don't need to.'

'I believe I do.'

'For old time's sake?' I let out a nervous laugh.

Leo viewed me with hard serious eyes. 'Because everybody lies.'

They did. I stared back. 'Tell me, Leo, how did you get this gig?'

He frowned, confounded.

'Out of all the police officers the Met could have chosen to send to Gloucestershire, *you* wind up here.'

Leo clicked his tongue, half-smiled. 'What are you saying, Sophie?'

'I'm saying that there's something off.' *You're* off.

'That's ridiculous.'

'Adam Hall has an almost mystical ability to ferret out people's weaknesses. Did he ferret out yours?'

'Now look here . . .'

'What's he got on you, Leo?'

His smile was kind. His eyes remained hard. 'I think you need to back up.'

'Me, back up? Did you bother to check Adam out at all?'

Silence spooled out between us. I drained the rest of my coffee and crushed the carton between my fingers. Leo did the same. It felt weirdly symbolic.

'You now have a little boy to consider,' Leo said, glancing in Rufus's direction. No threat. No warning. Unnerving just the same. 'I'm not seeking to destroy the new life you've built.' Leo spoke softly, resting a warm hand on my arm. A pivotal moment between us, I saw expectation in Leo's eyes. 'You know I'd take you back in a heartbeat.'

Shocked, I was lost for words. From the intensity in his expression, I knew this was no throwaway line. 'Leo, I . . .'

'There has never been anyone else,' he murmured.

'Then I'm sorry.' I listened to the sound of little children playing, the noise from a group of kids tramping past under the supervision of a games teacher with a booming voice. I was glad of the distraction. I had no words of comfort for Leo, and he knew it. I watched as the hope in his eyes faded to dull disappointment. He quickly assumed a back-to-business expression.

'I'm asking you to think very carefully about the man you share your life with.' Gone was the smile, the humour, replaced by a cold certainty that rocked me.

'Is there something you aren't telling me?' I asked.

'I can't discuss it.'

'But . . .'

'You know where to find me if you need me.'

He stood up and dropped the crushed paper cup into a bin. Without a word or backward glance, Leo strode back onto the path and out in the direction of the gates.

CHAPTER EIGHTY-TWO

Doubt is a maggoty affliction, burying deep, corrupting everything pure, clean and unsullied. Leo had inserted gut-wrenching doubt into my mind. Surely to God, Ben was not the biggest deceiver of all? Or was Leo trying to cynically discredit Ben in the fond hope I'd leave him and go running back?

Shaken at the very thought, I glanced at my watch. Without a second to lose, striding back through the park, I phoned Mum. She'd barely wished me 'Happy Birthday' before I asked if I could drop Rufus off. From the tension in my voice, she quickly caught on that something was wrong, which, after weeks of there being 'something wrong', was impressive.

'I need you to have him for several hours.'

She let out a sigh. I was interfering with her plans. A perfectionist, she would be in the middle of preparations for the party.

'It's important,' I said.

'Fine,' she said in a way that suggested it was not fine at all. 'When?'

'I can be with you within the hour.'

I hung up, dashed home and grabbed everything Mum would need: nappies and spare clothes and a couple of cartons of fruit puree I'd pre-prepared and chilled in the fridge, as well as expressed milk. The handover was messy due to the arrival of Auntie Fen. Making a noisy entrance, she was dressed in a dove-grey leather jacket and straight tailored trousers. She'd had her hair cut flatteringly short. Her skin positively glowed. She looked stunning. Wealth suited her.

'Sweetie, but it's your birthday,' Auntie Fen protested when she found out about my drop and go. I suspected her frustration was due to the fact we weren't popping open the champagne any time soon. Instead, she was going to be lumbered with a dribbling machine.

'We'll celebrate tomorrow,' I promised, fleeing to my car.

'What time can I expect you back?' I heard Mum call.

'Later,' I shouted. 'Oh,' I said, stopping mid-stride, bellowing over the roof of my car, 'if Ben drops by, hang on to Rufus, would you?'

'Sophie, what on—'

Before Mum could question me, I jumped in and drove away.

The devil, as the saying goes, is in the detail. I'd overlooked a detail so obvious I could kick myself for it.

It took me a little over an hour to reach my destination. On the way, I stopped off and bought crisps and chocolate, not for me, but for a boy who was now a man and who had seen something he shouldn't.

An uncommonly warm spring day, Lloyd was outside mowing the lawn with a petrol-powered mower. I pulled up outside the gate. Intent on what he was doing he didn't notice me at first. When he did, his face darkened and he stopped the engine.

'You,' he said, thundering towards me. At least he wasn't carrying a shotgun.

Bearing gifts, I raised my hands, showing that I'd come in peace. 'These are for Cody from Ben,' I said, smiling.

The fight went out of Lloyd. His gaze sharpened. 'Ben?'

'My baby's father.'

I couldn't read what travelled through his mind. He certainly seemed surprised. More significantly, he wasn't cross. Still, I had to be sure.

'Lloyd, is Ben a good person?'

'Damn funny question, if you don't mind my saying. Why are you asking me?'

'Because you're the only person who knew the brothers and Cody was the last person to see Phyllis alive.'

Lloyd stood rock solid for what seemed like an eternity.

'You kindly offered me a cup of tea last time I was here,' I said. 'Can I take you up on it now?'

* * *

We sat inside a room that wasn't quite sure what it was. A free-standing cooker and cracked sink indicated it was a kitchen. A wardrobe, its door ajar and clearly containing clothes, with a put-you-up bed next to it, suggested it was also a room for sleeping in. A phone attached to a wall indicated a landline. I sat on a wonky chair that didn't sit properly on the quarry tile floor at a table that looked as if it had been rescued from a skip.

'Where's Cody?' I asked Lloyd.

'Out and about.' The finality with which Lloyd spoke assured me that there was no way in hell I would get to speak to his grandson. 'Don't worry, I'll make sure he gets the chocolate and crisps,' he said, planting two mugs of tea down on the table. 'Sugar's in the jam jar.' He pushed it in my direction, offering me a spoon that was none too clean. I gingerly helped myself. He scraped back a chair and sat down opposite me.

'Where's your baby?' Lloyd asked.

'With my mother.'

He nodded approval. 'Ben qualified then?'

'He did.'

'Knew he would. Where's he living?'

I told him.

'Posh.' Lloyd raised his hairy eyebrows and lifted the mug to his lips, eyeing me warily over the brim. 'You live with him?'

'I do.'

Lloyd sipped and sat for what seemed like a long time. I watched and I waited. Finally, he spoke with a defeated smile. 'It makes no difference what I think or what Cody saw.'

I pitched forward. 'But he did see something?'

Lloyd gave me a slow look. I think he was working out whether he could trust me. 'Who threatened you?' I asked.

His eyes travelled over my head to the wall behind me. I twisted round to where a shotgun sat in a gun cabinet. The message clear: *I've got it covered.* 'It may make no difference to you but it would make all the difference to me,' I said.

Lloyd nodded slowly, grasping how much rode on his answer. I had the impression that he wasn't often asked for an opinion or advice. Perhaps it was the first time in a long time anyone had taken him seriously or expressed interest.

'Cody was a kid. He's not smart but he's not stupid and he's no liar.' Lloyd spoke firmly, as if daring me to disagree. 'He enjoys his bikes, has done ever since he was little. Used to ride up to the pub because people made a fuss of him. I'm not the fussing type,' Lloyd acknowledged. 'And he liked speeding down that hill,' Lloyd said, smiling fondly. 'The Hall boys built a den years ago and Cody would get up early, soon as it was light sometimes, and he'd camp there for hours on end.'

'The bivouac?'

Lloyd nodded. 'I'd often have to drag the child back to feed him. His mother upped and left,' he explained, in a dry tone that said, although it was irrelevant to what we were discussing, it was factually true. It also corroborated what Ben had told me. 'The morning Phyllis died was like any other morning for Cody. Except it wasn't.' Lloyd lifted the mug to his lips, took a deep drink and swallowed the beverage down as if it were neat whisky. 'He told me he'd heard noise, voices, *bad* voices, he told me.'

'An argument?'

'A blinder.'

'Between?'

'Phyllis and her youngest son, Adam.'

'Did he hear what it was about?'

'If he did, he couldn't put it into words. What he did understand was the hiding Adam gave his mother.'

There it was: Adam the serial abuser.

'How badly did he hurt her, Lloyd?'

'From what I gathered it was serious. To my mind, it's why Phyllis drove off — to get away from that mad young bastard.'

And any wounds she'd sustained would have been covered up by the injuries from the accident. Adam was responsible for his mother's death either by distressing her so much she fled or hurting her so badly she would have died anyway. It accounted for why Adam had never gone to the police and told them what he knew to be true about Ben; it would draw too much heat. So why risk it now? Answer: to extract as much loot as possible. With the trust fund nearing maturity, there would be a lot of money swilling about.

'You reported it?'

Lloyd viewed me as if I were stupid. 'It took me days to winkle it out of Cody and when I did, what was the point? Nobody would believe the word of a child like him over the word of a bereaved grown-up son.'

'But *you* believed Cody?'

'And I believed him when he told me that Adam Hall had threatened to burn the house down if he ever breathed a word.'

I suppressed a shudder. 'Adam saw him?'

'Caught him by the scruff of his neck. Would have wrung it too, I daresay, if he thought he could have got away with it, but Phyllis intervened.'

'She protected Cody?'

'She loved the lad.'

I stayed quiet. Everything Lloyd said served to emphasise that my fears about Adam were real.

'Last time I came you asked me if I was sent,' I reminded Lloyd.

'I remember.'

'Sent by whom?'

'Adam Hall.' He spat the name out between his cracked lips.

'He threatened you?'

'Never one to do his own dirty work, he was too slippery to come himself. Knows I can handle a twelve-bore,' Lloyd said, casting his wistful eyes over my head again. 'The little rat put a copper on to me.'

My pulse rocketed. My skin flashed hot then cold. 'A police officer?'

'S'right.' Lloyd glowered.

No, no, no. The room spun. I felt as if, in a moment of insobriety, I'd sent the wrong file to the wrong client and caused a financial meltdown. Barely capable of wrenching out the words, I asked, 'Was he tall, lean, blond and blue-eyed, in his early forties?'

Lloyd's brow creased. He shook his head, scratched his chin. 'Thick-set bloke. Buzz cut. No neck, like a rugby player.'

I gasped in surprise. 'Hicks, was that his name?'

Lloyd's eyes gleamed in recognition. A grin split his face wide. 'That's the one.'

CHAPTER EIGHTY-THREE

I exchanged phone numbers and asked Lloyd if he'd be prepared to make a statement to the police about Hicks.

'Gladly,' he said. 'I've about had enough of keeping my mouth shut.'

Thanking him, I made a fast getaway. Hicks was Adam's man on the inside, all information fed to Leo sanitised and designed to point the finger at Ben. God alone knew what the deal was. Why would a serving police officer allow himself to be corrupted by a loser like Adam Hall? How had their paths crossed? Then I recalled Adam dishing out advice about friends of theirs who'd had an extension built. Brooke mentioned they'd spent time in London. Was this how they'd connected, and some dodgy agreement made? Was Hicks getting a cut from the money Adam extorted?

But I was conflicted. Even if I proved that Hicks and Adam were working together, it would not save Ben.

Ben was culpable in the eyes of the law and a moral bankrupt in the eyes of people who strongly opposed assisted dying. The prospect of sacrificing one brother to bring the other to justice made me feel ill. Somehow, I had to find a way to protect Ben while putting a stop to Adam's trail of manipulation and destruction. After what Adam had done to his mother and my sister and with a question mark still hanging over Brooke's death, I had to bring him down.

I called Leo on my hands-free; an automated voice told me that my call was being connected. Impatiently, I drummed the steering wheel with my fingers. Leo was wrong about Ben. Misguided for sure, he didn't beat up women. He didn't threaten small children. Lloyd believed he was a good guy. In my heart, I knew he was.

'DC Hicks speaking.'

It felt as if someone had exploded a firework in my face. I swerved a little into the facing lane. Fortunately, nobody was driving towards me. Recovering as quickly as I could, I remembered Saskia's philosophy: *Time to woman the fuck up.*

'I was hoping to speak to DI Carpenter.' Short, Direct. Pleasant.

'He's on a rest day. Can I help, Miss Knox?'

'Not sure you can. Would you be kind enough to tell him I phoned? It's a matter of some urgency.' I squeaked, sounding excessively middle class.

'I'll let him know.' Not a whisper of suspicion. Not a single attempt to block me. Ice-cool under pressure. Returning the favour, I forced a grateful smile into my voice. 'Thank you so much.' It wasn't quite 'have a nice day', but close enough. Time to go after his partner in crime: Adam Hall.

Adam had left no forwarding address. He didn't need to. My aunt's decision to extend her visit, her new look, the shiny, preposterously girly expression in her eyes was the result of a new companion, or, in this case, a man accustomed to escorting older, wealthy and attractive women for monetary gain. To locate Adam, I only needed to find my aunt and I knew where she was.

Ellenborough Park Hotel is a fifteenth-century manor house set in ninety acres of grounds. Chosen for its chic country house living and old-school grandeur, it had been a popular destination for the rich and famous for decades and long before Soho House was out of nappies.

I drove up the long drive, parked in the designated parking area and strolled into Reception, a long, softly lit room with panelled wood floor, ecclesiastical windows and a vestry feel. At the far end: a large desk beneath a portrait of some ancient grandee. Beyond: an arched doorway begging the traveller to pass through and discover the other architectural delights on offer.

Had Adam been holed up in my aunt's suite, I might have had a problem gaining access. I didn't like to think about what might confront my tired eyes. But Adam was never a man to shy away from a good old game of conversational Cluedo. Explaining that I was meeting my aunt, Mrs Fenella Clinton-Gower (her last husband's surname), I was ushered through and found Adam alone in the Great Hall. As the name suggested it was a massive room with chandeliers and inglenook fireplace, cosy club chairs and sofas with cushions. Scenes depicting religious Christian rituals decorated an entire wall. Sitting in a corner below a stained-glass window, Adam was taking tea. This was not of the buttered teacake and mug of builder's variety. This was a three-storey stand of cute sandwiches, crusts removed, fruit scones, clotted cream and jam and, at the very top, a cream-stuffed éclair, strawberry French tarte and a glass of what looked like lemon posset. Tea, as a beverage, was almost incidental; Adam's preference a glass of pink fizz. Curiously civilised for what was going to be a deeply uncivilised conversation.

Adam looked up. His lips quirked into a smile, indicating he'd received a tip-off from his new best mate, Jared Hicks, and was expecting me. Dark glasses cloaked his eyes. I couldn't read the expression behind them, yet I suspected they danced with sport and amusement.

'For how long have you been shagging my aunt?' It sounded terribly rude in the spiritual confines of the room. Fortunately, we were alone.

Ignoring my question, he slathered cream on a scone and then liberally topped it with jam, the Devon way. 'Do take a seat.'

I sat or rather perched.

'Goodness, no baby,' he exclaimed. 'I thought the little thing was attached to you. What do witches call it? A familiar, I think.'

My cheeks blazed. 'I know what you did, and I know why you did it.'

'Must we talk in riddles?'

'Your part in your mother's death.'

'I wasn't there so how could I *play a part*?' He jabbed the air with his butter knife. 'Is this a desperate and depressingly cruel play to deflect from what my brother did?'

'You were there. You were seen.'

Adam clicked his tongue. 'By some deranged kid with a warped imagination?'

'You deny it?'

'Certainly do.'

'Then why send Jared Hicks to threaten the Breezes?'

Adam put down his knife, spread his hands. 'I'm shocked.'

'I don't believe you.'

'Nothing to do with me.'

He sounded bored, as if I'd got it all wrong. To hell with that. 'Just like it wasn't you who hit my sister, or did God knows what to Brooke, or blackmailed Ben. For a man who does nothing you certainly know how to go places and get what you want.' And trample underfoot anyone who gets in your way.

He suppressed a yawn. 'Jealous?'

'Of a man who injures his mother so badly she's barely alive when she tries to escape? I don't know, maybe you killed her then shoved her into the car.' The last bit was a stretch, but the rest wasn't. Like I said, it was all in the detail, the one I'd overlooked. 'I'd love to know what the police — the local police, that is — would make of that crumbling piece of wall with the flecks of red paint on it from the Vauxhall Astra your mother drove. What did you do, Adam? Back the car into her, pile her back inside and send her on her merry way?'

I've never seen a cobra strike for real, only on film. Provoked, they dart at alarming speed, spit venom and stick their fangs in. Adam pitched forward faster than a viper. In a low threatening voice, he said, 'You really want to push it?'

'To the limit,' I said. 'It's called mutually-assured destruction. You lay off Ben and I'll lay off you.' I stood up. 'Send my regards to my aunt when you see her.' I strode out.

CHAPTER EIGHTY-FOUR

Mum was fretting. Not because I was late. Not because Rufus was grizzly. But because the tabatière, aka snuff box, circa King Emmanuel III of Italy, had gone missing. I did the maths: four hundred pounds' worth. Small, in relative terms, but spiteful and designed to distress.

'It's that bloody man, isn't it?' Mum ranted.

That *bloody man* had done a good deal worse than that.

Unless we had snuffbox fairies, I conceded he probably had. A slim item, it would be very simple to pop into the back pocket of a pair of jeans.

'To think we threw our home and our hearts open to him,' Mum bleated.

Hearts an understatement. Seizing hold of Saskia's, he'd moved on to my aunt's. I asked Mum where she was.

'Left twenty minutes ago.'

'Did Auntie tell you that she and Adam are together?'

Mum's eyes popped. She looked as if a large chunk of Chelsea bun had travelled down the wrong way and got stuck in her windpipe. 'Oh God, oh God,' she exclaimed. 'What is she thinking? Has she any idea what the man is capable of?'

'You didn't tell her about Saskia?'

Mum shook her head and bit her lip. 'Saskia's so terribly sensitive. Should we warn Fen? Dear God, you don't think she'll bring him to the party, do you?' Mum's face was a picture of churning emotion.

Least of our problems. 'I think it very unlikely.' If Adam knew what was good for him, he'd hit the road first light.

'I hope you're right. What on earth will your father say?'

The sort of threat a harassed mother issues to naughty children, it felt faintly risible. Things were going to go a lot more pear-shaped than that.

CHAPTER EIGHTY-FIVE

When Ben got home, he noticed instantly that my day had been memorable for all the wrong reasons. Over stiff gin and tonics apiece, I told him about my visit to Lloyd and what Cody had witnessed.

'Adam beat up our mother?' Ben pressed a fist to his mouth.

I explained about the overheard row, the suspicious-looking dent in the pub wall car park.

There's silence that is peaceful, silence that is angry and silence you pay attention to. I paid attention. Ben looked like a man emerging from a house struck by a missile from which he is the sole survivor.

He drained his glass and poured another. When he was ready, I told him about Jared Hicks's threat to Lloyd and Cody. Ben almost choked.

'*Hicks*? Why would Hicks risk his career to protect my brother?'

I shook my head. 'I've no idea how their paths crossed. Maybe in London?' Then another thought zipped through my mind. What was it Adam had said? Something about his friends not being Ben's friends when they were growing up.

'We moved in different circles,' Adam had told me. Ben had also confirmed Adam's tendency to sofa-surf. *He used to hang out with all sorts back then.* Was it just possible that Jared Hicks was one of those old mates and had subsequently joined the police? Hicks wouldn't be the first police officer to allegedly cross to the other side. I put my theory to Ben.

'It's possible, I guess.' Ben's lips thinned. 'Think Leo's in on it?'

'No way. He couldn't afford to make another career mistake, not after Caron.'

'You've alerted him?'

I explained my thwarted attempt to get through to Leo, followed by my fraught conversation with Adam.

'And he didn't deny any of it?' Ben said, dark-eyed.

'He went on the attack.'

'Typical,' he hissed.

'That's when I threatened him with mutually-assured destruction.'

Ben blinked, perplexed.

'If another police service, West Mercia and the original police involved in the case, look to investigate a new allegation, it's bound to frighten the crap out of Adam,' I pointed out. 'While Cody might not be viewed as a plausible witness, Lloyd will, and he's agreed to make a statement and report Jared Hicks's threats. Once the truth is out about Hicks, especially if his relationship with Adam can be traced back, it will compromise the entire investigation into Brooke's death. Adam, discredited, will be forced to turn off the poisonous tap of information he's feeding, via Hicks, to Leo.'

'And then what happens? Adam moves on to ensnare some other unsuspecting woman?'

I prayed that karma was female and had a very special place in her soul for Adam Hall. 'I hate the idea of your brother moving on, but this is your best shot of extricating yourself.'

'Only if he acts in the way you think he will. I know him better than you.'

'And I know Leo better than you,' I said. 'I also understand how cops think and work. One bad apple like Jared Hicks can screw the entire case against you.'

Ben took another astringent swig of gin. 'Here's to rotten fruit then.'

CHAPTER EIGHTY-SIX

I didn't sleep well. I don't think Ben slept at all. In the early hours he got up, crept outside and put his car on charge.

Rufus was spark out. Ben was pottering about, waiting for Liam to arrive with his delivery of tiles. Party day, I couldn't say I was really feeling it. I got up, showered and dressed, and took my first cup of coffee at the end of the garden. Sparrows hopped about on our lawn. The wind had got up and the sky was the colour of old slate. I feared we were in for a heavy downpour.

Sleep deprivation is a curious phenomenon. It's generally agreed that the odd night won't impact negatively on your health. Repeated nights, however, can mess with your thinking processes. I hadn't slept properly in weeks. While my brain felt fried, my body felt strangely alert and on the lookout. I'd read that poor sleep could induce paranoia. My paranoia ran deep, and it had nothing to do with the hours I'd failed to clock up in preceding weeks.

I thought all about Adam, his misogyny and murderous cruelty and his manipulation of others to extort what he wanted.

I thought of Brooke, a thief and addict who'd met a lonely death.

I thought about Hicks, a dirty copper, in cahoots with Adam, reporting to Leo. Leo offering to take control of the situation with Saskia and provide a listening ear.

'*Leo*,' I cried aloud.

Like a train jumping a track onto another line, I'd been travelling down the wrong route. What if Leo's assertion that he was a changed man was a lie? What if he was in a corrupt partnership with Hicks? What might be the consequences for me of spurning Leo for a second time?

I shook my head. This was ridiculous. As I'd already insisted to Ben, Leo wouldn't jeopardise his career, not in the wake of Caron's death, not after his mentor had been convicted, not after 'lessons had been learned'. Hicks was connected to Adam, and Hicks was Leo's colleague; it didn't mean that Leo was corrupt or involved in some grand conspiracy.

The noise of a vehicle pulling into our drive brought me back to my senses. I listened as a vehicle door opened and closed, boots on gravel. Liam, I realised.

After eight, I phoned the police number again. Once I'd spoken to Leo, I'd feel better, more sorted.

It didn't connect.

The 'number unavailable' tone cut through the damp air.

The hardest part is telling yourself what you already know to be true. I dropped my mug and ran as if my son's life depended upon it.

Tearing across the lawn and through the back door of the house, I shouted to Ben several times. There was no reply and no sign of him. Upstairs, there was no sign of Rufus. Heart rocketing, I tore back downstairs and ran out of the front door and onto the drive in time to see my car taking off at speed. Instinctively, I knew Rufus was inside. Letting out a scream, I tore off after it.

Our lane is not long. On the left, high up on a bank, there's a row of new builds, with only one way in or out. Beyond the wide entrance to the development the road narrows to a single track. Approaching from the opposite direction, a big white van, popular with tradesmen.

I waved my hands frantically. 'STOP HIM. BLOCK HIM IN.'

Bewildered, the van driver dropped the sandwich he was eating and swerved, clipping the front of my car, slowing it down yet failing to bring it to a halt.

'Fucking moron,' the driver yelled out of an open window, pulling over into the gated entrance to another property.

Before he climbed out to inspect the damage, I put on a spurt. Eyes popping, pulse hammering and lungs bursting, I wrenched open the passenger door and jumped, breathless, into the seat beside him.

'What the—'

'DRIVE. My baby's in that car.'

His eyes rolled in astonishment. 'You serious?'

'Deadly. For God's sake, step on it.'

CHAPTER EIGHTY-SEVEN

In a dramatic U-turn that had me reaching for the grab rail, we hung a left and careered onto the London Road in the direction of Lechlade. All sorts of horrors buzzed around inside my head like hornets in a jam jar. What if Rufus wasn't strapped in? What if he'd been shoved in the back without being secured into his car seat, or thrown into the foot well? His little head, I thought wildly, the anterior fontanelle, the soft spot between the bones of a baby's skull, was not yet fused. Vulnerable, open to serious injury, an accident could leave him brain-damaged.

If he survived.

The van driver floored it as we hit a straight stretch.

'Who took your baby?' He had to yell over the roar from an old engine that was being thrashed to within an inch of its life.

Up until half an hour ago, I'd have named Adam as prime suspect. Minutes ago: Hicks. Seconds ago: Leo. Confused, I couldn't call it.

I gasped as we tore around a brutal bend to the right and then switched back to the left. It felt as if my insides were being clawed. Instantly, I was reminded of Louise. What if heartbroken Elliott was so bent out of shape after Louise's miscarriage, he'd done something dangerously stupid?

'I don't know,' I replied.

'How old is the kid?'

'Five months.'

'Hold tight.'

The van surged forward as the sky burst open, unleashing a heavy torrent of rain. After dry weather the road was greasy. The tyres of the van had a hard time gripping the surface. I clung on, nails digging into my thighs and prayed the prayer of the desperate, begging my car to stay on the road, that Rufus would be safe, that he would survive whatever happened, that I would not be punished for making such lousy personal choices.

Rain beat down, hammering the top of the van. Hail too.

'Flash flood,' the driver muttered. I could barely hear him over the fast drum of windscreen wipers.

We tore past a development of park homes and flew by the turning to Meysey Hampton. Another bend and we were down a hill, followed by another bend and a sign for Cotswold Water Park. *SLOW* signs punctuated the tarmac along a road that had double white lines running down the centre.

Up ahead, a milk tanker trundling along, complying stoically to the forty mile an hour limit.

'Shit,' the van driver let out.

I gaped as I watched my car veer to overtake on a bend.

'He can't possibly see what's ahead,' I yelled, my knuckles pressed to my mouth.

'Fuck, he's not going to make it,' the van driver let out.

Everything slowed.

With a blast of horn, the milk tanker trundled on.

A Maserati on the other side of the road braked, skidded and braked again.

Fishtailing, my car mounted a thick verge, shot through a hedge and disappeared from view.

The van was barely stationary when I threw the passenger door open and exploded onto the wet road. Tearing through the pouring rain, I took the same path as my car and plunged down a bank, slipping and sliding, oblivious to fern, nettles and brambles clawing at my skirt. A deep, deadly scar had been cut into the landscape by the other vehicle. I couldn't tell how many young trees it had mowed down, how many times it had overturned, how badly its occupants were injured.

Oh God, oh God.

Gripped with maternal madness — this had to be karma, punishment by the universe. My guilt. My fault. One life for another.

But not Rufus, whose life has only just begun.

Not my baby.

Not my son.

Drenched through, my clothes were plastered to my skin and mud splattered the backs of my legs, weighing down my shoes, turning them to concrete. I could barely see through the driving rain. Terror of what I might find scythed through me like a sharpened blade. Close behind, the van driver was calling the emergency services, his deep voice edged with alarm, barely keeping it together as he rattled off details. *Location. RTA. Two occupants. Baby. Five months old.*

A slip down the vertiginous slope could prove fatal. Still, I hurtled, rolling an ankle on the way, the pain so eye-wateringly intense I gasped, but kept moving.

Halfway down the steep scree, I spotted the wreck. It had travelled an astonishing distance and into a clearing. Surrounded by glass and debris, the mangled car was upside down, smoking in the pale, wet morning light. Cold crept into my bones.

I scanned for movement.

Nothing.

I prayed for sound, however faint, however brief, yet all was quiet as if every bird had already fallen silent in mourning.

Bile flooded the back of my throat. My pulse hammered and my chest felt tight. There was a weird sensation in my head, like I was going to stroke out. Closer now, on solid ground, I sped up and then my eyes flared and my legs almost gave way. At a distance, a body lay face down in the dirt, one arm flung out as if reaching, too late, for redemption. No sign of my son – he must be trapped inside the vehicle.

This was bad but not as bad as the smell from a full tank of petrol. It clung to the wet air, noxious and threatening, like a death sentence waiting to be delivered.

'Christ,' the van driver let out. Right behind me, he had caught its poisonous odour too.

I had to get to Rufus; had to before the whole thing went up in flames. Cold fear coursing down my spine, I started forward. No more than a few paces, a body slammed into mine, knocking the air out of my lungs and bringing me down. I was pinned to the ground with earth in my eyes, blood and iron in my mouth.

'Let me go, you bastard.'

'It's about to light up, woman.'

I didn't care. I couldn't survive without Rufus. I couldn't live in the knowledge that I hadn't tried to reach my baby. 'LET. ME. GO.'

'There's nothing you can do,' the man pleaded.

Lifting my chin, searching through a blur of tears, a cry, feral and inhuman, ripped from the back of my throat.

'RUFUS.'

CHAPTER EIGHTY-EIGHT

Agonised, I twisted my body and lashed out with an elbow, jabbing the van driver and hero of the hour, full in the face. Startled, he let go with an earthy expletive. Digging into the soft earth on my forearms, I wriggled free and, scuttling to my feet, sprinted and stumbled and sprinted again.

'Rufus, Rufus,' I screamed. If the power of mother love could be bottled, it would save him. It had to.

Eyes raking the carnage through the rain, the unbearable stink of petrol slammed into my eyes, nose and throat. Smoke seeped from the engine, thicker and blacker. Closing in, my heart almost gave out. Rufus's car seat was roughly twenty feet from the accident and facing down. Clutching my stomach, I vomited on the spot.

'Get back,' I heard someone behind me yell.

I did the opposite.

CHAPTER EIGHTY-NINE

Fearing the worst, I rolled the car seat over. Rufus remained strapped in; eyes closed. Grass stains covered his Babygro. There was dirt on his tiny hands. He had a cut to his forehead where his face had planted into the earth. Blood on his cheeks.

But he was breathing.

I picked up the carrier and, in terror, hobbled on my wrecked ankle as far and as fast as I could towards the tree line. Popping, crackling and spitting, it was as if a firework display erupted behind me. Suddenly a great whoosh and a wall of heat burst across my back, scorching my neck. The dark wet morning exploded with light. I glanced over my shoulder and saw bright yellow flames ripping through my car.

Opening his eyes, Rufus let out a cry.

I stared at him in awe. The most glorious sound I'd ever heard, I burst into tears.

CHAPTER NINETY

The field was awash with emergency services. Two police officers were questioning the bewildered van driver; another was trying to speak to me. The rain had eased and there was some protection from the trees, but we were all soaked. Peeling off my fleece, I'd covered Rufus as best I could.

Once a clear-eyed rookie police officer, PC Cairns, had established my name, I gabbled an account that sounded as ludicrous to my ears as it must have sounded to him. 'My partner, Ben, I've no idea where he is,' I cried. I named names. I made allegations. Into the mix, I threw the investigation into Brooke Gentry's death. 'The person driving my car,' I began, looking in the direction of where a small crowd of emergency workers were gathered, 'is he . . . ?' I trailed off.

'I don't have that information, Sophie,' Cairns replied.

'Has the casualty been identified?'

'I don't have that information either.' Calm and kind, he held my hand until a paramedic reached us and examined Rufus.

'Will he be all right?' I was filled with panic at the thought he might not be.

'Luckily, he had a soft landing. Had it been concrete or tarmac . . .' She looked up with a steady gaze. I swallowed, letting her know she didn't need to spell it out. 'Babies are tougher than you think,' she said in a soft voice. 'We'll give him the once-over in hospital to be certain. Now what about you?'

'I rolled my ankle.'

She examined it. 'Looks like a nasty sprain,' she declared and applied a compression bandage.

A helicopter landed in a neighbouring field ready to transport Rufus and me to Cheltenham General. As I was preparing to leave, a crackle on the police officer's comms alerted Cairns to fresh information. He stood up and walked away then turned and looked at me. 'Yes,' he said, 'I'll let her know.'

I gave a jolt. 'Know what?'

'Your partner, Ben Taylor, is being taken to hospital.'

My heart plunged. Cairns read three questions in my expression. *Why? How? When?*

'He was at home when he was attacked. You didn't see him?'

I shook my head in dismay. I'd looked but not hard enough.

'A workman found him.'

Liam, I realised, my relief short-lived. 'Is Ben badly hurt?'

'Took a nasty knock to the head.'

'But he'll recover?'

'I'm not a medic. You'll need to speak to a doctor. Seems that you're going to the right place for a catch-up.'

Numbed, I stared across the field to the other side of my burnt-out car. A number of boots on the ground, including scenes of crimes officers, there was a lot of activity. That's when I noticed the body bag.

CHAPTER NINETY-ONE

I'd never flown in a helicopter and absolutely hated it. We landed near Cheltenham racecourse and were transported by ambulance to Paediatrics where Rufus was seen by a young consultant who also happened to know Ben. Promising to find out where he was and, more importantly, how he was, she gave Rufus a thorough examination and, to be on the safe side, suggested we stay in for the night for observation.

'Police will want to talk to you,' she said.

'Can you stall them? I need to catch my breath.' Which was true. I also wanted to think how best to protect Ben. How far would the police investigation extend? How wide would it go? Would they be linking up with the Met? And where did Leo figure? Surely . . .

I was still staring at Rufus in wonder when she returned an hour later and told me which ward and room Ben was in.

'He was badly concussed,' she said, 'but he's in the land of the living.'

Reluctantly leaving Rufus with a nurse, I found Ben easily, the large number of police officers milling around the door to his room the giveaway. A middle-aged man, with short grey hair, searching hazel eyes and an uncompromising expression, stepped forward. In plain clothes, he had DCI written all over him.

'Are you Sophie Knox?' he asked.

'I am.'

'DCI Allerton,' he said, 'You've had a nasty experience. Baby okay?'

'Seems so.'

'Nothing short of a miracle,' Allerton said. 'I expect you want to speak to your other half.' He indicated the door with a jerk of his head. 'All right, if we speak afterwards — if you're not too tired?'

Too wired to be tired. I explained I'd already spoken to an attending police officer. 'And I really need to get back to my baby.'

'Noted,' Allerton said with a friendly smile. 'I've got the basic shout lines, but it would be very helpful if we could take a statement sooner than later.'

'Have you discovered the identity of the driver?' I asked.

'Formal identification hasn't yet taken place.'

'But . . .'

Allerton rested a hand on my arm. 'You'll be the first to know when it's been established, I promise.'

I slipped into Ben's room. He looked to be asleep. His lips were pale and there was blood on his pillow. Hearing me, he slowly came to and opened his eyes; the pupils dilated. 'Thank God,' he said, with a wan smile. 'They said Rufus survived.'

'He's fine. Better than you, by the look of it.' I sat on Ben's bed and held his hand.

'My head bangs but no fracture. Fortunately, I was struck from behind.'

'Not sure I call that fortunate.'

'The back of your head is quite solid.'

'What's the damage?'

'A super-glued wound.'

'What happened, Ben?'

'I answered the door to Hicks.'

My mind returned to the muddy field, the body bag. 'You let him in?' I was shocked.

'I wanted to confront him, see what he had to say for himself.'

'Good God, Ben.'

'It was the only way to find out about the connection to my brother and what they had planned,' Ben insisted. 'We went into my study and, apart from blinding pain, that's the last thing I remember.'

The door had been closed I recalled. While I was yelling Ben's name, he was lying unconscious. Hicks must have attacked Ben and then hunted for Rufus. Hang on, I thought.

'Did you see a vehicle when you opened the front door?'

Ben placed a hand against his temple. 'Come to think of it, no.'

I hadn't seen one either. Had Hicks parked farther away and walked? If so, the police would discover the vehicle. There was a more obvious explanation. I was seized with sudden nausea. 'Think someone dropped him off?'

'I guess it's a possibility.'

'Did Hicks have Leo with him?' And was this the reason Leo hadn't picked up my call?

Ben's gaze held mine. He knew what I was saying and understood how much it cost me to say it.

'As far as I recall, which,' Ben said, smiling sadly, squeezing my hand, 'isn't very far at all, no.'

I thought about that. Ben's amnesia was concerning. A gap in the commentary, there were a couple of likely scenarios. Adam had dropped his old pal, Hicks, off and Hicks had driven away with Rufus; Adam had abducted Rufus leaving Hicks to escape. Either way, one of them was dead. Without a positive identification of the driver, I remained in the dark.

And I still couldn't rule out Leo's involvement.

I filled Ben in on what had happened from when I ran in from the garden.

'Christ, you could have been killed on that road.'

I'd been too upset to give it a thought. 'Have you given a statement to the police, Ben?'

'The medics are holding them off, although they know that DC Jared Hicks attacked me.'

I met Ben's eye.

He sighed in resignation. 'The truth is going to eventually come out, isn't it?'

I gave his hand a squeeze. 'And if it does, we face it together.'

CHAPTER NINETY-TWO

I insisted on checking in with Rufus and giving him a feed before I gave a statement to the police.

Having squared it with hospital staff, DCI Allerton showed me into a private room with two beds and chairs. There was another police officer with him. Six feet tall. Sandy hair. Hooded eyes. Prominent jaw. Allerton introduced him as DCI Reece Kenney from the Met. Over a three-hour drive away, Kenney had wasted little time to reach the hospital, the police acting fast when it was one of its own; the biggest confirmation, to my mind, that a police officer was lying in the mortuary. Based on history, unappealing thoughts crossed my mind: was Kenney a mate of Hicks? And, as bad, *if* Leo was involved, was Kenney Leo's mate? Was this going to be a covering reputation exercise?

Allerton sat on one of the beds. Kenney took a chair and I another. The surroundings made it feel slightly surreal.

Allerton set the conversational ball rolling by asking after Ben's health.

'Badly concussed,' I answered.

'Not in a fit state to answer questions?' Kenney's grey-green eyes swept mine.

'The doctors are the best judge,' I replied evenly. 'He seemed confused when I spoke to him, although not about his attacker. Have you picked up Hicks?'

'Not yet.'

Then it wasn't his body in the mortuary. I shuddered inside with fear. *Can't be Leo. Can't be Leo.* 'You've spoken to Adam Hall? Dr Taylor's brother,' I clarified.

'Should we?'

'Hall and Hicks are friends. There's no way Hall isn't involved. He's a thoroughly bad person.'

'You have evidence of that?'

'He abuses women. You can ask my sister.' I blanched as I said it. Saskia was really going to kill me.

Allerton requested her contact number, which I supplied. It was imperative I got to her first to warn her.

'Returning to Hall,' Allerton said, 'I gather from PC Cairns there's quite some background in the lead-up to Rufus's abduction.' Allerton steepled his fingers beneath his chin. 'Can you go over it again?'

I took it from the top, starting with Adam and Brooke's arrival. As soon as I mentioned Brooke Gentry's name, Kenney pitched in: 'She was your guest?'

'With her boyfriend, Adam Hall.' I told them how, later, Adam and Brooke had moved in with my parents.

'Why?' Kenney interjected.

'Because Adam Hall is a manipulative user,' I said, 'and my parents are kind people.'

Kenney nodded for me to continue.

'Brooke didn't stay long at my parents' home. She left following an argument with Adam Hall.'

'About?' Allerton asked.

'I don't know. I wasn't there. My mother told me she'd overheard Brooke complaining that it was "not part of the deal".'

'She said those exact words?'

'You'd need to confirm it with my mother but, as I understand it, yes. Not long afterwards we received a visit

379

from the police to say that Brooke Gentry had gone missing and later that she'd committed suicide.'

Kenney frowned and broke in again. 'Police?'

'From the Met. DI Leo Carpenter and DC Jared Hicks — the man who attacked Ben,' I said with emphasis.

Kenney's eyes flickered, a thin smile playing on his lips. He glanced at Allerton who met his eye. I caught a hint of a silent exchange but couldn't grasp its meaning.

'What am I missing?' I asked, mentally braced.

'Leo Carpenter and Jared Hicks are no longer police officers.'

I thought the floor might leap up to meet me. Had I heard correctly? Is that really what Kenney said? From the expression on my face, Kenney clearly felt the need to explain.

'Dismissed from the Met early last year for gross misconduct.'

Stunned, I looked from one police officer to the other. My head swam. 'But Leo Carpenter had a warrant card.'

'You saw it?'

I thought back. Leo flashed it so fast. Had I seen what I expected to see? Had my brain filled in any potential gaps because I had no reason to suspect otherwise? 'What did he do?' Sickened inside, I suspected the answer before Kenney had a chance to reply.

'Carpenter had a history of corruption extending over a number of years.'

Lester's man all along. Chilled to my core, I realised Leo hadn't changed at all. I asked for specifics.

Kenney answered. 'Carpenter had an inappropriate sexual relationship with a woman after responding to a report of domestic abuse.'

I flushed with sudden anger for trusting Leo when history dictated otherwise. Red flags around his behaviour were there right from the start. He and Hicks were in this together. That's why they'd always conducted interviews at home, never in a police station, why they'd led us to believe that police in Gloucestershire were in the picture but that this was principally a Met investigation, all done to head me off and give their lie greater credence. It was why Leo had reacted with genuine shock when I'd reported Adam's abuse of Saskia; a big complication that he'd suddenly been forced to factor in and steer, by offering to personally speak to her. I saw how the entire conspiracy had clung to a knife-edge — a measure of their desperation. Had Saskia gone to the police the plot could have unravelled and gone south faster than it took to flip a coin. One big fabrication and yet I couldn't fathom why a disparate group of people would take such a risk or how they connected. It was as if I had most of the ingredients to make a Sachertorte but didn't have any flour.

Struggling to contain my consternation, I said, 'And Hicks, what was he dismissed for?'

'Sharing pictures of female victims of abuse with his mates.'

I gaped, incredulous. 'Why weren't they sent to prison?'

'Their cases never went to trial.'

'Why the hell not?'

'I can't answer,' Kenney replied, tight-faced. 'Wasn't my call.' Allerton took a studious interest in his nails.

'Then whose call was it?' I demanded.

Neither answered. Three words sprang to mind: limit reputational damage. I'd seen it before and here it was again. Nothing substantive had altered.

'We have been through hell as a family,' I exploded.

'Appreciated,' Kenney said.

'My partner was seriously injured. He could have been killed.'

'Understood.'

And then another thought hit home, one that might save Ben. 'The whole Brooke Gentry missing and suicide story.'

'What about it?'

'Was it all one big lie?' I had to be certain.

The air felt charged. Electric. This time, Kenney answered. 'Brooke Gentry was driving your car, Sophie.'

I stared, incredulous. 'No, no, that can't be right.'

'While Hicks attacked Ben, Gentry took your child.'

'And she's dead?'

Both police officers nodded.

Good. I didn't say it but, God help me, I thought it.

CHAPTER NINETY-THREE

'Stealing a child is next level. Why were you and your family specifically targeted, do you think?' Sharp-eyed, Allerton posed the question.

Leo's voice slipped into my ear, unbidden: *What interests me is the why of it.* It was a question I longed to put to *him*.

'Revenge,' I said.

It sounded dramatic to my ears. To the two men sitting in front of me it was probably tediously run of the mill. I remembered the expression in Leo's eyes in the park only yesterday. Was it one last attempt to force Ben to come clean and make me leave him? A cynical plan to further mess with my mind? Or was Leo intending to continue the deception and turn up like the cavalry to *save* my son while extorting money from behind the scenes? Sparking inside, I suddenly realised what lay at the heart of it.

'Leo Carpenter was my fiancé eight years ago,' I admitted. 'You probably recall the Caron Street case.' My mouth felt bone dry.

Both officers braced. They were familiar with the murder, if not the detail. 'Leo Carpenter was Lester's Street's close friend,' I told them.

'How close?' Kenney probed.

'Enough for him to defend Street's actions. It's why I walked out on Leo three days before our wedding.'

Allerton raised an eyebrow at Kenney. 'Vengeful lover scenario?'

'Throw in child abduction to up the ante,' Kenney batted back.

I watched and listened like an old-school City trader observing the communication on the floor regarding the value of a bond at the stock exchange. They were both off-beam. The truth was an awful lot simpler.

Allerton suggested a break and slipped outside in search of tea. A ruse for Kenney to winkle out more information, one for which I was prepared.

Changing direction, I appealed to Kenney. 'You *will* find Carpenter and Hicks, won't you?'

'They won't be able to stay off the radar for long,' Kenney assured me. 'We're already breaking down doors.'

And walls and ceilings and floors, I hoped.

Affecting a reflective expression, Kenney touched the bottom of his chin with a ballpoint pen. 'I'm struggling to understand why Carpenter and Hicks would go to so much trouble to set up a bogus investigation. At any point you or Ben could have found them out.'

'Obviously a gamble they were prepared to take.'

'Why do you think that was?'

'Because in a couple of months' time there will be over five point two million pounds to be had.'

Kenney's jaw jutted out. His sharp features contracted.

'Shall we wait for DCI Allerton?' I said with a pleasant smile. 'It will save me repeating it.'

By the time Allerton returned, bearing paper cartons of tea the colour of radiator water, Kenney was almost cracking a tooth. He quickly picked up the conversational slack and brought Allerton up to speed.

'Five point two million quid?' Allerton repeated, open-mouthed.

'Ben's inheritance from his uncle.' I explained about the nature of the trust.

'And Adam?'

The question was as dangerous now as it was then. One misstep from me and I'd set the police on a train of investigation I didn't want them to follow.

'Whatever amount his uncle bequeathed to him has run out.'

Kenney said, 'You're alleging that Adam Hall, aided and abetted by Leo Carpenter and Jared Hicks, orchestrated the kidnap plot?'

So many human connections and agendas, yet it sounded about right. And Adam had maintained control all the way through; it accounted for his incredible mileage in my dad's car. 'Yes,' I said firmly.

Gathering momentum, I reported everything that had happened during Adam and Brooke's stay. I spared no detail, including the blade in the sink, Adam pressuring his brother to give him money destined for the garden-room extension and the night I'd found him way too close to my baby's cot at my parents' home.

'Rufus was obviously taken in order to blackmail us.' Thoughts of what might have been shot chills from the base of my neck all along my spine, down my shins and out through my toes.

'Because Hall felt short-changed from a sizeable inheritance?' Allerton said.

'Adam Hall never forgave Ben.' I took care to avoid mentioning the dark events at the family home. Adam wouldn't want that aired any more than Ben.

'That's quite some scenario.'

Equally unconvinced, Kenney looked at Allerton and raised an eyebrow.

'You allege that Hicks was Hall's friend?' Kenney said.

'I don't know but that's my guess, possibly from when they were adolescents.' I had a sudden image of Adam fleeing to Jared following the fatal row with his mother. If I was

385

correct, neither Adam, nor Hicks were going to own up to that.

'Let me get this straight,' Kenney pressed, frowning, 'you're alleging that Hicks moved to London and became a police officer?'

'While staying in contact with Adam Hall. Surely, you can check?'

'And Hicks just happens to team up with Carpenter?' Kenney's voice was riddled with cynicism.

'Corrupt police officers are like iron filings to magnets,' I said. 'They find each other.' Just like Lester had attracted Leo.

Neither Allerton nor Kenney disagreed.

'Without hard evidence it will be difficult to make Hall's role stick,' Allerton murmured to Kenney. 'He might simply have mentioned the money to Hicks who saw an opportunity for him and Carpenter to get their hands on it.'

'Depends on what's on their phones.' I hadn't lived with a police officer without acquiring basic knowledge.

'Let's see what Carpenter and Hicks have to say for themselves when we finally catch up with them,' Kenney said. 'Rats in a sack bite hard and deep.'

I flashed a smile. I liked him a lot more than when we'd first been introduced.

CHAPTER NINETY-FOUR

I'd all but forgotten about the birthday celebration at my parents' home. Remembering with a bump, I phoned Mum in a panic from a payphone.

'Sophie,' she burst out. 'Where on—'

Before she could get out another word, I launched in like a rugby player diving for a messy tackle, gave her the gist and finished with: 'We're being kept in overnight at Cheltenham General.' Predictably, Mum's first concern was Rufus, followed by Ben and then me.

I set her mind at rest on all counts.

'And you say that Brooke Gentry was driving the car?' she asked, aghast.

I confirmed she was.

'And she's dead?'

'Yes.'

Mum fell quiet for a moment. 'I can't believe any of it,' she said, eventually finding her voice. 'How could she?'

A good question and one yet to be answered. I wondered if Brooke had been selected because it was thought, as a woman, she'd be able to handle my baby better. Not that she'd shown a smidgeon of interest in Rufus all the time she'd spent with us. 'I'm so sorry about the party, Mum. I know you went to a lot of trouble.'

'It will freeze. More importantly, Adam Hall's latest activities.'

'What activities?'

'You don't know?'

'Not a clue.' I'd been a bit tied up. This I didn't say.

'He attacked Auntie Fen.'

In a day of shocks, you'd think I'd be immune. I wasn't.

'Oh my God, is she all right?'

'Barely. She's at the facial trauma unit at the Nuffield with your father. Adam completely lost his temper. Loosened a tooth, I gather.'

A sure sign Adam was feeling the heat. 'Have the police been notified?'

'Auntie Fen, God bless her, managed to call while Adam was trying to make off in her Aston.'

'And where's Adam now?'

'In custody.'

'Thank God.' I was certain Allerton and Kenney would be interested in having a chat.

'Horrible, horrible man,' Mum exclaimed.

'How's Saskia taken the news?'

'She's at the police station right now filing a report. By the time we're done with him, Adam Hall will never ever set foot in the Cotswolds again.'

CHAPTER NINETY-FIVE

The police kept us informed with intermittent updates. Leo and Hicks were picked up in Essex within twenty-four hours of the botched kidnap. After Allerton had charged Adam Hall with assault, Kenney and his team questioned him about the attempted abduction of his nephew.

A day after Ben's discharge, a meeting was arranged at our home. Police sat on one sofa in our sitting room, us on the other, Rufus in my lap.

'Hicks has been a lot more talkative than his co-conspirators,' Kenney informed us. I looked straight ahead, not daring to glance at Ben. Fortunately, his knee didn't jitter.

'You were right about Hicks and Hall's long-standing friendship,' Kenney continued, looking at me, 'although communication in the intervening years was intermittent until around twelve months ago.'

I gave a start. Around the time I moved in with Ben and the time Hicks and Leo had lost their jobs, their reputations, their everything. There would have been added emotional pressure in Leo's case due to the death of his mother.

'Convenient timing,' Ben observed cynically.

Kenney nodded. 'The imminent date for your trust fund to mature, set everything in motion,' he confirmed.

'Essentially, Hall, Hicks and Carpenter realised they had a common cause.'

'A case of mutual self-interest,' Allerton commented.

I didn't dare look at Ben. Adam had an additional reason to destroy him. Would he do so now he was backed into a corner?

'What about Brooke?' I cut in.

'Yes,' Ben said, glancing at me. 'I understand how and why the three men conspired, but where does Gentry feature?'

'Carpenter pulled Gentry in for drugs offences several years ago.'

'She was booked?' I asked.

'No.'

'Cautioned?'

Kenney shook his head.

'Making her indebted to him.'

'One way of putting it.'

'Did you know that Brooke Gentry was a wannabe actor?' Allerton interjected.

'A failed actor,' Kenney said through thin lips. 'Didn't make the grade with drama school.'

'We had no idea,' Ben said, shooting a glance at me.

'She certainly played her role with conviction,' I said, remembering the programme for a West End play I'd found in her belongings.

'Unfortunately, it also got her killed,' Allerton reported dryly.

'She was used?' Which didn't surprise me. Vulnerable, emotionally unstable and indebted to Leo for deliberately omitting to charge her for drugs' offences, she was effectively a pawn in the men's hands.

'Neither Carpenter nor Hall intended her to get her share of the money, according to Hicks,' Allerton said.

And once she was introduced to Hall, her judgement was obscured.

She never saw what was really going down. 'Had she ever been to the States?' I asked.

'No,' Allerton replied. 'It was simply part of a cover story.'

'What about my brother?' Ben asked.

'He had a visa, courtesy of a sponsor.'

I remembered the fierce light in Adam's eyes when describing the music hotspots he'd visited. A dreamer to the last and one who imagined having a shedload of money and didn't give a damn how he got his paws on it.

Kenney turned his gaze to Ben, a penetrating light in his eyes. 'During the course of our investigation, we came across the unfortunate and tragic events surrounding your parents, Dr Taylor.'

I swallowed. Was this it? Had Adam grassed? Was this the moment that Ben was nailed for a crime he committed over a decade before?

'Yes?' Ben said, sombre.

'It's been alleged that you provided the drugs that killed your father, and you administered the fatal dose, not your mother.'

My breath caught in the back of my throat. I looked straight ahead, willing Ben to deny it.

'A grave accusation if it were true,' Ben said.

'You seem unsurprised.' Kenney leant forward fractionally.

'Because I've heard it all before,' Ben said, his voice weary.

'From?'

'My brother.'

'It was Leo Carpenter who made the accusation.'

'Then he is simply repeating my brother's words,' Ben said smoothly. 'And my brother has already been thoroughly discredited.

'Studying to be a doctor so that I could save lives and help people like my father, I was nearly a hundred miles away at the time. I didn't drive. I had no access to drugs. I think you'll find my movements were thoroughly investigated.'

Kenney's top lip twitched a smile. 'I'm sorry I had to ask.'

'Fair enough,' Ben said with more composure than I could summon up.

'Was the abduction of my son, Adam's plan or a nasty idea cooked up by two bent coppers?' Grain in my voice, I addressed Allerton who flinched at the obvious slight.

He looked to Kenney to answer. 'As you might imagine, each is blaming the other.'

But Adam had nobody to blame other than himself for assaulting my aunt and sister. 'What's the situation with my aunt?' I tipped forward in my seat, alert to the answer.

'Adam Hall has been charged with GBH with regard to Mrs Clinton-Gower.'

'And what about the kidnap plot?' Ben asked.

Kenney met Ben's eye with a level gaze. 'The abduction of your son will result in custodial sentences for the perpetrators.'

Bye-bye Adam Hall, Leo Carpenter and his sidekick, Jared Hicks.

CHAPTER NINETY-SIX

One Sunday in May, we christened our new garden room by throwing lunch for my parents and sister. With me supporting him, rose-cheeked Rufus sat up on my knee. He'd rarely been out of my sight since that awful day I thought I'd lost him. Auntie Fen had taken herself off to the Italian lakes with one of her ex-husbands to recuperate while awaiting further treatment for a fractured cheekbone. The sale of the flat was going through. Saskia had already made the home hers. I'd visited Louise and, although Elliott had not seen Ben, they'd spoken on the phone and patched things up. I also phoned Lloyd and brought him up to speed on recent events.

'Always knew Adam Hall had it coming to him and I can't say I'm sorry,' Lloyd said.

In a couple of weeks, I was destined to return to work part-time. Adam Hall, Leo Carpenter and Jared Hicks were remanded in custody, their trials due in Crown Court the following year. These were the broad brushstrokes of our lives.

Underneath, we were played out, drained and exhausted.

You don't have to be Brooke Gentry to assume a role. We are all actors in our own carefully scripted stories. All of us lie, mostly to protect ourselves and project the best version, sometimes to protect others; we each have sides we'd prefer the world never saw. All of us have secrets, too. Ben knew his secret was safe with me, as was mine with him. We were stronger as a couple because of it.

As disturbing as it was, I privately thought it possible that Adam might step back into our lives one day. But with a multi-million-pound windfall to look forward to, more than enough to secure our son's future, there was plenty of money to ensure (legally, of course) that Adam never troubled our family again. I always was a numbers girl.

THE END

ACKNOWLEDGEMENTS

As ever, my thanks go to my fantastic agent, Broo Doherty at DHH for her editorial input and enthusiasm for the story and for my other fantastic editor, Kate Lyall Grant, at Joffe. Once again, 'Team Joffe' has swung into action so thank you to all who met up to discuss the cover, marketing and promotion and then promoted! I'm indebted to my eagle-eyed copy editor Sarah Tranter for picking up my blunders and correcting them. As always, she's an absolute delight to work with.

Cirencester Antiques Centre deserves a special mention for allowing me to skulk around and ask questions, particularly in relation to the snuff box mentioned in the story. A glorious historical treat of a place, I can't recommend it highly enough.

Huge thanks (again) to Graham Bartlett, writer, former senior police officer and detective and expert advisor, for talking me down from an impossibly high ledge of fear after I thought I'd tanked my own plot. This is called writer paranoia so he should add counselling to his skill set.

Thank you to my first reader, Ian, who always takes his life in his hands when he delivers constructive criticism. Thanks also to my lovely family for your support and love over many years.

Finally, the reviewers and readers who have taken the time and trouble to read my stories, to you, a big, heartfelt thank you.

THE JOFFE BOOKS STORY

We began in 2014 when Jasper agreed to publish his mum's much-rejected romance novel and it became a bestseller.

Since then we've grown into the largest independent publisher in the UK. We're extremely proud to publish some of the very best writers in the world, including Joy Ellis, Faith Martin, Caro Ramsay, Helen Forrester, Simon Brett and Robert Goddard. Everyone at Joffe Books loves reading and we never forget that it all begins with the magic of an author telling a story.

We are proud to publish talented first-time authors, as well as established writers whose books we love introducing to a new generation of readers.

We won Trade Publisher of the Year at the Independent Publishing Awards in 2023 and Best Publisher Award in 2024 at the People's Book Prize. We have been shortlisted for Independent Publisher of the Year at the British Book Awards for the last five years, and were shortlisted for the Diversity and Inclusivity Award at the 2022 Independent Publishing Awards. In 2023 we were shortlisted for Publisher of the Year at the RNA Industry Awards, and in 2024 we were shortlisted at the CWA Daggers for the Best Crime and Mystery Publisher.

We built this company with your help, and we love to hear from you, so please email us about absolutely anything bookish at feedback@joffebooks.com.

If you want to receive free books every Friday and hear about all our new releases, join our mailing list here: www.joffe-books.com/freebooks.

And when you tell your friends about us, just remember: it's pronounced Joffe as in coffee or toffee!